My Vietnam War

E.E. "Doc" Murdock

H.O.T. Press

Published by
H.O.T. Press
Los Angeles, CA
www.hotpresspublishing.com
Publishing fine books since 1983

ISBN: 0-923178-23-6
ISBN-13: 978-0-923178-23-9

Acknowledgments

I am indebted to the members of the Ojai Writing Workshop who provided valuable feedback as I worked through the many drafts of this book. And of course, without the help of Zoe, this book would not exist.

What It Is and What It Isn't

This is a novel. That means there are events in this story that never really happened—at least not quite in the way I'm going to tell them. I'm going to tell this story as if you were there with me as it happened, seeing it as I did. Is that possible? I don't know, but it seems like the only way I can make you understand what it was like over there.

Now that the disclaimers have been taken care of, I can tell you what *is* true. In the spring of 1967 (the year that turned out to be the deadliest of the Vietnam War), I and every other American male of my age was trying to decide what to do when the dreaded draft notice arrived in the mail:

Greetings: You are hereby ordered to report for induction into the armed forces of the United States of America.

In 1967, if you received that oh-so-official-looking and oh-so-ominous-sounding letter, chances are you would soon find yourself in Vietnam. This is the story of that year, 1967, only one year in a war that went on for ten, but it was a year that changed my life, and changed me. Forever.

One more thing before I begin: all of the character names in this novel have been changed to protect both the innocent *and* the guilty (even though most of the latter are dead, or have completed their prison sentences which means they are, in some ways, free).

How can you prove we are not sleeping and this is not just a dream?

René Descartes

(From my Philosophy 112 textbook, *Introduction to Modern Philosophy* by Edwin Tompkins.)

Book One
The Watcher

1

Life and Death at Wong's Bar

I am the watcher. I sit at the end of the bar. From here, I can watch the chaos of Wong's Bar go down. Plenty of chaos to watch at Wong's Bar, soldiers gambling ferociously at the antique-looking dice table, soldiers lusting after Wong's cute little girls for hire, soldiers drinking hard just to get drunk, soldiers smoking pot to find or to forget.

Hidden away in one of Saigon's poorer districts, Wong's Bar is supposed to be off limits, but it's always crowded with U.S. soldiers. I'd be willing to bet that most every American soldier in Saigon has made a visit to this place, or at least heard about it. My old pal Brent and I, both freshly-minted soldiers in this man's army, discovered Wong's Bar not long after we landed in Vietnam. We've been coming here just about every night since. There's no signboard out front, but everybody calls this place Wong's Bar because it's run by an irritable dried-up little old Chinese guy who goes by the name of Wong. Wong keeps a close eye on things. Here day and night, so I don't think he sleeps. He's always scowling at us soldiers and tugging on his wrinkled old earlobes. Evidently, there's an old Chinese belief that the length of your ears predicts how long you'll live. I watch Wong dart here and there, passing out drinks, collecting money, berating the girls in their own Vietnamese language. I suspect he's telling them to sell more drinks, sell more sex. Hurry, hurry. He's sharp, old Wong. He saw the rapid American buildup after the Gulf of Tonkin "incident" and was ready for us.

My attention is drawn to some shouting over at the dice table. Looks like trouble brewing over there, but it's so noisy—soldiers talking loud, laughing loud, arguing loud—that I can't hear what started it. Probably the usual thing, an accusation of cheating. A lot of money changes hands at that dice table, so there are a lot of fights when somebody thinks they've been cheated (which they probably have been). Wong doesn't want to get hurt, and he doesn't want the MPs or the White

Mice (the white-helmeted and white-gloved Saigon police) coming around, so he lets the boys take care of it themselves. Fairly entertaining to see how hard those guys work at their gambling. The dice game goes on twenty-four hours a day, and every throw of the dice brings forth a burst of loud yelling: a few yell with joy at having won, but most yell curses at the dice, the shooter, their bad luck. They're utterly captivated by the game, all of them pushed up close against the table, crowded together elbow to elbow, all leaning forward to see those dice roll, every hand gripping the rail, every eye focused on those two little rolling cubes. Hypnotized, I'd call it.

I switch my watching to the area where Wong's girls are stationed. Plenty of entertainment over there too, lots of soldiers lusting after Wong's girls. The girls are "available," for a price. Different kind of hypnotism is going on with those guys, something more innate, more hormonal. The soldiers come here to be around girls. Here, they can talk to a pretty girl and maybe take one of them to a back room—if they have enough money in their pocket. They crack slyly-dirty jokes (which the girls don't get), and they brag about who or what they were back home (which the girls don't care about). In other words, they do what boys always do when confronted with a pretty girl. And we *are* all still boys, despite our snappy military uniforms and our eight weeks of Basic Training. As I look around, I don't see a single guy in this place that's much over twenty. All barely out of high school, but here we are, pretending to be soldiers in a hot and humid country that none of us ever heard of before the Washington politicians got on TV and starting ranting about how important it was to our national security.

Uh oh, better not let yourself start thinking like that. You're starting to get into your analytical mode again, like you're above it all. Face it, you are not above it all, even if you are the watcher. You're the same age as them, homesick like them, and worried about getting killed in this war, just like they are. But I have a solution. Get drunk. Drink enough booze, and it shuts off the old brain, at least for a while. I pick up my drink and slug down the entire glassful. I shake the glass at Wong and he's quick to refill it.

Uh oh, looks like another fight about to commence. Two guys are after the same girl. It ends up with the guys nose to nose, chins held high, fists rigidly at the ready. This is usually when the first punch comes, but this time, these two seem to be stuck in their confrontational poses. Is it going to be nothing but a glaring match? After a few overly-long moments of serious, if drunken, glaring, one of them launches a two-handed chest push. Surprisingly, there's no response from the pushed guy. Is he going to back down? No, wait, it was a ruse. He fires a sneaky wait-til-the-guy-looks-away sucker punch. Punched guy goes down, and that starts the really big fight when the other soldiers from the attacked guy's unit jump in, quickly followed by an equal and opposite reaction from the attacker's unit. I settle in to watch a good fight, but it turns out to be mostly pushing and stumbling and telegraphed wind-up wallops that usually miss. Fortunately for them, they don't have to continue fighting very long because they soon knock over a table that has a bunch of partly-full glasses on it, and the other soldiers quickly pull them apart before they can spill any more of Wong's expensive drinks. A few last insults are traded by the two original fighters, followed by a bit of pretending to try to break free to get at the other guy, but soon the ritual is complete. They straighten their uniforms, wipe away the blood under their noses with a manly back-of-the-hand swipe, and go back to wooing.

So there you have it. Typical night at Wong's Bar, Saigon, Vietnam. Gambling and girls, arguments and fights. My nightly entertainment. My self-designated task is to sit here at the edge and watch it. And there's always a new group to watch because unlike Brent and me—currently stationed in Saigon on rear-echelon support duty—most of these young American soldiers are just passing through. They're being held in local bases while they undergo what's known as "Indoctrination Training." When that's over, they'll be sent to where the fighting is. They know that, so when they finally do get a night out on the town, at liberty, for the moment, from rigid rules and badgering non-coms, they hit places like this to try to be as noisy and boisterous and irresponsible as possible. This'll be a night they'll always remember, that night when they finally became an adult, that night when they drank and fought and screwed foreign girls, that night they were finally far enough from home to be free to do whatever the hell they wanted to. But it will be a night they won't write home about—nobody back home would want to know what America's finest really do in their free time.

That thought makes me wonder what the people back home would think of this joint. I imagine they would describe it in one word: sleazy. Wong's Bar just about defines sleazy: a stifling-hot concrete box with no door and no glass in the one front window which means the mosquitoes get to wander in and make a feast out of me because I'm usually too drunk to notice. There's a distinctive smell to Wong's Bar, a mixture of sweat and urine that you notice the moment you walk through the door. But tonight I'm also picking up a drifting odor of Old Spice after-shave lotion. Amazing to think these soldiers would douse themselves with Old Spice before going to see a prostitute. Old habits, I guess.

With the temporary lull in the fighting entertainment, I turn my attention back to my drinking. I plant my elbows on the rough surface of the long bar that seems to have been hacked out of a tree trunk. I'm ready to get into some *serious* drinking. Between my elbows is my personal, almost-clean glass that Wong keeps behind the bar for me.

Wong keeps my glass filled with what he calls "house drink," a good-tasting, but bad-acting, booze and herbs mixture the soldiers call "love punch" because it tends to make you woozy and amorous at the same time. Wong thinks the woozy part cuts down on the number of fights, and the amorous part stimulates Wong's main business, his going-to-the-back-room-with-a-young-Vietnamese-girl business.

Brent and I have only been "in country" (as they say) for a couple of months, but this place has become our regular hangout. We come here as soon as we get off work at "the warehouse," the U.S. Army's central Saigon food supply storage and shipping facility. Brent and I joined up together, went through Basic together, and then, once we got here, Brent got us both jobs at the food warehouse. We're the lift-and-grunt guys, part of the Army's hoard of behind-the-lines manual laborers who help keep the war going. Our little part in the grand scheme of things is to load the trucks with cases of packaged and canned foods that are used to feed the "real" troops. I come here most every night to do my drinking and my watching. Brent comes here to sell pot to the other soldiers. Even though we haven't been in this country very long, Brent is getting to be known as the guy who has access to some of the best marijuana in Saigon.

Tell you the truth, the drunken carryings on of the soldiers is starting to lose its entertainment value for me, but I do like to watch Wong's young girls in action. I can't help but wonder how such beautiful young things ended up in a place like this. And Wong's girls *really are* beautiful. They're beautiful because they're all young, and young is beautiful anywhere in the world. How young? Well, let me put it this way: Wong wouldn't have a girl in the place unless she was young enough to be considered illegal back home in the states. That's what American boy-soldiers seem to like, so that's what Wong provides: a trip to the back room with a beautiful too-young girl, a few moments of heaven before their scheduled trip to the hell of war. I asked Brent where Wong could have found young girls willing to sell their bodies to American soldiers. He said Wong brings them in from the countryside. Pays their parents to let him take them to Saigon. Parents happy, young American soldiers happy, girls happy. And believe it or not, the girls really do seem happy. I like to listen to their giggly mix of English and Vietnamese as they do their "jobs." True, they are now in the hooker biz in the big city, but if you try hard enough, you can still see, and hear, the country in them. Look beyond their slinky long white silk dresses and you'll see simple Vietnamese country girls, excited to be in the big city, making young men happy while they earn money to support their folks back home on the farm. Although they may have been forced into, or attracted into, this fast-paced life of fun and sex, none of them seem hard or especially callous. They laugh freely and easily at the dumb jokes the young soldiers make at their expense. Back at the barracks, the soldiers refer to them as "boom-boom girls." A vulgar name, I think, for such pretty young things. Brent says the girls are just pretending, but I think they do like us. Or maybe that's just what I prefer to believe.

I turn back to my drinking. Get enough of Wong's booze in me, and I can almost forget where I am and how I stupidly let Brent talk me into avoiding the draft by joining up. But at least I'm out of hot and sleepy little Mesa, Arizona. After Basic, when they told me I was going to be sent to Vietnam, I thought, well, if I'm going to have the bad luck to arrive at draft age in 1967, right when there's an actual war going on, at least I'll get to go to a foreign country and see some new things, encounter some new experiences. And so far, I *am* having new experiences, but they're not exactly the kind I expected. My "experience" is slaving away all day in an oven-hot food-supply warehouse, and then getting stoned every night in a sleazy bar/whorehouse in the saddest part of this frantically spread-out city. But in time, even new and novel experiences become routine, and coming here every night has become routine for Brent and me. Brent keeps himself busy with his dope-dealing business, while I keep myself busy with my watching and my businesslike drinking. Wong knows I come here to drink—not to gamble, not to fight, not to get laid. I come here to get drunk enough to make my damn brain shut up its endless thinking, thinking, thinking, at least for a few hours. Every time I drink my glass down to the last inch or so, old Wong is quick to refill it. With each refill, he takes more money from the pile of genuine U.S. dollar bills that are scattered in front of my glass. I don't know how much money he takes, and it doesn't matter; if my pile runs out, I can always get more from Brent. Brent makes us a lot of money. Tonight, he's at a back table with a couple of his customers, the two very-drunk sailors who a while ago walked in yelling, "Does anybody know where we can get a shitload of really good Vietnamese grass?" Brent has his Army shirt off, as he almost always does, and as usual he has the short sleeves of his Army T-shirt rolled up to show off his formidable biceps. He thinks providing advance warning of his physical capabilities is a way to avoid fights, but he's ended up in so many fights since we started coming to Wong's Bar, I think it actually does the opposite—sort of like when a young gunfighter shows off his pearl-handled revolvers.

Good old Brent. Watching him tonight, I realize he still looks and acts about the same as he did when he was selling pot back in Arizona, putting on his glad-handed salesman act, making everybody like him. Brent is a go-getter who knows what he wants and knows how to get it. Tonight, he seems to be working extra hard at his "job," talking fast, laughing loud, passing around free sample joints, and giving every single potential customer his famous I'm-your-Godamm-best-friend slap on the back along with his put-er-there-buddy handshake that will just about break your damn hand. His Army-green T-shirt shows the energy he puts into his salesmanship: it's so sweat-wet it looks almost black. And of course, he's got his pack of Luckies carefully rolled into his left sleeve just like he always did back home. As I watch him, it hits me that he could just as well be back home sitting in his favorite Washington Street bar/whorehouse over in Phoenix. But that's Brent all over. Get sent to the most dangerous place in the world? No problem, just go right on doing what you were already doing back home.

Well, let Brent stay busy making money if that's what he likes to do. Me, I'll just sit back and drink and watch the action. I see a young soldier talking to one of the girls. He seems to be telling her a joke because she's giggling non-stop. The girls have learned a little English, and they've learned how to giggle appropriately at the soldiers' stupid jokes. The guy manages to get his hand up under her pretty white dress, and she giggles even more as she tries to push him away. I know why she's giggling like that: she has nothing on underneath that fine white dress. None of them do. But old Wong is not about to let the guy get away with that. He's there in a flash, shaking his finger at the guy and chattering at him in Chinese—probably Chinese curse words. Then, he switches to his down-to-business version of fairly-understandable English: "No free feel 'til money in hand." He holds out his hand and waits. The guy produces the cash, slugs down the required number of Wong's expensive drinks, and then—and only then—does he finally get to take the girl to one of the back rooms. That's where he will get what he paid for, ten minutes of bliss, on the clock.

Ah well, time to move my brain as far away from this reality as possible. I light up a joint and shout at Wong to put on an American record. He goes to do it. This time, he puts the Purple Haze record on. It's one of my favorites, and Wong knows it. He cranks the volume up all the way, I sit back to listen to the song. I don't know how Wong got his hands on a few American records, but they've been played so many times I've come to recognize the scratches as if they're part of the music. The song, along with the scratches and warbles, comes out of the one big old cloth-covered speaker that Wong has got mounted up in the corner of his moldy, fly-speckled ceiling. Back home, Brent and I used to listen to the Purple Haze song all the time. Funny what memories a song can trigger. I remember a night when Brent and I were in a car yelling out the words to that song right along with Jimi. When was that? Oh yeah, it must have been that time Brent salvaged a ratty old used-to-be-red-but-now-sun-faded-to-almost-white Corvette from his dad's junkyard. The car had been wrecked pretty bad, but Brent figured he could get it fixed up. First, he got out the torch and cut the top off of it. He patted the top of the threadbare driver's seat and said, Now we got us a convertible. Then he tried to rebuild the mashed-in and badly cracked Vette's fiberglass body using Bondo. He made a mess of the used-to-be-smooth lines of the car. After he gave up on that, we went to work on the engine. Turned out it ran just fine once we rebuilt the fuel pump and put on a new starter motor. We stayed awake until late in the night trying to get the Vette ready for the road, both of us flyin' high on the Bennies we'd got from that doctor Brent found in Phoenix who'd prescribe any kind of amphetamines we wanted for ten bucks a script. By the time we finally got the poor old Vette running, dawn couldn't have been far away. We scavenged some pretty good tires off of other cars in the junkyard and slapped on a Texas license plate from Brent's collection of supposedly-still-valid plates. Brent used a crowbar to rip an 8-track out of a wrecked Dodge Dart, hung the old tape player under the Corvette's dash using a bent-up wire coat hanger, ran a couple of electrical wires to the big old battery we'd "borrowed" out of his dad's pickup truck, and we were off to Vegas with a brand new tape of Jimi howling his Purple Haze song at us. We shouted the words right back at him, all three of us howling at the strange yellow sliver of moon that seemed to be beckoning us toward Sin City. Somehow, we made it out of Phoenix without getting arrested, and then it was flat out across the desert, passing all the other cars on the road like they were parked. Brent was enjoying pushing the Vette hard to see what it could do. When we got up into the hills, he decided to see if he could double the marked speed limits around the curves of twisty, turny route 93. Too easy. The Vette was hugging the road like a desperate lover. Brent said, Let's try tripling it. My stoned-out brain was having vaguely disturbing thoughts like, is this the night Brent finally gets me killed? Sure enough, it wasn't long before we went into a spin, and then we were flying off the road backwards. It all seemed to happen in slow motion, like it was happening to somebody else. There was the sound of tearing metal that turned out to be a guard rail, and then it was over the edge and down into a sandy ravine. We slid to a stop in a cloud of dust. Brent turned to look at me and started laughing like a maniac, describing, between hysterical laugh gasps, how scared my eyes looked. I ignored him, and we got out to check the damage. Brent didn't think it looked too bad. That's the advantage, he said, of driving a pre-wrecked car. That got him started laughing again. I pointed out that as funny as it was, the back end of the car was completely smashed in because of going backwards through a damn guard rail, and we were now stuck axle-deep in the desert sand. We crawled back up to the road, and it seemed like only a few minutes before a bunch of cowboys just off work and heading out for their weekend binge came by. Two pickup loads of 'em, heading for Vegas. One of the trucks had a winch, and after they got us back up on the road, we all stood around looking at the smashed-in

Vette. It wouldn't budge because Brent's Bondoed back end had gotten pushed down on top of the rear wheels. One of the cowboys got a *really big* sledge hammer out of the back of his truck, and holding it up to show us, volunteered to "fix" the Corvette. He was strong, that cowboy. Only took him a dozen hits or so to pretty much knock off the whole rear end of the car's fiberglass body. After the "fixing" job was done, we passed around their bottle, all of them taking turns pounding us on the back for being such ga-dam good ol' boys despite our long hair. Then they suggested we all caravan together to Vegas to see if we couldn't rip the heart out of that glittery old town. One of them got his pickup in front of us, and the other one followed close behind. Somehow we limped into Vegas and parked the vehicles next to some bushes in the dirt parking lot behind the Stardust casino. We formed a circle and sat there in the dirt to drain what was left of the whiskey. Then, we put our hands together in the center of the circle and made a solemn vow to show that town what real fun was like—or damn well die tryin'. Most of that night in Vegas is a blur, but I do remember watching Brent help those cowboys break up some bus benches to make a really big bonfire. That must have been why we were running from the cops through that back alley that smelled like . . .

Aw, what the hell. That was then, this is now. You shouldn't even be thinking about home. Brent keeps telling me to forget that back-home shit. He says we're in Vee-et-nam now, so we got to make the most of it. He says we got to grab life by the balls and twist. That's Brent all over. He doesn't spend his time thinking about the whys and the whatfors and the whatifs. He doesn't waste a single second thinking about *if only*, or about *what if you had* . . .

There you go again. More thinking. You've got to stop all this useless thinking. Just let yourself go with the music. Good song. Fits what's going on in this incomprehensible country. A purple haze. The song ends, but I'm still swaying with the memory of it. I'm finally starting to feel the strong anesthetizing effect of Wong's mysterious home brew and the familiar, pleasant, separate-from-the-world feeling that comes from Brent's strong Vietnamese pot. I yell at Wong to put that song back on. He does, and Jimi goes back to belting out his message. I get it. His purple haze is in my brain too. It means the booze is working good now. I'm starting to feel even more disengaged as I look around at the madness of what goes on in Wong's Bar. The place is so crazy it makes me smile. Everybody is madly "doing things," drinking, smoking pot, gambling, grabbing at the girls, all of them trying to get in as much sin as they can before they get sent to the front.

Something makes me turn toward the front door. What's this? A young rosy-cheeked soldier is standing in the doorway. Never seen him in here before. Looks like he's stunned by the noisy pandemonium of the place. Doesn't know whether to enter or not. You can tell he's fresh from Basic Training, probably just landed in Saigon, probably out on his first pass off the base. He's wide-eyed and grinning. But he's not stoned—if anybody can tell that, I can. He's . . . what's the right word? Innocent, that's it. Give him a battered straw hat and a bamboo fishing pole, and he could have walked right off the cover of an old Saturday Evening Post magazine. I like him right away. A nice kid, I'm sure of it. Maybe from Iowa. Someplace like that. I should talk to him. Ask him how are things back there in the Great Midwest. How's the corn crop this year, old buddy? I chuckle at the look of him. Actually, I'm probably laughing at myself, at the memory of how I looked when I first got to his country. I probably had that same fresh-to-Vietnam, dumb-as-a-pebble look that day I stepped off that big silver airplane and stood blinking out there on the steaming hot tarmac of the Bien Hoa Air Base—curious, if not exactly eager, but ready for new experiences in this very-foreign-feeling place. The kid just stands there in the doorway, taking it all in. How did a young innocent-looking guy like that end up in the most sinful place in Saigon? What makes him think it's safe to enter a place like this? He's braver than I would have been back then. He looks around, grins at the sight of the pretty girls, and comes to the bar to buy a drink. I nod to him. He nods back, pays for his drink, and heads straight for the dice table. Uh oh, not a good idea. Right away, I'm worried about him. He doesn't have a clue what he's getting into. I should get right up off this stool and go over there to rescue him. But I don't. The booze and the dope and the music are all telling me none of it matters anyhow. I stick to my watcher job and watch him. He puts down his money and leans in with the rest of the crowd to watch the dice roll. He loses, puts down more money. He seems to know the game. Maybe he'll be all right after all. At first, he seems to be enjoying himself, still smiling as he loses more and more money. He's trying to be good-natured about it. Probably doesn't want to make a big fuss. But then a look of concern crosses his face. Is he getting suspicious? He should be. Brent says that dice game is a game of who can cheat the best. He loses again and before the shooter—a burly Marine with a missing-front-tooth smile that isn't really a smile but more like a challenge—can throw the dice again, the kid leans forward and holds up his hand. The look on his face is now that of a puzzled young student in class wanting to ask the teacher a question. The other gamblers all turn to stare at him. He's still smiling and looking shy as he says something, but with all the noise and Jimi's yelling about purple haze, I can't hear what it is. He's pointing at the dice. He's probably saying he's a bit suspicious of those funny-acting dice. The missing-tooth Marine, who I assume owns those funny-acting dice, yells at the kid, loud enough for me to hear, loud enough for everybody in the place to hear: "What the fuck do you know about it? So you lost your money. Shut up and take it like a man." But the kid doesn't shut up. You can tell he's a little scared, but he stands his ground. He's brave, you have to give him that, even if he is a bit foolhardy. I tell myself I really should try to get up and go over there to try to save him. I could put my arm over his shoulder and bring him back to the bar with me. I could buy him a drink and explain about what goes on at that gambling table. But I'm too late. The place has suddenly gotten very quiet. Even Jimi is taking a breath between verses, as if he too is waiting to see what's going to happen. The kid says right out loud that he wants to take a closer look at those dice. The Marine pockets the dice and comes around the table, not smiling anymore. Oh, shit. I hope the kid knows how to defend himself. Another gambler quickly produces another pair of dice, and they all turn back to their game of chance. Everybody else in the place goes back to their loud talking. They know there's going to be a fight, a serious fight, and they don't want to get involved I expect the Marine to come at the kid swinging those big fists of his, but no, all of a sudden he's gotten friendly. All smiles, and acting a lot drunker than he was a minute ago. He drunkenly gives the kid a big one-armed bear hug while he whispers something in the kid's ear. Kid listens, then pushes away. Looks down at his stomach. Face changes to surprise, then concern. Did that Marine do something to him? Did I miss something that just happened?

The Marine, still smiling, still acting drunk, looks around.

I look him in the eyes to let him know I'm watching him.

He hesitates. Is he going to come after me now? No, he heads for the door, moving fast, and disappears into the night. I look back at the kid. He's still looking down at his stomach, touching it. I can tell something is wrong with him, but what? His legs seem to lose strength, and he abruptly sits down on the floor. He's swaying back and forth, looking down at his stomach, puzzled. He tries to pull himself up by grabbing at the pant legs of the gamblers, but they're all too caught up in the frenzy of their dice game to bother with him. They push him away with their feet. He slumps back and lies there staring up at the ceiling, blinking. The constantly moving feet of the agitated gamblers keep stepping on him until eventually he gets rolled under the dice table. Now his eyes are closed. Is he just resting? Did that Marine hurt him somehow? I look around to see if anybody else has noticed. Nobody has. In the noisy madness of Wong's Bar, no one ever notices anything besides what they're into themselves. Or if they do, they don't care: everybody who comes in here is used to seeing passed-out drunks on the floor, and they often get shoved under tables. But I know the kid hasn't had that much to drink. Something is definitely wrong with him. I stagger to my feet and manage to stay upright long enough to get there. I get down on my hands and knees and squeeze past the gambler's legs to get under the table with the kid. Right away, I can see he's in trouble. I don't know a damn thing about death, but the kid's paper-white face makes me think he might actually be dying right there in front of me. My stoned-out brain is telling me I ought to do something about it, but I can't seem to get my head on straight enough to figure out what. I roll him up on his side, and that's when I see it: the front of his shirt is all bloody. I pull up his shirt. There's a tiny little hole in his gut. His life blood is spurting out of that little hole: spurt, spurt, spurt. I stare at the blood that's being spurted onto the concrete floor. I try to make my mind comprehend it. Did that Marine stab him? But it's such a little bitty hole. Can all that blood be coming out of that tiny little hole? Maybe that Marine was just trying to tell the kid to back off. Gave him a little poke with something sharp. But it must have hit an artery or something, because the kid is rapidly losing blood, real blood. It's making a little river on the concrete floor that wanders away toward the other end of the dice table. Wet cigarette butts are floating along in it like little toy submarines. The little river of blood continues on until it finds its lake, a low spot in the concrete. But the lake is already filled with a pool of yellowish liquid that's gradually turning darker as the blood flows into it. What is that yellow stuff? It takes my booze-and-dope-slowed brain a minute to figure it out, but then I recognize it by its smell: it's piss. I stare at the nervous legs of the gamblers all around me and try to get my mind to work clearly. Above me, the gamblers shout out their bets. Then, a sudden quiet as the dice roll, followed by loud questions. Is it an eight? Is it? Then cheers, mixed in with the curses of the losers. It dawns on me that those damn gamblers must not be willing to stop gambling long enough even to go out to the latrine ditch in back. They must just whip it out under the table and let it go right there onto the floor. They're so caught up in their mad game, they're not willing to stop throwing those little cubes for even the few minutes it would take to go outside and piss, not willing to stop tossing those damned dice for a second. While they watch the dice roll across the felt of the table, they let their dicks hang out and piss under the table, not thinking about anything but those dice, hoping for that magical eight-the-hard way, every mother's son of them believing they are the one lucky stiff who's about to hit it rich and rake in that huge pile of booze-sticky bills, not one of them stopping to realize they damned sure were not lucky enough to avoid getting drafted and sent to the most dangerous place on earth.

I drag my thoughts away from that image. I have to make my brain concentrate. The Iowa kid is in trouble, and I should be doing something about it. I stare at the little lake of blood and piss and realize I should get the hell out from under this table before somebody whips it out and lets their piss go right onto the top of my head. I start to crawl out, but then it hits me: if I leave, I'm just like them. I can't leave the kid under here all alone. I have to do something for him. But what can I do? His pale white face must mean he's lost a lot of blood. Is he bleeding inside too? What am I supposed to do about that? I'm feeling a lot more sober as I roll the kid over onto his back. Is he breathing? I lean down close to his face. I feel little puffs of air against my cheek. He *is* breathing, but just barely. I reach out and pull at the pants legs of the gambling soldiers. I yell up at them: "Help me! There's a hurt kid down here." But they pretend not to hear me. They're too caught up in the game. Shouting. Hoping. I push my head out between the gambler's legs and yell at Brent. But he can't hear me. The shouting and cursing and laughing of all the soldiers is too loud. Jimi's singing is too loud, and I'm too stoned, and it's all too confusing. I yell and yell at Brent until he finally glances my way. I frantically wave for him to come help.

He leaves his two customers to walk over. He leans down. "What the hell are you doing under there, Scotty? Are you drunk again?"

I shake my head. "I'm not drunk. Not very." I point at the kid. "He's hurt. Bleeding. We have to do something."

Brent leans in for a closer look. He grabs my arm and tries to pull me out. "Get out of there quick. It's too late. That guy is dead."

"No, Brent, listen. He was breathing. A little anyhow. But he's hurt bad. We've got to do something."

Brent won't let go of my arm. "Damn it, Scotty, it's none of our business. Stay out of it. I'm right in the middle of a big deal. Let me finish, and we'll get the hell out of here."

I shake off his grip. "No, we can't just leave him under here to get pissed on. We should do something. Call for help or something."

He shakes his head. "I can't afford to get involved right now." He points at the two sailors back at the table. "This deal means some real money for us. Those sailors are off a ship that's pulling out tonight. They want me to deliver a big load of weed to their ship. And they've got the cash. Collected it from everybody on the ship. Give me a few minutes to set a price, and then we'll go." He hurries back to his deal making. I stare at the kid and try to get my brain to make some sense out of this. Can Brent be right? Can this kid really be dying? Just because of that little tiny hole in his stomach? I put my ear close to his mouth. I don't feel anything. Has he stopped breathing? I frantically try pushing on his chest to get some air into him, but that doesn't seem to help. I even blow air into his mouth, like I've seen people on TV do, but that doesn't have any effect either. If he's breathing at all now, I can't detect it. I keep thinking, this can't be happening. You're in a bar in Saigon. You're surrounded by a bunch of American soldiers who are too busy drinking, or too busy hitting on Wong's girls, or too busy throwing those damned dice to help this kid who's an American soldier just like them, an innocent kid whose blood is leaking out of him right here under this table, and you don't have a clue what to do to help him.

Somebody yells the MPs are coming, and everybody runs for the door. Brent pulls me out from under the table. Jerks me to my feet. Forces me out into the street, and we all run off into the night. I look back, feeling like a shit for leaving that kid behind, like I'm one of the cockroaches that run for the dark corners of Wong's back hallway when somebody turns on the light. We all hide in an alley, everybody whispering, giggling drunkenly, as if this hiding from the MPs is a fun kid's game. Brent is farther back in the alley, completing his deal with the sailors. I feel angry at him, angry at them all. I keep thinking about that poor kid under that damned dice table. Why wasn't a single one of them willing to help him? I crawl to the edge of the building and look out. The street is deserted except for an MP jeep parked in front of Wong's. Then, the MPs come out. Two MPs have got the kid under the arms, dragging him backwards. His heels are leaving two furrows in the dirt street. They throw him in the back of their jeep and roar off down the street, raising a hell of a big cloud of dust as they go. I stand up and watch the jeep disappear around the next corner. The others push past me, in a hurry to get back into the bar. I'm left standing alone in the middle of the street, waving the dust away from my face, hoping the kid is still alive, even though I'm pretty sure he's not. That's when the reality of it hits me: that poor kid was no younger and no older than we are, no different than any of us really, just another American soldier far from home. He probably got drafted and sent to this far-away foreign land to fight in a war that he knew nothing about. And now he's dead before he even got to see any of it. I think about how bad he's going to be missed by his folks back home, and maybe missed especially bad by his girlfriend, if he had a girlfriend, who will probably be left alone at his graveside, standing there sobbing her eyes out in a driving rain long after everybody else has left the cemetery.

I slowly walk back into the bar and take my place on my stool. Wong has refilled my special glass right up to the brim, and it doesn't look like he even took any of my money after doing it. I look at him, and he makes eye contact with me, which is unusual for him. But then he quickly turns away. I drain the entire glass of booze and light up another joint. Wong is quickly back to refill my glass. This time he does take some money, quite a bit of it. He goes away, and just for me, he starts the Purple Haze song playing again. I stare down into the dark liquid Wong poured into my glass. It seems to be vibrating with the beat of the music. I decide to think about nothing else but what is in my glass. I focus on the ripples on top of the rich brown liquid. It's fascinating how they reflect the light.

2

Saigon Fable

Back in Basic Training, they said if you get sent to a foreign country you should behave in a way that upholds the honor of the U.S. Army. One thing for sure, you're not behaving in a way that upholds the honor of the U.S. Army. You seem to be lying on a floor. You are hearing noise. Shouting. Loud music. Is it still the same night, the night when that kid got hurt at the dice table? MPs came. Dragged him off. You went back inside. You tried to make the reality of what happened go away by engaging in some *real serious* drinking. You slugged down glass after glass of Wong's amorous-making, woozy-making house drink. Damn stuff sneaks up on you. Might be best to take a little nap. Let the old brain have a nice little rest. Close eyes. Try to sleep. But the concrete floor is hard, and there's a smell. What *is* that smell? You open your eyes. Something smelly stuck to floor. Throw-up? Yours? No matter. Ignore it. Take nap. But it's hard to nap with so much noise going on. Shouting Arguing. All too loud. Music starts, scratchy, distorted music, fading in and out as it tries to find its way into your brain. Hey, that song sounds familiar. It's trying to penetrate your tired brain, but it's getting all mixed up with the yelling and laughing and cursing and complaining and threatening. "I'll smash your fuckin' face in." "Oh yeah, you and who else?" A glass shatters. Must be another fight. You brush the glass splinters out of your hair. Yelling gets louder. Cursing gets meaner. The music tries to compete, but it's all gabled. But familiar. Some kind of radio-type American rock. Trouble is, the music is so loud it can make a person's head hurt. You put your fingers in your ears, but it doesn't work. Still too loud. And a crappy song besides. The kind of music Brent calls teeny-bopper music. "Turn it off!" Uh oh. Did you yell that out loud?

A face appears. Looks down at you. Your blurry eyes try to focus. It's a Vietnamese face. A pretty Vietnamese girl face. "Hello, pretty girl face." Did you say that out loud too? Pretty girl face comes closer. Must be one of Wong's girls, but she doesn't seem familiar. If only you could make your eyes focus, you might recognize her. Maybe she's a new girl. If only you could make your tongue talk, you could ask her why she looks so sad. She sits down on the floor next to you. Hello, pretty girl. Want to share my floor? She takes your hand. Her hand is small, delicate, a caring hand, a hand that wants you to be happy, to be at peace, to not be so worried all the time. Who is she? Even with your blurry eyes, you can tell she's more beautiful than any girl you've seen in the entire twenty years of your wasted life. She's thin, exotic, almost dream-like in her white silk dress. Her pretty face leans close to your face. Is she going to kiss you? With the bedlam of the noisy bar all around the two of you—men drinking, men gambling, men shouting, men fighting, men not upholding the honor of the U.S. Army—she seems to be going to kiss you. Nice.

But wait. No, she's only whispering something in your ear: "You want story, soldier?"

A story? Sure, a story would be nice too. Then the kissing.

Long time ago, poor man go to forest. Family starve. He want find wood. Trade wood for food. But when he get to forest place wood all gone. Trees all cut down. He walk and walk, but see no tree. Then he see one tree all alone. It look like very good tree. Man very happy. He think, I cut down tree. Take back to village. Get food for family. Man get ready to hit tree with ax, but very beautiful woman come right out of air. She stand in front of tree. She say, Stop! No cut down tree. I spirit of forest. I live in tree. Last tree left. She disappear. Strange smell left behind, like flower, sweet flower man never smell before. Man drop ax and rub eyes. Did he really see spirit? Maybe he imagine her. He not want to make spirit of forest mad, but he need tree. Else family starve. He start to hit tree with ax, but spirit come back, right out of air again. She say, No cut down tree. I give you better thing. I give you horse. Man think horse very good. He think I take horse back to village. Trade for much food. But he think maybe spirit try to trick him. He say, First let me see horse. Spirit make horse. It come right out of air, like magic. To man, it look like very good horse. Man very happy, but he not let on. He think he good trader so maybe he get more. He say, Horse look old. I rather have tree. He get ready to hit tree with ax. Sprit say, Stop! This no ordinary horse. This magic horse. Hit horse with stick three times. You see. Man find stick. Hit side of horse three times. Magic thing happen. Gold coins fall out back side of horse. Man very happy. Try to pick up gold coins, but they gone. Man get angry that spirit trick him. Spirit say, That only to show. You not cut down tree, next time horse make real gold. You keep horse. You keep gold. Man agree. Lead horse away quick before spirit change mind. Man walk on road. He walk and walk, long time. Come to inn. He hungry. He think I stop. Get food. Get drink. Man eat and eat and drink and drink. Time come to pay. Innkeeper say, Give me money. Man lead innkeeper outside and tell him stand behind horse. He say, Here is pay. Man hit side of horse three times with stick. But what come out of back side of horse not gold coins. It big smelly pile phân bón land on innkeeper foot. Innkeeper very angry. He beat man very bad with stick and take horse as pay for food and drink. Man go back to forest to find spirit that trick him. He find place, but tree gone. Only big pile phân bón there.

Her story is over. It was a funny story, and it makes you feel a little better. She manages to get you up off the floor and into a chair. She gently explains that the rule is you have to pay money. She signals to Wong. Wong comes and you give him money. He goes away. She brings your hand up to her cheek. Your hand is getting wet. Is she crying? Why is she crying? She helps you to your feet, and you put your arm over her shoulders. She's strong, very strong. She helps you stagger down the narrow hallway until you get to a battered wooden door with peeling paint. She opens it and guides you inside. It's a small room. So this is where the girls bring the soldier boys. Such a grimy little space for doing what used to be called making love. A narrow little bed is pushed up against the wall. No other furniture. But why would there be anything but a bed in a room like this? This room is where the pretend loving takes place. No need for anything but a bed. It's dark in the room, except for a bit of flicking light coming from a candle on a cardboard box near the door. A little carved-wood Buddha sits cross-legged behind the candle. The Buddha has a fat tummy. Why do Buddhas in this country all have fat tummies? The people don't have fat tummies. The little Buddha is smiling. Why is he smiling? Does he know what goes on in this room? The girl leads you to the bed. She helps you take off your clothes. Thank you, nice girl. Better to not have clothes on. Too hot for clothes. She pushes you down onto the narrow little bed. She stands there looking down at you. You stare up at her. What happens next? Isn't she going to lie down too? She pulls her silken dress over her head and carefully hangs it on a big nail that's been pounded into the wall. She turns to face you. You blink your eyes to clear them: this you want to see clearly. Her slim little naked body is a shimmering marvel in the dim flickering candlelight. It's a beautiful body, more beautiful than you ever imagined a body could be. So thin. So delicate. Her skin looks so smooth and delicious you want to reach out and touch it all over. But why doesn't she come to the bed? Isn't that what's supposed to happen? She just stands there. Is she giving you a chance to look at her body before the next part happens? But wait, you told yourself you didn't want to do the next part. You don't want to be just another sweaty American who pays a bunch of money to climb on top of one of Wong's little girls. You don't want to be just another ten-minute trick. You promised yourself your first time should be something special. But maybe this girl is not one of Wong's girls. You've never seen her before. She seems so young. Maybe she's a local girl who just wandered in. But what would she be doing in a place like this? No, she has to be one of Wong's girls. Must be new, just in from the countryside. But if she is one of Wong's girls, why doesn't she come to the bed? Why is she just standing there looking at you? Okay, you should just look at her too. She's very nice to look at. You want to examine every inch of her lovely body. But then you notice her eyes. Dark eyes. Those eyes are watching you closely. What are those eyes looking for? Are they trying to see inside your brain? Don't bother, pretty girl. Not much in there anymore. That brain in there used to be smart. Smartest kid in the whole damn high school. That's what everybody said, but now there's nothing much in there but boozed-out, drugged-out, worn-out mush. You want to look at her nice body some more, but you can't seem to look away from her eyes. Why is she looking at you like that? And why isn't she in a hurry? Brent always complains that whenever he goes to the back rooms with one of Wong's girls, they use their tricks to get you to finish quick, and then they put their pretty white dresses back on and go back out to the bar to get the next guy. But this girl is not doing that. This girl is just standing there. Her eyes are calm, but intense, as if they're trying to tell you something. Those dark staring eyes are enough to make a drunk guy not so drunk anymore. What is she seeing? Just another naked young soldier, one more soldier come from far away to make war on her country, or is she seeing through the pretense, seeing the real you, the lonely, much-less-experienced-with-girls-than-he-pretends-to-be guy who isn't quite sure how the hell he ended up as an American soldier in some God-forsaken hot and steamy country halfway around the world from his home in Arizona? Those eyes may be seeing too much. You have to look away.

As if that was a signal, she comes to the bed. Is this it? Is it going to happen now? Is what you've been wanting, but resisting, for all these years going to happen now? Maybe you should just let it happen. You're no longer in Arizona, no longer the lonely, moody outcast. And besides, the girl you thought you were waiting for is probably meeting cool new guys back there at her fancy eastern college. She's probably already forgotten about you. You said you wanted to do something different with your life. Okay, here's your chance to do it.

She lies down next to you. You hold your breath. What is she going to do? But she doesn't do anything. She just lies there, staring at you. What are you supposed to do now? How does this work? Are you supposed to grab her and begin? Or is she supposed to grab you? Maybe she's waiting until you're ready. Are you ready? Actually, you are feeling a little shy. But why should *you* feel shy? She's the girl. You're the guy. She's the one at risk, completely naked, in bed with a foreign soldier who is also naked. She's entirely vulnerable. In fact, she's so young and so thin, she looks fragile. Not only that, but in her country, what she's doing is undoubtedly considered to be shameful. But her eyes are not ashamed. Now you are the one that feels ashamed. You tell yourself you should stop your damn foolish lusting long enough to ask yourself just what did you intend to do to this fragile young girl? You know the answer to that question. You know very well what you intended to do. Well, it's what you're supposed to do, isn't it? Isn't it what all the other soldiers do to these girls in these back rooms? Isn't it what these girls are paid to let you do to them? So, why aren't you doing it? You should have gone ahead and done it the moment she took off her dress. Even though you've never done it before, you know how to do it, so why hesitate now? But still, you're unsure. All you can do is stare at her eyes. Those dark eyes calmly gaze at you. You're forced to turn away. You turn onto your back and look up at the ceiling. Parts of it are peeling away and hanging down like thick cobwebs. It reminds you of where you are; a grimy little room in the back of a sleazy bar/whorehouse in Saigon. You tell yourself to snap out of it and enjoy this. You paid good money for this, so shouldn't you at least enjoy looking at her body? You turn back to face her and let your eyes wander over her entire naked body. Beautiful. Just beautiful. You try to find another word, but there isn't one. Beautiful is the only word for her. And young. And pure-looking. Yes, pure is a good word for how she looks. Her body is as innocent-looking as the body of a child. But that thought startles you. Just how young is this girl? In the flickering light of the candles, it's hard to be sure, but she looks pretty damn young. You sit up to look at her more closely. There's no doubt about it: she is young, *very* young. She's very thin, and her breasts are too undeveloped to really be considered a woman, even in this insane country where lots of child-women earn American dollars by selling their bodies. The dead giveaway is that she has almost no hair down there between her legs, only a dark triangle of beginning fuzziness, not even enough to hide the shallow crevice that leads downward. Crevice? That's something you never noticed in the pictures of naked women. Maybe it's usually hidden by their pubic hair. Do all women have that kind of crevice? Or only young girls? You're fascinated by it. You can't take your eyes off of it. It's as if it's drawing your whole being toward the magic place it leads to. You tell yourself to stop looking at that place. And stop thinking about her age. Either do it or don't. It's a straightforward process. No great mystery. Natural even. All you have to do is climb on top of her and enter where that crevice is leading you. You should just go ahead and do what she undoubtedly wants you to do, what she's probably waiting for you to do. But although she is undeniably exquisite, and overwhelmingly enticing, you still hesitate. Why? Is it her youth? A word creeps into your mind: forbidden. This is a child. Back home they would call her "jail-bait." Back in America you could be put in prison for what you're thinking about doing with this young girl. You try to push such thoughts out of your mind. This is not America. This is Vietnam. The rules are different here. You try to tell yourself she couldn't be *that* young, could she? She seems entirely feminine, despite her apparent youth. And besides, even if she is very young, she's undoubtedly as sexually experienced as any of the other girls here. But the more you look at her, the more doubts you have. She doesn't seem to be at all like the other girls. Maybe this is her first time too. Was she forced into this? You imagine somebody threatening her, maybe holding her family hostage unless she does it. Or maybe it's her parents who are making her do this. They need money. She's a good girl, loyal to them, wanting to help them. You lie back down. You tell yourself to just stay where you are and look at her body. It is enough. She's so beautiful, you should be content to just look at her and enjoy this moment. Your mind tries to put her essence into some kind of words. She's . . . flawless. Yes, that's the word, flawless. She's perfect, as if no man has ever touched her before this moment. Is that possible? Such perfection hardly seems possible here in Wong's dingy little back room. No, she can't be just another one of Wong's girls, but if that's so, what is she doing here?

She waits, still calmly watching you, allowing you to look at her body all you want. The situation is very confusing. You begin to doubt this is even real. That last joint you smoked must have been a lot more potent than you thought. Or maybe Wong put something in that last drink. Maybe it knocked you out. Maybe this is a dream. Otherwise, how could such a lovely young girl, a dream of perfection, really be here lying naked next to you? But it feels real. You can feel the warm moist air of the room. You can feel the damp pressure of your own naked body against the mattress. Yes, it all seems completely real. And she seems real too, more real and more wonderful than anything that's ever happened to you in your entire life. Okay, this must not be a dream. She's just waiting, waiting for you to start. But if that's it, why isn't she in a hurry? If she's here to provide sex for money, why isn't she urging you to do it and get it over with? She isn't doing anything, and she hasn't uttered a word since the two of you entered this room. You have to decide what to do before it's too late. Brent says Wong has a time limit when one of his girls takes a soldier to a back room. When your time is up, she'll get up and leave. So why aren't you doing it? Every part of you wants to make love to her, but for some reason you just can't bring yourself to begin.

Finally, apparently sensing your uncertainty, she reaches out to pull you close. You put your arms around her. So this is it. It's about to finally happen. Your whole body is ready for it. You feel her lovely little breasts against your chest, firm and cool. Cool? How can that be in this terrible wet heat? But she doesn't do anything else. She just holds you.

You know you should get started, make some kind of move, see how she reacts. You cautiously put your arm between your two bodies and slowly begin to move your hand down toward that thin triangle of girlish hair you saw between her legs. You move your hand down very slowly, almost apologetically, but just as the tips of your fingers cautiously begin to touch the first few delicate hairs, she gently moves your hand away and whispers, "Shh, shh." Why did she do that? What does shh mean? Does it mean she really *doesn't* want you to make love to her? Maybe it's her way of telling you she's too young. It would be wonderful to make love to this beautiful young girl, but you can't. She's only a child. You tell yourself to be content just lying here with her. Do you really feel content? You do feel somewhat content. Your feeling of agitated worry that's normally lurking inside you seems to be gone. How odd. Maybe you're even feeling a little bit happy. It's like remembering an old feeling, a feeling you haven't had for a long time, maybe not since you were a child. You allow that feeling to grow, and soon you're getting so comfortable, you begin to feel sleepy. But you don't want to go to sleep. You don't want to let this moment go. You are determined to keep your arms around her and try not to go to sleep. You're afraid if you don't hold on tight, she might disappear into the night and go back to whatever dream she came from. You turn your head to stare up at the ceiling. In the flickering candlelight, you see what looks like a face up there. You know it's only the rusty stain of an old roof leak, but it looks like the face of some kind of demon. You don't like it. You feel the edge of worry starting to creep back into your brain.

As if she senses your worry, she snuggles closer. She begins to whisper in your ear. "You should no be here. You wrong for this place."

What did she mean by that? You shouldn't be here? Where? In this room? In this country? You try to push away the cobwebs of drugs and alcohol to figure out what she's saying.

"You no fit here. Much danger for you." Her voice is urgent.

Danger? That's for sure. There's a war going on here, isn't there? But maybe that's not what she meant. Maybe she somehow understands that you are no soldier, no killer of men. You consider how to explain it to her. You want to tell her how you ended up here, how your old pal Brent convinced you to join up to avoid getting drafted and sent to Vietnam. You begin: "Back home . . . in America, when you get to a certain age, you get drafted. Into the Army, you know? You don't have a choice. So my friend Brent said if we—"

She puts her finger to your lips. "You listen," she whispers. "I tell. You no sleep."

"Okay," you whisper back. "I won't go to sleep. I promise."

She begins to tell you another story:

Man catch soft-shell turtle. Bring turtle home to eat. Tell servant girl kill turtle. Cook turtle for supper. Man go. Servant girl get out knife. Make knife sharp. Start water boil. But turtle talk. Say, Please no kill. I hurt no one. Eat only green plants next to river. No eat flesh. Only plant. Please let go. Someday you get reward. Girl have knife in hand. It good and sharp. Must kill turtle. Master say want eat turtle for supper. Turtle say, Please. Take me to river. Servant girl look at knife in hand. Throw down knife. Hide turtle in cloth sack. Take turtle to river. Let turtle go into water. When master find out, he very angry. He tell girl go away from house. Never return. Poor girl thrown out on street. Only clothes on back. Man tell neighbors not hire her. Girl have nowhere to go. Cold rain come. She go to river to hide under wooden bridge. Girl have no food to eat. No blanket. She get very cold. She get very weak. She get sick and have terrible fever. She sure she going to die. Turtle come up out of water. See girl under bridge. Turtle come up on land. Begin cover girl with mud. Special mud from bottom of river. Make girl warm. Soon girl feel better. Turtle bring girl fine green water plant and good white water root to eat. Girl soon feel better. People see turtle help girl by river. Bring other people to see. It miracle, they say. Master of girl come. He see miracle too. He say he sorry. He take girl back to house and let her be like daughter. He tell people he never eat turtle again.

She finishes her story, and stares into your eyes. What is that look? A question? Is she asking if you understand? Were you supposed to get something special out of that story? It was a story about being kind to animals. Okay, it was a nice story, but why did she want to make sure you stayed awake to hear it? It was only a story about a servant girl who saved some turtle. But what was that about you being in much danger? Does the story have something to do with that? You try to think of something to say, anything to make her happy. "Nice story," you say. "Poor little servant girl. She got thrown out and got sick. All she did was save the . . ."

Again, she puts her delicate finger to your lips. "You listen." Her eyes are urgent. "Time come. Great danger. You save turtle."

What a strange thing to say. A time will come when you're supposed to save some damn turtle? Does she think she's some kind of fortune teller? What's she up to? She's watching you. Those eyes. So dark, so intense. What is she trying to say? But maybe she didn't mean it literally, that thing about saving a turtle. Maybe she just meant you should be kind to all animals. Nothing wrong with that idea. Being kind to animals is probably part of their Buddhist tradition. Maybe that's all she meant by it. But what was that about not belonging here?

She looks deep into your eyes. Such penetrating eyes. "You

remember. Yes?"

You nod. "Sure, be kind to animals. Especially turtles. Nothing wrong with that idea."

She lies back down next to you. She strokes your cheek. "You sleep now." She begins to whisper into your ear again. Is it another story? Something about mysterious creatures that live in the jungle, creatures that move silently like the mists, more felt than seen. Her whispered stories are hypnotic. They're making you feel very sleepy.

You open your eyes. Something is wrong. Your sleepy peacefulness is gone. The old lurking anxiety that has long lived inside your mind has returned, once again trying to invade every part of you. What has happened? Why are you sweating? Are you in danger? Then you remember: the girl! You reach out for her, but your hands find nothing but the wadded-up pillow. That sweat-stained pillow is trying to deny that she was ever here. It's trying to tell you she wasn't real, that you dreamed her. Can that be? It's dark. This must be the same night. The usual noises are coming from the street outside, shrill arguing voices, a dog barking in the distance, a motorbike passing with harsh overconfident loudness. You realize your head hurts. How can it hurt so much? Did you really drink *that* much last night? Think. Try to remember. You were in Wong's Bar. Something bad happened. You were *taken* to this room. A girl, a wonderful storyteller girl. But where did she go? Why did she have to leave? You feel a terrible emptiness, the kind of emptiness that comes when the last of your hopes have been abandoned. You're hung over, dizzy, feeling like crap from head to toe. You feel like you're about to throw up, and you don't care if you do. It's all meaningless anyhow. Pain is meaningless. This war is meaningless. Being a soldier is . . . not meaningless, worse than meaningless—stupid and wrong. You should not be here. She said that, and she was right. You're not a soldier, never will be. Somehow she knew that, knew the reality of your situation. And now you're left alone, lying in a sad little bed, feeling empty, empty of expectations, empty of purpose, empty of confidence, empty of hope. Anything you had, or thought you had, before this moment is gone. Your aspirations have been revealed for what they were, naive self-delusions, childish fantasies that should have been given up long ago. That realization drains you of hope. Any hope she gave you is gone too because she's gone. You stare up into the darkness. That rusty stain up there. Looks like a face that's somberly staring down at you. You saw it before in the candlelight. But wait, what happened to the candlelight? You look around the room. No candle. No carved wooden Buddha. Nothing but the scuffed wooden floor, the pessimistic stained wooden walls, a cracked, unpainted wooden door that looks like it's been kicked open one too many times. The sad little room is telling you that *this* is the true reality, telling you that your dreamy fantasy of being in a magical world with a beautiful storytelling princess was just that, a fantasy. You are nothing but what you always were, a confused young American, often depressed, generally uncertain, directionless as ever, and stuck for at least a year in Vietnam, the last place in the world you want to be. And that for damned sure is no dream. All you feel is dread, an intimidating feeling of foreboding that hides deep within you. And although you may not want to admit it, you've had such feelings before. Sometimes it unexpectedly overtook you when you were out on your long solitary hikes in the desert. It came on at night when the moody desert sounds talked to you about your wasted life, your pointless existence. But the next morning, the hot desert sun and the clear cold reality of pragmatic cactus plants and restless coyotes tracks all around your campsite were enough to push the feeling away—for a while, anyhow. But here, in this forlorn country, you can't seem to find any way to shake the feeling. It won't leave you alone even when you're at the warehouse surrounded by the other soldier-workers. It's there with you when you walk the streets among the Vietnamese people. It infiltrates you, possesses you, and you know it's going to get worse and worse until you finally give up and face the fact that it's not going to go away until you can pour enough booze into your body and inhale enough strong Vietnamese pot smoke into your lungs to convince your brain that you are serious about not wanting to hear any more of that shit so it will finally oblige by shutting the whole damn thing down to the extent that you can once again be absolutely sure that nothing at all matters anyhow.

No, no, no, you can't allow those dark depressing feelings to take you over again, not now, not after you just had a wonderful night in bed with a wonderfully mysterious storytelling girl. You tell yourself that although you are in a strange foreign country, a country being devastated by an insane war, it's also an exciting country, with interesting foreign people, including a wonderful girl. So don't just lie there letting those damned old dark feelings consume you. Get up and go find her!

You sit up. The room reels. Hang onto something. It usually calms down in a few minutes. You wait. The world stabilizes. You pull on your pants. Your wallet falls to the floor. You check it. Most of your money is gone, but you knew it would be. It doesn't matter. Somehow you make it to your feet. Your head fills up with angry pressure. It hurts more than is possible. You lean against the wall and wait for the pain to go away. But it doesn't go away. Maybe something inside your head is broken. Maybe your head will hurt like this from now on. You look back down at the narrow little bed. A depression in the middle of the worn-out mattress shows where you were lying, where the two of you were lying.

You fall to your knees to smell it, and you're in luck: some of her scent is still there, only a tiny bit, but it *is* her. You try to remember what it was about her scent that was so wonderful. There on your knees, you pray for the essence of her to come back. You want it. You need it. You close your eyes and concentrate, and finally, the essence of her begins to clarify deep inside your mind, the way stirred-up water settles out and gradually becomes clear. It is her aroma; it is her. You take in a deep breath of her. You allow the scent of her to fill you. It's deep and arousing, like some kind of exotic, but maybe poisonous, forest flower. You take in as much of her as your lungs can hold. You hold your breath. You don't want her to get away. You stay there on your knees, grateful that at least this part of her remains. But how long can you hold your breath? You begin to grow dizzy, but you resist breathing, not wanting to lose this last remnant of her. But then your body fails you; it wants air, even if you don't. You're forced to let your breath out. It comes out in a whoosh, and you know that the last essence of her is gone, drifted away to mix in with the stale air of the room; her wonderful fragrance has been gobbled up by the smell of old, wet cigarette butts, by the booze-tinged sweat of the prior inhabitants of the room, by the motorbike exhaust fumes that seep in from the street. But you are absolutely sure it *was* her scent that was there on the bed, if only for a moment. It means she really was here earlier tonight, in this very bed. But if she really *was* here, *why* was she here? She couldn't have been one of Wong's girls, could she? She wasn't at all like them. You look toward the door. Why did she pick you out of all the other young soldiers who hang out in Wong's Bar? Maybe she came to find *you*. Maybe she planned all along to bring *you* back to this room. Maybe, to her, you are somehow special. Didn't she say something like that? You try to remember. She didn't speak much, mostly just told stories. But maybe her stories were more than just stories; maybe they held answers. Maybe that young Vietnamese girl knows something you don't know, something that can save you. You have to find her. You struggle to your feet again. Uh oh, still dizzy. Everything in the room is moving. Fight it. You have to go back out there and find her. Everything depends on it. You stagger out of the room and down the hallway to the bar. The bar is still crowded: gamblers still gambling, soldiers still talking to the girls. Is she among them? No, only the usual girls. They look tired. Must be getting close to dawn. Brent is not here. Did he already leave for the warehouse without you? No, it's still dark outside. Music begins to blast out of the big old speaker up by the ceiling. What is it? Light my fire? Morrison? Whoever it is, he's too loud. Painful to your ears, to your brain. You put your fingers in your ears and lean back against the wall. Maybe you should try to make it to your usual bar stool, your watching place. You could get a drink to steady your nerves, then look for her afterwards. No! Stop thinking like that. You have to find her. You may be woozy and feeling sick, but you can't pass out now. You have to keep looking. Where is Wong? He'll know where the girl went. He *has* to know. You find him just outside the front door. He's trying to drag an unconscious black soldier out into the street. You pull at Wong's arm, but the little Chinese man won't look at you. He's grunting and sweating as he rolls the heavy soldier off of the concrete porch. Finally, when he's finished, he turns to you. He's not happy to see you; you can tell that by the sour look on his face. He has a dirty towel over his shoulder that reeks of the same kind of sour as that look on his face. He wipes his sweating forehead with it.

You ask him where the sad girl went.

He says, "What girl?"

You say, "The strange beautiful girl with the sad face who sat under the table with me last night and held my hand and whispered a funny story into my ear about a horse that pooped gold coins instead of horse shit. Only she didn't say horse shit, she said *phân bón*. Wong, what does *phân bón* mean?"

Wong just stares at you. He doesn't smile. Wong never smiles. He says, "No such horse. No such girl. You go back sleep."

Wong is not telling you the truth. He knows there was a beautiful young girl, but he won't admit it. He even knows who she is, but for some reason, he won't say. He goes behind the bar and won't come back even though you demand it. You chase after him, but he ignores you no matter how much you beg. Where is she? Why won't Wong tell you? You have to find her. Everything depends on it. You try to think what to do, but your brain isn't working very well. Maybe Wong is right. Maybe you should go back to sleep. You can try to find her later. You stagger your way down the hall and back into the room. It's hot in the shabby little room, stifling. You kick off your pants and fall into the bed. You're about to fall asleep when you smell it: her wonderfully intoxicating aroma has returned. It proves she was real. The filthy mattress no longer smells of sweat and sex; it smells *like her*. Her magical odor has become part of the bed, part of the entire room. You sleepily let yourself merge with her scent and soon you find yourself in the silence of a treeless field covered in exotic flowers, the kind of flowers you can only find in an enchanted forest.

3

Kids and Business

I hear giggling. I open my eyes. Sunlight is coming through the papered-over window. It must be morning. I turn over onto my side and discover the room is full of little boys, sitting cross-legged on the old wooden floor. They're in a circle, like little Indians. They seem to be worshipping a big pile of very green plants stacked in the middle of their circle. It's pot, dark green and strong smelling. Looks like Brent got his hands on some really good grass this time. I'm amazed at how many large buds are still in the pile. He usually pulls the best buds out and sells them separately. The stuff looks so potent I wonder if the kids are getting high just handling it. But where is Brent? I spot him. He's also sitting on the floor. He's got his own pile of dope, two small piles actually, and he's mixing them together, using both hands. I wave to get his attention. "Hey Brent, what's up? Who are these kids?"

The little boys turn to look at me. Some of them giggle. I guess they think it's funny to see a confused, naked American waking up.

Brent stands up to bark at them: "Hey, back to work. I'm not paying you to sit on your duffs. Move it!"

They go back to work. Now I see what they're up to. Brent has them rolling joints. He must have got a new shipment in, and it must be good stuff because it looks like he's planning to sell it a joint at a time.

"Faster," he yells. "Pick up the pace. Move. Move!" He circles around them like a papa wolf, scowling at them, berating them. He picks up a few of the finished joints to inspect them. "They're too big," he complains. "You're wasting it. You think this shit grows on trees?"

He laughs at his own joke, but the kids don't get it. He gets serious again and shakes his finger at them. "Keep it moving. And if I catch anybody eating any of this shit, I'll cut your damned tongues out."

The kids giggle and poke at each other. They lean close together to whisper secrets in their own strange language: *Nuean mong deong.*

I know they don't have to bother whispering: Brent doesn't speak a word of Vietnamese, even though sometimes he pretends to. "Hey!" he yells. "Knock off that whisperin'. I'm warnin' you. I got a Vietnamese language book. I can look up anything you're sayin'."

They get very quiet. Did they understand what he meant? Did they believe him? Maybe they think he does have a magic book, one that will instantly translate what they're saying into English. But I know Brent doesn't have a translation book. In fact, I haven't seen Brent pick up a book since high school. Maybe he'd like to know a little of their language, for business purposes, but it's not likely he'd actually bother to try to learn it. But I *would* like to learn more of their language. I've tried, but it's a hard language to pick up from just listening. You think you've learned a word, but then you find out with a slightly different intonation it can mean something completely different. What I need is a teacher. I wonder if that storyteller girl would be willing to teach me her language. If I can find her, I'll ask her.

Brent comes to sit on the edge of my bed. "How ya feelin', old buddy?

"Headache."

"I'm not surprised. You really hung one on last night."

"There was a girl. Did you see her?"

"A girl?"

"Yeah, there was a girl here last night. Didn't you see her?"

"What girl? I didn't see any girl."

"You didn't? She was a beautiful young Vietnamese girl. She told me a story."

Brent laughs again. "This town is full of beautiful girls, my old pal, and they'll all tell you a story if you let 'em. Did she get your money?"

"I guess so, but that doesn't matter. She told me a wonderful story about a magic horse."

"I bet. And I bet she told you that was why she needed the money. Scotty, you never learn. Get your ass out of that bed. We'll find you another girl."

"She was . . . nice. We have to find her."

Brent nods, but his attention is still on the kids. He spots one of them whispering to his neighbor. "Hey, didn't I say to knock that off?" He turns back to me. "Listen, Scotty. I made a couple of real good deals last night. This here shipment is just the start of it. Wait 'til you hear."

"So tell me."

He glances back at the kids again.

I say, "They don't understand half of what we say."

"I'll fill you in later." He jumps to his feet. "Hey, what the hell are you kids starin' at? Pay attention to what you're doin'. You think I'm payin' you to just sit there? Move it!" I watch Brent in action. He circles around the kids, berating them, bopping a few of them on top of their little heads to make the point. They just giggle, but they do speed up. He stops behind one of the youngest, a serious looking boy with a dirty face. He grabs up a handful of joints and holds them up in front of the kid's face. "Damn it, you're makin' 'em too big. These are to sell, not to give your damned mother as a present." He throws down the joints and continues to move around the circle, growling. He stops in front of a skinny little kid who's missing one of his hands. He picks up a few of that kid's joints. "Now this is how to do it. Look at this. Lefty's joints are half the size of any of yours. Lefty rolls better joints than any of you, and he's only got one hand. Show 'em, Lefty."

The kid he's calling Lefty dutifully picks up a cigarette paper and uses it scoop up some of the weed. Then, he creates the joint by rolling it against the stump of his missing hand. One lick, another roll up the arm, and it's a perfect joint. Amazing.

Brent takes the joint and holds it up to show me. "Look at this, Scotty. This kid is a joint-rolling machine. And with only one hand. How about that?" He pats the kid on the head.

Lefty beams with pride. He's missing one of his front teeth. I wonder if he's young enough to still be shedding baby teeth. Or maybe it got knocked out. They must live rough lives, these street kids.

Brent gets ahold of Lefty's right wrist and to show me the kid's stump. "Picked up a funny looking metal canister, didn't you, Lefty? When he was still a baby. Boom. No more hand. Isn't that right, Lefty?

Lefty nods and smiles cheerfully.

"That's why we call you Lefty, isn't it?"

The kid nods again. He won't stop smiling.

Brent moves on to inspect the other kids' joints.

Lefty stares at me. "You Mer-can?" he asks.

"You bet," I say.

"Where part Mer-ca?"

"I'm from a state out west."

I glance at Brent who's frowning at me, his hands on his hips. He thinks I'm distracting them from their job.

"It's called Arizona."

"Air-zo-na?"

"Right," I say. "Deserts. Cactus. Cowboys."

He squeals. "Cowboy! I know cowboy."

The other boys also get interested. They all look at me expectantly.

I sit up. Uh oh, still dizzy. I must have had a lot more of Wong's wicked punch last night than I thought. I wait for the room to settle down. I hang onto the edge of the bed. I feel like I'm balanced on the edge of a cliff. Everything in the room is moving. I see wavering little boys, a wavering Brent over in the corner, back at his task of mixing dope. "Jeez, Captain, sea's a bit rough today, eh? Hold 'er steady now. You've got a man about to fall overboard." I laugh at my own joke, and the kids look at me with curiosity. I shake my head to clear it. Oops, that wasn't a good idea. Makes me even more dizzy. Makes me want to throw up. Better not do that. The kids are watching. Not good for kids to see a naked American soldier throwing up. As the room slows down, I see that Lefty is still watching me. He's a cute little kid. I smile at him to show him I'm friendly, that I like little kids.

Lefty grins at me. "You know cowboy?"

I manage to stand up and steady myself by leaning with one hand on the wall. "Do I know about cowboys? Damn right I know about cowboys. I knew lots of cowboys. Back in Arizona."

That makes Lefty very happy. "Tell cowboy. Tell story."

A story? Let's see. Do I know any stories about cowboys? I saw all the cowboy movies when I was his age, but can I remember any of them? How does he even know about cowboys? He can't have seen a cowboy movie. Do they even have movies in this deranged country?

The other kids chime in: "Story! Story!"

Brent looks up from his dope-mixing. "Hey! Knock it off."

"It's all right," I say. "I'll tell them a story to keep them occupied. They can work and listen at the same time."

Brent makes a grumpy sound and goes back to his mixing. He's tearing big chunks off of a tightly packed ki bale. Must be cheap local stuff. He's mixing the cheap stuff with the good stuff. I'd like to try some of that good-looking weed before he gets it all watered down, but I decide not to bother him right now. He'll give me some later.

"Cowboy story," says Lefty to get my attention back. "Tell story."

The others are watching me with eager eyes. They want me to tell a story about the America they imagine. What would Arizona look like to them if they could go there? They would not believe their eyes. They would see boys their age dressed in fine new clothes, going to clean, well-furnished schools. Probably, these little boys have never seen the inside of a school. I wonder if they are orphans. Maybe they have to do things like this just to survive. Brent probably pays them a dong coin, which is worth essentially nothing, for each joint they roll. But to these poor kids any coin must be like real treasure, something they can trade for a little bit of food. Their grinning and expectant faces make them seem like babies. Have they heard about the war going on in the jungles outside of this city? Do they know that's why we're here? If this war goes on long enough, will these little kids end up carrying a gun someday? I shake off that thought. There is no way this ridiculous war can go on much longer. What would be the point?

"Give me a joint," I demand. "As payment."

Lefty looks through his pile. He's taking the task seriously. He picks out what he must think is an especially good one and holds it out to me. I imagine it must be a big sacrifice for him, a penny lost.

Brent scowls, but he doesn't interfere.

"So, " I say, "you want a story, do you?"

"Yes," says Lefty, serious now, "cowboy story."

The other boys are also looking at me: little brown faces, all waiting for my response.

"You see shootout?" asks Lefty. "In Air-zo-na place?"

One of the kids produces a match, and I light up the joint. I take a deep drag. While still holding my breath, I whisper, "Have I seen shootouts?" I blow out what remains of the smoke. "You bet I've seen shootouts. In Arizona, we see lots of shootouts. Just about every day."

Brent rolls his eyes. "If you're feeling up to it now, why don't you put some clothes on?"

"It's too hot."

The kids snicker. They don't care if I wear clothes or not. They understand. It's hot in their country, day or night. They hardly wear any clothes either. Only tattered shorts. No shirts, and not a single pair of shoes among the lot of 'em. A circle of dirty little feet in front of a very expensive pile of weeds.

Brent shakes his head and goes back to mixing dope.

I feel the first whispers of the marijuana's strength as the cannabis finds its way from my lungs into my bloodstream. Good stuff. I can tell already. Powerful stuff. Makes me realize I'm hungry. How long since I've eaten anything?

"Shootout?" prods Lefty.

I nod, and take another hit, hold it down for as long as I can, then begin: "Okay, there was this one time out West. Two guys faced each other down in a saloon."

"Sa-loon? What is sa-loon?" asks Lefty.

"See, you're distracting them," says Brent.

I see that he's right. "Okay, now listen, kids," I say as gently as I can, "you have to keep working, or I won't be able to tell the story."

They all immediately go back to work, but they're still glancing up at me, wanting me to go on.

"A saloon is a bar. A place where men gather to drink. Like this place." I point toward the wall. "Like Wong's Bar."

I'm not sure they completely understand, but they're all waiting for me to go on. "It was in this Arizona town. Called Tombstone."

Lefty pauses his joint-rolling. "What toom-stone?"

"Keep working, slave," growls Brent.

Lefty goes back to rolling joints, but he keeps glancing up at me, waiting for an answer.

"It's the name of a town in Arizona," I say. "A rough town. Named for all the gravestones they had there. Gravestones. You know, the stone they put on top of your grave. When you die. They had a lot of tombstones in this town. That's how rough a town it was."

They all nod like they know what I'm talking about. Maybe they do. Maybe they know more about death and dying than I do.

"Six-gun?" demands Lefty. "Cowboy six-gun?"

"Of course they had six-shooters. Everybody in Arizona carries a six-shooter. Right here." I slap my bare hip to show them where. I get a mean look on my face. "Okay, here's how it went down. These two hombres have both got six-shooters. Real mean hombres." I growl. "Mean, I'm telling you. Real mean. You didn't mess with these guys. Steely eyes, both of them." I squint my eyes and try to make them look steely. "Long handlebar mustaches."

"What han-de-bar?" asks Lefty. He's looking at me with wide eyes, curious eyes. They are still the eyes of a child, despite the hard life he must live on the streets.

The other kids are also waiting. They're curious, happy, I suspect, for the simple pleasure of being told a story by an American soldier who actually pays attention to them.

"Keep working, you rug rats," yells Brent. "Or I'll sell you to the rag man."

The kids giggle and return to their task. But they're all still glancing up at me, wanting me to go on. I take another hit off the joint. This batch of marijuana seems to be a lot stronger than usual. I wonder where Brent got it. It's making everything in the room very vivid. The shafts of sunlight streaming through the holes in the window paper are being broken into a rainbow of colors. I blow smoke toward the light and it swirls through it, disturbing the colors, changing them to more subtle hues. I look back at the kids. They're still waiting, watching me, wondering why I stopped. I try to focus, but before I can continue with my story, Brent starts grouching at me. "Damn it, Scotty, you're slowing them down with your dumb stories. I got a schedule to meet tonight. And it's almost dawn. We still have to get to the warehouse on time, remember?"

"I'm keeping them entertained," I insist. "We got to keep the workers happy, don't we?"

Brent shakes his head and goes back to his task.

I take a few steps toward the kids. Uh oh, I'm still dizzy. Maybe I'd better sit back down on the bed.

But I miss and end up sitting on the floor.

The kids look concerned, but I wave my hand to show them I'm all right. I crawl to them and squeeze into the circle next to Lefty. "I'll help them roll joints," I say to Brent, "while I tell them stories to keep them happy."

The kids glance at each other and giggle. What must they think of this naked American soldier who joins their circle?

Lefty reaches out to touch my hair. Maybe he's never seen blonde hair this close before. I lean closer to let him do it. He stares into my eyes, as if he can't quite believe how pale my eyes are. Maybe he's asking himself, How can eyes turn blue? Maybe he thinks I'm some kind of freak: yellow hair, pale blue eyes, too tall and skinny for an American, skin too white for anybody. I glance at Brent and realize he looks a bit more like them. It's his Italian heritage: dark eyes, olive skin—not as dark as theirs, but not so different from them, really. Maybe that's why they trust him.

Lefty nudges me. "Shootout?"

I try to focus. "Okay, two mean hombres. Like I said. One of them, this one cowboy, is . . . uh, standing at the bar. That's it. He's twisting his handlebar mustache."

"Han-de-bar?" asks Lefty again.

"Oh, right. I forgot to tell you. Uh, a handlebar mustache is . . ." I pick up a long piece of the pot. It has a few small buds clinging to it. "Like this." I stick it up under my nose and hold it in place with my upper lip. I stroke it on both sides, as if it's a drooping-down mustache.

The boys break out into squeals of laughter. They get it. Smart kids.

Brent yells, "Hey!"

They quiet down.

I drop the branch back onto the pile and take another hit off my joint. It's really starting to work now. I'm feeling lighter, calmer, much less worried than usual. But maybe it's not just the dope. Maybe it's the kids. I like them. I start to float up toward the ceiling, but Lefty touches my arm. Is he trying to hold me down? No, he's just waiting for the story. The other kids are waiting too, so I can't float away. No dreaming yet. I have responsibilities. I'm the storyteller. "Okay, it's like this. The hombre at the bar is gettin' mean drunk. He's been drinking shots of red-eye all day." I look at the kids. They're quiet. Have I lost my audience? No, they're looking at each other. They must be wondering what red-eye is. "Red-eye. Rot gut. It's this kind of strong drink. Like . . . real strong whiskey. Every cowboy worth his salt drinks it."

The kids nod to each other. They know about men drinking.

I point. "All of a sudden, this other big guy comes in through the swinging doors. Oh, my God, it's Black Bart! The sworn enemy of Cactus Jack." I look back at the kids. "Cactus Jack is the guy at the bar."

The kids' eyes are wide. Their mouths are open. They've all stopped rolling joints.

I pick up a little bit of weed and start to roll a joint. "We have to keep rolling, right? We can roll joints and have the story at the same time. Yes?"

They go back to rolling, and Brent nods his approval.

"So, these two cowpokes stand there, eyeballing each other. Their hands are close to their six-shooters, ready to slap leather." I jump up to enact the scene, stumble and almost fall down, but Lefty steadies me with a hand on my leg. Good kid.

I put my right hand down next to my imaginary six-shooter, ready to slap leather. I get a snarly look on my face. "The two cowpokes are trying to stare each other down. Who will blink first?" I pause to build up the tension. I try to make my voice sound deep and urgent: "Then, as if on some kind of signal, both men go for their guns at the same time." I quickdraw and point my finger at the door. I yell, "Pow! Pow!"

The kids are gleeful. They point their pretend gun fingers at each other and mimic my words: "Pow! Pow!"

But I stop their frivolity by holding up both hands. "Guess what?"

The kids don't know what. They wait, eyes wide.

"They both got shot," I say, pointing to my own chest. "Right through the heart. Dead, both of 'em. How about that?"

The kids are frowning. "Dead?" says Lefty.

I can see he's disappointed. He doesn't want the story to be over.

"But one of them is not quite dead," I quickly add.

The kids yell. "Yay!"

"Somehow, Cactus Jack is alive. He struggles to his feet." I stagger, then spread my legs wide, getting into my best gunfighter pose. I keep my imaginary revolver in my hand as I waver from side to side.

"Cactus Jack staggers forward. He's trying to make it to the door." I take a faltering step forward. "His left hand covers his wound. He's trying to stop the blood that's pouring out of him." I look down at my chest. "But it's no use. He can't stop the bleeding. Blood is running down his legs and into his boots." I look down at my bare feet. "He's a goner," I say, and stagger backwards.

The kids yell: "Yay!"

"There's blood everywhere." I point at the floor. "The blood is mixing in with the deep sawdust on the floor."

"Yay!"

"Okay, that's enough," says Brent. "We got to finish this up and get to the warehouse. Get your clothes on."

I carefully put my imaginary gun back into my imaginary holster. "Clothes? Really? Do I have to?"

"Yes, and be quick about it. It's time we got moving. I'll go get a bag for this dope. You keep watch to make sure these damn kids don't steal any of it. I'll be right back." He goes out the door.

"More story," whispers Lefty.

I put my finger to my lips. I whisper, "Cactus Jack is still alive, but just barely. He staggers toward the door, bleeding real bad now." I take a drag off the joint as if I was an old time gunfighter taking his last hit off of a good old hand-rolled cigarette. I leave the joint in my mouth, letting it hang out the corner. I close one eye against the sting of the smoke. "Cactus Jack is watching all the other men in the place. He knows they're all out to get him." I roll my one open eye at the kids and yell, "They all go for their guns!"

The kids all raise their right hands and point their gun fingers at me—all except Lefty, of course; he points his left-hand gun finger at me.

"Pow! Pow! Pow!" they all shout in unison.

I stagger. I fall face-first into the big pile of dope.

The kids scream with delight and pound on my bare back with their little fists.

I'm laughing so hard I can't get my breath.

They're still shooting me: "Pow! Pow! Pow!"

Their shrill voices are making my head hurt. I roll over onto my back, scattering kids. I'm staring up at the ceiling, trying to catch my breath.

But it gives the kids the chance to start tickling me. Their hands are all over me, running up and down my ribs like tickling ants. I try to push their little hands away, but they won't stop, and I can't stop laughing. I can't get my breath. The room spinning. The joint is still in my mouth, but it's getting short and hot, but I can't seem to make my hand move up to do anything about it. Now the ceiling joins the spinning party. That strange stain-face on the ceiling is staring down at me, seeming to move closer and then farther away. For the first time, I think it might be a woman's face.

The door opens and Brent comes back in. "What the hell are you doing, Scotty? Get off of that dope."

From where I am, he looks very tall standing up there.

He helps me up and brushes off the pieces of dope that are sticking to my sweaty body. He takes the roach out of my mouth and helps me back to bed. I realize I'm feeling very tired. My head hurts like hell, and my stomach feels like there's something seriously wrong inside of it.

Brent stands there above me, looking down at me, shaking his head.

I grin at him. "Nice kids," I whisper.

"Yeah," he agrees. "Nice kids. But we got to get going. The warehouse, remember?"

"Just give me a minute. I don't feel so good."

"Well, you'd better get it together, Scotty. I'll get rid of these kids and lock up the dope. Then we got to go."

"Right, right. Just give me a minute."

I close my eyes. Maybe I can catch a few quick winks before he comes back, but as soon as I close my eyes, my damn brain goes right back into its same old regret routine, remembering:

4

Memory: How I Ended up Here

It was an unusually warm afternoon in March, the kind of day you sometimes get in Arizona in the spring, a day that warns of the blistering hot summer that's soon to come. Brent and I were out working in his dad's auto salvage yard, shirtless and sweating hard. We'd used the old Ferguson tractor to push a wrecked 4-wheel drive pickup onto its side, and we were trying to wrestle the stubborn, rusted transmission out of it. Damn tranny wouldn't budge. It was stuck good, all the bolts rusted solid from years and years of sitting out there in his dad's weedy back lot. Finally, Brent got tired of busting his knuckles and gave the damn thing a hell of a whack with his sledge hammer. It still didn't come loose. All his whack did was break the transfer case, the part of the tranny we were after in the first place. When Brent saw the crack in the transfer case, it put him over the edge. He flew completely off the handle and started smashing the thing to bits, yelling out every curse he could think of. I backed off. Better part of valor. Give him time to let off steam. He banged away at that tranny for quite a while, pretty much bashing the whole thing all to hell, ruining anything on it that might have once been salvageable. Finally, he threw down the sledge and turned away, sweating and still growling under his breath. He glared up at the hot sun, as if he wished he could give it a good whack too. I waited, leaning against one of the tractor's big back wheels. Brent glanced at me and did one of his who-gives-a-shit shrugs. He sat down on the ground and lit up a cigarette.

I waited a couple of beats, then: "So, what was that all about?"

He blew cigarette smoke up into the air and didn't reply. He picked up a rock and threw it at the truck. "Worthless piece of crap." He turned and stared at me, scowling.

What was that look for? Was he accusing me of something? It wasn't my fault the damned tranny wouldn't come loose

He used his cigarette to point at me. "Listen, Scotty, about this college thing. We got to talk."

So that was it. His angry blowup was actually about me going off to college, about me doing something without him. But why should he care? We both knew he had no interest in college, hated the very idea of it. He hadn't said much to me since the day before when I'd casually mentioned that I was going to take a class at the U, but I should have known sooner or later he'd get around to trying to talk me out of it. I half expected this kind of blowup when I first told him about it, but he hadn't said a word. Now, it was finally going to come out. I knew he was about to go into a rant about the hated subject of school: school is a waste of time, the teachers are all full of crap, the classes are boring, the textbooks don't teach you a damn thing that will ever be of the slightest use in the real world. Then, he would get into an anti-college rant. College? Are you nuts? College is an even dumber idea than high school. Nothing more than a way to waste years and years of your life learning stuff you'll never ever think about again. I decided to head him off before he could get going. "Listen, Brent, I'm only taking one class. And I'm not going far, just over to Tempe. I can still help you and your dad out here, at least on weekends."

He put on one of his grumpier faces before taking another drag off of his cigarette. He blew the smoke out angrily and shook his head with what looked to me like real irritation, not one of his put-on acts. "I don't give a shit if you help out here or not. My old man thinks two of us working out here during the slow winter months is one too many anyhow. It's just that college is such a dumb idea. Listen, Scotty, take it from me, you'd be wasting your time with this college thing. I'm givin' it to you straight. We got other stuff to do, more important stuff."

"Important stuff? Like what, for example?"

"Like our dope business, for example. Did you forget about that?"

"Not *our* dope business, *your* dope business. All I do is tag along. You do all the selling." He shook his head, but how could he disagree? Selling pot was all his idea in the first place. I only started growing the stuff in my secret spot up in the mountains because I was curious about how to do it. After a while, he said I was getting so good at growing pot, we should start selling it. He pointed out we had a lot more than we could smoke ourselves. That's when he came up with his grand plan to give the stuff to his friends so they could become small-time dealers. We would be the wholesalers. Let them take the risks while we reap the rewards. But it was never a profitable business. His friends either smoked the pot themselves, or quickly blew whatever profits they did make on girls and cars and partying, so we rarely got paid. But Brent kept on providing them with the stuff, if for no other reason than he wanted to think of himself as the local top dog in the marijuana business, the biggest dope-dealing fish in our little pond of Mesa, Arizona.

He shrugged. "Okay, I'm the dealer, but you're the master grower. We wouldn't have a business without your expertise, right? You like that part, don't you? Growing it?"

"Growing is okay. I've learned a lot. But the business part is boring. Besides we don't make enough money to justify the risk."

"Right, right. I couldn't agree with you more. So I got a new plan."

Uh, oh, another grand Brent plan. "What is it this time?" I said, playing along, even though I wasn't really much interested in hearing yet another of his grandiose schemes because they always ended up having a boring, or arduous, or dangerous role for me.

"Can't tell you here." He looked around like somebody might be listening, but he knew as well as I did nobody was around. His old man was the only other person there, and he always stayed close to the office to answer the phone and take care of any walk-in customers.

Brent finished his cigarette and ground it out in the dirt. "Let's knock off and go get a beer. I'll tell you all about my new plan. Wait 'til you hear. It's the best."

"What about the transmission?" I pointed at the truck. "What're you gonna to tell your dad?"

"Screw it. We'll find another tranny tomorrow."

He obviously wasn't going to say anything more about his grand new scheme until he was good and ready. Whenever Brent hatched a big new plan, he always took his time to put it all together in his head before he presented it to me with a big flourish. But this time, he did have me wondering. What kind of plan could it be that he couldn't talk to me about it out here in the junkyard? The junkyard was the one place where we *could* talk, where we *had always* talked, since we were little kids. We'd talked about anything and everything out there, from cars (his second most favorite topic), to how to score with girls (his favorite topic), to the meaning of life (my topic). Maybe he really was worried there might be some customers snooping around somewhere amid the rows of stacked-up wrecked cars and trucks. I looked around, just in case, but there was nobody in sight, nothing but sun and sky and weeds, nothing but the same old smashed up, stacked up, ruined cars. There were rusting piles of axles and tailpipes and teetering stacks of hopelessly bent doors and trunk lids, all of it lying right where it had probably been lying since before I was born. It made me think about how long I had been hanging out with Brent in that place of rust and ruin. Just about all of my Arizona life, ever since my mom and I moved to Mesa from Illinois and Brent beat me up on the playground my first day in grade school (his way of making friends). That same day, after school, he led me out to the edge of town to show me his dad's junkyard. Right off, it looked to me like a cool place to hang out. And it was. We made up fun games to play in the make-believe canyons between the cliff walls of stacked-up cars and in the network of secret tunnels we created by digging under the three side-by-side tire-less faded yellow school buses. Our favorite game was soldiers, search and destroy the enemy. My favorite strategy was the lying-in-wait strategy, hiding in perfect camouflaged silence in ever more innovative junkyard hiding places. We "killed" each other over and over again, first with squirt guns, then later with Red Ryder BB guns that left a little red welt to prove you'd really been hit. Even way back then, when I first saw it, the junkyard was run down and disorganized, already infiltrated with tough weeds that were finding a way to grow right up through the rusted out, fused together, piles of random-metal crap. But there was something about the junkyard that I liked: the weirdness of looking at once-valuable and highly-prized cars that had ended up discarded and forgotten. The cars were strewn about the weedy field, seemingly randomly. Some of them looked in pretty good shape, but that only meant their engines had blown. It was clear they would never again be loved. They looked forlorn, as if they had given up any hope of rescue, and they were slowly sinking into the earth, as if being consumed by it. Most of all, I liked the aloneness of the place. After school, Brent would wander through the junkyard scavenging parts for his ever-growing fleet of not-quite-running old cars, and that gave me the chance to be alone. I'd sit in the front seat of one of the old doors-missing, ragged-topped convertibles doing my homework, or maybe just thinking. Customers almost never made it out to the back lot. The truth was, for the past few years, it had been getting more and more uncommon to see customers anywhere in the wrecking yard. Brent's father was a moody guy, a stealth drinker who didn't talk much, but when he did talk it was usually to complain that the junked car business was not what it used to be. Brent and I knew why, but we never said it out loud: more and more people were buying European and Japanese cars, and Brent's dad wouldn't have a junked foreign car on his lot. Didn't believe in them, didn't believe the foreign car buying "fad" would last. The few customers who did come by to get parts for their old American-made junkers almost always stayed up front where Brent's dad had arranged the best stuff—generators, alternators, starter motors, radiators, wheels, pulleys, and other stuff like that—in wooden racks out behind the sales office. I had never been able to figure out how Brent's dad could make enough money selling those few items to keep food on his family's table, even though it was only the two of them since Brent's mom had died and Brent's little sister had managed to get herself pregnant at fifteen so she could force some poor sucker to marry her in order to escape from a falling-down old house at the edge of a junkyard. At the time, I wondered if she did it mostly to escape the endless washing of her dad's and brother's filthy, oil-soaked overalls.

Brent lit up another cigarette and seemed content to just sit there and smoke it. He'd picked up a stick and was drawing odd little designs in the dirt with it. I knew he was trying to wait me out, expecting my curiosity would get the better of me. He was sure that sooner or later I'd go along with him to a bar to hear about his grand new plan. But this time, I wasn't going for it. I didn't care what his new plan was, I was going to college. If he wanted to just sit there and wait, it was fine with me. I could play that game too. A light breeze picked up. It was coming up the ravine from the lower part of the junkyard, the place for vehicles that had long-ago been stripped of anything that might be remotely useful. It brought the familiar smell of old oil, a smell you don't get used to, no matter how long you're around it. Old crankcase oil. Old gearbox oil. Over the years, the dry Arizona air had solidified all that old oil into a kind of sticky gum. Even though I had smelled that smell just about every day of my life since I came to Arizona, I suddenly realized that smell said *old*. It said *tired*. It said *worn out*. I realized it was a smell that should not be smelled by a young person like me. That kind of smell was meant for old people, old mechanics, old junkyard dealers like Brent's dad. Such smells should not be smelled by a guy only a couple of years out of high school, a guy just getting started in the world. That day, the old oil smell and the tired-out feel of the old junkyard made me even more aware that I had been wasting my life ever since I'd finished high school. I looked over at Brent and wondered if he had ever thought about what that smell of old oil said about us. Probably not. He'd been around that smell since he was born. But I smelled it clearly that day. I realized that old oil smell was warning me, telling me I'd been doing the same old things for way too long. It told me I'd been just hanging around, working for peanuts in his dad's junk business, selling a little pot, drinking just to get drunk, taking drugs just to get stoned. What the hell was I was doing with my life? Was I waiting for something to happen? Like what? Nothing was going to happen as long as I kept on doing the same old things. Maybe Brent was right about college being a waste of time, but at least it was doing something, and doing something had to be better than doing nothing.

"Okay, you're right," said Brent, bringing me back. "Our dope business isn't goin' anywhere in this slo-mo town." He tried to take one last drag off of his cigarette, but he'd smoked it down to the filter without noticing. He looked at the burned cigarette filter in disgust and flipped it away into the weeds.

He stood up and nodded grimly, as if he was agreeing with me that college was a good idea after all. But I knew better. He was just preparing his next argument. He picked up his sledge hammer and gave the truck another whack, but not so hard this time: this whack wasn't a destructive whack; it was more of a thoughtful whack. Then, he leaned on the sledge's handle and looked off into the distance, "Listen, Scotty, I'm tellin' you, this time I really do have it all figured out. No kiddin'. My new plan is sure-fire."

"Yeah, right," I said, trying to sound as sarcastic as possible. "Your plan is always sure-fire. Remember your last can't-miss plan? Smuggling Bennies in from Mexico inside the frame of that old Buick?"

He shrugged. "Hey, it worked didn't it? The border police didn't suspect that innocent-lookin' girl we used as a mule, did they? Man, I wish I coulda been there to see her driving up to the border checkpoint in that big old black Buick."

"Yeah, it worked alright, but why didn't you seal the pills in plastic bags instead of just pouring them into the frame."

"Hey, how was I supposed to know it was gonna rain? It hardly ever rains down there in November. Anyhow, this plan is nothing like that plan. This one is big." He raised his eyebrows like he does when he means, This one is so good you'll be wide-eyed surprised.

But this time I wasn't about to play the wide-eyed surprised game, no matter how big his plan was. I was going to start college, and he wasn't going to talk me out of it. In fact, although I hadn't told him, I'd already signed up for my first class, a philosophy class. Modern Philosophy 112. I'd signed up for it just to prove to myself I could be a real college student, even if I couldn't afford to go full time yet.

"Come on," he said. He swung the big sledge hammer up onto his shoulder. "Let me buy you that beer, and I'll tell you all about it."

"No thanks. I've got plans."

"He squinted at me. "Plans? Bullshit. You got no plans. You haven't even gone out on a date since Miss Fancy Pants, dumped you."

I ignored him, but I knew he was going to keep on pushing it.

"I suppose your plan is to head out into the desert again. Camping out by yourself, as usual. Poor little Scotty, all alone, wandering around in the desert since his girlfriend went off to a fancy eastern college."

"She was never my girlfriend."

"Yeah, but you wanted her to be. You chased her around like a little puppy dog for two years."

"I never chased her. We liked to talk, that's all."

"Right, talk. In other words, you never once got her into the sack."

"She's Catholic."

"So? What does that mean, that she's got the Pope and the Holy Mary standing guard in front of her precious hole?"

"Drop it."

"Glad to. Forget her. Let's scare up a few girls that know how to spread their legs. Let's go have some fun."

"Like I said, I've got plans."

"Plans. I bet. Out there communing with cactus and coyotes."

I ignored him. I wasn't about to let him talk me into another night of drunken pointlessness, using the fake IDs he'd made for us to hit the downtown Phoenix bars, just so he could pick up some drunk girl. I never could figure out what pleasure he got out of scoring with some girl he didn't give a shit about.

He pointed in the general direction of Phoenix. "Ready?"

I stood up. "Like I said, I got plans. And tonight it's not camping out. Tonight I'm headin' up to the res as soon as it gets dark. That secret place on the Verde I told you about."

"Fishing? And you talk to me about boring? Sitting in the dirt staring at a cork floating in a river? Now that's what I call boring."

"You don't catch trout with a cork. I'll find you later. We can talk then." I picked up my tools and headed for the tools shack.

But Brent caught up and got ahold of my elbow. "No, no, if you're goin' fishin', then I'm goin' fishin' too. Let's go."

I shook off his wrestler-strong grip, and as we walked back to the tool shack, I tried to talk him out of coming along. I knew he'd just use the opportunity to try to talk about whatever his latest grand plan was.

But this time he was more insistent than usual. He said he would just tag along, that he had nuthin' else to do.

So he really was going to go fishing with me. That was a real surprise. Brent hated fishing. He'd once told me fishing was about the dumbest thing man had ever invented, said if you wanted a fish, you should go to a store and buy one of the damn things. If he was willing to go along fishing with me, it should have told me this new grand plan was something especially big.

As we drove up to the river, he didn't seem interested in talking to me. He was muttering to himself as he searched the dial of my old truck's radio. He was complaining, as usual, about how hard it was to find good rock music in the midst of all the currently-popular crappy teeny-bopper music like the Beatles—the dumbbell "Beatles for Brains," as he called them. I knew what he was looking for: he was intently searching the radio dial for the acid rock he liked. The real music, he called it, the music for *us*, not the music for *them*. *Them*, in his mind referred to pretty much everybody besides him and me, but he especially put the kids who had been popular back in high school into the "them" category. He liked to sarcastically describe *them* as trained seals, dutifully getting good grades because their parents wanted them to, going to stupid school-sponsored events like football games and prom dances as they tried to be "Oh so popular." It was the main thing we agreed on; I wasn't the slightest bit interested in becoming one of *them* either. He restlessly cranked the radio dial back and forth, stopping only when he hit one of the staticy pirate rock-and-roll broadcasts from the other side of the border. We'd heard talk that some of those Mexican radio stations were so powerful they could reach far-away places like Kansas, or Illinois, or even Moscow. The rumor was that the Russian government was always trying to jam those broadcasts of decadent Western rock-and-roll music, but the stations were just too powerful. Maybe they did reach all the way to Moscow, but in much-closer Arizona, those pirate stations always faded in and out, and even when you could hear them, they sounded like they were coming from inside a big tin can. Brent finally found the gravel-voiced Wolfman, and for a change, it was coming in fairly clear. Wolfman Jack was the disc jockey's name, and he only broadcasted in the evening. He said it was because that's when the ionosphere cooled down enough so his radio signal could bounce around the planet. The crazy guy loved to talk about his really big transmitter. Said it was the biggest and most powerful transmitter in the world, made just for his secret station. He claimed it was so powerful birds flying too close to the antenna would drop to the ground dead. No one knew exactly where his broadcasting station was, but the rumor was it was hidden somewhere in the Mexican desert, very close to the Arizona border. The Wolfman said it was built like a fortress and was surrounded by rows and rows of barbed wire. He claimed to have a force of armed guards with machine guns lest anyone try to break in and stop his broadcasts. None of his claims were likely to be true, but wherever his broadcast studio was, the Wolfman was Brent's favorite DJ. He played exactly the kind of rock music Brent loved. Sometimes when we were driving around late at night, Brent would say we should drive down into Mexico and try to find the guy (we never did). As we drove up into the mountains that night, the Wolfman entertained us with good music. But then he got into a long crazy rant about what he called bubble-gum music, meaningless repetitive non-musical music. He said most of the listening public only went for mordida, the worthless crap radio DJs are paid to play. Then, he went into his usual non-stop selling. He started with his "famous" weight-control pills that were supposed to be able to make you put on weight or lose weight, whichever you wanted. Then, it was his baby chicken eggs. He said you could grow 'em up and then eat 'em. Next, it was Florex pills to "put some zing in your thing." His own personal favorite product was mail-order roach clips. He said they were totally legal. You used them to clip the roach's tiny little legs before you threw 'em out the window. Finally, he got back to putting on good music. He started with Jefferson Airplane, then Big Brother and Janis, and then the Animals, "We Gotta Get out of This Place." Brent put his feet up on the dash and sang along really loud, mimicking Burdon's raspy smoker's voice as he play-acted the fingering of an invisible guitar. His eyes were closed, and I could tell he was fully into his act, singing away at the top of his lungs like he didn't have a care in the world. The music drifted in and out through the static that sometimes got so bad the song was barely recognizable, but that didn't matter because we both already knew the song by heart. Brent kept on jabbing my shoulder with his finger each time he sang the line about getting out of this place until I finally said, "Right, right. I get it." Very funny. He'd actually found a song on the radio to help him make his point: we gotta get out of boring old Arizona. It made me realize his grand plan must involve going somewhere else. The coast? LA? San Fran? But with no money in our pockets, and no contacts in those places, that probably wasn't his big plan. So what was it? I pushed away my curiosity and tried to keep my focus on my upcoming college class. The class started in a week, and I wasn't about to get caught up in some grandiose scheme of Brent's that would make me miss it. No way. Not this time.

When we got to the river, I did the fishing while Brent sat on the bank chewing on a weed and tossing stones far out into the water, probably trying to scare away the fish so we could get back to talking. I tried to ignore him, but eventually I got fed up. "Damn it, Brent, quit that. I'm trying to catch a few trouts for our supper here. If you're hungry, quit scaring the fish away so I can catch one."

He threw one last rock and edged a little closer to me to make sure I could hear him above the gurgling sound of the river. "Listen, Scotty, you and I both know the pot business around here is crap."

So that was it. His plan had to do with our pot business. I expected him to continue on, to lay it out for me in all its glorious detail, but he didn't. Apparently, he still wasn't ready. He just leaned back on his elbows and didn't say another word. He was content, for the moment, to stare out across the river at the first few stars that were popping out in the darkening sky.

I finally caught a couple of smallish trout, and he followed me back up to my truck where I built a small mesquite fire—big enough to cook on, but not big enough to attract the attention of the Indian police who would chase us out and take the fish for themselves. I cooked the fish in my old black skillet, and as usual, Brent complained that I'd undercooked the fish. "You left them practically raw," he said. "And your old iron skillet makes 'em taste like rust."

But I noticed he ate his fish up plenty quick. After we finished eating, neither of us said a word for a while. He smoked, while I looked up at the stars. Eventually, the fire died down to crackling red coals.

"Okay," I said, "let's have it."

"What?"

"Come on, you know you only came out here with me so you could tell me about this new grand plan of yours."

"Well, if you really want to know, it's that we got to change our lives. Mesa, Arizona is a small potatoes, small-minds town."

"You think you're telling me something I don't know?"

"The thing is, we're wasting our time here selling dope to small-time dopes. And then there's this war thing. We got to make sure we don't get sent to Vietnam."

That got my attention. I'd been trying not to think about that. "And you've figured out a way to avoid getting drafted?"

"You bet I have. I talked to this guy."

"What guy?"

"Just a guy. He joined up, put in his hitch, and came back home. The girls around here all think he's some kind of war hero, but he told me all he did was lay around at some base down in Florida. The guy told me there were hot chicks down there. You hearing what I'm sayin'? Florida? Hot chicks? The guy said he spent his weekends at the beach playin' with the locals, hot girls in teeny little bikinis."

Brent waited for me to give him a reaction, so of course I made sure I didn't. I could already see where he was going.

"So, say somethin'."

I kept my mouth shut and stared up at the stars. Join up? Could he really be suggesting that? With a war going on over there in Vietnam? Like everybody else my age, I had been thinking a lot about the inevitability of getting drafted, but the generals and politicians on TV had been saying the war over there was almost won. Some were even saying they would end the draft soon. The only problem was, they'd been saying that for a long time.

"Listen to me, Scotty. I'm layin' it on you true."

He again paused to wait for my reaction, and but I didn't give him one. I was going to college. I would worry about the draft later.

But Brent wasn't going to give up that easy. He moved closer. "So here's my plan. I checked it all out. If you get drafted, they say it's for damn sure you'll end up getting your ass shot off in Vietnam. But if you join up, you get to name your job and where you get sent. How about that? And you only have to be in for two years. We'll ask for that base in Florida, and we'll have a ball down there. Get laid every day." When I still didn't respond, he said, "Are you listening, Scotty? I'm serious."

And he did look serious, dead serious, and that wasn't like him. I figured it had to be another one his trial balloons. He liked to float his crazy ideas out there in the air in front of me, just to see how I'd react. He couldn't really be thinking about joining the Army. Brent, a soldier? No way. I decided not to even give his trial balloon a chance to launch. "Not me," I said. "I already told you, I'm going to college."

He shook his head and put on his best you-just-don't-get-it frown. "That college trick doesn't work anymore, Scotty. They're gonna start drafting everybody now, even college students. Things are goin' from bad to worse over there. Every guy our age is gonna get drafted and end up in Vietnam."

"If we signed up, we'd probably still end up over there."

He shook his head, and kept shaking it longer than was necessary.

"Absolutely not. I guarantee it. Like I said, I checked it out good."

"How did you check it out?"

"I went to the recruiting office over in Phoenix and asked 'em. They said it straight out. If you sign up, you get to name your own training, and that means you get to go to some base stateside. That's what the man said. Think about it, Scotty. Don't I always figure out a way to work things? This is gonna be a walk in the park. We sign up, name our own deal, and stay out of the draft. The fact is, they need more support guys than fighters. They'll agree to anything to get you to sign up."

I tried to imagine Brent as a soldier. Brent was a tough guy, and he liked a good fight, but he hated authority. If a teacher at school tried to discipline him, he told them to stick it up their ass. He wouldn't last ten minutes in the Army, no matter where they stationed him.

But once Brent has an idea in his head, there's no stopping him. I knew I was in for a non-stop convincing session.

"I'm tellin' you, Scotty, this is the right move. If we don't do something, we *will* end up in Vietnam. Guys like us are getting killed over there every day. The war is goin' bad. That's what this guy told me. A lot worse than they're telling us. They need more cannon fodder over there. You want to end up in Vietnam? Gettin' killed? We got to sign up before that happens to us."

I tried once more to get through to him. "No, Brent, you're not listening to me. I'm going to college. My class starts next week."

He started jabbing his finger in my direction, getting louder with each jab: "I'm tellin' you, Scotty, we can't let 'em draft us. We do that and we're fucked. We got to act and act quick while they're still makin' these deals for signin' up."

I kept my mouth shut and concentrated on eating my fish while he went on talking about sunny Florida. "Hey, man," he said, it's a place we've never been. Someplace new for the both of us. You'd like that, wouldn't you? You're always sayin' you wanna get out of here."

It's true, I was ready to get out of Arizona, but I was determined not to hook into his scheme. He always made his big plans sound good, but something always went wrong.

I decided it was time to just lay back and look up at the stars. I always enjoyed watching the movement of the constellations across the sky. I pointed. "Look up there, Brent. See that pattern of stars, the ones that look like a bent-up W? That's Cassiopeia."

He stared at me, frowning. "Stars? Damn it, Scotty, who cares about stars? This is somethin' we got to think serious about."

"C'mon," I said, "just look at her. She's sitting in a chair up there. Doesn't it look like a chair?"

He shook his head in disgust, but he did look up.

I pointed out each of the stars that made up her chair. "The constellation is named for Cassiopeia. She was this legendary queen. A queen among the gods. Her beauty was known throughout the land. But her beauty got to her, and she became really vain. One day she boasted that she was even more beautiful than the sea nymphs."

Brent interrupted my story: "What's a sea nymph?"

"Some type of minor sea goddess, I guess. Anyhow, the sea nymphs heard about Cassiopeia bragging about her beauty, and they got really pissed off. They went to Poseidon, the god of the sea, and demanded she be punished. Poseidon didn't want to do it. I think he secretly kind of liked her. But in the end, the pressure got to him, and he sent a horrible sea monster named Cetus to her land. The monster tore up Cassiopeia's whole country."

Brent lit up a joint while he thought about it. Finally, he said, "What a load of unimportant crap. I suppose you read that in a book. Why do you waste your time reading about that kind of shit?"

I gave up. He wasn't interested in anything that hinted even vaguely of school. He smoked his joint and refused to look up at the sky.

But just when I thought he'd forgotten all about my story, he handed me the joint and said, "What kind of monster?"

I took a hit and handed it back to him. When I couldn't hold my breath anymore, I whispered, "A whale."

"What?" He looked incredulous. "A whale? That's no kind of monster. Whales only eat fish."

I let out the rest of the smoke. "Whales don't eat fish. They eat krill."

"What's a krill?"

"Krill is this little tiny stuff whales eat. They strain it out of the water through their baleens."

"What the hell is a bay-leen?"

"Some kind of strainer thing. Inside their mouths, I think."

"They eat little tiny stuff?"

"That's right."

"If that's all they eat, how do they get so big?"

"They eat a lot of it."

"They must." He handed me the joint again.

I took a hit.

He was still looking up at the stars. "And how could a whale tear up a country?"

I blew out what remained of the smoke. "I don't know. Do you want to hear the rest of this story or not?"

He shrugged, so I went on. "Anyhow, after the monster, Cetus, tore things up, you'd think that would have been the end of it. But no, as far as the sea nymphs were concerned, her country may have got torn up, but Cassiopeia herself got off scot-free. So they went to the other gods and made a big stink about it. Finally, to get the sea nymphs off their backs, the other gods put Cassiopeia up into the heavens tied to a chair. I pointed up at the constellation again. "So now she has to stay there forever. That's her, sitting up there in her chair."

Brent took back the joint. "I still don't see how a whale can tear up a country." He took a big hit.

"It's a legend. Legends don't have to make sense."

He gave the joint back to me, and then he went silent. I could almost hear the gears turning in his head. What was he thinking now?

Finally, he turned to me. "Listen, Scotty, there's another reason. The guy said they stayed drunk the whole time because they couldn't get any dope down there in Florida. We could start a whole new dope business there. We'd have the market all to ourselves. We'd get rich."

"Let me get this straight. You're saying we should join the Army so we can sell dope to the other soldiers?"

"Damn straight. I mean, mainly we got to join up to keep from getting sent to Nam, but also because the Army is where shit is happenin' right now. Listen, Scotty, sellin' dope is what we do, right? It's what we're good at, about the only thing we are good at. That's our business, and a businessman has got to go where the market leads. Right now, our business is leading us to the Army. I'll tell you somethin' else; sooner or later all our customers are gonna get drafted, and unless we go with 'em we'll be out of business."

Was he making a joke? It didn't seem like it.

"Think about it, Scotty, we could be the kings of pot in the Army. You know how to grow it, and I know how to sell it. We could make some boo coo bucks while we put in our hitch."

That stopped me cold. So this was his grand plan? Join the Army to become a bigger dope dealer? I decided it was time to clam up completely. When Brent got going on some nutty idea like that, there was no talking him out of it. And when he got his mind set on something, it was supposed to be my role to just go along with it. He saw himself as the grand planner, and I was supposed to be the number one go-alonger. But not this time. He could go ahead and join the Army if he wanted to. But not me. I was going to college.

No need for me to tell you the details of how he talked me into signing up. He continued to work on me, like he always did, and in the end, of course he pulled out the big one, the ice memory: "God damn it, Scotty, Don't you realize I'm trying to help you? Didn't I go under the ice for you? Didn't I risk my life to save your sorry ass?"

It was true, I did owe him my life. He really did go under the ice to save me back when we were kids, but it was his fault I fell through the ice in the first place. It was him that talked me into hitching all the way up to the mountains in the middle of the winter just because he wanted to see snow. And it was him that brought along the fruit jar half full of whiskey he'd stole from his father's secret stash. We started out by drinking the booze, taking turns slugging it down. We did a lot of gagging and spitting and making sour faces, but somehow we got it all down. And we kept it down by challenging each other not to be such a wimp as to throw it back up. From then on, the day became a battle of drunken dares: who could kick the most dead limbs off a fallen-down tree (he won), who could break a limb off that dead tree by butting it with your head (he won that one too because I wouldn't even try it). The final one was his dare of how far we could slide out onto the cracking ice of that frozen river. I said I would go first because I was a fast runner, and it was the one dare I might actually win. Besides, a dare was a dare, and had to be responded to, or you'd forever be labeled as the biggest chicken: Cluck, cluck, cluck. I took a long run at it and did a really good slide that took me out almost to the middle of the river. But of course, as soon as I came to a stop, the ice broke, and I went through. Before I could even understand what was happening, I was under the ice feeling the current taking me downstream. I could see the bright silvery ice above me, and I clawed at it, but it was no use. I had the sudden awareness that the dim sunlight shining through that thick layer of ice was the last thing I was ever going to see, and for some dumb reason I kept trying to reach for that light. Then, I felt Brent's strong grip on my arm. He must have run out onto the ice as soon as he saw me fall through. Drunk as he was, he didn't hesitate: he jumped in after me. You had to give him that; he didn't for a second worry about his own life. And somehow in the dim light under that ice, he found me. I was confused and scared and probably only half conscious, but I felt him dragging me back to the hole in the ice. He pushed me right back up onto solid ice. As soon as I realized I was out, I scrambled across the ice like a frenzied turtle trying to get away from that dreadful hole. When I reached the shore, I looked back, but I couldn't see Brent. For a second, I thought he must have been pulled under and drowned. But then his head popped up out of the hole. He was struggling to pull himself out, trying to grab onto the ice, but he kept on slipping back into the water. I wanted to go help him, but I was so numb from the cold I didn't think I could even move. Besides, I figured if I went back out there, I'd just go though the ice again, and then we'd both be dead. His head kept on popping up, and each time he yelled at me to go find a stick to pull him out. I somehow got to my feet, and I did manage to find a big stick, but I was damned sure I didn't want to go out onto that ice again. To this day, I wonder how he knew I'd be willing go back out there to save him. How did he know I wouldn't be too scared? Standing there on the shore with that stick in my hand, I almost decided it would be better to run for help. I told myself there was really nothing I could do for him: the ice was too thin to support both of us. But there were no houses nearby. I thought about running out to the highway and trying to flag down a car, but I knew it would take too long. Even if I did find help, by the time we got back, it would be too late. I knew what that icy-cold water felt like. He would slip into unconsciousness soon. So even though I was half frozen myself, and shaking uncontrollably because of a strong north wind that was whistling through my wet clothes, I crawled back out there onto that creaking ice. Brent was still trying to pull himself out, but I could see he was getting weaker by the moment. I took the stick and crawled as close to the hole as I dared, staying flat on my stomach. I held the stick out to him. He caught it and even though his pulling on the stick started dragging me closer and closer to that terrible hole, I held on long enough for him to pull himself out. I wanted to hurry and get off the ice, but he just sat there shivering, staring at the hole. Then he started laughing. He socked my shoulder, hard, and then he threw his arm across my shoulders and let out a huge loud laugh. It was like a laugh and a yell at the same time, and it echoed across the snowy valley and back to us. "Well, here we are, old buddy," he said. "A couple of half-drowned rats, drunk as skunks and freezing our asses off. But we're alive, aren't we? I saved you and you saved me. How about that? It means we're brothers now. Like the Indians. Blood brothers." There were tears in his eyes, but he was grinning.

I had the feeling his words about us being brothers, and his rare display of emotion, meant he was thinking about his little brother who'd got run over by a car when he was only a little toddler. Brent was supposed to be watching the kid, but he got distracted by something or other, and the next thing he knew there was a screech of tires. He ran out to the road to find his little brother dead, pinned underneath a car along with his bright-yellow plastic big-wheel rider. Maybe Brent thought his saving me was like saving his little brother. Maybe I was supposed to take his brother's place. I still remember the odd feeling it gave me. Even though I was so cold I could hardly think straight, for some reason his "adopting" me worried me, as if playing the role of his little brother might carry some kind of heavy responsibility.

We pretty much stuck together ever since that day we were under the ice. He seemed to feel responsible for me. Hardly ever let me out of his sight. He watched over me like I really was his little brother, protected me, gave me money, and eventually forced his dad to pay me a small salary so we could continue to hang out together in the junkyard. When we got to high school a few years later, the other students, and even the teachers, couldn't figure out why we were pals. They said we couldn't be more dissimilar. The school counselor, a tall thin man with unnaturally black hair told me I shouldn't be hanging around with Brent, that sooner or later he would get me into trouble. He said Brent and I didn't have a damn thing in common. He described

Brent as a moody outcast from the wrong side of the tracks, a tough guy who would always be looking for trouble and finding it. He said I, on the other hand, had promise. He described me as one of the smartest students in the school. He pointed out that I was also a good athlete, had made the cross-country squad, even though I had to quit the team before the end of the season to keep from losing my salary from Brent's dad. That counselor said I was a bright fellow who could go far in the world, if I made the right choices. And hanging out with Brent was definitely not the right choice. Later, back in class, I thought about it and realized something important: that counselor may have had an advanced degree in counseling or something, but he didn't understand friendship. He said Brent and I didn't have a damn thing in common, but he was wrong. We had something in common that counselor would never understand: we were under the ice together; we both should have been dead, but we weren't because we'd stuck together.

After that night of fishing and talking, Brent worked on me every time we were together, cajoling me, badgering me, describing how much fun we would have in the Army. He embellished his story more with every telling: not only hot girls in bikinis, but exciting new places to see and fun new things to do. He said he had it all worked out. There was so much money to be made selling dope to the other soldiers, we'd be rich by the time we got out. I wasn't interested in selling dope to soldiers, and I doubted we'd be meeting many hot girls in bikinis at any Army base I'd ever heard of. But every time we were together, he came up with another reason his plan was perfect.

I tried to ignore him, tried to keep my focus on my one college class, which I was enjoying. The class was addressing some of the questions that had made me sign up for a philosophy class in the first place. Ever since that time I was under the ice, looking up at the strange silvery sun that was shining down through the ice, scratching at it with my fingernails as I desperately tried to keep ahold of my young life for one more second, I had wanted to understand more about life and death. In the very first class session, the professor quoted an old-time British philosopher named Hogben who'd said, No problem of philosophy is more fundamental than the meaning of life. The professor wrote what Hogben said on the blackboard, and then he turned back and pointed his piece of chalk at us. He said, Life is what matters to us humans. Then we die and none of it matters anymore. I knew immediately that I had signed up for the right class. That Hogben guy had it right on: none of the stuff we do every day matters; what matters is that we are alive. That first day in the philosophy class gave me a lot to think about, but I knew I couldn't explain any of it to Brent. He'd just tell me to knock off the school crap. He'd say the important thing was how we were going to keep ourselves from getting drafted and sent to Vietnam.

In the end, the horrors of Vietnam they were showing on the TV news every night told me he was right: I had to do something, or I'd be sure to end up over there. They were starting to draft everybody our age, so it was either sign up or get drafted. I decided to at least go along with Brent to the Army recruitment office to see what they would say. So, one fine spring afternoon, after we had knocked off work at the junkyard, I went with Brent to the downtown Phoenix recruiting office, got the man's assurances we would be assigned somewhere nice and safe, maybe even Florida, signed on the dotted line, endured the recruiters iron-gripped congratulatory handshake and Brent's hearty clap on my back, and walked out the door a soon-to-be soldier in the U.S. Army. I remember walking back to Brent's ratty old illegally-parked and unregistered Camero thinking that the paper I had just signed could well have been my own death warrant.

A few weeks later, Brent and I were at a base in Missouri, not Florida. I stumbled through the make-believe hell they call Basic Training, and after that was over, an elderly captain called me in to give me my assignment. He gestured for me to sit down, and he didn't even look at me as he read one word from the paper, "Vietnam."

I jumped to my feet. "Now wait a minute. The recruiting officer said if I volunteered for the draft I could choose my own assignment."

At least that got him to finally look up at me. He made an odd sound in his throat, maybe a stifled laugh. He had a smile on his face. Had I said something funny? Maybe he'd heard that same complaint so many times it had become a kind of running joke to him.

But then his smile disappeared, and he put on a serious and concerned look that I assumed must have been his half-hearted attempt at compassion. He said, "Son, that recruiting officer had no business making that kind of promise to you."

He had a gentle drawl like he was from the South. Maybe he was a nice man. I held my hands out to him and pleaded: "But, sir, if you can't believe what the official Army recruiting officer tells you, who in this army can you believe? Isn't there some kind of appeal process?"

Apparently there wasn't, because he sat back in his chair and drawled, "Who the hell cares what he said or didn't say, soldier. And who the hell cares what you want anyhow? You go where we tell you to go. Now get the hell out of my office and go pack your shit."

So that was it: no laid-back assignment in Florida, no hot girls in teeny bikinis; I was bound for Vietnam, like just about everybody else I had gone through Basic Training with.

When the sarge came to the barracks to bring me my dispatching papers, he acted like he was happy for me. "Congratulations, soldier, you bound for the big time. Vee-at-nam. Where the action is."

I took the papers from him without a word and started packing up my stuff. At least I wouldn't have to put up with his bullshit anymore. I finished packing and went to the brig to see Brent. He was sitting on his cot, looking sad and pissed off. Basic Training was over for me, but he was still only a week into his two week stretch in the brig. It was his second visit to the camp prison cells, this time for doing more than his usual refusal to follow orders; this time he had threatened to rip off a staff-sergeant's stripes and stuff them up "your fancy sergeant ass."

I told him the news. I was being sent to Vietnam. "Not Florida," I emphasized, "Vietnam."

Surprisingly, that cheered him up. "Great!" he said. "I'll go too." He jumped up and came to talk to me through the bars. He pointed at me and winked. "I got to keep an eye on you, don't I?"

He stuck his hand through the bars to shake on it, but the MP at the desk half stood up and pointed a white Billy club at him: "Keep your damn hands inside the bars," he growled. "I told you before."

Brent gave the MP the finger and mouthed "F you."

Surprisingly, the MP didn't do anything about it. He just sat down and went back to reading his newspaper.

Brent seemed as happy as I'd seen him in a long time. "No shit, man. That's great. Lots of action over there. I been hearin' all about it. It's just what we need after being stuck . . . in this shit-hole place!"

He said those last few words plenty loud enough for the MP at the desk to hear, but the guy still didn't look up.

"All we got to do is keep our heads down over there for one lousy year, and we'll be done with it. Hey, it'll be fun. We'll hook up with some of the local girls over there. Get laid every day!" Again, he said the words plenty loud enough for the MP to hear, but the MP was obviously ignoring him.

"You think that's all Vietnam is?" I said. "Fun? Girls and action? Did you forget there's a war going on over there?"

He waved my words off and half turned away from the MP. He whispered behind the back of his hand, "Lighten up, Scotty. This'll be even better than Florida. Remember how I told you we needed to go where the dope business is? Well, I been hearing everybody over there is smoking pot. I betcha Vietnam is the hottest dope market in the world. We'll make a fortune over there."

That was Brent. He sure knew how to roll with the punches. Every other recruit, including me, was scared to death, figuring we were being sent to die in a very dangerous foreign war. But not Brent. I don't think he was even capable of conceiving of his own death; he was going to live forever—and have fun doing it.

Brent immediately volunteered to go to Vietnam, and that got him out of the brig. They suspended his sentence, patted him on the back, and said, Good lad. We need more patriotic men like you.

When you finish Basic Training, if you're heading for a foreign assignment, they give you a few weeks leave before it's time to ship out. Brent used his time to party. He hung out in the local bars using his brand-new uniform to attract girls. I hid my uniform in my bottom dresser drawer and went back to my philosophy class. The university semester had been going forward without me, but I hadn't bothered to drop the class, so I figured I might was well go back and get as much out of it as I could. I didn't tell the professor where I'd been, but it was a pretty big class, so he probably hadn't even noticed my absence. I hadn't gotten to know any of the other students so nobody expressed any curiosity about where I'd been. It left me feeling even more like an outsider than before. I enjoyed being back in the philosophy class, but the atmosphere on campus had changed while I was gone: the buildings were now plastered with even more anti-war posters, and there were now anti-war rallies on campus nearly every day. The posters were saying the Vietnam War was an immoral war, more immoral even than other wars. One day, walking across campus after class to get to my car, I saw a student standing on the lip of the central campus fountain shouting through a crackly megaphone. He was yelling about the immorality of the Vietnam war, and he seemed really angry about it. He yelled at everyone who passed, trying to get them to join his one-man demonstration. I ignored his ear-blasting entreaties and walked on past. But I didn't go far. I stood in the shadow of the Student Union building and watched him. Soon, he began to have some success at getting some of the students to stop. It wasn't long before he had a small crowd gathered around the base of the fountain. He started a chant, "Hey, hey, LBJ, how many kids did you kill today?" The students eagerly joined in. "Hey, hey, LBJ, how many kids did you kill today?"

I hurried on, not quite sure what to make of it all. I had the uneasy feeling that if I had stuck around, the less-than-enthusiastic look on my face might have given away the fact that I had signed up to be one of the baby killers they were all yelling about.

I didn't make it far down the sidewalk before a very attractive girl moved quickly to block my way. Her eyes were just about as angry as the boy back at the fountain, and I had a quick rush of adrenaline, wondering if she had somehow found out about me.

She forced a flyer into my hands and said, "Join us, before they get you too."

I knew what she meant: she could see I was about draft age. What she didn't know was that she was too late; they'd already got me.

But I didn't say that. I just thanked her for the flyer and hurried on. As I walked, I looked at her flyer, not really reading it, thinking more about her and what she was representing. She was very pretty, but what struck me the most was how sincere and honest she seemed. She had looked into my eyes without any pretense or guile. She truly believed in what she was doing, and I admired that. For the briefest moment, I considered going back to talk to her. Maybe I could suggest we go to the fountain together and join in the shouting. Or we could go somewhere else. Have some coffee in the Student Union or something. Just talk, maybe. Of course, I didn't do that. I kept on walking. What would I have to say to her? She would probably want to talk about the war. What would I say if she asked me how I was going to avoid the draft?

Safely back in my car, I sat in the front seat reading her flyer. It said the Vietnam War was being "staged" in a backward country that didn't want us there in the first place. I reread the flyer a couple of times, not quite sure how I should feel about it. There was something about that girl and her flyer that disturbed me. It wasn't because she was protesting against a war that I had signed up to participate in—I understood where she was coming from, even if she wouldn't understand why I was doing what I was doing—but why had she and so many of the other students come to distrust our government? I had to admit I hadn't been paying much attention to politics. The ease with which that young fellow had gathered together an angry crowd of students to yell out their protests made me wonder if something fundamental had been happening in America while I was off exploring the inner workings of my own head out in the Arizona desert. Of course, I *had* noticed the stenciled words "THE WAR" at the bottom of every stop sign in town and the increasing proliferation of the peace sign, the three intersecting lines inside a circle. It was appearing everywhere: spray-painted on walls, magic-markered on traffic signs, hurriedly painted on colorful Volkswagen buses. Other than noticing those hints that the anti-war movement was gaining some momentum, I hadn't paid much attention. But on the ASU campus, I thought I was seeing something much more significant than peace sign graffiti; I was seeing real anger at the government. I was aware that a lot of the dopers Brent sold pot to tended to ramble on about the "damn politicians" who, they all agreed, were "only out for themselves." But the sudden appearance of so much overt and angry anti-war activity on the ASU campus got me to wondering if something bigger was going on in America; maybe the mistrust of politicians had already been inside those students, and maybe this new war, being fought for some kind of vague "domino-theory" reasons in some dinky little far-off country, had brought that mistrust and resentment of our government to the surface. The angry words in her flyer reminded me of the explosive anger that had led to the chaos and violence of the Watts riots in LA that had been shown so vividly on TV. It was clear that the fires and the looting in LA had been expressions of anger at "the establishment." Now, I was getting the feeling that the growing anti-war sentiment among the students was very similar to that kind of anti-establishment anger. As I reread her flyer, it finally brought home to me the fix I was in. I *really was* about to go to Vietnam to participate in a war that many were saying was wrong. For the first time, I asked myself if *I* trusted the government; did I truly believe they were sending me over there for good and true reasons, that we *had to* go to Vietnam to stop Godless Communism before it could spread to our shores? The politicians on TV were saying that was the justification for the war. They called it the "domino theory." They kept on warning us that if Vietnam fell into the hands of the Communists, who knows what country would be next? Japan? Us? Did anybody really believe that? So why were we fighting a war over there in a far-off place like Vietnam? What was really at stake? I was pretty sure my new superiors in the U.S. Army would not be interested in answering such questions. In fact, they probably wouldn't appreciate me even asking them. If I'd learned anything in Basic, it was not to question orders. Our drill sergeant always emphasized that our superiors knew better than we did. But did they really? Weren't they too just following orders from higher up? I wadded up the flyer and dropped it on the car seat next to me. What did it matter? I was committed to go to Vietnam, so I'd soon get the chance to find out for myself what was going on over there. I was doing what Brent always warned me against, thinking too much. I looked out the car window and tried to think about something else. It was a nice warm blue-sky day. There was nobody about except for a policeman putting tickets on the windshields of the student cars who had parked past the two hour limit. It made me think about my policeman father. He'd served as a Navy shore patrolman in World War Two. If he was still alive, what would he think about those student war protesters? He had never talked about the big war he had been in, and now I wondered why he hadn't. I couldn't remember him ever mentioning anything about it. He never even talked about anyone he'd served with. I knew his ship had been involved in the invasion at Normandy, and he'd been in France. Was he assigned to keep the peace in France after the U.S. combat troops landed? I didn't know. I couldn't even remember how I knew he'd been in France during the war. Did my mother tell me that? Now, looking at that cop passing out parking tickets, I wondered what a former soldier and policeman like my father would think about these students shouting insults aimed at our President. What would he think about them calling an American war immoral? I wished he was still alive so we could talk about it.

After that day, I began to hang out on campus almost every day, even when I didn't have to go to my class. I didn't really have anything else to do. I was totally bored with Brent's constant partying, and besides, if I hung out with Brent, it would have put me back in contact with the guys I had gone to high school with, guys who were struggling with their own decisions about what to do about the draft. Whenever I ran into any of them, they always asked me why I had joined up. They didn't believe me when I said I'd joined up because I didn't know what else to do. They preferred Brent's explanation, that we had joined up to have fun, to go to a new place, to meet new girls. Most of them said that's what they were going to do too. Join up. Either that, or they were going to wait and hope the war was over before they got drafted. Some of them talked about running away to Canada, but I had the feeling they wouldn't really do that.

On the ASU campus, there were anti-war rallies every day. I found them interesting. There was folk singing, which I enjoyed a lot, and some pretty good oratory. There were even some clever skits designed to show how evil Uncle Sam was: a student in an Uncle Sam suit strutted around in an outrageously-tall stars-and-stripes top-hat cynically trading money for arms, even as he sent boys like me to their deaths. I admired those students: they were serious about their beliefs, and they weren't afraid to show it. Some of the boys were even burning their draft cards, even though the police were often there taking pictures of them. I didn't join any of the demonstrations, but I went every day to watch. I kept my distance, staying in the background so nobody could draw me into the protests or ask me any questions. Staying well back from the main group of protesters was a good idea anyhow, unless you wanted to end up surrounded by the riot police that usually arrived mid-afternoon, and if you were lucky enough to get away without being arrested, you'd end up stumbling away from the campus teary-eyed and half-blind from the tear gas they routinely used on the protesting students. Whenever the police came and started laying down tear gas, I put my wet handkerchief over my face and retreated to the building where my philosophy class was held. I figured I really was registered for that class, so I had the right to be in that building even if my class wasn't meeting that day. I wandered the halls, and I sometimes hung out near classroom doors to hear what was being discussed in the other classes. Most of the lectures were pretty boring, but I eventually discovered the film classes that met every day in an auditorium-type classroom. They showed very old films and some foreign films. Although I had never been much interested in movies, I was curious about what kind of films they would show in a university class, so one day, after they turned down the lights, I slipped in and sat down in the back row. A movie titled "Wild Strawberries" was just starting. The actors in the film were speaking in another language, Swedish I think. There were English translations printed at the bottom of the screen that were hard to read because the printing was white, and the movie itself was in stark black and white. The movie seemed kind of scary to me, but the students in the class seemed to think it was funny. Sometimes they burst out laughing for reasons I couldn't figure out. Like this one scene that was on a street corner. There was a big clock that didn't have any hands on it. The man in the movie was looking at the clock, trying to figure out what time it was. The students in the class thought that was funny too. Then, a shiny-black horse-drawn hearse came along, but it couldn't go past the corner because its wheel got caught on the cobblestone curb. It kept on trying to go forward, but it couldn't because of the stuck wheel. It kept on trying, bumping and bumping against the curb until the back door of the hearse finally sprung open and a black coffin slid out the back. When it hit the pavement, the coffin lid popped open, and the man saw that the dead body in the casket was him. The students also laughed at that. Why were they laughing? It seemed really scary and disturbing to me.

The next day, I went back to that auditorium and again, sat in the back row. This time the movie wasn't in black and white like that Swedish film, it was a German film, and it was in color. When my eyes got used to the dark, I realized I was the only person in the auditorium. Where were the students? Wasn't this the normal time for the class? I wondered if I should leave. I wasn't registered for the class, and I wasn't a "real" student either: I was an about-to-be-soldier, soon to be heading for Vietnam, exactly the kind of person the students on campus were protesting against. I decided that maybe they were just running through the film, getting it ready for a later class. The movie seemed strange, but interesting, so I figured there wouldn't be any harm in staying put for a while to see what it was all about. Turns out, it was about two puppets that were inside a little stage that looked like a box draped with black curtains. It seemed to me that the black-draped box looked a lot like the black-draped windows of that horse-drawn hearse that had been in the Swedish movie the day before. Maybe they were going to show this film to compare it with the Swedish film. In that film, the man was being forced to do things he didn't want to do, and now, they were showing a movie about how somebody pulls the strings of puppets to make them do things they didn't want to do. As I watched the puppet movie that day, it hit me that I was like that too: I was doing things in my life that I didn't want to do. The draft board and other high-up officials in hiding were pulling my strings, making me do whatever they wanted, making me go to Vietnam to fight in a war I was beginning to have doubts about. The students were all saying this war was morally wrong, and I was beginning to wonder if they weren't right. In the film, I couldn't see any strings controlling the puppets. Of course, there were no real strings making me be a soldier, but like the puppets in the movie, I really had no choice. The puppets in the movie started to hit each other. They started out slapping each other with their white glove-like hands, but then they started hitting each other with sticks. It wasn't long before they escalated from sticks to big clubs, then to knives. Eventually, one of them pulled out a rifle and shot the other puppet dead. The killer puppet put the murdered puppet in a casket and nailed down the lid. Then, he got a really big nail and started hammering the nail down through the center of the casket. Then, the movie was inside the casket, so I was seeing that big nail come down right at my face. I couldn't move because I was supposed to be dead, but I knew I wasn't because I could see the big nail coming right down at my eye, coming closer and closer with each bang of the hammer that echoed very loud inside my casket. I jumped up and ran out of the theater. As I ran down the hallway, I was sure the "real" students up there in the projection booth had somehow found out I was heading for Vietnam. They'd tricked me into coming into a dark empty auditorium so they could scare the wits out of me with that awful movie. I never went back to that auditorium.

When the weekend came — our last weekend before we had to report to the Army bus that would take us to a Vietnam-bound airplane — Brent and I went up to my secret growing spot in the mountains to harvest what was left of our pot plants. With the coming of the warmer weather, my little watering spring had all but dried up, which meant most of the plants were already dead. But there were a fair number of buds that could be salvaged. While we were trimming the plants, I mentioned the campus demonstrations. I told him they were getting bigger every day.

He wasn't much interested. "Who gives a shit about their damn protests? Those candy-ass students can shout and march and demonstrate until their faces turn blue. Won't change a thing. All we got to worry about, old buddy, is how to make money off this war."

"And keep ourselves from getting killed," I added.

"Don't worry about that," he said, focusing on his pot-trimming task. "I'm workin' on that angle too."

Our plane full of new recruits left the states early in the morning. We refueled in the Philippines before the last hop to Vietnam, and then we were supposed to land at the big Bien Hoa Air Base outside of Saigon, but the pilot had a hell of time getting us down on the ground, because every time we got lined up with the runway, a jet bomber would push in line ahead of us. We circled around for quite a while, waiting for our turn, until finally we were able to move in behind a B-52 that was moving about as slow as we were because it was trailing fire from two of its engines. Everybody on our plane, all green and untested like me, some of them still white-headed from where they'd buzzed off all of their hair, scrambled over to that side of the plane to see it. They pushed their noses up against the windows like they were kids on their first trip away from home. For some of them, it probably was. We finally landed, and from the moment I got off that plane and set my foot on that hot tarmac, I knew I was in over my head. Mostly, I was focused on trying to figure out how to breathe the hot, wet air. If the air wasn't already bad enough, every time another jet idled past, it left a trail of stinking, toxic-smelling fumes. Everybody seemed to be having trouble with it. There was a lot of throat clearing and eye rubbing. That thick, wet, jet-fumes-filled air smelled so bad it was all I could do to keep from puking. They made us stand in formation under a hazy sun on that hot asphalt runway for a long time. I guess we were waiting for somebody to come and tell us what to do next. I was surrounded by the other newly arrived soldiers, but I felt very alone. Brent wasn't on my plane because he had been assigned to a penalty platoon as part of his suspended sentence and they were scheduled to come in on a later plane. I looked around to try to take my mind off of the bad air. The base seemed huge, with lots and lots of buildings, and there were American soldiers all over the place. Some of the soldiers were marching in formation, to nowhere in particular as far as I could tell. Their formations were about as ragged as they had been back in Basic, but they didn't seem all that unhappy about having to march under the hot sun. Maybe they were excited to be away from their parents and in a foreign country. They chanted cheerfully as they marched:

> They say in the Army the pay is just fine
> Give you a hundred and take back ninety-nine
> Sound off one two. Sound off three four.

Another group went by, sounding off even louder, as if they were competing with the first group:

> They say in the Army the shoes are just fine
> You ask for eleven they give you size nine
> Sound off one two. Sound off three four.

They continued to march, their chants often drowned out by the screams of jet bombers and fighters taking off. Nearby, shirtless soldiers were hard at work building sandbag walls against the narrow white clapboard buildings that looked exactly like the ones we had been barracked in back in Basic Training. If it wasn't for that hot wet air, it would have been hard to believe I really was in a foreign land. Although being in a brand new place should have been exciting to me, I got a sinking feeling that it might not be the big adventure I had hoped for. I was all dressed up like a genuine soldier, but I sure didn't feel like one. I looked at the others who had been on the plane with me. What did they think of this air base, of Vietnam, of the war? Did they also have doubts about why we were here? Back in Basic, I had never heard anybody talk about why the U.S. military was in Vietnam. Maybe they didn't think about it. Besides, except for that one damaged bomber that we had followed in, and the fact that they were stacking sandbags around the buildings, there was no sign that there *was* a war going on here. As I stood there watching it all, waiting for somebody to order me to do something, I was having a hard time imagining myself joining the busy soldiers I saw marching and sandbagging. I felt about as out of place as a kindergartner who'd just stumbled into the men's locker room. For about the hundredth time, I wondered how I had let Brent talk me into this. I was no soldier. But I knew I would have to at least go through the motions while I was here; I was committed to be in Vietnam for the duration of my sentence (or tour, as the Army likes to call it). Seeing the extent of the buildup at the huge Bien Hoa Air Base, I wondered what those student anti-war protesters back home would think of it: all the men, all the airplanes, all the seemingly endless rows and rows of white two-story buildings. As I looked at it all, my mind was saying, what the hell is *this* all about? Is this dinky little country really worth all this? And then, that thought made me wonder if those anti-war protesters had actually gotten to me. Even though I had kept myself distant from the protests, I had listened carefully to the points they were making. The protesters were asking why we were fighting a war in such a faraway unknown little country. They kept on saying, how could a nothing place like Vietnam really be all that important to our national defense? I tried to shake off those kinds of thoughts. I was a soldier now, not a war-protester. I had made the commitment to come see it for myself, and now I was in it. What good would it do me to be always thinking about the meaning of everything? I hadn't even thought twice about running off to Canada like some were doing. And I was not interested in doing anything dishonest like faking a back injury, or expressing a preference for boys over girls. I had just gone along with Brent's plan of adventure and profit because I knew it was time to do something, and in that moment, I was convinced doing *something* was better than doing *nothing*. As I stood there sweating on that hot runway, I wondered what Brent would think when he got there. He'd probably see all these soldiers as pot customers. He'd take in a big deep breath of the foul air and say, Hey now, this is just what we needed, Scotty old pal. New territory to conquer.

5

The Streets of Saigon

"Hey, what the hell are you still doing in that damn bed? Brent is hovering over me, frowning and tapping the face of his watch. "Dawn has sprung, my lad. Nighttime playtime is hereby officially kaput, over and done with. Time to get back to the reality of the U.S. Army."

I don't move. I stare up at the face on the ceiling. "Look up there, Brent. It looks like a face."

He glances up at it. "It's a water spot. Leaky roof."

"Yeah, but doesn't it look like a face? Staring down at us?"

"No, it doesn't. Get dressed. We got to move."

"I don't think I can do it today, Brent. I'm sick."

He laughs his usual short sarcastic laugh. "You're just hung over, my drunken friend. But hung over or not, we got to get a move on or old Fart-Ass will rip us a new asshole." He tosses my soldier clothes at me. "Did I land us our cushy jobs at the warehouse for nothing?"

"Cushy? Are you kidding? In that hot as hell warehouse?"

"Hey, workin' is better than bein' dead. Am I right or am I right?"

"I'm serious, Brent. I feel like shit."

"I bet. With what you been puttin' into your body, who wouldn't be? But sick or not, we got to get to the warehouse."

I respond with my best groan.

"Hey, I did my part, didn't I? Didn't I keep us from getting sent to the front to get our asses blown off? Now you got to get out of that sack and do your part."

"All right, hang on. I'm coming." I sit up and pull my pants on. I put on my shoes and stand up. Uh oh, still woozy. I put both hands against the wall and wait for the room to slow down.

Brent is impatient. "C'mon, c'mon, get your act together, Scotty. We're runnin' late as hell."

I manage to get my wrinkled-up Army shirt on and I follow Brent down the narrow hall. I'm so dizzy I can barely keep going forward. Man, how much did I have to drink last night? Brent leads us through the bar, which is the hard part for me because there are no walls to lean against. I focus on keeping my balance, arms out wide, taking small steps, aiming for the front door. I'm trying not to throw up on Wong's floor, even though I know nobody would notice because its been thrown up on so many times before. As we go through the barroom,

Wong stops wiping glasses long enough to watch us go by. Nobody else seems to notice us: all the other soldiers are either still sitting at the tables hitting on Wong's girls, or they're hard at work at the dice table, still caught up in the madness of their non-stop gambling. I make it to the door and lean against the frame while I take one last look back, hoping to spot my storyteller girl. She's not there.

Brent hurries off in the direction of the warehouse, expecting me to keep up, but the thick steam-bath air and the angry, high-pitched, headache-inducing whine of the whizzing-past motor scooters is not helping my head any. The street is already full of people, even though the sun has just come up. Despite how bad I feel, the sight of all the hurrying-past Vietnamese people cheers me up a little. I tell myself to snap out of it: this is a foreign country, just where you wanted to be. You said you wanted to go somewhere different, do something different. Well, here you are. At least you're out of boring old Mesa, Arizona. I try to keep up with Brent, but he's moving too fast, and soon he gets lost among the crowds. Okay with me; I'd rather slow down and look at the people. I always enjoy being out in the Saigon streets, seeing what the locals are up to. They go about their business, just regular folks doing whatever they do. As usual, they all seem to be in a hurry. It's as if they're all late for some very important meeting, but more likely, they're just busy by nature. And just about every one of them is carrying something, boxes, cloth bags, U.S. Army Jerry cans they probably bought on the thriving military-equipment black market. An old man is carrying a heavy-looking clay pot that must be filled with liquid. You can tell the pot has liquid in it by the way he carries it close to his chest and how it makes him wobble as he walks.

And then there are the heavy-duty movers, old men on bicycles. I watch one of them as he weaves his way through the crowd. He's got so much loaded onto his bicycle, both in front of and behind his seat, it seems impossibly top-heavy. Why doesn't he tip over? He wobbles on down the street, barely avoiding running into the other people, seeming to be always about to lose control, but he never does. It's as if he's doing some kind of amazing circus act. I spot Brent ahead. He's able to move fast because the locals see him coming and stay out of his way. They always stay out of the way of any American soldier. Even though we're not armed, the locals act as if we are. I try to smile to show them I'm no threat, but they don't smile back. They look down at the ground and move to the side of the road until I pass.

I catch up with Brent, but as soon as we pass out of the bar district and into the much more crowded shopping district, he gets ahead of me again. I especially like the shopping street with its waves of people and waves of odors: burning incense, a strong smell that can make you sneeze if you get too close, piles of flowers that offer a much more gentle and appealing smell, and an amazing variety of food smells, most of them almost hidden beneath the pleasant odors of sweet ripe fruit. The sellers line both sides of the street with big baskets full of things I recognize, like carrots and potatoes and onions, but also other types of vegetables I don't recognize: bundles of something that looks like weeds, and strange root vegetables. Part of the block is reserved for clothing venders. They've set up tented stalls, and they've made them a little bit colorful by hanging out flapping-in-the-wind, flag-like, narrow strips of bright cloth. I'm not sure what those strips of cloth might mean. It may have something to do with what they're selling, but if so, I can't figure it out. Maybe it's just intended to attract attention, to lure potential buyers in, like a fisherman's colorful lure is used to attract fish.

I hurry to catch up with Brent again, and soon we're surrounded by a flock of young boys. A few are about eight or nine years old, like Brent's dope-rolling kids, but most of them are much younger. They gather around us, their dirty little hands held out to us. They're cute little barefoot beggars in shorts. They overwhelm me with their high-pitched chatter and their adorable, expectant grins. They're all very much alike, all black-eyed and black-haired, and they're all short with flat tummies, skinny legs, and stick-thin wrists. And all so suntanned they're brown as berries. They see our U.S. Army uniforms as a signal to beg for the Hershey's chocolate Tropical candy bars that some soldiers get in their sundries kits (a flyer in the package says the candy bars were designed especially for use in Vietnam — guaranteed to not melt in your pocket despite the wet Vietnam heat). On the rare occasion a soldier does give one up, I've noticed that the kids never eat them right away like American kids would. So what do they do with them? Share them with their siblings? Trade them for other things? Sometimes older kids beg for the Pall Mall or Lucky Strike cigarettes the front-line soldiers get in their field-ration packs, and sometimes I see a little kid smoking. But not very often. I expect the cigarettes are like money for them. I often see those American cigarettes for sale in the shopping-street food stalls, so I bet the kids trade the cigarettes for food. Brent shoos the kids away, and as I watch them disappear into the crowds of people, I wonder if they have homes to go to.

With the way my head feels, there's no way I can keep up with Brent's fast pace. When he walks, he walks fast. He strides right on down the middle of the street. Even if you didn't know him, you could tell by his walk that he's not afraid of anyone or anything. He's always been a faster walker than me, always impatient to get where he's going. But his fast walking isn't because he has longer legs than me; the truth is, although I'm a lot thinner, we're about the same height. But Brent always wanted to be taller than me. When we were little kids, he'd regularly make me stand up against his dad's garage wall to be measured. He'd make a pencil mark on the white wall to show where the top of my head came to. When it was his turn, he'd stretch himself up as tall as he could and make me mark his height. Then, he'd step back and say, See there, I'm still taller than you, and I always will be. Even though we were the same age, it was like he was trying to will his body to grow just fast enough to stay a little bit taller than me. I never once mentioned that I knew he was going up on his tiptoes before we did the measuring. If he wanted to be the tallest one, it didn't matter to me one way or the other. And he made sure I knew which one of us was the toughest too. We had our scraps—who remembers over what—and he always won, never hurting me much, just dominating me enough to show which one of us was the boss. He *was* plenty strong, no denying that. A lot stronger than me, and a lot stronger than just about any other kid in town. He got that way from throwing around heavy transmissions and other heavy crap like that in his father's auto wrecking yard. Been doing it his whole life. But it wasn't just his muscles that made him tough. It takes more than strength to be tough; it takes a tough attitude, and a willingness to get hurt and still not back down. Brent had that too. He's loose-limbed and lanky, like all the really tough guys are, and everybody in school was afraid of him. For good reason: he had a short fuse. He was ready to fight at the slightest provocation. Nobody messed with Brent, and because I was his best friend, nobody messed with me either.

As I go down the shopping street, I'm feeling better and better. This walking fast in the morning air is beginning to make me think I might actually survive this day. But that thought reminds me of what it's going to be like slaving away all day in that damn hot warehouse, and my confidence drains away. With the shape I'm in, I can't imagine how I'm going to get through another long hot day of work.

I slow my pace to try to catch my breath. I look ahead and see that Brent hasn't noticed that I've fallen behind again. He's probably lost in his head, probably dreaming up some new scheme. Brent's always been like that, a strategizer and a schemer. Even when we were kids, he was always looking for an edge, a way to take advantage of any situation. In my college philosophy class, the professor said there are different types of people, different personalities, and they can be classified. He said a philosopher named Soren Kierkegaard had described one special type of person as "self-realized," the type who's not bound by society's rules. I knew immediately he was talking about Brent. I always knew Brent was like that, I just didn't know there was a name for it. Self-realized. Not bound by society's rules. That's Brent all over. I sometimes wish I could be more like him, but I know I never will be.

I pass by a family of three that's selling live chickens. A young woman is doing the selling, an older man (grandpa?) is taking the money. A naked toddler is lying on a blanket, and he's got a circle of wetness around his butt. The seller-family has hung their chickens upside down, and the upside-down chickens turn their heads to stare at me as I pass. I wonder if they have any idea of their fate.

I pass an old woman' stall who's selling what looks like used clothes. All of her stuff looks pretty much worn out, and nobody is buying any of it. She also has piles of shoddy hand-made stuff like sandals and pointed conical hats. She sees me looking at the conical hats and picks up a dusty yellow one that seems to be made of woven straw. She gives me a cackling smile that revels her few remaining teeth that are dark red. Brent says it's from chewing betel nuts. She moves faster than I would have thought possible and tries to put the hat on my head. But she's so short, she can't reach up high enough to do it. I try to hold her off, shaking my head. I say, "Nou, nou," which is a word I've heard the girls at Wong's use when the boys get too rough. I'm pretty sure it means no, or maybe it means I don't want to—something like that. But the old woman is insistent. She's struggling really hard to reach high enough to get that hat onto my head, so I eventually feel sorry for her and take off my Army-issue boonie hat and lean over so she can put the straw hat on my head. She pulls it down firmly and stands back to admire it. I can barely see past the brim of the damn thing, but I stand there patiently and smile at her. I expect the silly thing makes me look like a nut, but she looks at me with satisfaction, nodding and smiling and jabbering something in happy-sounding Vietnamese. She's probably telling me how good it looks on me. I glance around and notice that some of the other sellers are watching me, waiting to see what I'm going to do. I fish into my pocket and hold out some coins to her. What else can I do? She takes as much as she wants and steps back, satisfied that she's made a good sale. She undoubtedly charged me a lot more than the usual price, but I don't care. I know I'm supposed to dicker over prices in this country, but I've never developed the knack for it. I bow and thank her, as if I'm the one who came out ahead of the deal. Maybe I did. Maybe the silly hat gives me exactly the look I should adopt if I want to blend in with the locals.

My mouth feels dry and sticky. How long has it been since I had anything to drink? They tell us not to drink the local water, but I'm damn thirsty. I spot a dried-up old guy who's selling some kind of milky-looking drink out of a big pottery jug. Maybe it's some kind of homemade liquor. Whatever the stuff is, the locals must really like it because there's a line waiting to get some. I get in line too.

"What the hell are you doing, Scotty?"

I turn around. It's Brent. He's come back for me.

"Uh, I was thirsty. I thought I'd give the local drink a try."

Brent just shakes his head and leads me away. "No time for your nonsense this morning, Scotty. You gotta get your ass in gear." But then he stops and stares at me. "What is that ridiculous thing on your head?"

"It's a hat. A locals hat. I just bought it. Do you like it?"

He jerks it off my head and throws it to the ground. "For Christ's sake, Scotty. You want everybody to think you're a damn idiot?"

He gets me by the arm and pulls me on down the street. I want to go back to retrieve my new hat, but he's got a really tight grip on my arm. I look back at the hat. It's still lying in the middle of the street. I should just zip back and get it before somebody else notices it. But before I can act, a young girl, probably no older than six or seven, runs out and grabs it. She runs away, grinning and holding the hat up over her head with both hands: a lucky find, a prize left behind by the tall American. I wonder if she's taking it to her father. I hope so. At least he might be able to make good use of it. But then I realize the father of a girl that age will be off fighting in the war, on one side or the other. Maybe her mother will get the hat, if she's not off fighting in the war too.

I see a group of four young American soldiers coming toward us. I stop to watch them go by. They're acting excited and talking so loud, so I figure they must be out on their first off-base passes. They hurry by with only the vaguest of nods in my direction. Maybe they're a little embarrassed to be seen on a local's shopping street, but more likely it's only that their minds are already thinking about the off-limits bars. They're heading for the sin-for-pay places they've heard about. Their faces are rosy with anticipation as their eyes search every streetside business for the much-rumored whorehouses where they've heard the oh-so-young Vietnamese girls will do it for a red MPC (Military Payment Certificate) dollar. Sooner or later, I expect they'll find Wong's Bar, or one of the other similar places, and they *will* find the young girls they're looking for, except they'll have to pay for their time with those girls in genuine U.S. greenback dollars, and it'll cost them a hell of a lot more than one buck. (Better write home and tell mom to send a care package full of dollar bills, and don't ask why.)

When I turn back, I see Brent waiting for me. He's scowling. "For Christ's sake, Scotty, do you have to keep stopping every ten feet?"

I give him a snappy salute. "Yessir. Coming, sir."

He shakes his head and turns away. He starts moving even faster now, and I have to hurry to keep up. I know he's right: we have to get to the hated place, the 2nd Brigade Support Battalion U.S. Army Food Warehouse, the warehouse from hell. It's overseen by the hard-stripe sergeant from hell, Sergeant Fart-Ass Farkas. Right now, that warehouse is the last place on this planet I want to be, and Fart-Ass Farkas is the last person in the world I want to see. I can't imagine facing him with this aching head and flip-flopping stomach. How much *did* I have to drink last night? I only have a vague memory of it. There was trouble at the gambling table. Some kid got hurt bad. And after that it was a long night of boozing and dope-smoking. But there's a good memory mixed in, the memory of *her*, my mysterious dream girl. It's like she magically came out of nowhere to save me. But then she went away just as magically. I wish I could go back and look for her, but I know Brent is right; we do have to go to the warehouse. It's our Army assignment, and we're lucky to have it because it's far from the war. Sergeant Fart-Ass never fails to remind us that if we lose our warehouse jobs, it's the jungle for us. He especially has it out for me. He follows me around, constantly warning me in his Ah'm-from-Arkansas-an-proud-of-it way of talking: "Do yar wark and mind yar Ps and Qs, boay, or it's tha gaw-dam jungle for y'all. Up to you, boay." Nobody at the warehouse wants to lose their rear-echelon job because nobody wants to go to the jungle. The jungle is where the war is. We hear stories about the jungle war every day, frightening and gruesome stories about death hiding behind every tree. So we all keep our mouths shut and do our jobs, sweating our days away loading cases of food into the trucks for all the other American soldiers to eat. We have to submit to being under the thumb of Sergeant Farkas because we don't want to end up in one of the many body bags that are rumored to be coming back from the jungles. Everyone says they're trying to play down the number of American deaths, but the word is the death count is rising fast. They say the body bags are quickly hustled out of sight and lined up on the concrete floor of a hidden-away back hanger out at the Bien Hoa Air Base. It's known as Hanger X, and it's supposed to be the place where they pretty-up the poor sucker's body as best they can before they ship him back to the states in a fancy flag-draped coffin. It may be true, or it may not be. How would I know? All we get is rumors. One day it's rumors that the war is going badly. The next day it's rumors that the war is almost over.

So I work at the warehouse and do whatever Sergeant Farkas tells me to do because I'm not interested in finding out what this war is really all about. I know I'm not the hero type. Some of the guys at the warehouse put on a lot of bravado when they talk about the war. They say they're ready to go to the front right now, if called upon. But I don't see them volunteering. They put up with the heat and the back-breaking work and Farkas's insults, just like I do, in order to stay right where they are, in the rear echelon. But maybe I'm wrong about them. What do I know? Maybe they *are* hero types. Maybe they really are ready to go out into that jungle and die for their country. Me, I keep quiet during those kinds of discussions. Why? Because if somebody gave me a gun and said, Shoot that enemy guy, I'm not sure I could do it. I've been thinking about that a lot lately. I always wondered if the other guys at Basic thought about it. They all seemed gung-ho enough, all ready and willing to stab the man-shaped gunny sack with a bayonet. The sarge made us do it, probably to test our gung-honess, even though I don't think the Army even uses bayonets anymore. Maybe it was a test to see how we'd react, a nasty little test made up by our nasty little five-foot-seven drill sergeant who, short as he was, had a voice big enough for two men. He lined us up and shouted, "Stab the gook. Stab the shit out of him!" Everybody took their turn at running up and stabbing the straw gook. When it came my turn, I stabbed him too, but as usual, the sergeant didn't think I did it with enough gusto, so I had to do it again. He made me stab the poor old straw guy over and over again while the others watched. Would they be so eager to stab the straw guy if it was a real person? Who knows? I never asked them. The truth is, I've never had a very clear idea of how other people think. That's one of the reasons I took that philosophy class at the U. I enjoyed that class, and that's why I brought the class textbook here with me. The book says a lot of those old-time philosophers spent their time thinking about those same kind of things: why we humans do what we do, why we think the things we think, why we believe in the things we believe in. Reading about those philosophers made me feel like I wasn't such an oddball after all; turns out, there are other people who think about the same kinds of things I spend my time thinking about. When I get back (if I get back), I want to finish that philosophy class, and maybe even take more philosophy classes. Maybe I'll even take some psychology classes.

I shake off my unsettling thoughts about killing people and think going back to Wong's tonight after work. Maybe my storyteller girl only comes in late at night. I'll stay there all night tonight and wait for her. The barracks officer is one of Brent's best dope customers, so if we show up late back at the barracks, or don't show up at all, he just marks us down as present and accounted for.

I look ahead and see that Brent still hasn't noticed I've fallen behind again. He must have some new deal cooking in his head. He's always working on his next big dope deal, figuring, calculating, working out the plan. He's been like that ever since we arrived in Saigon. As soon as he saw the barefoot kids selling their crooked little hand-rolled joints to the soldiers in the streets outside of the military bases, he knew he was right; we had arrived in exactly the right place at exactly the right time to make our fortunes. He was sure the dope business, or "the biz," as he calls it, was ripe for taking over. With the MPs always lurking about, he figured American soldiers would trust one of their own more than they would trust those kids. And he was right. The soldiers were even willing to pay a little more for the stuff, as long as we supplied it to them on the QT. At first, he just made his quiet deals in the barracks bathroom. He was making a few bucks, but it was too small-time for Brent. He wanted to grow his "biz," make some real money. So one day we went looking for the big time.

6

Memory:
Looking for the Big-Time

On our first day off from the warehouse since arriving in Vietnam, I was looking forward to sleeping in for a change. But Brent woke me up early. "Saddle up, my man," he said. "We got to hit the streets. We got to find more volume." For days, he'd been grumbling about needing to find a cheaper and more reliable source for the pot he'd been selling to the other GIs. "Buying the pot on the street is too expensive," he said. "Can't mark the shit up enough to make a decent profit."

So we left the military compound and went off wandering through Saigon. Brent led and I followed, as usual. He didn't seem to be heading anywhere in particular, just walking down one back street after another. I had no idea if he actually had a plan about where he might find his illusive "better source," but I didn't mind going for a long walk; it was my first chance to see more of Saigon. Eventually, we found a poorer section of the city where the streets were no longer paved and the buildings were all raw rain-stained concrete boxes with makeshift scrapwood doors and no glass in any of the windows. The few locals we did see, old men and old women mostly, moved to the side of the road to watch us pass by. The farther we went, the more dangerous it seemed to me. But if Brent felt any danger, he didn't let on. He said, "The guy told me the bigger dope dealers hang out in the back streets."

Just like Brent. He hears some scuttlebutt from "some guy" and off we go to find it. So why did he think this neighborhood was the right neighborhood? Had "the guy" told him to look for a rutted, dusty, scary-looking deserted street? I was ready to turn back when we saw a tall thin kid coming out of a building. Brent hurried ahead to talk to him, but I held back. I didn't like the look of him. He was dressed like the local businessmen, standard black pants and short-sleeved white shirt, but he was a teenager, way too young to be a businessman. Unlike most of the locals, his clothes looked crisp and fresh. His pants had a sharp crease in front, and his shirt had shining pearl-like buttons. Most surprising of all, his clothes actually fit him, as if they were tailored. He was wearing a tan-colored beret, the first beret I'd seen in Vietnam except for the military berets some of the U.S. airborne forces wore. I decided he was trying to affect a look that back home we might call hoodlum-stylish, and that worried me.

Brent went right up to him and said, "Hey, bud, know where we can score some dope around here?"

I cringed. To me, it was like saying, Hey, hoodlum kid, want to cut our throats for the few American dollars we might have in our pockets?

The kid just stared at him.

Brent repeated his question: "You look like somebody who knows his way around. We're looking for pot. Marijuana, *comprende*?"

The boy finally smiled, but I couldn't see his eyes behind his too-dark glasses, so it was hard to say what that smile meant. It could have simply meant he was happy to have run into two such perfect victims.

"You want smoke?" he said cheerfully.

Brent nodded, still smiling. "Yeah, what you got?"

"I got all," said the boy. "You name, I got."

"We want lots," said Brent. "We sellers. You *comprende*?"

That stopped the kid. For a moment, he seemed confused. I wasn't sure whether it was Brent's street Spanish that confused him, or the fact that we wanted the dope to sell rather than use. But he quickly recovered, and the smile was right back on his face. "You come," he said. He turned and waved for us to follow.

Brent was ready to follow the kid, but I tried to hold him back. "Jesus, Brent. Don't you think we'd better find out where this kid wants to take us? After all, he might just be leading us into—"

Brent shushed me and whispered, "This is what we've been looking for. He's going to lead us to the big time dealers."

"You don't know that. He could be planning to roll us."

The kid stopped and waved to us. "You come. You come."

Brent pried my hand off his arm. "Now don't get paranoid on me, Scotty. I can handle this. Let's go."

He called to the boy: "Wait up, we're coming."

The boy started down the street with Brent right on his heels. I was left standing by myself in the middle of the street. I looked back in the direction we'd come. Could I find my way back alone? Not a chance. I had no choice but to hurry and catch up with them.

As we walked, the boy kept up a steady chatter: "Good cỏ dại. You like. *L'herbe, hein*? You like, *c'est vrai*?"

He was speaking a kind of rough Asian-accented French, mixed with English. I remembered enough from my high-school French classes to mostly figure out what he was saying. He was mostly telling us over and over that he had good *herbe* (weed), and that we'd like it a lot. He jabbered away, giving us constant assurances that he knew what he was talking about. He said he was *savoir* (in the know). He was quite the back-street linguist, but I had the feeling he was keeping up his non-stop kindergarten English and distorted French in order to keep us from asking any questions. I felt like he was luring us along, as if he wanted anybody who might be watching to see he was fully in charge of these two dumb Americans. It was like he was tossing out doggy treats, a non-stop stream of encouraging words, to keep us foolish puppies following him. His whole lighthearted, but clearly agitated manner, convinced me he was leading us to where his friends were waiting to kill us and take our money. They would probably cut us into bits and pieces and then feed what remained to the scrawny street dogs that scurried away to hide under porches as soon as they saw us coming.

"My name Mar-lon," said the kid, pointing at himself and grinning at me. "Like American actor, Brando, no? Some say me look like, yes?"

He didn't look anything like Marlon Brando. To me, Brando looked somewhat Italian. How could a Vietnamese boy think he looked Italian?

He held his hand up next to his mouth, as if he was about to tell us a secret. "Me know main people." He winked. "Me, how you say, *cousin*? Premier Thiệu. Nguyen Thieu. Head of all country."

So this back-street know-it-all kid was trying to convince us he was somehow related to the head of the country. But as far as I knew, the president of the country was some Vietnamese General named Ky. But who could know for sure? They seemed to change leaders a lot ever since that first monk had burned himself to death in downtown Saigon.

Mar-lon, the president's pretend cousin, kept us moving, and he kept up his constant chatter. He was trying to convince us that he too was going to be somebody really important someday, just as soon as somebody named Nguyen-something-or-other took power, and somebody else, also named Nguyen-something-or-other, lost power. All I got out of it was that everybody who was anybody in this strange country must be named Nguyen. Eventually, we came to a normal Saigon-type paved street with regular Vietnamese people walking back and forth on it, and people riding bicycles, like normal. I was happy to see them. Maybe this Mar-lon character wasn't leading us to our doom after all. He was walking right down the middle of the street as if he owned it. But when a pedicab came, he stepped aside to let it pass. The pedicab was piloted by a sweating, scrawny shirtless old man, and inside it, sitting calmly under the tattered cloth shade, was a white man in a white suit. The man looked impossibly cool in the stifling heat. Mar-lon doffed his beret to the passenger, but the man didn't show any sign that he had even noticed us. That didn't seem to bother Mar-lon. He went right back to strutting down the middle of the street, with us in tow. Mar-lon's fancy clothes, his attitude, and his acting like this was his own turf, got me to thinking maybe he really did know something about getting marijuana. As unlikely as it seemed, maybe this skinny, strutting, bragging kid who thought he looked like Marlon Brando was the local version of a big-time dope dealer. Maybe this time, one of

Brent's grand plans was actually going to work out. But where was this kid leading us? My question was soon answered. He led us to a rain-stained concrete building that had once been painted white. It had wide concrete steps that led up to an entrance with two tall wooden doors. Each door had a carved dragon head on it, the two dragons facing each other as if they were fiercely guarding the entrance. Mar-lon skipped right up the steps and pulled open one of the heavy doors. He did a funny little bow and gestured with one hand for us to enter. Inside was a large, high-ceilinged room with a floor made out of smoothly polished, earth-colored stone tiles. There were maybe a dozen tables scattered around the room, in no discernible pattern. Each table was covered with a crisp, clean white tablecloth, and every table was accompanied by four black wrought-iron chairs with surprisingly clean-looking white seat cushions. It looked a lot like my idea of what a fancy restaurant in New York, or maybe Paris, would look like. But there was no food on any of the tables, only glasses. It was pretty dark in the large room because the windows were covered with heavy ceiling-to-floor drapes, but I could see well enough to realize the men seated at the tables were all white men, and they were all wearing white suits, just like the men I had seen in the pedicabs. Except for Mar-lon, there was not one Vietnamese in the place. So many men in nearly identical white suites sitting at tables with clean white tablecloths made the place look staged, like maybe something out of an old Humphrey Bogart movie. Who were these men, and why had Mar-lon brought us there?

Mar-lon put his finger to his lips to tell us to be quiet. He took off his beret and led us toward a back table where a short dark-haired man in an extraordinarily-clean white suit sat reading a newspaper. When we got closer, I could see he was reading a French newspaper. Was this guy French? Was everybody in the place French?

Mar-lon put up a hand for us to wait, then he slowly, almost apologetically, approached the man. He waited a moment, then cleared his throat. The man lowered his newspaper and looked at Mar-lon, not smiling. Mar-lon leaned close to the man and whispered something to him, pointing at us. The man stared at us over the top of his glasses for only a brief moment before shaking his head and going back to reading his newspaper. Mar-lon came back toward us, looking sheepish. "He say not today. Maybe we come back tomorrow when he—"

But Brent didn't let him finish whatever he was about to say. He pushed past Mar-lon and went to the man's table. I quickly followed, hoping Brent wasn't about to get us into big trouble. Without asking permission, Brent pulled back a chair. Against the stone floor, the chair's metal legs made a screeching sound that seemed very loud in the quiet high-ceilinged room. Most of the other men in the room turned to look. I thought it might be a good idea to do what Mar-lon had suggested and just leave quietly, but Brent sat right down and scooted the chair forward, making that screeching sound again.

The man lowered his newspaper and stared at Brent.

Brent stuck out his hand. "I'm Brent. This is my pal, Scotty. Are you the dope guy we're looking for?"

The Frenchman, if he was a Frenchman, didn't shake hands, but he did put down his newspaper. He stared at Brent, expressionless. Then, he looked at me and nodded toward the other chair.

I sat down and kept my mouth shut.

The man turned his attention back to Brent. He folded his hands together and rested them on the table as he silently stared at Brent. I was struck by the man's hands. They were both badly scarred, as if they had been burned in a fire a long time ago. He had plain silver rings on both of his little fingers, and the shiny rings contrasted starkly with the red and rumpled flesh of his burned fingers. I had the feeling he knew the effect his scarred hands would have on people.

Mar-lon came up next to the man and whispered something in French. Despite my two years of high-school French, I couldn't be sure of everything he was saying, except I did recognize the words "*fous,*" which means crazy, "*vente.*" which means sell, and "*stupide,*" which needs no translation. The man waved him away, and Mar-lon went to stand against the wall, arms folded, keeping his eyes on us. The Frenchman didn't say a word. He just stared at Brent. And Brent wasn't saying anything either, so I decided to break the ice. I pointed to the man's half-empty glass on the table. "Is this a bar? I could use a drink."

The Frenchman turned to me, and for the first time, he smiled. He shook his head. "Members only." His accent indicated he *was* French.

He turned back to Brent. "I am told you are looking for large quantities of marijuana." He spoke very slowly, but his English very clear despite the heavy French accent.

"That's right," said Brent. "We're looking for a solid supply."

"And I am told you plan to resell it."

Brent put his elbows on the table and put on his "let's-do-business" look. "Yeah, we got a little pot business goin' back at the base. Nothing big so far, but we got plans." He kept his eyes fixed on the Frenchman.

For some reason, Brent's words seemed to strike the Frenchman as funny. He smiled broadly and sat back in his chair. Maybe he was thinking we had no idea what we were getting into, which was, of course, absolutely true.

Brent picked up on the smile too. "Yeah, you may think we're small time. But like I said, we got plans. Big plans. You may think the American soldiers will keep right on buying your weed from the kids on the street, but they're getting nervous about it. The word around the barracks is that the MPs are gonna crack down on it. The soldiers worry about what might be in those joints the kids are selling them. Bottom line is, they'd rather buy it from us, somebody they can trust."

It was the most words in one string I'd heard Brent speak in a long time, maybe ever. It was clear he had prepared that speech in advance.

The Frenchman was no longer smiling. He was studying Brent's face. He went on staring at Brent for so long, I started to get anxious again. If this guy really was a big-time dope supplier, maybe Brent's speech had made him think we could be competition for him. Maybe he was thinking about how to get rid of us.

As if to confirm my suspicions, he waved to Mar-lon. *"La voiture."*

Mar-lon brought the Frenchman a white linen hat that was just as clean as his suit, and then he hurried out through the front door. The Frenchman put on the hat and stood up. "Let's go," he said. He headed for the front door, and an aged Vietnamese man appeared out of nowhere to open it for him. As we followed the Frenchman, I leaned close to Brent and whispered, "He said the French word for car. We can't let these guys take us somewhere in a car."

"A car?" said Brent. "Great. It means this guy really is big time." He hurried to keep up with the Frenchman, and out the door we went, the old Vietnamese doorman bowing to each of us in turn.

We stood on the burning-hot concrete front porch, presumably waiting for a car. I couldn't stop thinking I should just walk away. Now that we were on a regular paved Saigon street, I figured I could find my way back to the base on my own. I looked at the Frenchman. He was completely silent, not looking at all hot as he should have been, wearing a suit under that hot sun. I glanced at Brent. He seemed to be calmly watching the traffic go by, but I knew better; he was in his head, thinking about his next move, strategizing, as always.

Finally, a dirty, off-white four-door Citroen came up the street toward us, moving fast, scattering pedestrians as it came. I'd never seen a Citroen in Saigon. It pulled up to the curb, and Mar-lon, jumped out to open the back door for us. Brent hopped right in. I hesitated. There was something I didn't like about this whole scene. Where was this mysterious Frenchman going to take us?

Brent leaned out and shouted at me: "Let's go, Scotty. Quit stalling."

So I did what I always do: where Brent leads, I follow, like I'm a mindless idiot instead of supposedly the smartest kid in our high school. I got in, and the kid slammed the door closed, hard, as if he wanted to make sure we were shut in tight. He opened the front passenger door for the Frenchman to get in and then closed it much more gently than he had closed my door.

I looked the inside of the car over. It was not new, but at one time it had been pretty fancy, with tan leather seats and polished wood trim. But it had no air-conditioning, so with the tinted windows rolled up, it was hot as hell in there.

Mar-lon got into the driver's seat, started the car, and took off fast. I sat there smelling the almost overpowering smell of the car's leather seats, thinking I shouldn't be doing this. I should have just done my job at the warehouse until my hitch was over. Then, I could go back to college and finish that philosophy class. I told myself when we got back to the barracks—if we were lucky enough to ever get back to the barracks—I would dig out the philosophy textbook from that class and occupy myself reading it instead of traipsing around after Brent.

Mar-lon was driving like a maniac, laying on the horn, using the car as a weapon to drive the pedestrians out of our way. He hardly slowed, even when he came close to flattening somebody. I was learning Vietnamese pedestrians can move fast when they have to.

I held onto the edge of the seat and looked out through my darkened side window thinking I should just jump out and make a run for it. I decided to get ahold of the door handle, just in case. That's when I discovered there wasn't one. There was only a hole where the handle had once been. There was also no window crank handle. It was obvious they had been removed to keep anybody from getting out. The back seat was a trap, and we were the mice caught in it. I nudged Brent, but he ignored me. He was gazing out the window as if he was on a pleasant sightseeing trip through the city. I reached across him and pointed to the two holes where his door handle and window crank had been removed. I whispered. "They've got us trapped in here. Don't you get it?"

He shrugged, put on his who-cares look, and whispered back, "You think I can't handle these guys. Calm down."

"But who knows where they're taking us?"

He glanced at the Frenchman. "Pipe down. They'll hear you. This is what we spent all day looking for. Just calm down."

Brent was probably right about being able to handle Mar-lon and the Frenchman if it came to a fight, but what if they had guns? And what if they took us to where their friends were waiting? What if they were taking us out of the city? Maybe the Frenchman had a special ditch out in the countryside where he disposed of his competition.

I kept my eyes on the buildings we were passing, hoping to see something that might give me the slightest hint about where we were, but I didn't recognize anything. The only signs I saw were in Vietnamese which meant we were nowhere near the American military district. But at least there were still a lot of people in the street. I could only hope they wouldn't kill us in front of so many people. As we raced on, Mar-lon jabbered away in French, but the Frenchman never once responded. He was an odd duck, that Frenchman: scarred hands, silent and looking straight ahead. What was he thinking about?

We hadn't gone all that far before the boy-driver pulled up in front of a two-story concrete building. It had a metal door, painted black, and yellow-tinted glass in all the windows. One more thing to worry about. The French guy was taking us inside a prison-like concrete building with a formidable-looking metal door.

Mar-lon came around and opened my door. I jumped out quick, glad to be out of that trap.

As the Frenchman led us up the steps to the building's front door, I realized this might be my last chance to make a run for it. We were still in the city. He hadn't taken us out into the country to kill us. I decided to go along with it, but stay alert.

The Frenchman unlocked the metal door's two locks, with two different keys, and led us inside. He locked the door behind us and led us up a stairway to a room that was completely empty except for a beat-up gray metal desk and two metal chairs. The Frenchman jerked the chain of a ceiling fan, and the blades—made of interwoven cane that had yellowed with age—lazily began to turn. The yellow-tinted windows gave the room a sickly cast, but the Frenchman swung open the window to let in some fresh air. That was good. If worse came to worse, I could jump out that window.

The Frenchman went to sit behind the desk, and Brent immediately sat down in the only other chair.

I stayed near the door, watching that ceiling fan wobble precariously overhead. It was hanging from a thin wire that looked like it was sure to break sooner or later.

Mar-lon stayed in the middle of the doorway, arms crossed. Was he making sure we didn't make a run for it? Whenever I looked his way, he put on a big smile for me. Hard to tell what he might be thinking behind those dark sunglasses.

Looking comfortable and fully in charge behind his desk, the Frenchman unbuttoned the front of his white suit jacket and took off his hat. He put the hat down on the desk, folded his hands together, and told Brent how much a kilo of marijuana would cost.

The guy sure didn't waste any time getting down to business.

Brent said that was too much.

The Frenchman said, "Take it or leave it."

It was a lot less than we had been paying, so of course Brent quickly agreed. I could hardly believe what I was hearing. It sounded as if this French guy really was going to set us up in the dope business. It looked like this time one of Brent's grand plans was actually going to work out.

The Frenchman said Mar-lon would bring the deliveries and pick up the payments. If the payments were not received right on time, the supply would immediately be cut off.

Brent limited his responses to, "Uh huh, right," and "okay, I get it."

The Frenchman turned to Mar-lon and said something in French. I think it was about how much to get.

As Mar-lon hurried out the door, the Frenchman opened one of the desk drawers and took out some papers. He began to read. It was like he had forgotten about us. Brent must have assumed the interview was over. He stood up and put out his hand. "Okay then, we have a deal."

The Frenchman glanced up at him and shook his head. "No need for that. When I make a deal, I adhere to it."

I couldn't help thinking, Is that really all there is to it? Are we really going to be in the pot-selling business in a foreign country right in the middle of a war?

Mar-lon was back, all smiles. He was carrying a large black plastic bag. Was that big bag full of marijuana?

Mar-lon said, "We go," and out the door he went. We followed him down the stairs and back out to the car. He had the bag over his shoulder as he opened the car's back door for us. He didn't seem at all worried that someone might see him carrying it. If it was marijuana in that bag, everybody in that part of town must have known what the Frenchman and his kid cohort were up to, but they either didn't care or were afraid to say anything about it to the police.

Once we were in the car, the kid handed the bag to Brent and hurried around to get into the driver's seat. Brent had the bag open and was looking inside before the kid had even got the car started. He grinned and held open the bag for me to look. It was mostly bud clumps, obviously much better stuff than we had been getting from the Vietnamese kids on the street. And it smelled strong too, as if it had been recently picked. I tried to reach in and grab a bud to nibble on, but Brent pulled the bag away. He shook his head and glanced at the driver who was watching us in his rear view mirror.

The kid put the car in gear and took off fast.

I sat back and tried not to worry. Brent was checking the bag's contents, so there was nothing for me to do but look out the window. More concrete buildings, more bikes and pedicabs, more people scurrying to get out of our way. The hanging advertising signs were still only in Vietnamese, and I still had no idea where we were.

Mar-lon turned off the main street and roared down a narrow dirt side street. Dust floated up from the floorboards every time the car hit a bump. Now where was he taking us? Clearly, we couldn't go back to the base. No way we could just walk right in through the guard gate carrying a big bag of marijuana. So where were we going to hide it? It had to be worth a lot of money, and I was pretty sure the Frenchman wouldn't be happy if we lost it. I wanted to ask Brent where we were going to hide it, but I knew the driver-kid, Mar-lon, would be listening.

Mar-lon was driving way too fast, turning down one side street after another. I was holding on tight, but Brent didn't even seem to notice. He was still sorting through the bag's contents. I could imagine what was going on in his head: so many ounces, how much per ounce; How much to charge if we sold it by the lid versus how much we could charge if we sold it by the joint.

Mar-lon seemed to enjoy roaring down narrow dusty streets, scattering pedestrians and coating all of the nearby houses with a good thick layer of dust while he jabbered over his shoulder to us about what a great man the Frenchman was, and how lucky we were that he had led us to the Frenchman, and how we should always do whatever the Frenchman told us to do. "Un homme noble," he kept repeating. "Un homme noble." He touched the side of his head with one finger. "He smart man. Know thing nobody else know." We turned into a street with houses on both sides that looked like concrete cubes. All of them small, no glass in any of the windows. Mar-lon brought the Citroen to a stop in front of one of the concrete-cube buildings. It seemed to be some kind of business. American soldiers were standing around out front talking to young-looking Vietnamese girls, every one them wearing a long slinky white dress. The place had a wide doorway, but no door. I wondered if that meant the place never closed. Mar-lon jumped out and ran around to open the car's back doors for us.

Why were we stopping here? Was he going to show us something, or was he just stopping off for a quick one?

Mar-lon let us out of the car and waved for us to follow him into the building.

Brent followed right behind him, carrying the black plastic bag over his shoulder, Santa Claus like.

Once inside, I was amazed to see that the place was packed with American soldiers, a lot of then young buzz-cuts just in from Basic. There was a rough wooden bar that looked like it could have been made out of tree, but no soldiers were at that bar; they were all either gambling at an antique-looking polished-wood dice table, or they were sitting at a cluster of round metal tables talking to young girls. Like the girls out front, they were wearing the same type of long white dresses that might well have been made out of silk.

Brent called to me to get my attention. He was standing at the far end of the bar with Mar-lon. They were talking to a little dried-up man that looked Chinese, and although he looked very old, he was standing quite erect, as if he wanted to show us Americans that he was very proud and not to be taken lightly.

I went over to where they were. Brent put his hand on the little Chinese man's shoulder and said, "Meet Wong, our new business partner."

7

Headless Humans

As I continue to follow Brent toward the warehouse, it amazes me to realize it's only been a couple of months since the Frenchman set Brent up to be the dope seller at Wong's Bar. It seems like we've been here a lot longer than that.

We pass out of the shopping street, getting closer to the military district where our warehouse is, and the crowds thin out a little so we can move faster. In fact, it seems to me there are *a lot* fewer people on the street than normal. It's so unusual not to be surrounded by locals when on a Saigon street, it makes me a little nervous. There were lots of people in the shopping street back there, so what's keeping the people away from this area? I stop, and Brent also stops. The deserted street must have made the never-worried Brent a little nervous.

I say, "What the hell? No people. Do you think it's a trap?"

Brent shakes his head. "Naw, not in broad daylight."

He's got his brave face on, but he also knows something is wrong.

I say, "Let's go back and find another route."

He shakes his head again. "That would make us even later. Something must've been going on here earlier. Maybe the police cleared out this street. Whatever it was, it's all over now."

I don't think Brent's easy explanation can account for the fact that there's not one single person on the street. He goes on, striding down the middle of the street. I make sure to keep up with him, but I keep my eyes on the rooftops on both sides. I look ahead and see what looks like people lying in the street. They're strung out across the whole width of the narrow street, like a barrier. I stop. "What the hell? Are they dead?"

Brent doesn't reply. He goes a little closer, moving cautiously.

I follow, but hanging back. So that's why we hadn't seen any locals. They must know about these bodies and are staying away. But how long have they been here? Since last night? Where are the police?

As we get closer, I see the horrible truth: the bodies have no heads. That's enough for me; I'm ready to get the hell out of here. Now!

I grab Brent's arm to try to pull him back, but he's curious. He shakes off my hand and goes closer.

I stay where I am, trying to think it through. Somebody killed these men and cut off their heads. I can't see any blood on the street, so they must have been killed somewhere else and brought here. The bodies are not army or police: no uniforms on any of them. They're all dressed in the standard Vietnamese business attire, dark pants and white shirts, except now the whole upper parts of their white shirts are stained dark red. They seem so lifeless, so non-human. Without their heads, they look more like damaged and discarded store mannequins. Who are they? The way they're so carefully laid out across the street is obviously intended to send some kind of message. But what is the message? A warning? If so, who is the warning intended for? Us Americans?

Brent walks right up to the line of bodies and looks down at them.

I slowly come up beside him.

"No heads," he says, as if he's not sure I noticed.

"Right," I say. "I can see that. Let's get the hell out of here."

"Okay," is all he says. He steps over the nearest body and goes on.

That leaves me standing on the other side of the body barrier. Should I step over them like he did? For some reason, I can't do it. I'm stuck. Common sense tells me I'm no safer on this side of the string of bodies than on the other, but I can't make my feet step over them. It seems sort of disrespectful. I don't know the rules about the dead in this country.

Brent finally notices I'm not following and turns back to yell at me: "Jesus, Scotty, come on. Get a move on. We're late as hell."

I have no choice but to step over the bodies and run to catch up with him. I stay close to Brent, keeping a close eye on every window in every building we pass. Now, the area seems old and maybe threatening. The walls of the buildings are cracked, Above us, dangerous-looking electric wires hang down. The wires criss-cross the street above us, all of them emanating from one leaning wooden utility pole to end up under the eves of the roofs in bird-nest-like bundles so hopelessly messed up it's hard to believe anybody could ever figure it all out. Roof tiles are chipped and blackened by mold and could break off at any moment and come falling down on us.

I start walking even faster that Brent, almost running, until we're out of that street. The next street is as busy with pedestrians as ever, so I relax a bit and ask Brent, "What do you think that was all about? Headless bodies? Right here in Saigon?"

Brent shrugs. "Who knows? There's a war going on, remember? You think we won't see more dead bodies before we get out of this country?" He walks on, maintaining his long-striding pace and hanging onto his hard-ass attitude. I'm sure he has no idea what those headless bodies were all about, but he's not interested in speculating about it. It's as if he's already forgotten about them. Even as a kid, he had an amazing ability to push bad stuff out of his mind. Put him in a tough situation, and he'll always act nonchalant, like it's no big deal. Whatever he really thinks about danger, or fear, or any other negative emotions — what he refers to as "bullshit emotions" — he keeps to himself.

8

The Ticking Clock

At the warehouse, Sergeant Farkas is waiting for us. He's leaning against the wall at the clock-in station, arms folded, nailing us with his hard-ass eyes as we approach. When we try to sign in, he stops us by putting his fat hands against our chests. He snarls, "Ten-hut!" I snap to attention, but Brent just stares at Farkas, not hiding his impatience. Brent wasn't willing to stand at anything like real attention back in Basic, and he's not about to do it for a lowly supply sergeant like Farkas. The sarge keeps us standing there while he dresses us down in his exaggerated Arkansas drawl, saying how we're always late and "nuthin' but lazy bums when ya'll do get here." He shakes his head. "Hard as ah try, I jes can't seem to turn ya'll into good soldiers. You boays keep on gettin' here late, I might havta send ya'all back to the work placement officer." He pauses for a couple of seconds to let that sink in before he gets to his most somber pronouncement: "And ya'll know wot that means. It'll be that bad ol jungle fer ya'll." He acts real sad about how a terrible thing like that might happen to us because "Without a damn doubt, ya'll er so damn dumb you'd likely as not get yourselves killed yur first day out thar."

I keep my eyes locked on the "Work Keeps US Strong" poster on the wall behind him to make sure I don't look directly at him, because hung over as I am, I'd probably start giggling. I don't dare look at, or even think about, his wide booze-pockmarked nose or his beady little pig eyes because I'm sure it would send me straight into an absurdity attack about how an idiot like this ever got put in charge of anything. He's yelling really loud to make sure everyone in the place can hear him, and he's trying hard to keep his big sagging belly sucked in. But I shouldn't have noticed his belly because I start to imagine him being poured into his uniform one lump at a time, like a walking, talking sack of Arkansas potatoes. But somehow I keep a straight face as he rants on. He's really getting into it now, red in the face and throwing out quite a bit of his famous spit every time he uses a word that starts with *T*: "Ya *T*wo asswipes er gonna show up lait wan *T*wo many *T*imes. I'm bout *T*a put both of ya boots on ree-port." (He calls every soldier in the warehouse a boot even if they aren't fresh out of boot camp.) Finally, he demands to know why we're late. I think about telling him we got delayed by those headless bodies in the street, but I don't. I say, "Sorry, Sarge, but I'm real sick." I stick out my tongue and try to look sickly, instead of just hung over.

He looks real close at my eyes, which I'm sure are really bloodshot.

"Ya doan look sick ta me. Ya looks lak a hung over limp-dick pogue who can't hold his likker. That's wot ya look lak to me."

It's the first time I've heard the sarge use the word "pogue." It's a derogatory Marine term for soldiers like me who mange to get ourselves assigned to any kind of non-combat, far-from-danger support capacity. I'm surprised he's using that term because somebody might remind him that he's one too. I've heard Farkas use other Marine terms like that, even though he's not a Marine, so maybe he wishes he could have been one. Brent talked to a guy who said Farkas has been in the Army practically his whole life, and he's been in supply from the start. If so, it's hard to figure how he ended up in Vietnam. Maybe he volunteered to come over here to prove to his drinking buddies back in Arkansas just how brave he was; but of course, being a supply sergeant, he knew he'd never have to see any action.

He jabs me in the chest with his fat finger to get my attention and demands I fess up that I'd been "Out all night boozin' and whorin'."

"Hey, lay off, Sarge," says Brent. "Scotty here really is sick. I been nursemaidin' him all night."

But Farkas isn't going for it. He starts jabbing me in the chest again and is just getting into a whole new stream of insults when Brent does something you should never do with this particular sergeant: he moves between us and ends up nose-to-nose with Farkas. "Back off, Sarge," he says. "If I say Scotty's been sick, then he has." His voice is real low, the words coming from deep in his throat.

I've seen this before: Brent is ready to explode. If Farkas doesn't back off, Brent will knock him on his ass, and then we'll be in real trouble. I try to think about how to stop this, but Farkas has already hooked in. He tightens his fists and lifts up his flabby chin.

Brent doesn't seem at all intimidated. He says, "And don't you be callin' my buddy those kinds of names, or you'll answer to me."

Farkas hesitates. He must know it would be a big mistake to take Brent on. I figure old Fart-Ass must go at least two-sixty, and Brent can't weigh more than one-eighty, dripping wet. But you can tell when a guy knows about fighting, and Brent has that look.

I decide to just wait. I'm sure Farkas will back down. I can tell he's more than a little scared of Brent, and besides, Brent has something on him. Turns out, Farkas likes very young girls, so Brent provides them. "Borrows" them from Wong. Trouble is, one night with Farkas and the girls won't go back again. Once when Brent was having fun imitating Farkas's Arkansas drawl, he said, "Old fart-ass goes through them young girls "lak a hot knaf through malted butta". It's probably costing

Brent a bundle to keep Farkas in young girls, but Brent thinks of it as an investment to make sure we get to keep our nice safe jobs at the warehouse. Not that Brent would be afraid to go to the front. I've never seen him afraid of anything. One night, I saw him take on a whole gang of leather-jacketed punks at a drive-in movie when they gave me some shit about brushing up against one of their fancy custom cars. He pushed me aside and was instantly willing to fight them, one at a time or all together. He was so crazy ready to fight, he started punching the side of the offended car over and over again with his bare fists. He hit that car so hard, it actually made a big dent in it. That made them think twice about taking him on. No, it it's definitely not fear that's keeping Brent out of combat; he just doesn't want to leave Saigon and lose his fast-growing dope business. So generally, he keeps his mouth shut and does whatever it takes to keep Farkas happy. But not this time. Thinking he's protecting me, Brent seems ready to take Farkas on, no matter what the consequences are. And Farkas is also acting like he's ready to have a go at Brent. For a long moment, they're stuck in their face to face stare-down, playing the who'll-blink-first game. Brent is clearly ready to fight, but he's staying relatively calm. Farkas, on the other hand, is not calm. I can see the sweat circles under his armpits growing bigger, and it looks like he's losing the battle to hold in his big pot belly.

In the end, of course it's Farkas that blinks first. He looks around, probably checking to see if any of the other guys are watching. Maybe he thinks he can get out of this if nobody else is looking. Unfortunately for him, a few guys on their way to take their carts to the loading docks notice what's going on and stop to watch. Now Farkas is in trouble. He's scared of Brent, but he can't let anybody see him back down from a private. Finally, he does the damnedest thing: he starts growling. I'm not kidding. He's actually growling, deep in his throat, like a damned pit bull dog or something. It's a low growl at first, then it gets louder, plenty loud enough for the guys over by the loading docks to hear. I can see he's ready to blow, and I know Brent won't back down, so I decide I'd better do something quick. I don't want to see Brent get any more brig time. He got brig time back in boot camp for threatening a superior officer. Who knows what he'd get for actually striking a superior in a war zone. I squeeze in between them and say in as whiny a voice as I can muster, "Aw, come on, Sarge, give us a break. It's like he said, I was sick all night. But I'm feeling better now. Just let us go to work."

Farkas turns to me, happy to take on somebody he knows he can intimidate. "Ya bet yur ass yur gonna get *Ta* work, sick or not. Ahll be watching ya, Private. That sick shit don't cut no ice with me. Ya pull your weight round here, or it's the jungle for ya. Ya har me?"

"Loud and clear, Sergeant," I say as I grab Brent's arm to pull him away. I keep a good hold on him as we head back into the warehouse.

At first he comes along without resisting, but I can see he's in his head thinking about it, deciding. He stops and looks back.

I know I won't be able to hold him if he decides to go back and punch Farkas. "Let it go," I whisper.

He jerks his arm away. "You shoulda let me knock his fuckin' teeth out. I've about had it with that fat pig."

"Right, and they'd give you six months per tooth. You want to spend the rest of this war in the brig? What about our pot sales at Wong's?"

He stares at me, then glances back toward Farkas. He laughs and punches me in the shoulder, harder than I would have liked, but at least I know it's over, for the moment.

As soon as Farkas goes into his office, we go punch in and grab two lists out of the orders box. Brent's list sends him off toward the packaged goods and mine sends me down the canned fruit aisle.

By the time I'm halfway through my first list, I'm already soaked with sweat. The warehouse gets stifling hot when the sun gets high enough to radiate straight down on the steel roof. You can tell whether it's cloudy or sunny outside by how much heat comes through the steel roof. Today the top of my head is so hot I know there must not be a cloud in the sky. But the strange thing is, no matter how hot it gets, the gray concrete floor under my feet is always cold. It's like being in a big oven set on broil, but with your feet on ice. I'm pretty sure sooner or later it's going to fry my brains out, but at least my feet will be cool.

Sergeant Farkas doesn't care how hot it gets in the warehouse. He won't let us take off our shirts. He doesn't even like it when we unbutton our shirts. He says we have to maintain "proppa military dee-core-um." That's a laugh. Within an hour we're all walking around in shirts that look like wet rags and pants that look like we peed in them. Sergeant Farkas doesn't have to deal with the heat. He stays in his air conditioned office watching us through his observation window. He keeps his eye on us using his great big, military-issue binoculars, looking for what he calls "gaw dam shirkers" and "weaklins" who can't cut it. He has his three hundred cases per hour rule, and he makes damn sure everybody maintains it. He watches us all day long through those binoculars to see who's slowing down, and every night he goes over the order lists to see if anybody fell below the required average. Let me tell you, it's damn hard to maintain three hundred cases per hour. We have to pull the heavy carts through the boiling-hot warehouse picking up individual cases of whatever crap is on our order list, and then we have to drag the overloaded cart all the way back up to the truck-loading docks where the loaders pack the shit into the trucks for the various Saigon-area base kitchens and PXs. Then, to make sure we don't drop below Farkas's three hundred cases per hour average, we have to hurry and grab another list and start the process all over again. No breaks or slowing down allowed. The only break you get is to go to the bathroom or to grab a quick lunch, and even then you have to maintain your three hundred cases per hour. I think Fart-Ass Farkas spends all day watching through those big old binoculars just because he likes to see us suffer. I think he gets off on it. And he never fails to let us know he has the power of life and death over us. That three hundred cases per hour rule is our sword of Damocles. Of course, Fart Ass Farkas wouldn't have a clue who Damocles was (Dam-o-claus who?), or what the sword-hanging-above-your-head-by-a-thread metaphor means. Old Fart-Ass isn't so good with metaphors. What he is good at is reminding us that all he has to do is put our name on THE LIST and "Baam" (as he says), "ya'll er dun fer." Off to the jungle we'd go, off to the front to "git yur daem fool head blowed off."

After loading up the cases of canned fruit, I flip to the next page of my list and see I've gotten lucky: there's a large number of smaller or lighter cases on the list, things like breakfast cereal and Jell-O that can be loaded fast. Good. I need a break. I'm thirsty as hell, and I have to pee. I drop off my cart and head for the restroom. I drink a half dozen cups of water at the water cooler, and then take my time peeing.

As usual, the rest-room cleanup lady—a dried-up, bent-over old Vietnamese woman—mops around my feet under the urinal while I pee. I don't think she cares all that much about looking at our dicks (she's already seen them all); I think she does it to try to get a reaction out of us. The new guys do talk about it, but after a while, they get used to it like everybody else. Now, we hardly even notice she's there.

As I zip up my pants, I turn to look at her. She's moving away, busily mopping around the stalls. I wonder if she lives around here. Maybe she knows something about those headless bodies. I say, "Excuse me, Missus. Can I ask you a question,"

She ignores me and keeps on mopping.

I move in front of her. "Don't be afraid. I only want to ask you a question."

She looks up, snorts, shakes her head, and goes back to mopping in the other direction.

What did that snort mean? That she doesn't want to talk to me? I decide to ask her anyhow. I get in front of her again. "I saw some dead men in the street this morning. Do you know who they were?"

She keeps on mopping, moving away from me, heading toward the back of the long narrow room.

Maybe she doesn't speak English. I follow her, trying to think how to explain my question with gestures or something.

She turns back to me. He face is angry. "What you want?"

So she *does* speak English. She's so short, and so bent over, she has to look up at me sideways, but I can tell she's not scared of me. She looks right at me, and her old eyes are not as dull as you'd think they'd be. I wonder where she learned English. From just listening to us soldiers at the warehouse?

"Who were those dead men lying in the street this morning?" I ask, as gently as I can. "They all had their heads cut off. Why?"

"Not know." She looks away and goes back to mopping, but in the other direction, toward the front of the room.

I hurry to get in front of her again. "You must know. All of your people were staying away from that street this morning. Nobody came to look at the bodies. It was like no one was even curious."

She mops right past me. Is she heading for the door? I catch her arm to keep her from getting away. It feels like there's nothing but bones inside of her dry wrinkled skin. "Tell me. I think you know."

She doesn't look at me, but she says two quick words that sound like, "Chin thuk."

"In English," I say. "Say it in English. Who were they?"

"Big shot."

"Big shots? Like men in charge?"

She nods, still not looking at me.

"Do you mean they were government officials?"

She nods again.

So they *were* Vietnamese government officials. Maybe they were men the U.S. military placed in high positions after the coop. Most everybody knows the U.S. was behind the coop, and their deaths are a warning about cooperating with the Americans. "Why were they killed?" I ask "Was it a warning?"

She shrugs.

Another soldier comes in to take a leak. The old woman goes to mop around his feet as he pees.

I wait until he leaves, then go up to her again. "One more question. Why did they cut off their heads?"

She doesn't look up, but she does mumble something that sounds like, "Thin duong."

"What does that mean?"

"Christian."

"What? You mean they were all Christians?"

She glances up at the ceiling. "Christian no go up." She spits on the floor and mops it up so quick it's like it never happened at all. What did that spit mean? Does she hate Christians? Or maybe she hates government officials. Or maybe she was thinking about Americans interfering with the Vietnamese government. But then I have doubts about whether it meant anything at all. Maybe she was just spitting at a dirt spot on the floor, adding some moisture to help clean it up.

I watch her as she goes on with her mopping. She always uses the same back and forth motion, doing it in such a precise rhythm it's like a metronome; you could hum a tune in time with it.

Once again, I move in front of her. "Christians no go up? What does that mean? Christians don't get to go up where? To heaven?"

She keeps on mopping, but as she moves away from me she mumbles, "No head, no go up."

At last I understand, or at least I think I do. She must be saying the men who were executed were Christians, and somebody cut their heads off because they think Christians won't get to go to their heaven if they no longer have a head. I'd heard there were Christians among the Vietnamese, or at least some that claimed they were, and it makes sense the U.S. military would pick them for their sham Vietnamese government.

I leave the restroom and go back to work, but as I load up my next cart, I'm still thinking about her words. What had the killers heard about our Christian heaven? Had they heard the old story about the beautiful cloud up there in the sky where Christians go (if they've been good)? Do they have a vision of Christians sitting up there in peace, gazing down at all this madness? The killers must assume that with no head, those Christians would be stuck down here on earth forever. With no head (and therefore no eyes) those Christians wouldn't be able to find the pearly gates. With no head (and therefore no mouth), they wouldn't be able to tell old Saint Peter that they were good boys, even if they weren't. And what about us soldiers? Uh, excuse me, Mister Peter, sir, if we kill people because we were told to, are we still good boys? And what if the enemy starts cutting all of our heads off? With no eyes to see our way to salvation, and no mouth to proclaim our innocence, even if we do get into heaven, we'll have to wander around that land of the righteous where we know we don't really belong, even if our parents and our preachers and our commanders say we do. I shake off those crazy thoughts and focus on loading my cart. I wonder where Brent is. I should tell him what I found out.

I find him in the canned soup aisle. Before I can tell him what I just learned, he takes the opportunity to grouch to me about getting an order with a lot of heavy cases of soup on it. "Why don't I ever get the good orders with lightweight things?"

I interrupt his grumbling to tell him what the old woman said.

"Makes sense," he says with a shrug. "Some of the other guys heard about the dead bodies in the street. One guy said he'd heard they were Saigon city officials. He thought it might be a protest against the U.S. military requiring all Saigon residents to carry official identity cards."

"The old lady said they were Christians, and they cut their heads off to keep them from going to our heaven."

He laughs. "Great. If they think we're Christians, they'll be cutting *our* heads off next. You and me better get the word out we don't believe any of that religious crap." He heads on down the aisle, still grumbling about how heavy cases of canned soup are. I go back to work, wondering what they did with those men's heads.

I'm just finishing loading the last few heavy items of yet another order list onto my cart when I hear Farkas's shrill toots on his lunchtime whistle. I hurry to drag my cart up to the loading docks, and then I head for the lunch room. You have to get there pretty fast or all the sandwiches will be gone. The tall, red-faced spec-4 who delivers the sandwiches doesn't hang around long enough to make sure everybody gets one; he just dumps them on the lunchroom table and takes off. Farkas has the key to the lunchroom, so he gets in there first and locks the door. He sits in there by himself and eats all he wants, and only then does he unlock the door and blow his lunchtime whistle. Half the time, all I get is a "splat sandwich," which is our derogatory nickname for a thin slice of artificially-yellow Velveeta cheese stuck between two pieces of plain white bread. Turns out today I didn't have to worry about it because Brent got there early and grabbed four of the better sandwiches for the two of us. He's sitting at one of the back tables guarding them from the other guys. He waves me over. I sit down, and he leans close to whisper, "Listen, Scotty, we'd better be on our toes because—"

Before he can finish saying whatever warning it was, Farkas comes and stands in the doorway. Uh oh, he has *that look* on his face, the look that tells me he's looking for somebody to pick on. Is it me? Maybe he isn't through with us about being late this morning. He been coming into the lunch room quite a bit lately to pick on somebody. And when he's in a bad mood, we have to watch out. He can really go after a guy.

I keep my head down and focus on my sandwich, and everybody else does the same thing. We're all *very* engrossed in eating.

"You!"

Everybody looks up.

Farkas is pointing at Phil.

It looks like today's victim is going to be Phil. Phil is a tall lanky guy with a ruddy face and what they call "jug-handle" ears, the kind that stand out from the sides of your head. He's a good worker, but he always looks worn out. The other day, Brent told me why: Phil keeps a girl in a hooch out by the river. He spends all his free time out there with her.

Phil looks up at the sergeant, wide-eyed. He points to his own chest with a scared look on his face.

As far as I can remember, Farkas has never gone after him before because Phil keeps quiet and does whatever he's told to do.

Farkas walks right up to Phil and just stands there, arms crossed, looking down at him.

Phil says, "What?"

Mistake. He should have just kept his mouth shut and put on a real sorry look for whatever it was he might have done wrong.

"I jest looked at yore card, sonny-boay. Ya been lat twace this week."

Phil shrugs. "Sorry, Sarge. I was, uh, hung up."

Another mistake. He should have said he was sick, like I did, or else he should have just kept his mouth shut and let Farkas rant for a while. Farkas is always hoping somebody will come back at him, and this time he takes Phil's wimpy response as coming back at him. "Hung up?" he says. "Ah bet ya'll was hung up. Ah bet ya got yur dick stuck'n your little slant-eye's pussy, didn't ya?"

So Farkas has somehow found out about the girl. Phil is in big trouble.

Phil gets red in the face, but he doesn't respond. He just looks down at the table. Good for him. Now, if he'll just keep his mouth shut and let Farkas rant on for a while.

And Farkas does go on. He's talking really loud to make sure everybody in the room can hear every word he says.

Now I know he was just waiting until we were all in the lunchroom so we could all watch his big show as he went after Phil.

"Ya jest couldn't stan Ta pull it out in time Ta get Ta yur job, could ya?" Farkas's famous T-spit is flying all over the front of Phil, even on his face.

Phil is doing a pretty good job of not flinching, but how long will he be able to hold out?

"The Army's payin' ya good money Ta do yur job, boay. She that good a lay, boay? So good ya forgot all bout yur job?"

Phil glances up at Farkas, and for a second, it looks like he's going to take the bait, but then he thinks better of it and keeps his eyes down.

But Farkas knows his victim. He can tell by Phil's reaction he's struck a nerve. As dumb as he seems, Sergeant Farkas can get a pretty good read on people when he wants to. He leans down close to Phil, close enough to make sure Phil gets hit right in the face by plenty of spit. "No? Ya gonna Tell me *no*, boay? Ya gonna Tell me it Tain't True?" He moves in so close his nose is almost touching Phil's, and he gets a real concerned look on his fat face. "Now don' ya be Tellin' me she be so gaw-dam good a lay ya'd risk yur job fer her? Risk goin' to the jungle fer her, would ya? Got ya that pussy-whipped, has she, boay? Got ya down on your knees lickin' her pussy day and night so you can't even get in here Ta do yur job? That it, boay?"

Phil stands up so quick his chair falls over backwards. His face is a deep red now. "Now wait a minute, Sarge. You shouldn't be saying things like that about her. You don't know her. She's a good person."

Oh no, Phil is actually going to hook in. But why? Everybody knows

Farkas only does these things to try to get a rise out of you. Stare right through him, and give him a bunch of meek Yes Sirs, and chances are he'll finish putting on his little show and go pick on somebody else.

Farkas stands up straight and smiles. He knows he's hooked his fish. Everybody in the room knows Phil is done for.

I whisper to Brent: "Why is Phil hooking in?"

Brent leans close and whispers, "She's pregnant. Phil's been tryin' to get a marriage permit."

All I can say is, "Oh, shit. He's a goner."

Slowly, as if he really, really doesn't want to do what he's about to do, Phil points a finger at Farkas and stammers, "I'd rather you didn't talk . . . that way . . . about my woman, Sarge." He's looking straight into Farkas's eyes, and we all know what that means: it means Farkas can now say this soldier was challenging his authority. It means Phil is a dead duck. He's out of here. It's the jungle for him, for sure.

It's dead quiet in the room.

At first, Farkas doesn't do anything. He's holding it back, letting the tension build for effect. Gradually, the usual snarl on his face turns into a smile. "So, it's true," he says, putting an exaggerated shocked look on his face. "She *has* got ya pussy-whipped. Smelly little slant-eye, and she's got ya down on yur knees lappin' it up."

Phil grits his teeth and holds his ground.

They're stuck that way, face to face, and everybody in the room holds their breath. Phil hasn't done anything yet that could get him thrown in the brig, but he's close. I'm hoping he'll think twice about what he's doing and just back down. He's a good enough worker, if he'll just roll over this time and show he's sorry like a good little puppy, Farkas might relent. But I can see Phil is not going to do that. He's a soft-spoken fellow with soft brown eyes and the kind of quietly friendly face that most people would probably take as gullible, but I make him out to be a pretty steadfast guy. He's the kind of nice guy the hard-asses would probably call "GL" (gutless), but I have the feeling there's more to him than shows on the surface.

For a few moments, Phil doesn't do anything, just stands there scowling at Farkas.

Nobody in the room is eating; they're all waiting to see what Farkas will do with his new plaything.

"Aw, now lookit what I dun," says Farkas in his most phony apologetic voice. "Ah went and hurt the little boay's feelin's. Aw, what can ah do *Ta* make it up to ya, boay? C'mre." Farkas pulls out a chair and sits down, very close to Phil. He pats his lap. "Now, now, com'on over here an have a sit. Let me make it up *Ta* ya."

Phil doesn't move.

"Now, don be lak that, boay. Sit down here and lemme show ya how sorry ah am that ah hurt yore little feelins." He pats his lap again.

Phil looks away. Thankfully, he doesn't say a word. I'm thinking maybe if he can come up with a joke or something, he might still be able to wiggle out of this. Sure, he'd have to do some serious apologizing, crawl on his belly for a few days, but if he really cares about his Vietnamese girl friend, it might be worth it.

But Phil isn't going to do that. He's gone way past saying he's sorry. He just stands there, his clenched fists down at his sides. Too bad.

Farkas looks around at the rest of us, grinning. "Hey, anybody got a baby bottle? Maybe tha little boay needs some milk *Ta* make him feel betta." He turns back to Phil. "Or maybe tha little boy doan take to the bottle. Maybe the little boay goes for the breast feedin'." He pulls up his sweaty shirt and pushes out his chest like he's inviting Phil to suck on a tit. He's so fat he actually does have breasts, like a woman. He puts both of his hands under his breasts and lifts them up. He shakes them, making a kind of kissing sound with his lips.

That gets a few chuckles from the men which encourages Farkas even more. "Want some, little boay?" He shakes his breasts again. "Git on ova here and suck on this here tit. How 'bout it?"

Phil just stares at him, his face red with suppressed anger.

Farkas waits, still shaking his breasts, still grinning.

It hits me that Farkas doesn't know how to get out of this situation any more than Phil does. Maybe, if somebody did something right now, they might be able to save Phil's ass. Make a joke maybe. Get everybody laughing.

I start to stand up, but Brent senses what I'm about to do. He grabs my elbow and pulls me back down.

"Stay out of it," he whispers between clenched teeth.

But it's too late. Farkas has seen my move. He turns toward me. "Wot's this? Somebody else wanna suck somma ma milk?"

I shake off Brent's grip and stand up. I'm standing there, exchanging stares with Farkas, thinking I probably should do what Brent said, just sit back down again and keep my eyes on the table. I don't really owe Phil anything; I've never exchanged more than two words with him. But part of me knows this isn't about Phil; it's about how far we can let Farkas go. Phil hasn't done anything wrong that's related to his job here. He does his work, maintains his three hundred cases per hour, and keeps his mouth shut, like the rest of us. Somebody has to draw a line. Otherwise, Farkas will keep on pulling this shit. Sooner or later, he'll do something like this to every one of us. I put a grin on my face and say, "Come on, Sarge, lay off. Phil's got girl trouble. Isn't that bad enough?"

Everybody laughs. Everybody except Farkas, that is. He pulls down his shirt and leans back in his chair. I can see he's been caught a bit off guard, and he's trying to decide how to come back at me.

But Phil's too dumb, or more likely, too proud, to see his chance at escape. He says, "You don't have to stand up for me, Scotty. This is none of your business. I can take care of myself."

I shrug. "Naw, it's not that, Phil. I was just appreciating Sarge's humor. Good joke, Sarge. Real funny. But I guess we'd all better get back to work now."

Brent jumps up. "Right. Joke time's over. Time to get back to work. Let's go everybody."

The others catch on quick. They all get up and grab their sandwiches and head for the door. On my way out, I swing by where Phil is standing and push him out of the room ahead of me. Farkas stays where he is, his eyes nailing me, watching me go.

Outside the lunchroom, Phil is not happy with me. "You think you have to take care of me? You think I'm afraid of that asshole?"

Brent steps between us. "Shut your trap, Phil. Get your ass back into that warehouse and load cases like you've never loaded that shit before. If you're lucky, maybe Fart-Ass will calm down and you can hang onto this job. You'd better hope so if you want to stay here in Saigon with your mama-san."

Phil comes right back at him: "You tellin' me what to do, Brent? I can decide for myself what I should or shouldn't—"

Brent puts a hand against Phil's chest and pushes him backward. "Get the fuck outta my sight, and go to work before I knock your stupid fuckin' head off. My pal Scotty here maybe saved your bacon. You should be down on your God damn knees thankin' him."

Phil seems to be trying to decide whether he wants to take Brent on, but I don't let him even consider it. I grab his arm and pull him toward the lined-up carts. "Come on, Phil. We can't let Farkas split us up like this. Let's just go back to work."

For just a moment, I'm afraid he's going to go back and fight Brent, or even worse, go back into the lunch room and have it out with Farkas. But then he seems to make a decision. He grabs the tow-handle of the nearest cart and goes careening off down the aisle with it. He doesn't get far before he scrapes the leading edge of the cart against a tall stack of cases of paper napkins. The whole stack teeters and looks like it's just about to come tumbling down. Phil doesn't seem to notice and goes on, so I run to stabilize the stack before it tips over.

Brent comes up next to me and helps me straighten out the stack. "Nice try, Scotty," he whispers, "but it won't work. Phil's a goner."

I shrug and go to get a cart.

Brent follows me. "And you'd better hope you're not gone with him. Why the hell did you have to go and stick your nose into it?"

"Somebody had to. Fart-Ass is getting out of line. Lately he's getting way too—"

Brent shushes me. Farkas is coming out of the lunch room. He sees us and stops. He stares at us. He's moving his lips like he's muttering to himself

Brent and I both grab our carts and hurry back into the warehouse.

Once we're out of sight, Brent chuckles and slaps me on the back. That was a dumb move, Scotty, but pretty fast thinkin'." Hey, how'd you like it when old Fart-Ass squeezed his own tits? He's got bigger knockers than any of the girls at Wong's."

I smile to show Brent I appreciate his joke, but now I'm starting to get worried about how Farkas will get back at me. Sooner or later, even if he's under Brent's thumb, he'll find a way to get me. I know him. He'll think I one-upped him, showed him up in front of the other guys, so he'll have to even the score. He's like an elephant: he won't forget.

Brent heads off down the aisle, still chuckling.

I look at the first item on my list: twenty cases of Spam. I head off toward the canned Spam section. As I load the Spam, I think about Phil. How did he get himself involved with a Vietnamese girl? And what made him think they would let him marry her? The Army thinks it's okay to screw the local girls, as long as you don't get VD, but they told us at Indoctrination Training that serious relationships with the locals could turn into a political issue. Farkas knows that too, so he has Phil dead to rights. Brent is right, Farkas will get Phil sent out of Saigon, and Phil won't be able to do a damn thing about it. I realize I don't know Phil all that well. I don't think anybody does. For the most part, he keeps to himself. He'll carry on a friendly conversation if you offer it when the two of you happen to be loading cases from the same stack, but that's the extent of it. I've only chatted with him briefly a couple of times, about nothing really—the heat in the building, about how tired our backs get when we have the bad luck to get a list with a lot of cases of heavy shit on it, but he pretty much responds with one-liners like, Sure is, or You got that right. As I pass the canned fruit and canned vegetables aisle, I notice Phil is down there loading his cart. I quickly flip through the pages of my order sheets and discover an order for a ten cases of canned peaches. I hurry down to that section and start loading up the peaches. I'm right next to Phil, but I don't say anything to him. I don't even look at him.

He stops what he's doing and stares at me. "You didn't have to do that," he says. "I can take care of myself."

I stop loading cases and look at him as if I just noticed he's there. His face is very red. Is he pissed off, or embarrassed?

"Aw, forget it," I say. "The thing is, we've gotta keep a leash on Farkas. We gotta stick together. If we let him get away with pickin' us off one by one, we're done for."

Phil frowns, but he doesn't reply. He goes back to loading cases.

"Where you from?" I ask.

"Kansas." He keeps on loading, not looking at me.

"That right? Kansas? You grow up on a farm or something?"

"Yeah."

"Well, everybody gets drafted nowadays. Even farmers."

"I signed up."

He must have caught my questioning look because he adds, "It was the right thing to do. Every boy in my high school graduating class joined up."

Now, he *is* looking at me. He's waiting for my reaction.

Okay, if he wants a reaction, I'll give him one. I laugh and say, "Why? Did you think all you farmers were going to come over here and stop Godless communism in its tracks?"

From the surprised look on his face, I can tell he doesn't think it's a joking matter.

"Just a joke," I say and go back to loading up my cart.

He stares at me for a few seconds, then goes back to loading his cart. He finishes and goes off down the aisle without another word.

Now he probably thinks I was putting him down, but I wasn't. Not really. Most of the other soldiers make sarcastic jokes about the politicians and generals, but I know there are also some like Phil, boys that signed up specifically because there *was* a war going on. They felt their country needed them, so they did the right thing and joined up. The drunken carouser types that hang out at Wong's Bar make fun of soldiers like Phil, calling them "gung hos," or "hot to trots," but I actually respect guys like Phil. At least they're doing something they believe in. What are the rest of us doing here? We're just putting in our short time because we couldn't figure out how to get out of the draft. Now Phil will undoubtedly have me pegged as one of *them*, one of the unpatriotic jerks who don't support our leaders in Washington who, he must believe, know better than we do about what's going on in this part of the world. I should go catch up with him and tell him I respect his position, even if I don't agree with it. But I don't. What would be the point of carrying it any further? He believes what he wants to believe, and I believe . . . hell, I don't know what I believe. On the surface of it, this war seems like an idiotic idea: invading some stupid little country halfway around the world just because some people in our government think it has strategic value. But they taught us in high school history class that no invading army has ever been victorious in the long run, not even the Romans, so why are we really here? Back home, the leaders of the anti-war protesters were saying the politicians in Washington start these kinds of wars just to get reelected, and the generals go along with it to get in on the glory. But can that really be true? Would politicians and generals really start a war in such a faraway place, a war in which American boys are sure to get killed, if there wasn't a good reason for it? At times, I hear some of the older soldiers talk about this war being pointless. But maybe they just think it's cool to make fun of their officers and the politicians back home. But despite their smart-ass talk, I'm sure they'd go to the front and fight if they were ordered to. Not one of them wants to look like a chicken. I've even heard some of them say it doesn't matter why we're here, we have to wipe out the enemy to show them Americans can't be beat. When I hear their talk about wiping out the enemy, it gets me to wondering who the enemy really is. Who are the Viet Cong? Are they invaders from the north like they keep telling us, or are they just regular Vietnamese people who just don't like us being in their country? I sometimes wish I had somebody to talk to about it. I tried to talk to Brent, but he just said it wasn't our job to think about the whys and wherefores of it. He said, "Our job is just to keep on sending out food to the poor bastards to eat until they get shot. Besides, we're making money, aren't we? Lots of money. That's the great thing about war, everybody makes money off of it. So why shouldn't we get some of it too?" A hard slap on my back told me the subject was closed. But I still can't stop thinking about it. I don't want to believe this war is only about money. There must be another reason why we're here, and it's sure not because this little backwater country has any strategic value. One thing is for sure, the extent of our military commitment here is amazing. I look around at the incredible number of soldiers here, and the military trucks on the streets, and the planes and helicopters that are always flying over, and it seems to me the war is getting bigger and bigger every day. Back home, the politicians on TV are supposedly saying the war will be over soon, but the rumors that fly around this warehouse all say more and more of our soldiers are getting killed, and the enemy is getting stronger, not weaker. I tell myself to stop thinking about it. Brent is right: it's not my job to worry about such things. If nobody else cares what it all means, why should I? I should do what Brent says: keep my head down, do my job at the warehouse, make some money at Wong's, and have fun. It sure the hell doesn't matter what I think. It's obvious they're going to keep this war going no matter what anybody thinks. The word around here is that back home, the protests against this war are getting bigger and bigger, but it sure doesn't look like those protesters are having the slightest impact on what's going on here. Maybe this will be the war that goes on forever.

9

The Black Ball Drops

It isn't long before the MPs show up. I guess Brent was right, Phil was a short-timer. They escort Phil out the door while Farkas watches, grinning.

Uh oh, now it's my turn. They come back for me and lead me out the door. They put me in an MP jeep, and they take me only a short distance before they take me out and lead me into an office. The sign next to the door says it's the job-placement interviewer's office. They sit me in a chair and stand by the door staring at me.

So, I'm going to get a new assignment. Okay, time to plan out my strategy. I'll tell him I'd like to work in an office. I'll tell him I can type real good because I took a typing class in high school and got an A. If that doesn't do the trick, I'll tell him about all the years I worked in a junkyard and how much I know about tearing down vehicles.

He finally calls me in, but he doesn't give me a chance to tell him anything. He doesn't say a word to me. He doesn't even look at me. He just slams his rubber stamp down hard on my papers, pushes a copy of it to me, and that's that. The paper says I'm going to be shipped north, out of Saigon. As they say around here, the job-placement interviewer has dropped the black ball on me. The way he did it so matter-of-factly, without even asking me a single question, made me wonder if maybe he and Farkas were pals. Maybe Farkas told the Black-Ball Interviewer to send me to the most dangerous place possible.

The MPs take me back to the barracks and tell me I'm confined to quarters. I guess they think if somebody gets ordered to the front, he'll try to run away. But where is there to run to? I might try to go back to Wong's, if I got the chance, but only to try to find my storyteller girl. I'd tell her I have to go away for a while, but I'll be back. I'd tell her I'm going to try really hard to make it back to her in one piece.

But I know if I tried to get out of here, I'd be in big trouble, so I decide I might as well put the time to good advantage and read my philosophy textbook. I start with Kant. My book says Kant thought a lot about God. He said no one can really know whether there is a God, which seems kind of obvious, but maybe in his day it was a startling thing to say. Hegel, on the other hand, wasn't concerned with belief in God; he was more concerned with what, or who, people *thought* God was. I've read and reread the chapter on Hegel, and I have to admit, I'm still not sure I get what he's saying. Schopenhauer, on the other hand, I do get. He said the world is not a rational place. When I read that, I said right out loud, "That's for sure." My textbook says his philosophy appealed to people who wondered about the meaning of life. He also said the state should leave each man free to work out his own salvation. I assume that means he would have been against the draft.

I'm just getting into a section about a philosopher named Francis Herbert Bradley, who was strongly influenced by Kant and the German idealists, when two MPs I've never seen before come in through the door at the far end of the barracks. They march right up to my bunk, both of them looking real serious. They stand over me, scowling at me, until the taller one finally says, "You're in serious trouble, solider." He shakes a paper at me. This report says you refused to obey a superior's direct orders and threatened that same superior with physical violence."

I smile at the thought of Farkas writing such a ridiculous report. I get the two MPs to sit down on the next bunk while tell them about Sergeant Farkas. I tell them about the warehouse and its steel roof that radiates heat down on us workers and how Farkas hides out in his air-conditioned office watching us through his big old binoculars. I even tell them about how Farkas went after poor Phil and how he tried to get Phil to sit on his lap and suck his fatso girly tit.

That gets a quick laugh out of them, but then they quickly stifle their laughing and go back to their stone faces.

I then tell them about how I made a joke to try to help Phil out and that's really why Farkas has it in for me. I swear to them there is no truth to what Farkas said, that he's making it all up just to get me.

By the time I'm done, I'm pretty sure they believe my version of events. I don't think they want to lock me up in the brig just because of Farkas's phony report. Besides, I'm scheduled to be sent to the jungle, and I figure they need all the soldiers they can get there.

They stand up and the taller of the two says, "Good luck up there, son. Watch your ass."

They leave and they're hardly gone when Brent comes in. He's looking real pissed off, and the first thing he says is that he guarantees me he'll get revenge on Farkas if it's the last thing he ever does. He taps me on the chest and says, "Don't you worry, Scotty. I'll get you brought back here to Saigon real soon."

I don't want him to think I'm scared, so I say, "Actually, I wouldn't mind seeing some more of this country. We've been stuck in Saigon ever since we got here."

He says, "Can the fake bravery talk, Scotty. Just keep your head down until I can pull some strings to get you back here."

10

Transition: REMF to FNG

So, here I am, in the jungle. The small base I've been assigned to is on top of a little hill, and it's completely surrounded by jungle. This place is so different from Saigon, I might as well be in another country. All you can see in any directions is thick jungle, tall grasses, thick bushes, trees with vines growing around and through them. I have no idea why they put this base here. The dirt road I came in on ends at this base, so it's not at any kind of crossroads. Supposedly, we're near some kind of secret enemy trail that's just across the border in Cambodia. It's said to run all the way down from North Vietnam, and that's how the enemy infiltrates South Vietnam. But it could just be a rumor. The guys here refer to this place as "up country," but I think that just means anywhere that's not Saigon. They say we're at the western edge of the third Corps Tactical Zone (CTZ III), whatever that means. If I ask where exactly in Vietnam we are, they just make sarcastic cracks like, Who knows? or Out in the boonies. Or To hell and gone. This type of place is known as a Firebase (FB), but this particular FB could also be called a Fire Support Base (FSB), because we have a battery of two 155mm howitzers parked up at the highest point of our compound. We also have a helicopter Landing Zone (LZ), but in the short time I've been here, no helicopters have arrived. We have a mess tent, but you'd hardly know it was a tent because it's been all but buried in sand bags, like all the other tents here. We have a Tactical Operations Center (TOC) where a young, all-American-looking second lieutenant named Dasen has his partly underground office that's also completely buried in sandbags. The lieutenant is a clenched-jaw type of fellow, quiet, and maybe kind of moody, but I've never actually talked to him. He doesn't look all that much older than the rest of us, except he must be old enough to have finished college because behind his back, the old hands refer to him as a "shake-and-bake." It's their name for a guy the Army grabs right after he graduates from college and gets rushed through some kind of quick officer-training program. Then, they ship them off to Vietnam where they end up commanding combat troops even though they don't know anything about the country and not much about being an officer. We have an aid station (another sandbag-buried tent) and a medic, a young, kind of skinny fellow named Eric that everybody calls Doc Eric. He seems like a nice guy, fairly friendly, although he mostly keeps to himself. I've noticed he doesn't join in any of the ongoing poker games or participate in any of the horseshit that goes on here. By horseshit, I mean childish pranks like putting great big spiders or big snakes in your bed—things that reveal how young everybody here is.

It's not hard to describe what this place looks like. Besides our sandbag-surrounded tents, it's a flat patch of nothing. Just dusty devastated dirt. They tell me that before any troops arrived, it was plowed all to hell by Army engineering corps bulldozers. Those bulldozers guys must have been under orders to not leave a single trace of the jungle on this FB. So far, I haven't been outside the double rows of spiraled razor wire that surrounds this FB, but I expect if you were to see it from outside, it would look like a big oblong patch of churned-up dirt broken only by what must look like huge piles of sandbags. Inside those walls of sandbags are our tents. There are only a hundred or so of us here, and we all live inside those buried tents.

So, now I'm officially in the war and officially in danger, which means I'm no longer an REMF (Rear Echelon Mother Fucker) which is what the combat guys here call any soldier who isn't in direct danger from the enemy. They make it very clear they don't like the REMFs that somehow got themselves assigned to nice and safe supply duty back in Saigon. Now that I'm here, I'm no longer a REMF; now I'm a FNG (Fucking New Guy), which is one tiny little step up from REMF.

So far, it's not bad here. There haven't been any enemy attacks, so we're kept busy working out in the hot sun all day stacking sandbags or moving things around. Today, we're stacking more sandbags around the lieutenant's headquarters, which is already completely surrounded by sandbags. The guy next to me takes off his hat, wipes the sweat off his brow with his sleeve, and shades his eyes to look toward the west. "Boo-coo enemy right over there. In Cambodia. But we haven't seen hide nor hair of 'em. Guess we're not a prime target right now."

I look in that direction. "How do you know if you're a prime target"?

"You get attacked. No attacks so far, only probings."

I ask, "What's a probing?"

"Probings? Well, there are two types. At night, when you'd think it was too dark for anybody to see a damn thing, the enemy snipers hone in on us. They especially watch the latrines."

That makes me think about the fact that I've been heading for the latrine every night before going to bed. Nobody mentioned snipers.

The guy goes on. "Me, at night I use the shit can in our tent. Specially when there's a moon out."

I try to remember if I've been seeing a moon at night.

"The other type, well, it won't be long before you'll learn about that. Some nights, they shoot off a bunch of mortars at us."

Mortars? In the middle of the night? That sounds pretty scary. But this guy doesn't seem too worried about it.

He says, "They only fire off a dozen or so, and they usually miss. Nothin' to worry about. They're just tryin' to scare us.

I'm thinking, they *usually* miss? "Uh, trying to scare us?"

He looks up at the sun and puts his hat back on. "Pre-amble. Testin' our response. They shoot off a few mortars, and we fire our howitzers back at 'em. Gotta shoot back at 'em or we're in shit city. Let down one time, and they'll be on us like snot on a snot rag." He points to the west again. "Charlie's over there all right, and he knows right where we are. He'll drop by for a visit one of these days."

We go back to stacking sandbags. He doesn't seem too concerned, and I'm left wondering if maybe he was just trying to scare the FNG.

There are only two vehicles here, a big worn-out-looking truck that takes a crew out somewhere every morning for what they call "road security." I'm not sure what road security is, but I don't ask. If you're a FNG, you don't want to look any dumber than you actually are. The other vehicle is the lieutenant's jeep. This morning, the lieutenant told some of the guys to start it up and drive it around the camp. To keep it in good working condition, he said. A bunch of guys piled on, and they roared around the far end of the FB until they had created a sort of motocross course. They took turns driving to see who could go around the course the fastest. Eventually, they managed to turn the jeep over, and two of the guys got hurt bad enough that they had to go see Doc Eric. The jeep still works, but I don't suppose the lieutenant will be letting anybody drive it now.

We spend our free time inside our sandbag-buried hooches. Hooch is a Vietnamese word for house, but our hooches are nothing like a house. Being inside a sandbag-buried tent hooch is basically like being inside a cave that smells like burning lantern oil and dirty socks and sweaty men. My hooch-tent was built for two, but right now I'm sharing mine with three other guys. My three hoochmates are all white. The black soldiers have their own area, down at the lower edge of our big patch of dirt; but I don't think it's segregation—apparently, they stay over there by their own choice. All three of my hoochmates are recent high school grads, and by chance, all are from the Midwestern part of the U.S. I'm not going to tell you their real names, but I can tell you their nicknames (just about everybody here has a nickname). One guy is called Oh-Lee, pronounced as if there was a question mark after his name, sort of like it's his mother calling him in for supper. He's not all that tall, only a little taller than me, but he seems embarrassed to be tall so he slumps, his shoulders forward. He's the oldest son of a Norwegian family in Minnesota that owns some kind of small fishing resort. He talks really slow, as if he's planning every word before he says it. My second hoochmate is a little red-haired guy from Nebraska.

But he's not called "Red" because there was already a guy called Red on this FB. Instead, because he grew up on a farm, he's called The Farmer. He doesn't like being called The Farmer. He says he joined up to get away from all that. He says when he gets out, a farm would be the last place in the world he'd want to be. Him not liking to be called The Farmer guarantees that everybody is going to call him that. He's a frowner and a complainer. He has something cynical or disapproving to say about everything: the food is crap; our hootches are designed to make it as hot and stuffy inside as possible; the boots they give us are so bad we'd be better off going barefoot. My third hoochmate is a little older than the rest of us. He's kind of a dour guy, and he looks like one of those actors in the old black and white noir detective movies: tough, quiet, sour. But he's actually not as unfriendly as he looks. He's from St. Louis so they call him Saint Louee. But that's not the only reason; it's also because he seems to have taken on the duty of filling in the FNGs about camp rules and requirements. He's kind of harsh about it. He lays out the camp semi-official rules in a straightforward abrupt way, not wasting any words. I don't think it's an official assignment or anything, but he does it, and it is helpful to us new guys, so I guess that's why they call him *Saint* Louee. I've never once seen him smile or laugh. The main thing my hoochmates like to do is play poker. They built a rough little table out of scrap plywood and threw a cloth over it. Whenever they don't have other duties, they play poker, and they play for real money. They don't invite me to play, not that I would want to anyhow.

Tonight, I'm doing my first stint on perimeter guard duty. I'm sitting behind a wall of sandbags, staring out into the darkness through the spirals of sharp razor wire. The old M-14 they gave me is lying across my lap. I know I'm supposed to keep it in my hands at all times, but I get an uncomfortable feeling every time I hold it. I start thinking about what it's for: it's for killing people. When I feel how well it fits my hands, I start thinking about using it to shoot people. I wonder if I'd really do it. Do the others think about their rifles like that? Probably not. We all learned how to shoot a rifle in Basic Training, so they probably don't think there's any need to think about what it's used for. They obviously knew they were being trained to shoot humans, not just targets. I guess I should try to be more like that and not think about it. Brent says I think too much. But I can't get it out of my head that I have a loaded rifle in my hands, and the fact that we are in a war means I could probably shoot somebody out there in the darkness and nothing bad would happen to me. Shoot first and ask questions later; that's probably what anybody else would do. But would I actually shoot my rifle if I heard something out there? I'm not sure, but I am sure it's better to leave my rifle lying across my lap instead of holding it in my hands. That way I won't end up doing something hasty that I'd regret later. I wouldn't want to shoot and find out later I just killed a passing farmer, or somebody like that. At least I'm not alone out here on perimeter guard duty. They'd never put a FNG out here alone. Even though it's too dark to see them, I know there are guys in sandbagged holes on both sides of me, and I'm sure they *are* keeping *their* rifles in their hands. If there's any shooting to be done, I'll just let them do it. When the lieutenant told me he was putting me on perimeter guard duty, I asked him what my orders were. He just shook his head and stared at me like I'd asked the dumbest question he'd ever heard. Finally, he pointed in the general direction of the jungle and said my orders were to keep an eye on things out past "the wire" (which is what everybody calls the rolled up razor wire that surrounds the whole camp). I guess I'm supposed to be looking for movement. Or sounds.

As the night goes on, I start imagining that this will be the night they *will* come. A hoard of Viet Cong soldiers will come running right at me. The old hands say they will come, sooner or later, but they also say we have nothing to worry about because the daisy-chained and trip-wired Claymores will take care of Charlie if he tries to sneak up on us. Even though I'm a FNG, I know what a Claymore mine is. They showed us pictures of them in Indoctrination Training back in Saigon. They look like green slabs of metal with the words "Front – Toward Enemy" stenciled on them. Those words explain it all: they're a type of anti-personnel mine that are filled with a whole bunch metal bits. When they explode, they send those metal bits flying out toward the enemy. Saint Louee told me that over time, more and more of those Claymores have been planted out there beyond the wire, and a lot of them are daisy-chained together, so if the enemy comes, a hell of a lot of them will all go off at once. That would really be something to see, like the biggest fireworks show ever. Saint Louee told me it happened once already. He said one night, a little while before I got here, the Claymores started going off like crazy. Woke everybody up, and they all came running out with their rifles, some in their underwear, a few of them totally naked. But after all the Claymores had finished going off, the jungle was totally silent again. Nothing was moving out there. Everybody just went back to bed, and in the morning when they went out to look, there was nothing to be found. So what could have set off those Claymores that time? Was it the enemy testing the base's defenses? And why did everybody go back to bed? With the Claymores discharged, wouldn't that have been the perfect time for the enemy to attack? I guess it could have been an animal that set them off, but Saint Louee said there were no dead animals found. If it actually was an animal, then it's not a very reassuring story that the critter got away. I mean, when those things go off, aren't they supposed to kill anything within the kill pattern area? Maybe they're not as reliable as everybody thinks. Just one more thing for me to worry about. I stare into the darkness and imagine the enemy creeping around out there. I'm sure they're out there. They have to be. We're the only base in this area, so why wouldn't they be watching us? They're out there watching and waiting, evaluating us, waiting for the exact right moment to attack. Maybe they've already cut the Claymore trip wires. Maybe there will be nothing to stop them, nothing but me and this old M-14 rifle. Now I smell pot smoke. The other guys must think guard duty is so boring it's a good time to get stoned. That means they're not going to be very vigilant. I'm glad I was smart enough not to smoke any pot tonight. I lean forward to try to see through the darkness. I listen for any little sound. But maybe the enemy knows how to move around out there without making a sound. That gets me to thinking about what it must be like for them in that dark jungle. The vegetation looks so thick, I imagine it would give you a closed-in, claustrophobic feeling. Branches and prickly things would always be grabbing at your clothes, grabbing at *you*. You could get so caught up in the tangles of those vines and brambles you might get completely stuck and never get out. I've overheard the guys who come back from patrols talk about the jungle. They talk about it in whispered, almost reverent, voices. Their whispered conversations make the jungle seem scarier to me than if they came back and told horror stories. I shake off that scary kind of thinking. What do I know about the jungle? Maybe I'm just imagining things. Maybe there are not many enemies in this area. They say that except for the occasional mortar attacks, there's been no sign of the enemy. There *was* some talk around camp a few days ago about one patrol did have some kind of run-in with the local villagers. I heard a couple of guys whispering about some kind of squabble over a pig. They were saying some villagers got shot. I asked Saint Louee about it, but he told me to stay out of it. "Things like that happen."

I said, "Things happen? What kind of things?"

He just shook his head and walked away, which isn't like him. I guess a FNG isn't supposed to ask those kinds of questions.

The one good thing about being on peripheral guard duty is that it's quiet. Except for the background hum of millions of crickets, there's total silence. It's the first real peace and quiet I've had since I came here. It's like the Arizona desert, quiet. I like the quiet. It was one of the main reasons I spent so much time alone out in the desert. But now I do hear something. A whistle. Must have been the call of a night bird, close by. Is it calling to it's mate? Sure enough, the reply whistle soon comes, but softer and farther away. I'm glad she answered him. Better to have someone with you out there in that dark jungle. I listen for them to call to each other again, but here's no sound except for the usual background hum of millions of crickets. But then the crickets stop. What the hell? It's almost like my thought about them made them stop. I pick up my rifle and point it out into the darkness. I wonder if the other guys on perimeter duty heard the crickets stop and are also pointing their rifles out into the darkness. But time goes by and nothing happens, and gradually the crickets start up again. But what could have made them stop? Was somebody moving around out there? Is it the enemy moving in? I keep my rifle aimed into the darkness, and take quick little breaths. The enemy *is* out there. I'm sure of it. They probably move through the jungle like the animals do, silent, and not leaving any trace they had been there, not even bending over a single blade of grass. It's their domain, not ours. Quite a bit of time passes and nothing happens. I notice I'm holding onto my rifle too tight, and my hands are sweaty. I put the rifle down into my lap and tell myself to calm down and stop imagining things. Crickets might stop for any number of reasons. I try to think about something else. I try to remember how it felt to be at Wong's Bar. The smell of the place, the noise, the gamblers, the young soldiers lusting after the pretty girls. And what about that storyteller girl I met there? I was pretty drunk and really stoned that night, but I still remember her beautiful naked body in the dim light. And I remember the stories she told me. There was one about a magic horse. A funny story. And another one about a servant girl who saved a turtle. She said it was an important story, and that I should remember it. There will come a time, she said. Save the turtle, she said, but I'm still not sure what she meant by that. Now that I'm in the jungle, I wonder if maybe she grew up somewhere near here. Maybe her parents were farmers, scratching out an existence somewhere in the Vietnamese jungle. I can imagine her there, maybe helping her father plant things. Or maybe her job was to feed the chickens. I bet it was her mother that told her that story about the magic horse, and the one about the turtle. Bedtime stories. Or when she was being bathed. Bathing time would be just after sunset, after all the chores were done. There would be a warm rosy glow in the room from the setting sun. Her mother would be on her knees on the shack's dirt floor, telling those stories as she bathed her precious little girl who would be in an old tub. The mother would squeeze water from a sponge. It would run down over the girl's beautiful shoulders, over her smooth, unblemished skin. Her skin would be radiant in the glow of the sunset. Such a precious child, a treasure. But how would such a girl end up at Wong's Bar? She was way too young to be in a place like that. She should have been at home with her parents, helping her father take care of the farm, not hanging around in a sleazy place like Wong's. It's a mystery. Everything about her is a mystery. It makes me feel bad that I never got the chance to go back and see her again after that night. That damn Fart-Ass Farkas got me sent out of Saigon the very next day. I should try to get a letter through to Brent. Maybe he can find out who she is. But what if that was the only night she ever came to Wong's and nobody knows her?

Time seems to be moving too slow. I keep wanting to look at my watch to see if it's time for my relief to show up. But I know I'm not supposed to show any kind of light. They say there might be snipers out there watching us. I stare out into the darkness and imagine a sniper up in a tree out there somewhere. Is he watching me right now? There I go again, imagining things. Saint Louee said peripheral guard duty is no big deal. He said I have more to fear from the bugs than from the enemy. Well, he's right about that. There are plenty of bugs to worry about. The Vietnamese jungle must breed more bugs than anywhere on earth. You have to wear your helmet and flak jacket out here, and that means you're going to get hot and sweaty. Bugs like hot and sweaty. They get inside my clothes and bite me. I keep my collar buttoned up tight, but somehow they still manage to get in and bite the shit out of my neck. One thing for sure, the insecticide they gave me doesn't do a damn thing to stop them. I think it must have been made for American-type bugs. I'm starting to think the Vietnamese bugs like it, crave it even. And let me tell you, there sure is an amazing diversity of bugs here: big ones that look like they could chew your ear off, medium sized ones that bite meaner than they look, and little feathery ones, so tiny they're hard to even see. Those are the ones most likely to get you. You think they're so small they couldn't hurt a flea, but then they bite you and it hurts like hell. There are some so small you don't ever see them. They bite you in some sneaky way, bite you so soft and sweet you don't even feel it, and then the next day a big red welt comes up. And as if thinking about bugs makes it happen, I feel one crawling up the side of my neck. I slap at it, hard, but then I'm sorry I did because my slap made a noise. It wasn't much of a noise, but I bet those snipers out there are sensitive to any sound. I duck down behind the sand bags and wait for the shot to come. But nothing happens. It's still totally quiet. Then, I hear a snap. What the hell was that? It was like somebody out past the wire snapped their fingers. I again sit up and point my rifle out into the darkness. I listen. It's completely quiet out there, but I'm sure I really did hear something. Maybe it was an animal. The guys who've been out there say they hear things moving through the underbrush, but they never see them. They swear there are critters in the jungle that have *never* been seen by anybody, never been categorized by any scientist, critters so fast and sneaky no human will *ever* see them. I hear that night bird again, that same urgent call, and again comes the distant reply from another bird. I have the sudden scary thought that it might not be a bird. It could be an enemy signal. Is this the night they attack? I can feel my pulse thumping fast inside my helmet. Why am I so nervous? I have to calm down. Nothing has happened. Why would they attack tonight of all nights? The lieutenant would never put a FNG out here on guard duty if there was any real danger. But what if that bird call is actually a sniper up in a really tall tree? What if he's watching me? Unlike me, he won't think about who his target might be and whether I deserve to die or not. I'm the enemy, an invader from another land. He's probably taking out a bullet right now. I can see him doing it, slowly, methodically. He's been saving this one bullet for somebody special. Am I special? We all think we are, but are we really? If he shoots me, won't I just be another statistic, one more young soldier killed in Vietnam? Too bad, but then you reach a certain number of KIAs, what's one more? The young sniper licks the tip of his special bullet and carefully slides it into the chamber of his rifle. It's an old single-shot Soviet rifle, but it's accurate. He loves that rifle. He's polished the wood of that rifle's stock until he can see his own reflection in it. At night, in the darkness of his shack, he sometimes strokes that rifle to help himself get to sleep. Now he's going to get the chance to use his trusted weapon. The rifle fits against his shoulder perfectly. The feel of it in his hands is so familiar. He relaxes his shoulders, settles in, and takes his time aiming at where he heard that slap sound. He slowly lets out half of his breath and squeezes the trigger. The gun fires: such a perfect sound in the silence of the night. The bullet comes toward me, straight and true. It will arrive before I hear the sound of the shot. It will penetrate my head. The last thing on this earth I will feel will be that bullet coming out the other side of my head in an explosion of blood and flesh and brain matter. The bullet will bury itself in the ground, having done the job it was designed to do. The young sniper will be satisfied. He did his duty, and he did it well. But he will be disappointed that his bullet had to stop there. He hates to think about that special bullet being buried in the ground. He would have liked it better if that bullet had kept going after it left my head. If only that bullet could have gone tearing through the jungle, straight and true, so fast and powerful nothing could stop it. It might go all the way to Saigon where it could kill more Americans, kill them in the streets where he has seen them strutting along as if they owned the place, acting like they own the whole town, the whole country. Maybe the bullet might even kill that fat American sergeant who was eating Chink food in a streetside restaurant while the girl sat on his lap. She looks so young and so beautiful as she patiently waits for him to finish eating before going upstairs with him. She feels the bulge of him inside his pants, the heat and the sweat of him right through the thin white silk of her pretty dress. She wishes she was not there. She wishes she did not have to sit on the lap of this sweaty American sergeant. She wishes she was back with her family in the country, with her mother and father, and her little brother, the sniper.

11

The Fear

My relief finally comes. It's Oh-Lee, my hoochmate. He doesn't say why he's late. He doesn't even say hi, just hops over the sandbag wall, puts his rifle down, and sits there rubbing his eyes with the back of his hands. I guess he's in his usual just-waking-up grumpy mood, so I just say "See ya" and don't mention his being late. I hurry back to my hooch, running bent over in case that sniper is still watching me. When I get back to our hooch, I'm surprised to see the ARVN soldier who supplies this firebase with local weed and Cong souvenirs like broken Soviet-era rifles and cut-off human ears sitting on my bunk. I've never seen him in this camp at night before. He hands me a letter from Brent and demands payment for delivering it. I give him a handful of red MPC dollars. They aren't of any use to me out here anyhow. He takes off fast.

My two hoochmates are doing what they always do, playing poker at their rigged up plywood poker table. They ignore me, so I go lie on my bunk to read Brent's letter. It says Phil was supposed to be confined to barracks until his transfer papers were completed, but he went AWOL. The MPs found him right away. Brent says it was probably Farkas who told them Phil would be at his pregnant girlfriend's hooch. They found him hiding underneath her house, all covered in dirt and his hair infested with fleas from being under there with the mangy puppies she was raising for food. The MPs dragged Phil out and took him to the brig. They held him there for a while on the AWOL charge, which was legit, but they also added a charge for being at his girl's house which was off-limits. Brent's letter makes the point that the off-limits bit was a bullshit charge because just about every soldier in Saigon goes off limits to find girls, gambling, and dope. He writes that after a couple of days in the brig, they shipped Phil north to an area known for having a lot of enemy activity — very hot, as they say. As I itch my bug bites, I think about Phil being in the brig because of Farkas. But they never hold anybody very long on minor charges because they need everybody they can get up at the front (cannon fodder.) The letter says Phil didn't even survive a full week up there. Got killed before he was hardly even settled in. Apparently they sent him out on patrol before he had a clue what he was doing, and he got blown to shit when he stepped on a booby-trap. Brent says he tried to track down the girlfriend to give her some money, but she'd disappeared. Her family claimed they didn't know where she'd gone, but Brent figures she probably got sent out of the city to keep her half-American baby secret. I wonder what they do with unwanted American-fathered babies in Vietnam. I hope they don't kill them. I put away the letter and stare up at the tent roof thinking about the type of guy Phil was. Not the type to refuse to go to the front, even if it meant leaving his pregnant girlfriend. You'd have thought he'd do just about anything to stay with his girl and her forthcoming baby, maybe even fake a mental crackup or something. But such a thing would probably never even occur to him, patriotic farmer that he was. Some of the loudmouth boozers that hung out in Wong's Bar used to talk about what they were going to do when they got sent into combat. They all had their special boasts about how brave they'd be, and they all agreed that they'd never "turn chicken," like the cowards who come down with the so-called "battle fatigue." I have the feeling those guys would be as scared as I am to be out here in the jungle. But what do I know about bravery or cowardice? I wonder if any of the guys I went to high school with got drafted. Maybe some of them are here in Vietnam too. I guess I could write to my mother and ask. But she probably wouldn't know. I can't seem to make myself write to her. Maybe she watches the war on the evening TV news to see if she can see me. They show so much Vietnam War chaos and death on TV back home, maybe she thinks I'm already dead.

My thoughts are interrupted by a distant thump-like sound. What was that? A few seconds later, there's an explosion, and not all that far away. This must be it, the mortar attacks that guy told me about, the nighttime "probings." I glance over at my poker-playing hoochmates. They're grim faced, but they keep on playing. Are they really that brave, or are they just pretending? Another thump. That sound must come when the enemy sends a mortar skyward. How far away are they? How long will it take to get to us? I count it down: one thousand one, one thousand two, one thous . . . Then it hits. The sound of the explosion is muffled by the thick sandbag wall of our hooch, but I can tell it hit quite a ways farther down the hill. Another thump. I hold my breath and wait for it to hit. This one explodes a lot closer. It might have been where the black guy's hooches are. I hope it didn't hit any of them. Are the mortar shooters honing in on us, using the first few shots to find the range? Will the next one be the one that comes right down through my tent's roof? I hear the takeoff thump as the next mortar is sent skyward. I count it down, again holding my breath. I wonder if everyone else in this camp is holding their breath like I am. It hits. The explosion is much louder this time. A lot closer. Maybe over by the mess tent. I close my eyes and wait for the next one. I try to think about something else, about Wong's Bar, or about my storyteller girl. But that doesn't work: all I can think about is when the next one will come. I hear it launched. I wait. It hits, and this time the explosion is even louder. Where did it hit? Maybe over by the latrines. I think about the enemy out there in the jungle, squatting down, gathered around the mortar tube, each with his well-practiced task. Right now, they're aiming the next mortar at this camp, aiming at my hooch, aiming at *me*. They're telling themselves, now we've got the range, now we've got him. I hear the thump as the shell gets launched. I imagine it climbing higher and higher into the dark sky until it finally loses momentum. Then, it starts to curve downward, forming a mathematically beautiful arc as it begins its trip down to find me, down and down and down, picking up speed as it comes, faster and faster, unbelievably fast now, horribly fast, coming down straight and true, aiming directly for the very tent roof I'm looking up at right now. I close my eyes and wait for it. I swear I can hear the faint whistle it makes as it cuts through the quiet night. When it hits our hooch, the explosion will be unbelievably loud. There will be a flash. I'll see that flash of light even before the sound of the explosion breaks both of my eardrums. That bright flash of light will be the last thing I see before I die. The explosion comes. It's loud, and it's so close it sprays our tent roof with dirt. That one was too close, so close even the steel-nerved poker players stop their play and look up. They're still holding their cards in front of them, but the poker game has gone into freeze frame. They have to be thinking the same thing I am, will the next one be the one that kills me? Will this be my night to die? To see them holding so perfectly still like this gives me the oddest feeling that it's me creating it, as if I've somehow made everything stop, even time. It's like that thing about reality I read in my philosophy book, that philosopher, René Descartes, who said we each create our own reality. He said there's no way to prove we're not just a brain floating in a vat of liquid in a lab somewhere, dreaming reality. He said our only knowledge of reality is what our brain tells us, so there's no way to prove we're not making it all up. So maybe my brain changed the reality of falling mortars, and that's what is saving us. I close my eyes and concentrate. Make the next one miss. Make it miss. The next explosion is farther up the hill. I did it. I made it miss. I open my eyes and let the world start moving again. The poker players shake their heads and go back to their game without a word. They must think we lucked out this time, but I'm still holding my breath. What if I really did make that one miss? There are sure to be more. What if I can't hold this near-miss reality together any longer? The responsibility of keeping us all alive is too much. Why does it have to be me? I try to shake off that kind of thinking, but my mind seems to be stuck in low gear, grinding away at my nerves, saying over and over, this is how you will die, a pointless death in a pointless war in the middle of a bug-infested jungle. They will tell my mother a mortar fell on your son's head, and he died. But no one will care, not really. I haven't made any kind of mark on the world. They will just add one more to the count, and the war will go on. The fear causes my stomach to start acting up. I take a lot of fast deep breaths to keep myself from throwing up. I don't want to throw up in front of my hoochmates. Another mortar hits, not all that far away. I didn't even hear it being launched. What's the matter with me? Am I losing it? I try to focus. Where did that mortar hit? Are they working their way back toward our hooch, trying to get me? I look over at the poker players again. They're back to playing poker. They think it's over. Don't they realize that one was closer? But then, the howitzers start blasting away, throwing their huge exploding shells out into the darkness, aiming, I guess, toward wherever they think those mortar shooters are. No more mortars will come. Maybe the enemy ran away before the howitzers even started. How do they know when it's time to leave? Who is leading in this dance of death? I stare up at our sagging tent roof and wonder what good all our triple-thick walls of stacked-up sandbags are. Mortars come straight down out of the sky. There are no sandbags up there on top our tent roof. The enemy must figure all they have to do is keep on shooting off mortars, and sooner or later, they'll hit a tent roof. It makes me feel like I'm an unwilling player in a game of chance, but it's not like poker; this game of chance is deadly serious. It's like a problem they might have given us in high school math class: given an infinite number of mortars falling out of the sky, what are the chances that any one particular tent roof will be hit? The correct answer is, of course, that every roof will get hit sooner or later and everyone inside will die. Everybody here must know that, but I guess they all hope to be gone before their number comes up. Odds and hope. Is that what being in war is all about? Playing the odds? Heads you live, tails you die? Whenever I'm outside, I can't stop myself from calculating the number of square feet of dirt on this firebase, compared with the number of square feet of tent roofs. If others are doing the same calculations, nobody talks about it.

The poker players are back to their normal poker-playing behavior, complaining about the crummy hands they get. They now know they're not going to die tonight, so they can go back to acting normal, which is loud and crude. They slug down beer after beer and they nibble endlessly on the smelly dried fish sticks they buy from the villagers who come to the main gate every morning. Then, they start burping and farting their smelly fish-farts. They make jokes about who has the nastiest farts. They fill the hooch with their laughing and their complaining and their bad fart smells. But now that the mortar attack is over, my intestines have decided it's time to react. I have to scramble out of my bunk and hurry to the corner to squat over the damn stinking communal poop can. Now it's my turn to make bad smells. It's diarrhea, damned fear-induced, non-stop diarrhea. The poker players hold their noses and make stupid jokes about living in a pig sty. But there's nothing I can do about it. I'm stuck right where I am, squatting over the can until it's finally all over and done with. I limp back to bed, avoiding eye contact with my hoochmates. I lie down and turn away from them. They're cheerful now, making jokes again. They slap down their losing hands and complain like they always do, but I can tell they're not really all that upset about losing. I guess it's not such a big deal to lose a few bucks when a few moments ago they could have lost their lives, but they go right back to their poker game to avoid thinking about the danger. And the game bonds them together. Sometimes I think I should ask to join them, but I know they wouldn't want me. I'm the outsider, the fifth wheel, unneeded and unwanted. Nobody talks to me, except Saint Louee, and I think he looks at it like a job: train the new guy to make sure the FNG doesn't get the rest of us killed. It's been that way since I arrived at this firebase. Hardly anybody talks to me, and I'm not sure why. It's as if everybody on this firebase immediately decided not to like me. They seem to think I'm different from them, and I guess I am. I don't smoke cigarettes, even though the Army provides them for free, and I'm not interested in roughhousing or playing tricks on anybody. But how did they know that right away? Just because I'm quiet and keep to myself? Because I read my philosophy textbook a lot? Well, there's nothing I can do about how they feel, so I just keep to myself, even though I know it's taking me further and further away from everybody. While my hoochmates play their card games, I read my philosophy textbook. While they fart and make jokes, I take notes about logical positivism and neopragmatism and try to figure out what those things are. While they play seven-card draw with double draws on the end, I read and worry. They play poker, and apparently, they don't worry. I think about the war, and if they, or any of the other soldiers at this firebase think about the purpose of this war, they don't talk about it out loud.

I hear something and turn to see that it's Oh-Lee coming back from perimeter duty. He stands his rifle in the corner, tosses his helmet onto his bunk and hurries to join the poker game. Saint Louee asks him if anybody got hit. Oh-Lee says he doesn't think so, and they go right back to talking about poker. I'm shocked to realize I forgot he was out there during the mortar attack. What would it be like to be out there on the perimeter, huddled in a hole in the ground with those explosions going off all around you? Why didn't I once think about him being out there? Is that what happens to you here? You get so concerned about yourself, you forget about the danger to anybody else? But then I realize that while the mortar attack was going on, nether Saint Louee or The Farmer mentioned the fact that Oh-Lee was out there. They just kept on playing poker through it all. Didn't they care that their poker-playing buddy might get killed out there tonight? I turn back to face the wall, trying to block out their endless chatter about "getting hit by the deck" (being on a lucky streak), "cold decks" (the deck is stacked against you), hitting miracle inside straights (hitting the one card you needed to win), and God-damned airballs (missing all the cards you needed to win). Not one of them even mentions the mortar attack. Maybe they think if they don't talk about it they can convince themselves it was no big deal. Maybe they focus so intently on their poker game to make sure they don't get too scared. But I can't help but wonder if they do think about it after their nightly game of pretend chance is over. When they finally do hit the sack and turn off the lantern that hangs over the poker table, do they too stare up at our flimsy tent roof and think about dying? I know for a fact that both Oh-Lee and the Farmer have calendar sticks—wooden sticks with carved notches indicating how many days they have left before they can get out of here. Do they hold their notched calendar sticks tight in their sweaty hands and pray to whatever God they believe in to just let them survive one more night, to let them stay alive long enough to finish their hitches and get the hell out of this nightmare. They know as well as I do that sooner or later one of those mortars is going to land on somebody's tent. And what if it's ours? The next morning would the medic and maybe some kind of special death squad come in to clean up the mess? I guess they'd chopper out what's left of our bodies. The hole where our hooch used to be would be a place to be avoided. Everybody'd pretend the new hole in the ground is nothing special despite the nail-like wood splinters stabbed into the dirt and the ripped-open and scattered-about sandbags. Our personal possessions would be there, all torn up and stained with our blood, but nobody would look too close at that. Although they might be a bit quieter than usual the next day, I bet by the next night everybody would be right back to their poker games and their loud music and their cigarette chain-smoking and their non-stop beer drinking while they jabber on and on about hot girls and hot cars and the damn hot weather. It would be like it never happened.

Lieutenant Dasen's voice wakes me up. I turn over to see what's going on. He's asking for volunteers for a morning patrol. He's sending men out to chase after the mortar shooters. I swing my feet out of bed and surprise myself by holding up my hand. But the lieutenant ignores me. He picks The Farmer and Saint Louee. They get dressed and grab their gear and go out without a word. I quickly get dressed and follow them out. I want to see who the lieutenant picks to go out and chase the mortar shooters. Outside, it's still dark, but there's a bit of rosiness in the sky to the east, so dawn can't be far away. There's a mist in the air, but straight up overhead there's an almost-full moon trying to shine through thin clouds. The fact that the clouds are so thin must mean the much talked about rainy season that was supposed to have started weeks ago is still going to be missing in action. Even this early in the morning, I can tell it's going to be yet another hot and muggy day, same as every day since I got here. I look around to see if any of the hooches got hit in the mortar attack. It doesn't look like it, but one of the latrines obviously got hit. I can smell it from where I'm standing. The mortar's explosion must have scattered bits of our shit all over the place. Who knows how long this firebase will smell like human shit. Maybe forever. Other tired-looking soldiers start emerging from their hidey-hole hooches, all of them still sleepy and squinting to see though the mist. A few of them go to check out the blown-up latrine area. I don't know how they can stand to get so close to that smelly mess of splintered lumber and tangled, shit-stained toilet paper.

As the combat guys load up and get ready to head out to look for the elusive mortar shooters, I edge closer to hear what kind of instructions the lieutenant gives them. He doesn't say much, just tells them to go out and try to find where those mortar shooters were set up and then follow their trail. He says they should try to catch them before they can get back across the Cambodian border. He reminds them to be sure they don't go across the border into Cambodia. The squad leader asks how they're supposed to know if they've crossed the border, and a couple of the men chuckle. Maybe he asks that same question every time just to irritate the lieutenant. The lieutenant just tells them to use the maps, and that gets another chuckle out of the men. I don't suppose there are any border lines drawn out there in the jungle. But the enemy must know where the border is, and they must know we can't follow them there. The patrol files out through the gate, and the lieutenant heads back to his hooch. I decide to follow him, but I hesitate at his doorway. I want to ask him why he won't let me go out on patrol with the others, but maybe it's not appropriate for a new guy like me to ask. But why shouldn't I get to go out on patrol too? Don't I have as much right as anybody else to go out there and risk my life? That makes me decide to just forget it. I start to turn away, but then I hear his voice: "Yes?"

I peek in. He's sitting at his desk. "Excuse me, sir. I wanted to ask —"

"Why I didn't pick you to go on patrol? Cause you're not ready."

"Yes, sir. But maybe I could just carry a radio or something."

He shakes his head. "Takes special training to be a radio operator."

I guess he's right. I'm just not ready. I salute, ready to go out to start filling sandbags with the rest of the FNGs.

But he doesn't return my salute. He says, "They don't trust you."

I drop my salute. "They don't? I mean, who doesn't?"

"Nobody. They think you're one of those damn dumb college kids."

I'm not sure what that means. Back home we always thought the college kids were the smart ones. It sounds like he's saying out here college kids are the dumb ones. But didn't he go to college? I think about mentioning that, but decide against it. Instead, I say, "Uh, I'm not really a college kid, sir. I was only just getting started. One class."

"Oh yeah? What class?"

"A philosophy class."

He laughs a sarcastic laugh. "Philosophy? That's even worse. Tell them that and they for damned sure won't trust you. They'll think if something serious happens out there, instead of taking action you'll start thinking about the deeper meaning of it."

He has a point. Maybe that's what I would do. I can't think of anything to say, except, "Oh."

"So, after reading all that philosophy stuff, are you a pacifist?"

His question catches me off guard. I try to come up with an answer. "Uh, well, I guess I never really thought about it, sir. I never got into one single fight in school, but that was mostly because everybody was afraid of my pal Brent. He kind of . . . protected me."

The lieutenant stares at me. "I don't give a shit about whether you got into fights at school. I want to know if you'll shoot the enemy."

"Well, I'm not sure. I guess so."

He shakes his head and looks down at his desk. "Christ! Look what they're sending me now." He looks back up at me, and it's clear he's not happy with my answer. "I guess so isn't good enough, Private. You got to say, damn right, sir. Damn right I'd shoot them. I'd kill the shit out of 'em, sir." He shakes his head again. "And you wonder why the others don't trust you. Get the hell out of here."

He goes back to looking at his papers, mumbling to himself. I guess it means I'm dismissed, so I leave. I join the others who are already hard at work filling and stacking sandbags to replace the ones that got ripped apart by the mortars. But I can't stop thinking about what he asked me. What kind of a question is that to ask a new guy? Who wouldn't be scared and confused getting sent to a dangerous situation like this with no real training or experience? They pushed us through Basic Training so fast we hardly had time to learn which end of a rifle was which. How am I supposed to know what I'd do? Brent had me so convinced we could get some soft job away from the fighting, I never really had to think about it. The Army recruiter assured us that if we volunteered for the draft, we'd be sure to get a non-combat job. We'd just avoid getting drafted, put in our two years, and be done with it. But now look where I am. Right in the middle of the damn war, and my commanding officer is asking me if I would kill somebody if I had to. How would I know? I focus on filling sandbags and try not to think about it. There must be a lot of other guys in Vietnam who are not sure how they'd measure up in combat. I couldn't be all that different from *all* the others, could I? When I got sent to the front, I remember thinking I'd finally get the chance to find out what this war is all about. Well, I found out all right: it's about filling sand bags all day and hoping not to get killed by a mortar. It alternates between absolute fear and absolute boredom. I'm not getting to see any this country. and now it looks like I'm not going to ever see anything except for this patch of raw dirt they call a firebase.

I stop filling sandbags for a moment and look out toward the jungle. What would it feel like to be out there? It seems to me that by now the enemy mortar shooters must have learned our routine: after we fire off our howitzers, we go out and chase after them. So why doesn't the enemy just wait for us out there in the jungle and ambush us? Do our soldiers think about that when they go out? Or do they avoid thinking and just follow orders? The truth is, I have no idea what they think. Maybe they've gone out chasing after the mortar shooters so many times they just do it without thinking. Maybe it's gotten boring for them. Is that possible? If you do something dangerous often enough, can it really become boring? I guess because of how I responded to the lieutenant's question, I'll probably never get to find out. I'll just endlessly fill and stack sandbags until one of the enemy mortars lands on our tent roof, and that will be the end of it.

It's mid-morning before Lieutenant Dasen comes out to check on us. He pulls a few guys off of the sandbagging crew and tells them to see if they can find enough wood to rebuild the blown-up latrine.

One of the guys complains that we haven't even had breakfast yet.

The lieutenant says, "Okay, go ahead and get something to eat. But all these bags have to be replaced before tonight."

Everybody drops what they're doing and heads for the mess tent. I follow them, but I'm at the end of the line, so there's nothing left but a couple of dried-out unfrosted donuts. I know nobody wants me to join their table, so I take my donuts back to our empty hooch to get some reading done. If nobody wants to talk to me, fine, I'll just read my philosophy book and get smarter than any of them. I lie down on my cot and open the book at the square of toilet paper I use as a bookmark. The section is about a philosopher named Arthur Schopenhauer. So far, he's my favorite. He was a German, and my book describes him as a pessimist. It says he disagreed with earlier philosophers and almost all of his contemporaries. They thought the world could be analyzed through reason, but Schopenhauer disagreed. He said that in the face of a world filled with endless strife, we might as well forget about reason. He said there's no such thing as reason, and to think otherwise is naive. The book says Schopenhauer was about as pessimistic as you can get. He was pessimistic about the future of humanity, and he was an atheist to boot. He said don't expect any help from God to come along and save you, because there isn't any God. I have the feeling he was right. Whether I live or die here is going to be purely up to chance.

12

Security

I wake up. Somebody shook my shoulder. I open my eyes and turn over. Lieutenant Dasen is standing next to my bunk. He says, "Saddle, up, soldier. You're going out." He turns and walks out.

There was no mortar attack last night, so I have no idea why he's putting together a patrol and why all of a sudden he's decided to pick me. But I'm ready and willing. I get dressed quickly, feeling excited and only a little bit scared. I'm actually looking forward to getting off this firebase. I want to see something of this country, even if it means going out into the dreaded Vietnam jungle that everybody talks about in such hushed tones. After all, there isn't much to be scared of. Whenever a morning patrol goes out to chase after the mortar shooters, they always come back without ever having seen any sign of the enemy.

I get dressed quietly so as not to wake up my hoochmates. I look around. Do I need to take anything with me? I've got my helmet. Do I need anything else? Why didn't the lieutenant give me any instructions? I'm about to head out the doorway when I notice my M-14 standing in the corner behind my bunk. Except when I was on perimeter guard duty, my rifle has been standing there unused. Should I take it with me? The lieutenant didn't say. But then I realize how dumb I am. Of course I'm supposed to take my rifle. I'm going out on combat duty. I grab the rifle and hurry outside. The lieutenant doesn't look happy. "What's the holdup, soldier? Hurry up and get in the truck."

Behind him, the big six-wheeled truck is idling away next to the open gate, putting out steady, impatient-looking puffs of sooty diesel exhaust smoke. I can smell it from where I am.

I turn to Lieutenant Dasen. "Aren't I going out on patrol?"

My question seems to surprise him. He shakes his head with the same exasperated look he always gets whenever he's dealing with me. "Are you kidding? You? I'm putting you out on road security. I don't think you can get yourself in too much trouble there." He points at the truck. "Get a move on."

I run to the truck and climb up into the front seat. The driver stares at me like I did something idiotic. He uses his thumb to indicate I'm supposed to go around and get in the back.

I jump out and run around to the back of the truck. It has a canvas cover that's partly rolled back, and when I climb up, I see there's another guy already in there sitting with his back against the cab. I recognize him, but I've never talked to him. He's a spec-4, like just about every other soldier I've met in Vietnam. (To get to be a spec, a specialist, you need some kind of specialized training, but it can be training in just about anything, usually related to whatever assignment they give you. I'm still a private, so I guess the Army doesn't think loading cases of food into trucks in a warehouse in Saigon is enough training to be called a specialist. It doesn't much matter; a spec-4 is still pretty much a specialized private, still on the bottom rung of the ladder.) "Hey," I say. "How's it going?"

He glances at me. "No flak jacket?"

Damn, I guess his question means I should have brought my flak jacket. What else was I supposed to bring? It's not fair of the lieutenant to send me out without proper instructions. I'm trying to think of an excuse about why I forgot my flak jacket, but the guy looks away. I guess he doesn't care one way or the other. He's looking straight ahead and his eyes have that glazed-over, thinking-about-someplace-far-away look. Is he being unfriendly, or is he just bored? He's about my same age, kind of a handsome guy in an aw-shucks kind of way. He has light brown hair, and he's humming to himself. I don't recognize the tune.

I sit down next to him and stand my rifle up between my legs like he's doing. The strong smell of oiled canvas is almost overpowering, but the guy doesn't seem to mind, so I try to ignore it. The truck grinds into gear, and we rumble out of the compound onto the dusty road. We soon pick up speed, and the spec-4 isn't saying anything, so I decide to move toward the rear of the truck to get out from under the smelly canvas. Besides, I want to look at the scenery. I'm not going to miss my one chance to see what this country really looks like. But once I'm at the back of the truck, I find that I can hardly see anything because of the amount of dust the truck is kicking up. And the scenery is nothing but a blur of passing green jungle. From time to time, I do see a few people standing along the side of the road. They all have their noses down inside their shirts to avoid breathing our dust. I wonder what we look like to them, a huge six-wheeled monster truck rumbling down a narrow dirt road that was probably only used by walkers and bicycles until we showed up. I wonder if they hate us, not only because of the dust we're kicking up, but because we're such an outrageous imposing presence here. It must make them see as invaders that don't belong here. That thought makes me realize that if any enemies are hiding in the roadside jungle, I'd be an easy target. I decide to move back under the canvas. I sit next to the other guy again. The truck is so loud I'm not sure conversation is possible, but I try. "My name is Scott," I shout.

"Yeah, I know," he shouts back. "Scotty, the philosopher."

I smile to show him I don't take it as an insult, but it makes me wonder if all the guys think of me that way. I say, "Who calls me that?"

He shrugs. "Everybody. I think the lieutenant started it. I'm Jeff."

I decide it's no use trying to shout over the truck's noise, so we go on in silence, trying to hold ourselves upright as the truck sways back and forth on the rutted dirt road. After a while, the truck slides to a stop. It bring the chasing cloud of fine dust right into the back with us. I try to wave it away from my face, but it's no use. The dust smells and tastes like rotting vegetation. Must be what Vietnamese dust is made of

Jeff gets out quickly, so I follow him. We're barely out of the truck when it grinds into gear again and backs up into a place where a lot of bushes and small trees have previously been smashed flat. Then, the driver grinds it into a forward gear, and the big truck roars away, heading back toward the firebase.

I look around. So this is where I'm supposed to do road security, whatever that is. I don't see any tire tracks on the narrow dusty road except for the ones our truck made. There are a lot of footprints, though, most of them made by sandals, but also some made by bare feet. There are two shallow holes, one on each side of the road, with a wall of sandbags stacked up in front of each of them. A short distance on down the road is a thick bamboo pole pointing straight up. It's got a hinge at the base of it, so I guess we're supposed to lower the pole across the road to stop everybody who comes along. But what are we supposed to do after we stop them? Search them? As we were coming in, the only people I saw on the road were pedestrians and bicyclists. Are we supposed to stop them?

Jeff is heading for one of the holes, so I follow him and ask, "What are we supposed to do?"

He hops down into the hole and looks up at me. "Nothing. We sit in our holes until the pickup truck comes back to get us."

"That's it?" I say.

"That's it. We're supposed to lower the gate once in a while to check to see what's in their carts, but we don't."

"We don't?"

"Nope. We used to, but then a spec-5 showed up and said not to bother. He said there was no point in stopping anybody because they know we're here, so if they have anything they don't want us to see, they'll just go around us through the jungle."

"They put a sergeant out here?"

"Yeah. He was a hard-ass jungle humper who'd been up in the highlands where some really bad shit was goin' down. He told me he never expected to make it out of that place alive, and he wasn't about to get offed now when it was almost time for him to go home. He said his commanding officer did him a favor and got Lieutenant Dasen to reassign him here on this safe road security assignment for his last three weeks in Vietnam. All he could talk about was getting back to the states.

"So we just sit here all day?"

"That's about the size of it," says Jeff with a shrug. "Gets damn boring, but boring is better than dead. We're not supposed to move from this spot until the pickup crew comes back to get us. They usually get here about an hour before dark." He pulls a magazine out of his shirt and leans back against the dirt wall of his hole to read it.

I walk out into the middle of the road and look over the situation. The jungle is pretty close, all around. It makes me wonder why the sandbags are stacked up only on one side, the side next to the road. What if an attack comes from the jungle side? But Jeff says this is a safe assignment, so maybe it doesn't matter. Road security is not what I expected, but then I guess I didn't know what to expect. Maybe I expected a guard shack or something. The only thing here that suggests a checkpoint is that long bamboo pole on a swivel. It looks kind of flimsy. It sure wouldn't stop a vehicle, if one came along.

I hop down into my hole. The only thing in it is a partial roll of toilet paper and a porno magazine. Not hard to guess what the last occupant of this hole was doing to pass the time. The magazine is open to a page that shows a picture of a black guy with a big dick getting sucked off by an Asian girl. The guy looks bored. I look through the rest of the pages. Nothing but the usual screwing and sucking. I climb back out and see that Jeff is sitting on his sandbag wall, so I do the same. Some old people go past. They're wearing worn out clothes and their sandals seem to be made out of old tires. They don't make eye contact with us.

Jeff points at a slow-moving old man. "Hey, Scotty," he yells, "whatta ya think of our yokels? Pretty funny, eh?"

I nod, but I actually don't see anything funny about them. Yokels. I've heard some of the other guys use that term too. Probably short for local-yokels. I wonder where Jeff is from. He has a bit of a Southern accent. Maybe back where he came from they make fun of the local hillbillies. I decide to ask. I yell, "Why do you call them yokels?"

He shrugs. "I don't know. That's what all the guys call 'em. Or zits. I've heard some of the guys call 'em zits. Don't know why."

"What right do we have to call them names? It's their country."

Jeff looks hurt. "Aw, lighten up, man. It's just a joke."

I shrug and decide to let it go. I shouldn't have said anything. Now he'll probably tell the others, and they'll have me pegged as soft.

"Where you from?" I ask.

"Georgia. Small town, but not too far from Atlanta."

"What did you do back there?"

"Nothin. Odd jobs. Till I got drafted. But when I get back I'm gonna learn to play an electric guitar and get in a band. My little brother wrote me that he's starting one. He's learning to play the drums."

"Where you from?" he asks.

"Arizona."

He doesn't say anything else, so we just watch the yokels go by.

"Hey," yells Jeff. "They say you were in Saigon. How was that?"

"It was okay. A big, spread-out city."

He comes over to sit on my sandbag wall next to me. "Yeah, but aren't there good times there? I heard Saigon is a really wild place."

So I tell him a little about it. I tell him about the shopping street, the interesting people there. But he's not interested in that; he wants to know if there really are pretty girls there. Girls for the taking.

I tell him yes, there are plenty of girls. I tell him about Wong's Bar.

He listens, amazed, mouth half hanging open. I start to tell him about the bad shit that went on there, like the fights at the dice table and that innocent-looking kid who walked in one night, but he interrupts me. He wants to know more about the girls. "Are they pretty?"

I tell him yes, they are the prettiest girls in the world. Now he's really interested, so I keep it going: I tell him those girls really like us Americans. Not only that, but they know all the tricks. He laps that part up. He wants more. So I give him more, spicing it up a bit to make him happy. I tell him about the night one drunken guy made a bet he could screw every girl in the place nonstop, and how the guy went into the back with the girls, one after the other, and came back out to the bar saying he did it. But his pals wouldn't pay off. They laughed at him and said he was so drunk he probably just went back there and fell asleep. So he said he'd show them. This time they all put up the betting money in advance. Then, they took all of the girls into one of the back rooms and watched him screw them, one after the other. After he was done, they all slapped him on the back, all agreeing that by damn he really had done it, that he was a hell of a screwing machine.

Jeff looks off into the distance, thinking about it. Without another word, he goes back across the road and down into his hole, probably to fantasize about Wong's girls. If he hasn't had a leave to go to Saigon yet, he must be pretty new to Vietnam. Maybe he got shipped to the front as soon as he got in country. Now, because of my stories about the girls at Wong's Bar, he'll probably try really hard to stay alive long enough to go see them for himself. I think about telling him about the beautiful young girl who tells wonderful stories. No, I don't want anybody to know about her. She's mine.

An old man goes by. He has two live chickens hung around his neck, their feet tied together with a string. The chickens look at me, upside down. I remember some upside-down chickens looking at me like that back in the shopping street in Saigon. For some reason, that seems like a long time ago, but I guess it wasn't really. I wonder what these people think of me. I probably look bored. I am. But I'm not complaining; it's a heck of a lot better than stacking sandbags. The jungle looks dense all around, but the people going by look like farmers so there must some farms around here somewhere. Hard to believe anybody could hack enough of a clearing out of this dense jungle to start a farm. It sure would be different from farming back in Illinois. Wide open spaces there. Mostly corn fields in the part of Illinois I lived in. Back in Illinois, my father did real road security, not like this pretend road security. As a motorcycle cop, he secured the county feeder-roads that led to the main road, route 66. We lived in Springfield, the state capital, because it was about halfway between the two main cities that route 66 connected, Chicago and St. Louis. He was out there patrolling those roads on his motorcycle every day and a lot of nights. In the end, it was one of those roads he was securing that got him killed. The rainy night my mother got the call, I had just finished my homework and was getting ready to go to bed. I can still see the look of disbelief on her face. Whoever was on the other end of the line was probably explaining that he was dead, but she kept asking if he was hurt bad. I went to bed that night thinking he was only hurt. I imagined him lying in the hospital. A kid that age thinks that even if his father gets hurt, he'd be okay soon. At that age, I didn't have a clear concept in my head of what death was all about. The only death I had ever seen was the birds that kept on killing themselves by smashing into the big picture window in our living room. My mother let me bury the dead birds out by the alley and explained that the birds probably saw the reflection of the big maple tree in our front yard and thought they were flying to it. I wanted to cut that tree down so the birds wouldn't have to die, but she said no, it's just the way it is. Things die. The next morning, I found out my father was dead. Turns out, he was already dead when they found him next to his bent-up motorcycle. They told my mother that somebody in a car had run him over and driven away. Maybe it was an accident, or maybe somebody did it on purpose. Doesn't really matter, I guess. Dead is dead, however it happens. There was a big funeral. Cops came from everywhere. I can still remember the long, long line of somber cops in their dress uniforms parading past his casket. They gave me his bent-up police badge. It's the only thing I brought with me here besides my philosophy book. I should probably write to my mother and tell her I'm on road security now, like he was. Except she doesn't much like to talk about him. She doesn't like to talk about anything from back when we lived in Illinois. Painful memories I guess. I can't remember her ever mentioning him after we moved to Arizona to live in the creaky old house of her aging and supposedly-ill mother. Once we were there, we were both children of the grandmother, a moody old woman who mostly stayed in her curtains-drawn room at the end of the hall, a room that smelled of old dust and old lace and probably old memories too. I hardly ever saw either one of them. They stayed in that dark room, whispering together. As long as I was quiet, they let me do whatever I wanted to, so I mostly spent my time in the public library or hanging out with Brent in his dad's old junkyard.

More sad-looking locals shuffle by, kicking up dust that makes me sneeze. Old people mostly. Poor folks. Clothes about worn out, but fairly clean. All wearing old stained conical hats. The hat I bought back in Saigon was brand new. These people would probably be glad to have it, but Brent made me throw it away because he thought it made me look ridiculous. I have to agree that these people's conical hats do look kind of silly. Dressed all in black, and with those weird pointy hats, it's like they came out of some old-timey comic book. But the more I watch them as they go by, the more I like them. They seem like regular people; nothing scary about any of them. I have the feeling they're all hard workers, probably just trying to get by. If I could learn to speak their language, I would talk to them, learn more about their lives.

An old man sitting in a wooden-wheeled cart comes lumbering along. It's drawn by a tired-looking ox. I have the feeling that same cart could have been going down this same dirt road a thousand years ago. The cart is right in front of me, when suddenly, a B-52 bomber goes over, really low, its jet engines screaming so loud I have to put my hands over my ears.

Jeff pops up out of his hole. He shades his eyes with his hand and watches the B-52 disappear.

Soon, I hear the rumble of bombs. That plane must have dropped its bombing load not all that far north of here. I wait to see smoke rising up over the tops of the trees, but I can't see any, so maybe its bombing run was farther away than it seemed. Back in Saigon, at Wong's Bar, I heard some GIs refer to B-52s as "can openers." It was a joke. They call the little portable can openers that are included with field rations B-52s. Except this big airplane can opener is used to rip open the earth and kill people. I wonder what that B-52 was dropping its bombs on. Is there a town up there? Is the enemy that close? Did some people just die there?

The man in the ox cart didn't even look up. Are these people so used to war planes going over they don't even notice them anymore? Before we joined up, I remember sitting in Brent's living room eating TV dinners off of TV trays while we watched President Johnson's latest televised speech about the war in Vietnam. He said he was lifting the ban on bombing civilian "targets" in North Vietnam. He said he had ordered the air force to start bombing Hanoi and other North Vietnamese cities. Brent's dad said, "Good!" and told Brent to get up and change the channel to Hogan's Heroes. After the President's speech, the next day at school our history teacher told us that the intentional bombing of civilians was never a part of war until the first world war when a German Zeppelin dropped a bomb on a coastal city in England. He said only nine people were killed in that first air raid, but it opened up the concept that civilians might be intentionally killed as part of a war effort. He went on to say that despite the Zeppelin bombing raids in that war, the intentional killing of civilians didn't become normal practice until the second world war when huge numbers of civilians, including women and children, died in the air raids on England, Germany, and Japan. He said at least seven thousand babies in their cribs had been instantly vaporized in the atom bomb attack on Hiroshima, and there was a big discussion about that afterwards, especially in churches. People were asking why God would allow it. Good question. It makes me wonder if the pilots of those bombers think about who is down there. Do they wonder if there are babies in their cribs down there being blown to smithereens?

Jeff disappears back down into his hold, but I'm still looking up at the sky. Way up high, almost invisible in the hazy air, I see more bombers heading north. They leave long white trails behind, as if they're putting out sky-writing messages to prove to these people that the United States has powerful weapons that are true and real, real as metal, real as a toothache. The next time I see Brent, I'll have to tell him about how I was sitting out on road security when an ancient ox cart with wooden wheels went by just as a huge B-52 can opener went over and dropped some bombs not all that far away. I'll try to make him understand how surreal it was, and at the same time, how clear it made it that this is a real war and people are dying in it. But I know Brent: he'll just shrug and say something like, Hey, man, it's a war, real live life shit. People get in the way, they pay. I wonder what Brent is doing back there in Saigon. Having a grand old time I bet, and making money hand over fist. I keep thinking I should write him. Ask if he's seen my storyteller girl. I keep putting it off. What am I afraid of? That maybe he *has* seen her? That he's been taking her to that same back room?

I realize I've been holding my M-14 on my lap since I came out to sit on my sandbag wall. I didn't even think about it; I just kept it in my hands because . . . I don't know, just because that's what I thought I was supposed to do. It's an old weapon, but they say it will still do the job. Saint Louee told me it was a lucky rifle. Said the guy who had it before me once shot a Cong sniper out of a tree with it. I asked him if it was so lucky, why did he give it up? Saint Louee just shrugged and walked away. I guess that meant the guy was dead. Not so lucky after all. And here I am, out on this dusty road with that old rifle, acting like a real soldier for the first time. I watch the people go by and try to imagine if any of them could be dangerous. It seems like a ridiculous idea. How could old farmers be dangerous? But maybe I'm kidding myself. In Indoctrination Training, they said not to trust any Vietnamese. They said anybody could be an enemy agent, even women and children. Maybe so, maybe not, but I don't expect I'll be needing my old rifle to defend myself against these farmers. I lean it against the sandbag wall.

Pretty soon, Jeff pops back up out of his hole. He's rubbing his eyes with the backs of his hands. He's been sleeping over there. He yawns, and then he yells across the road to me: "Hey, Scotty, I had a dream."

"Oh yeah? What about?"

"There was a movie. My girl was up there on the big screen kissing some famous movie star."

I can think of anything to say except, "Is that right?"

"Maybe the dream means something about her. Do you think?"

I say, "I don't know. What do you think it meant?"

He looks off into the distance, and then says, "She stopped writing to me. Do you think it means she found somebody else?"

At first, I don't feel like answering him. He's been over there sound asleep, dreaming about his girl, while I had to keep watch on the road by myself. I'm supposed to be the new guy here. But then I relent and say, "Maybe the mail isn't getting through to us."

That idea doesn't do much to cheer him up. He sits down on his sandbag wall, looking glum. Unlike me, he keeps his rifle in his hands. "It's hard being so far away from her," he says. "Who knows what she could be up to back there. She likes to party and . . . well, you know."

I'm not sure what he means by "well, you know," but I guess it must mean she likes to fool around. Bottom line, he's not sure of her.

He says, "I sure hope she hasn't met a Jody."

A "Jody" is what they call a guy back home who steals your girl while you're in Nam. Back when I first got to Vietnam, I heard some marching soldiers at the Bien Hoa Air Base doing a marching song:

> Ain't no use in goin' home
> Jody's got your girl and gone
> Sound off one two
> Sound off three four

Jeff hops back down into his hole, and I go back to watching the people go by. It's getting hot. I could use a drink. Why didn't I think to bring a canteen? Or a beer. A beer would be nice right now, even though I haven't been drinking any alcohol since I shipped out of Saigon. Brent would be proud of me. He always said I drank too much, and now I'm not drinking booze at all. Interesting, I hadn't really thought about that until now. The sun is burning through the thin cloud cover, so I decide to try to get a bit of a tan. I strip off my shirt. I feel a bit vulnerable out here without my uniform shirt on, but the sun feels good. What do I have to be afraid of?

As the day goes on, there are fewer and fewer people on the road, but I see a young woman coming. She has two little kids in tow. I wonder what they tell their kids about us. Maybe they use us to scare the kids into behaving. Better be good or the big bad American soldiers will get you. One of the kids is dragging a nicely-carved little wooden man with a string that's tied around the carved man's neck.

I wave at him and say, "Where'd you get that little man, little man?"

He looks scared and hurries to catch up with his mother, dragging his hanged man behind him.

Another young woman comes close behind. She has a shawl over her head that mostly hides her face. Is she hiding from me? She's carrying something in a sling across her chest, a sort of cloth sack draped over her shoulder. There's something in that sack, and I'm curious to find out what it is. I pick up my rifle and hop off of my sandbag wall. I raise my hand to stop her, but she tries to hurry past me. I step forward and bar her way with the barrel of my rifle. "Hey, stop, lady. I'm not going to hurt you. I just want to see what you got in that sack."

She stares at the ground, not saying anything. She won't look at me.

I say, "Open up the sack."

She looks up at me, but her eyes tell me she doesn't understand.

I point at the sack with my rifle. It's the first time I've ever pointed a weapon, and it gives me an odd sense of power, as if I'm in command of the situation. "Show me what's in there, miss." I touch the top of the sack with the business end of my rifle

She finally understands. She opens up the top of the sack.

There's a baby in there. It doesn't move.

I lean in for a closer look. "Is it dead?"

She doesn't understand my words.

"The baby," I say, louder, "dead?"

Jeff pops his head up out of his hole and points his rifle at the woman. "What's going on?" he yells. "What did she do?"

I yell back, "This here woman has a baby in a sack. Looks dead."

My yelling at Jeff wakes the baby up. It begins to cry.

Jeff shakes his head. He disappears back down into his hole.

Oh shit, now I've done it. The kid wasn't dead, just sleeping, and I woke it up. "Sorry," I say. "I didn't mean to wake him. Is it a boy?"

She won't answer. She doesn't understand. She stares at the ground.

I back off and gesture with my rifle for her to pass.

She hurries away, and I go back to sit on my sandbag wall. That was dumb. Why did I do that? I can't quite believe I did such a thing. Is that how it works? They put you out here with a gun in your hands knowing sooner or later you'll use it. I still can't believe I did that. I tell myself I'll never do anything like that again. If I have to deal with any of these people, I'll leave my rifle leaning up against the sandbag wall where it belongs. That makes me realize I'm still holding it. What the hell am I doing? I lean it against the sandbag wall and turn my attention back to the people that are passing by. I smile at every one of them. But they don't smile back. They still won't make eye contact. Even with my shirt off and my rifle put aside, they still know who I am: I'm an American soldier, a foreign invader. Dangerous. Maybe the word has already gone out about me pointing my rifle at that lady. I wish I could tell them it was just a mistake. I thought the kid was dead. I've never seen a kid sleep that soundly. Imagine sleeping in a sack against your mother's chest like that. What a great way to travel, the soothing rocking motion of your mother's walking, listening to her heartbeat. Who wouldn't sleep like the dead if you could sleep like that?

Hours go by with hardly anybody passing. There's nothing to see and nothing to do, and the wet heat is making me sleepy. What with me staying awake all night worrying and thinking, I never get enough sleep. I'm sure Jeff is sound asleep over there in his hole, and that thought makes me even more sleepy. Luckily, a little boy comes along on the road to give me something to look at. He's about ten years old, barefoot, no shirt, ragged shorts. He's driving a skinny pink pig ahead of him by hitting the pig's back legs with a switch. That must hurt.

I yell at the kid: "Hey, quit that."

The kid stops to stare at me. The pig stops too. The kid makes a funny face by using his fingers to pull out the corners of his mouth.

I lean forward and pretend to growl at him like a bear. "Grrr."

He sticks out his tongue at me.

I laugh. He's not afraid of us foreign invaders.

He turns away and goes back to hitting the pig's back legs. The pig had been patiently waiting for the hitting to start again. It knows it's his job to get hit. They go on down the road.

More time goes by, and the sun gets so hot I worry that I might be getting sunburned. I put my shirt back on.

A young girl is coming. Like the little boy with the pig, she's barefoot, and like the little boy, she's wearing only shorts.

Jeff pops up out of his hole. He makes a wolf whistle. "Hey, baby. I got somethin' here for ya." He grabs his crotch.

The girl runs away.

I can't believe he did that. I bet that little girl isn't even ten, eleven at most, and Jeff is coming on to her. Her tits are barely even getting started, and he's getting all excited, whistling at her like she's a grown-up girl. Would he really do anything to her if he had the chance? Maybe he would. Maybe they like them young like that back in Georgia. But that thought makes me remember how young the girls back at Wong's were. They were young, but nowhere near as young as that little girl. I never did find out how old they were. Maybe my storyteller girl was . . .

I don't know, maybe only sixteen or so. And I was in bed with her, naked. No, she must have been older than that. There was no way for me to tell, not really. I decide not to think about her age and just think about how great it was to be with her that night. She told me stories. Strange stories about magic spirits and animals that can talk.

Jeff is still watching the little girl disappear on down the road when an elephant comes ambling up the road from that direction. I can't believe my eyes. It's an honest-to-God, real-life elephant. The only time I ever saw an elephant before was one time when I was a kid and my parents took me to a circus. The circus had trained elephants, parading around in a circle, trunk to tail, and each elephant was wearing a colorful hat that looked like a flower-pot. I remember feeling sorry for those elephants. I had the feeling somebody was forcing them to parade around and around every night with silly flower-pot hats on their heads. But this elephant is nothing like that; this is a real jungle elephant, and there's a teen-aged boy sitting on it, right behind its head. The boy is kicking the back of the beast's ears to keep it moving along.

Jeff runs out into the road to get a closer look. "It's an elephant," he yells to me. "It's a real damn elephant."

"I see it," I yell back. "Pretty cool."

It *is* a pretty cool thing to see a real live elephant. I didn't even know they had elephants in Vietnam. As it passes, I can smell the wild animal smell of the beast. Now this is what I wanted. Now I'm really seeing Vietnam. Getting a chance to see a real elephant makes the long day of boredom on the dusty road worth it. But then I realize the kid sitting on the elephant is about thirteen or fourteen. I've been watching people go by on this road all day, and I've never seen a boy anywhere near that old. In Indoctrination Training, they told us boys of that age are sometimes recruited by the enemy. He has a bundle of something tied up behind him. It looks like bamboo poles, but who knows what could be hidden inside that bundle of poles. I think about trying to stop him, but I quickly shake that thought off. It's just a boy on an elephant.

Jeff jogs along next to the elephant, hollering up at the boy, asking questions: "Hey, kid, where'd you get your elephant? How old is it? What do you use it for? I heard they can pull down big trees."

Of course, the boy doesn't answer—probably doesn't speak a word of English. He kicks hard at the elephant's ears to hurry it up. The huge animal speeds up and disappears down the road leaving only a cloud of dust behind. Jeff stops and stands there in the middle of the road watching it go. He looks disappointed. Did he want to go for a ride?

"Keep an eye on things," he yells. "I gotta go take a dump." He grabs his rifle and heads off into the jungle.

I'm still a little worried about that kid on the elephant and what they told us in Indoctrination Training. They made a big point of telling us how the enemy recruits young boys by threatening their families. I don't want to hide in my hole like a scaredy-cat just because of a kid on an elephant, but maybe I should be a little more cautious.

Not many people going by now, and the few that do all seem to be in more of a hurry than before. I wonder if it's because it's getting late in the day. Maybe they don't want to get caught out on the road in the dark. I have to agree with that: I wouldn't want to be out here in the dark either. With the jungle pushed in so close to the road and those mortar shooters moving around at night, I bet it would be really scary to be out here. Jeff said the pickup crew would come back for us before it gets dark. The sun is getting low in the sky, so they should be here soon.

Jeff seems to be taking a long time to do his business. I'm starting to get a bit worried, but then he comes back. He grins at me, like he's embarrassed about something. What does that grin mean? I'm beginning to think he's a bit of a strange guy, what with his whistling at that too-young shirtless girl and then disappearing into the woods.

He jumps back down into his hole, but then I hear a shout, and he jumps right back out again. "Snake!" he yells. He starts shooting down into his hole. He must have his M16 set on full automatic because he just keeps on blasting away. It fills the jungle with sound, unbelievably loud in contrast to the previous quiet.

Two old women that were coming up the road turn around and run back the way they came.

Finally, Jeff stops shooting, and then he notices the two old women running like hell. He points his rifle at them and makes "bang-bang" sounds. He laughs. He thinks it's funny, yokels running from gunfire in the middle of a war. Is that funny?

He hops back down into his hole and throws the dead snake out. I hear him mumbling to himself over there.

I listen to the silence of the jungle around us and wonder how far away all his shooting could have been heard. I decide maybe I'd better get down into my own hole. But I check it out first, now that I know there are snakes around. Something moves down there. What the hell? Is it a snake? How could two snakes get down into holes at the same time? Are the yokels throwing snakes into our holes? But how could they sneak up behind me and do that? I have the sudden thought that maybe they sent that elephant to distract us while they brought in the poisonous snakes. But when I look closer, I see it's not a snake. It's a turtle. I hop down into my hole to check it out. It's a little green turtle, not much bigger than the palm of my hand. Cute little fella. But how did it get down here? I pick it up, and it immediately ducks its little head back into its shell. I put it down on the ground, and watch it to see what it will do. After a few minutes, it peeks out at me. I lean closer and say, "Boo!" Its head disappears again. I've heard that if you flip a turtle over onto its back, it can't get itself upright again. I try it, and sure enough it immediately pops its little legs out and frantically tries to right itself. I watch it struggle for a few seconds, but then I feel sorry for it and turn it back upright again. The turtle pulls its legs back in, but not its head. It stares at me, like it's pissed off at me for doing that. Suddenly, I feel a bit silly. A grown-up person playing with a turtle. I stand up to see if Jeff is watching me. I can't see him. He's probably asleep down in his hole again. I squat down to look closer at the little turtle. It pulls its head back inside its shell. I peek in and see the reflection of its shiny little eyes in there. It's watching me from inside its shell. I decide I should toss the turtle into the bushes and let it go on its way. I pick it up, but then I worry that it wouldn't be good to just throw it. Wouldn't want to hurt the poor little thing. And then suddenly, a strong memory comes to me. It's part of the memory of *that* night, the night with my storyteller girl in that back room at Wong's. She told me a story about a turtle and said a time would come when I should save a turtle. She said it was important. And now, here I am, out in the jungle with a little turtle in my hand. Weird. It's like she knew. I look at the little turtle and its little eyes look back at me from inside its shell. In the story, the servant girl took the turtle back to the river to save it. Am I supposed to do that? But I couldn't do that even if I wanted to because there's no river around here. Or is there? I pick up the turtle and climb out of my hole. I get up on top of my sandbag wall and shade my eyes to look farther back into the jungle. There does seem to be something glistening in the distance. It could be water. But it's pretty far away. I glance over at Jeff's hole. He's being very quiet over there. How can a person sleep that much? The sun is down below the tree-line. That means the relief truck should be here soon to pick us up. I damned sure wouldn't want to miss it and have to spend the whole night out here alone. I should just toss the damned turtle into the bushes and let it go on its way. But I keep remembering how serious my storyteller girl was when she told me that story. She said I should take the turtle to water. She said it was important. It doesn't seem all that far to where that water is. I could just run the turtle over there and come right back. If I hear the truck coming, I could drop the turtle and run back fast. Aw, hell, why not? I grab my rifle and take off running. I run as fast as I can, dodging between bushes and trees and vines and ferns. But I'm getting fairly far from the road, and I'm not finding any water. I stop. The little turtle peeks out at me. Maybe I should just leave it here. Let it find its own way to water. But I'm sure I saw something that looked like water. I decide to go just a little bit farther. I go on, and then I see it, just ahead. It's a swampy area, but there are patches of standing water here and there. I hurry to one of the pools and slip the turtle in. I stay only long enough to watch it swim away, then I hurry back through the jungle.

I've got to get back to the road as fast as I can in case the truck comes. But going back, the jungle seems thicker than before. I start to worry that I might have somehow got started back in the wrong direction. I stop and look around. Nothing seems familiar. This is not like getting lost in the desert. Everything here looks the same, just green and more green. There are no hills or anything to use as landmarks. And the jungle seems especially thick here. I didn't run through any thick jungle like this. Or did I? Maybe I was just too focused on saving the turtle. Now I'm starting to think it wasn't such a good idea to take that little turtle to water. What if the truck comes while I'm wandering around in this jungle, lost? What the hell was I thinking? I listen for the truck, but all I can hear is silence. No crickets, no birds, nothing. When I used to hike in the Arizona desert, I learned it was easy to get lost and end up walking in circles, so I always kept my eye on a distant mountain peak to make sure I was going in one direction. But here, there are no hills. There are some trees that are taller than others. I pick out a tall palm tree in the distance and head for it. But then I come to a patch of thorn bushes so thick there's obviously no way through it. That worries me; I know I didn't run into any thorn bushes on my way to the water. Maybe I'm not even heading back toward the road. I could be going away from it, heading ever deeper into endless jungle. I work my way around the thorn bushes, but when I come out on the other side, I can't see that tall palm tree anymore. This is crazy. How could a tree that tall disappear? I have no choice but to keep going, hoping I'm still going toward the road. I begin to worry that I could be paralleling it. I stop and try to think it through. The setting sun is on my right. It was on my left when I was heading for the water, so I must be going in more or less the correct direction. I have to trust my old desert-hiking methods. If I just keep going, with the setting sun on my right, I'll have to hit the road sooner or later. I plunge on, fighting my way through the seemingly endless patches of underbrush. I'm sweating hard now, and I know it's not just because of the work it takes to make any headway; I'm really starting to get worried that I'll never find the road again. But then I burst out of the bushes and there it is, the road. What a relief. It's just a dusty old road, but I'm damn glad to see it. The frightening jungle is still on both sides of the road, but at least now I know I won't have to spend the night in there. I look in both directions. Which way is the checkpoint? Impossible to say. Nothing looks familiar, and there are no people on the road. The road is fairly straight here, so I can see quite a ways in both directions, but I don't see the checkpoint. How could I have missed the checkpoint by so much? I have the horrible thought that maybe this is not even the same road. It gives me that same weird feeling I had when I found the turtle in my hole, the feeling that the locals are playing tricks on me, trying to confuse me. I tell myself to calm down: the checkpoint couldn't have moved, and there can't be more than one road like this around here. I just came back to the road in a different place. All I have to do is go down the road until I get back to our checkpoint. But which way is it? If I pick the wrong direction, I could be heading away from the checkpoint. I think about yelling to see if Jeff can hear me, but I quickly push that thought away: no use yelling and letting the enemy know there's a lost American soldier out here. I tell myself to stay calm. This is no different from the many times you've been lost in the Arizona desert. What would you do if you *were* lost in the desert? You would look toward the setting sun. It's a hiking rule: always keep track of where the sun is. Okay, so use your brain and figure it out by using the sun. The setting sun was on my left when I headed for the water. And this morning when the truck brought us out here, the rising sun was behind us. That means if I head *away* from the setting sun, toward the east, at least I'll be going toward where the firebase is. That way, if I've chosen wrong and I'm going away from the checkpoint, I should run into the truck as it comes to pick us up. See there, all I had to do was think it through logically. More confident now, I run down the road toward the east. Soon, I see the sandbag walls of our checkpoint just ahead. My logic worked. That and my experience in the Arizona desert saved me. Feeling a bit silly that I was so worried, I slow down and try to act nonchalant. If Jeff asks where I went, I'll just say I went for a short walk to see a little of the countryside. No big deal.

Still, when I get back to the checkpoint, I immediately jump down into my hole. For some reason, now that it's starting to get dark and there are no people on the road, my stupid little hole in the ground feels safer than being up there sitting on the sandbag wall. I sit in my hole with my back against the dirt wall and realize I'm breathing too fast. I tell myself to calm down and breathe normally; there's nothing to be scared of now. Counting my breaths to keep them regular, I start wondering why that trip into the jungle scared me so much. Okay, so I got a little bit lost. Big deal. I've been lost in the desert many times, and I always found my way out. But then I remind myself that there's one big difference between getting lost in the desert and getting lost here: here there are enemies, enemies with guns. I stay in my hole and wish the pickup truck would hurry up and get here. It's starting to get dark. What could be holding up the truck? They *do* have to come for us, don't they? They wouldn't leave us out here all night. I start to think about how those enemy mortar shooters always sneak up on our firebase at night. Nighttime is their time to start moving around in the jungle. They know the jungle, I don't. I keep my rifle in my hands and wait. Time goes by, and it's almost completely dark now. I start thinking about that little turtle. How did it get all the way from that water to here? And how did it get down into my hole? And why was it in my hole at the same time as a snake got into Jeff's hole? Somebody must be playing tricks on us. But why? Although I know it wasn't very smart to go away from the road like that, I do feel good about saving that funny little turtle. I bet it's happy now swimming around in that swamp.

I start to wonder why I haven't heard anything from Jeff. Can he really sleep that much? I stand up and call across to him, keeping my voice almost to a whisper: "Hey, Jeff, shouldn't the pickup truck be here by now?" No answer. He must be sound asleep. Or did he run off into the woods again? It seems kind of strange that not one single person has gone by since Jeff shot that snake. The kid on the elephant went by, then Jeff shot the snake, and then the people stopped coming. But maybe that's normal. Maybe they don't like to be out on the road after dark. After all, there is a war going on. They probably make sure they're home long before it gets dark. Jeff said the pickup truck should get here before dark, but now it's almost dark. What if they aren't coming? No, the lieutenant wouldn't leave us out here. I try not to let my mind get carried away with worrying about it. Maybe the truck just had a breakdown or something. It's eerie that it's so quiet. I feel all alone out here, even though I know Jeff is right across the road, probably sound asleep, probably dreaming about his girl. I wonder why he isn't worried about the truck being late. Is he going to sleep all through the night? He couldn't be that good a sleeper, could he? I stand up and call to him again, louder this time: "Hey, Jeff. Wake up!" No answer. I duck back down again. Maybe he's not even over there. I should have checked on him when I came back from taking that turtle to water. So why didn't I? His hole is only a few steps across the road. You were scared, that's why. But what is there to be scared of? You've been here all day and haven't seen anybody except old men and old women and young women with kids. There's nothing to worry about. So what if the pickup crew is late. That probably happens sometimes. It's my first time out here, so I don't know the routine. Maybe they're always late. But the darker it gets, the more it feels like something isn't right. Is it possible the truck came while I was taking that turtle to water? Maybe the pickup crew came and picked up Jeff. If so, I'm going to be out here alone all night. All the guys back at the base will be laughing. They're teaching the FNG a lesson. I tell myself I should go over there to Jeff's hole and see if he's still there. But I can't seem to make myself move. I keep thinking about how that snake could have got down into Jeff's hole and how a turtle ended up in my hole at the same time. Jeff shot the snake. I took the turtle to water. The servant girl in that story did the same thing: she saved the turtle, and she got rewarded for it. My storyteller girl told me it was important to save the turtle. Is that why I took the chance on getting lost in the jungle just to save a stupid little turtle? But what if it was more than a story? Maybe it was a warning:

save the turtle *or else*. I try to tell myself I'm being ridiculous. That storyteller girl probably just likes to tell the stories she grew up with. She thinks they're important because they're lessons she learned as a child: be kind to the animals and you will be rewarded. I stand up in my hole and look around. It's almost completely dark now, and it's very quiet. It feels like quite a lot of time has passed since I got back from taking the turtle to water, but maybe it hasn't. I'd like to take a look at my watch, but nobody told me to bring along a flashlight. Why would I need a flashlight if the pickup crew is supposed to be here before dark? They must have come and gone while I was taking the turtle to water. But would the lieutenant let them leave a FNG out here all night? I tell myself there's only one way to find out: I've got to go over there and see if Jeff is asleep in his hole. I take a deep breath and climb out of my hole. It's getting too dark to see much, and the close-in bushes and trees look like hulking dark shapes. I take my rifle off safety, but then I feel silly for doing it. I tell myself to just pretend this is like being out in the desert at night. You weren't afraid of the dark in the desert; in fact, you liked being out there at night with the stars twinkling overhead and coyotes howling in the distance. But the desert is wide open; here, everything feels closed in. It comes right up to the edge of the road. Somebody could be a few feet away, hiding in those bushes, and you'd never know it. I slowly start across the road toward Jeff's hole, being careful not to make a sound. The night is warm, but I feel cold. I'm sweating. How can you feel cold and be sweating at the same time? I keep my rifle in my hands, my finger on the trigger. But then I hear something. A click. I stop moving. It was like somebody snapped their fingers, one quick snap, then total silence again. As the seconds go by, I start to wonder if I really heard it. Am I getting so nervous I'm making up sounds in my head? My hands feel so sweaty I have to keep a good grip on my rifle to keep from dropping it. Maybe I should just go back to my hole and wait. But I'm halfway across the road now, so I might as well go on. It's my responsibility to check on Jeff. That's what they taught us in Basic: always look out for your buddy. I go to Jeff's hole and look down. Jeff is down there. Thank goodness; it means the pickup truck hasn't come yet. It's so dark I can barely make him out. It looks like he's curled up in the fetal position. Asleep, just like I figured. How can he just lay there sleeping like a baby while I'm out here in the dark getting all up tight? You'd think that at least he could have warned me that the truck is sometimes late.

I whisper to him: "Hey, Jeff, wake up!"

No response.

What the hell? Can he be that sound a sleeper?

I jump down into the hole next to him and shake him. He doesn't respond. How can anybody be that sleepy? I have the sudden memory of that baby in the sling against that woman's chest, sound asleep, dead to the world. I shake Jeff again. He still doesn't move. I look at his face. There's a dark spot on his cheek. What is that? I touch it. It's wet. I reel backwards and fall against the side of the hole. I know what it is, but my brain doesn't want to believe it. It's blood.

I scramble out of the hole and run back across the road to my own hole. I jump down and huddle against the back wall, my rifle gripped tight in my hands. Jeff is dead. Or is he? Maybe I should have checked. See if he was breathing or something. No, he has to be dead. Somebody came and shot him in the head. He's dead. And soon, they will come back and shoot me. Then I will be dead too. I'm breathing too fast again, but this time I can't make it slow down. I feel shaky all over. My hands are shaking so hard I'm afraid I'll pull the trigger accidentally. If that happens, the sound of the shot will let the enemy know right where I am. But how could somebody have shot Jeff in the head, and I didn't hear it? It must have happened while I was taking that turtle to the water. It's almost like somebody put that turtle in my hole to get me away from the road so they could kill Jeff. But how could they know I would abandon my post to take the turtle to water? A wave of guilt floods my mind. Did Jeff die because I took the turtle to water? I left him here all alone and somebody killed him But what could I have done? If I had been here, they would have killed me too. But why did they kill him? Was it because he shot the snake? That doesn't make any sense. It's like he died because he shot the snake, and I'm alive because I did what my storyteller girl told me to do and saved the turtle. It's almost like she knew, like she was telling me that if I saved the turtle, I would be spared. But that's crazy. I have to calm down and quit thinking such crazy thoughts. It was only a story, a Vietnamese fairy tale. I should be focusing on what I should do now. But what can I do? Nothing. The enemy will come back, and then they will kill me too. But when they come, do I try to shoot them? But what if it's just a farmer walking by who decides to look down into my hole. What would the lieutenant tell me to do? I'm sure he'd say to shoot first and ask questions later. Maybe with Jeff lying dead over there, that's what anybody would do. Of course you should shoot them. They killed Jeff, and they will kill you too, if you let them. They don't care about killing people, so why should you? On the other hand, maybe it wouldn't do any good to shoot. There may be too many of them. You're all alone, and this is their country, not yours. Maybe if you throw down your rifle and give yourself up, they won't shoot you. That's it. When they come, I'll put up my hands and surrender. It's the most logical thing to do. I lean the rifle against the dirt wall. When they come, I'll say, I give up. See, I'm raising my hands. No gun. No, I'll say it in French. *J'abandonne!* I give up. Maybe they learned that phrase when all the French gave themselves up and left this crazy country. I sit perfectly still and wait for them to come. If only the pickup truck would have come. When it comes—if it ever does come—they will find two dead soldiers, both young, neither mattering much to the world. Add two more to the count. It's like it says in my philosophy textbook: in the end, there's nothing a person can do to change the fact that we live, then we die. Jeff shot a snake, so they killed him. You saved a silly little turtle, but that doesn't mean you don't have to die too. Or does it? That storyteller said you have to save the turtle, and I did. I whisper, "I did what you said. I saved the turtle." I realize I just said that out loud. A, I praying to a young prostitute? I must really be going crazy.

Time goes by, but for some reason, the enemy doesn't come to kill me. It's so quiet out there, so dark, I can't even tell if time is passing. I can't look at my watch because I don't have a flashlight. But what good would it do to look at your watch anyhow? Time doesn't matter now because . . . because maybe none of this is real. Maybe you fell asleep and this is all a dream. My philosophy textbook said everything could be a dream. Plato. Descartes. They both asked the same question, how can you prove it isn't all a dream?

I hear a sound, a deep sound. Far away, but coming closer. Is it part of the dream? I begin to hope it might be a truck engine, that it could be the pickup crew coming. Or is it the enemy coming? Does the enemy have trucks? I see lights bouncing across the tops of the trees. I stand up. Is it a vehicle? I pray that it is. Even if it's not the pickup crew, maybe I can flag down whoever it is and they'll take me out of here. The light comes closer. Now I can see it's two lights. Headlights. It *is* a vehicle. The suddenly-bright headlights blind me. I hear the squeal of brakes. I smell diesel exhaust. It must be the pickup detail. It has to be.

I grab my rifle and climb out of my hole. I hold up my hand to ward off the truck's bright lights. But is it really the pickup crew? Nobody is getting out. The truck just sits there, idling roughly. It's headlights bore two bright shafts of light through the dust. Finally, a squeaky truck door opens and somebody yells, "Come on, you guys. Let's go."

It *is* them. I'm saved. "I'm coming!," I yell. "Don't leave." I run to the truck and climb up into the front seat. I slam the door shut and try to calm down. I squeeze my hands together to make them shaking. I turn to look at my saviors. It's two black guys. I recognize them, but I don't know their names. By the green light of the dashboard gauges, I see that they're both staring at me, eyes wide open. I must look really scared.

The driver says," What's wrong, man?"

"It's Jeff," I say, trying to keep my voice from being too shaky. "He's dead. Somebody shot him. Right in the head."

Now their eyes get really wide. I expect them to ask questions, but they don't. The guy sitting next to me in the middle, the younger guy, turns to the driver and says, "Let's get the hell out of here."

"No, wait," I say. "Shouldn't we take Jeff's body back?"

The driver, a really big guy with a very loud voice, says, "Like hell." He slams the truck into reverse and backs up against the bushes, then goes forward, trying to turn the big truck around on the narrow road. He's in such a hurry, he grinds the gears trying to force the truck into reverse before it stops rolling.

I reach over and grab his wrist. "Wait. We can't just leave him here."

He shakes off my hand and points his big finger at my face. "You want him so bad, man, you go get him."

They both stare at me, waiting to see what I'm going to do.

I say, "I can't carry him by myself. But we have to get him, don't we?" My voice is all shaky and hoarse. I must sound like I'm begging. "What would the lieutenant say if we left him out here?"

The younger guy quietly says, "Okay, I'll help. Let's get him quick and get the hell out of here."

"Are you bullshittin' me?" says the driver. "You goin' out there?"

The younger guy says, "We don't even know if he's really dead. We got to make sure of that, at least."

The driver won't look at either of us. "Fine. Go ahead. It's your ass."

I take a deep breath and open the door. I can only hope whoever killed Jeff was scared off by the truck.

I run to Jeff's hole. The young black guy is right behind me. I start to climb down, but he doesn't follow me. He's standing up on the edge, staring down into the hole. The truck's headlights are fairly bright, but it's still pretty dark down in Jeff's hole. That's good because I don't want to look at Jeff's face anyhow. If he has a terrible hole in his head, I don't want to see it. I get ahold of Jeff's legs. I look up at the young black guy. "Come down here and help me. Hurry up."

"No way, man. Look at him." He points. "He's got no head." He turns and runs away.

I turn back to look at Jeff. It's unbelievable, but it's true: Jeff's head is gone, cut clean off. I stare at what's left of him. With no head, it doesn't really look like Jeff anymore; in fact, it doesn't look like anybody. I have the weird thought that the body is like a fake movie thing, not a real person at all. But then I realize Jeff had a head when I came to look at him earlier. I know he did because I touched the blood on the side of his face. It means they came back for his head *after* I'd gone back to my hole. It means they were here, watching. So why didn't they kill me too?

I hear the truck grind into gear. The engine revs. They're leaving.

I jump out of the hole and run after the truck. They're backing up down the road faster than I can run. The truck's headlights are blinding me, and I keep stumbling over potholes in the road. Finally, the driver backs into a small clearing. I'm barely able to jump up onto the running board before he grinds it into a forward gear, and we roar off down the road. Tree branches are slapping at me, trying to knock me off. All I can do is keep my head down and hang onto the door handle. Finally, the younger guy opens the door, which just about sends me flying. He grabs my arm and pulls me inside. I can barely catch my breath, but with what breath I have, I yell at the driver: "You son of a bitch. You were gonna leave me out there."

The driver won't look at me. He's leaning forward, straining to see out of the fogged-up windshield, wiping it with the back of his hand. He says, "Bullshit to that, man. You want me to stay out here and get my ass killed, Chuckie? I promised my momma I'd get back from this jive-assed white man's war in one piece. So fuck you, man. Fuck you."

I sit back and keep my mouth shut. Now I get it. So that's the way it is. They're black and I'm white, so to hell with me.

We roar on through the jungle night. Nobody says anything, until finally, the kid next to me says, "Sorry we're late, man. We got lost."

"Not our fault," says the driver angrily. "Somebody changed the road signs on us."

We go on in silence for a while, until I quietly say, "He shot a snake."

Neither of them replies, and I wonder why I said it out loud.

When we get back to camp, the driver says I have to be the one to go in to the lieutenant's hooch to tell him about Jeff.

I run into his tent and blurt it out: "Jeff is dead. They shot him."

The lieutenant stands up behind his desk. "What? Shot? On road security?" He looks toward the doorway, and then back at me. "But you're here, aren't you? If he got shot, why are you here? Were you asleep? You were, weren't you? Admit it."

"No, sir. I was awake all the time. I was."

"Oh yeah? What did you do when you heard the shot? You stayed where you were, didn't you? You didn't do a damn thing."

"No, sir," I say. "I didn't hear any shot."

The lieutenant leans across the desk toward me, but he can't find any words. His teeth are clamped, and he's glaring at me. He's clenches his fists, and for a moment I think he's going to crawl right across the desk and pound my face in. Instead, he pounds both fists on the desk. "Didn't hear the shot?" He pounds the desk again, even harder. "Then you were asleep, just like I thought. You can be court-martialed for sleeping on duty, soldier. You were sleeping on duty, and it resulted in the death of a comrade. You're in big trouble, soldier."

"No," I say quickly. "I wasn't asleep. Really. The reason I didn't hear the shot was I . . . I had to get out of my hole. But I was only gone for a few minutes."

The lieutenant stares at me. His eyes are narrowed. I can tell he doesn't believe a word I'm saying.

"So you're trying to tell me you had to go take a crap or something, and they used that exact moment to kill Jeff?"

"I'm telling you the truth, Lieutenant. I didn't sleep for one second, not even when the pickup crew didn't come on time."

He stares at me for a long moment. "Is he still out there?"

"Yes, sir. He's still down in his hole. I tried to get them to—"

"Shut up. Stay here. Don't move a God damn muscle until I get back." He runs around the desk and pushes past me.

I keep my eyes straight ahead.

He yells at the back of my head, "You hear me? Don't move. I'm not done with you."

He rushes out, and I hear him yelling outside.

He doesn't come back for quite a while, so I sit down to wait. I hear the truck start up. He must be sending some men out to get Jeff's body. I'll bet those guys aren't happy about having to go out there at night, especially after what's happened to Jeff.

I hear the truck pull out, and soon I hear the lieutenant coming back down the sloping entryway.

I cringe, waiting for whatever is next.

He yells, "Didn't I tell you to not move?"

I'd forgotten I was even sitting down. I jump up and go to attention.

He goes back behind his desk and sits down. He leans across the desk and stares at me.

I look past him. I can't take his accusing eyes.

He points his finger at me. "If you fell asleep, I'll have your ass. Jeff's death will be on your head." His yelling voice is so loud in the confined space I'm tempted to put my fingers in my ears. But I don't. I just continue to look past him. I try to keep my voice from shaking as I say, "I was wide awake the whole time, Lieutenant. I'm telling you the truth." I consider telling him about the turtle, but that would be too weird. He'd say, You left your post to save a damn turtle? I decide it's better to just keep my mouth shut. I am telling the truth. I wasn't asleep.

"Wide awake, eh? I bet. I know what you assholes do out there. Sleep and play with your puds. I outta—"

But I don't let him finish. "It wasn't my fault, Lieutenant!" All of my fear and regret and relief comes bursting out of me. My eyes are filling up with tears, but I don't care. I learn forward and look right at him. "Was it my fault the pickup crew didn't get there until after dark? You left us out there alone. Damn it, I was scared. They killed him, Lieutenant. They killed Jeff, and I don't know why they didn't kill me too. And then they came back and cut his head off, and I still didn't hear a thing. It was like they're ghosts or something." My voice is shaky, and I'm about to start crying. I bite my lip and turn away from him. I can barely keep myself from running out into the night.

"They cut his head off?" he asks quietly.

I nod, still looking away. I can't face him.

"Cut his damn head off. Jesus, he says, talking to himself now. "And they expect me to pacify this area. With what they send me? Dumb kids who don't know shit about anything. I told him to be careful out there. Didn't I tell him it was dangerous? Didn't I tell him to stay on his guard? But did he listen? Dumb shit. Gets himself killed, and for what? Road security. Safest assignment in the whole God-damned region." He looks up at me. "How am I gonna' explain it? Huh? How?" He jumps up and begins to pace behind his desk. "Dumb kids. Don't know shit about . . . ." He punches his fist into his other palm. "Damn it to hell." He turns back to me. "Well, don't just stand there. Sit your ass down."

I sit down. He doesn't look quite as angry now.

"And don't talk bullshit to me sayin' I left you out there. I didn't leave you out there. I sent those two boonies out right on time. Like I always do." He goes back to pacing, but then he stops right next to me and leans down close to my face. I can smell whiskey on his breath. "Right on time. You hear? They rolled out on time. I made sure of it. Is it my fault those two can't find their own asses with both hands?"

He paces for a while longer, but then he abruptly stops and heads for the doorway. "Come with me."

I follow him outside. He's heading for the perimeter wire. What's he up to? When we get to the wire, he doesn't even duck down behind the sandbag walls. He's pacing again, back and forth, right next to the razor wire. The nearby sentries stand up to see what's going on.

The lieutenant points out into the dark. "Look out there, damn it."

I look where he's pointing. Nothing but darkness. I can't believe he's yelling when we're so exposed. If there are snipers out there, they could pick us off just from his voice. He grabs my arm hard and jerks me closer to him. He makes me look where he's pointing. "You know what's out there? Do you? The enemy is out there. It's a war, God damn it. Damn it to hell, Scotty, can't I trust you boys to do anything right? You know what this means? I hadn't lost a God-damned man since I got here. Not a single man, except for the mortar casualties, and there's nothing I can do about that." He goes back to pacing. I look out into the dark night, hoping he's not right. I can only hope the enemy *is not* out there tonight. I half expect the shot to come at any minute. Is this how I'm going to die? Picked off in the middle of the night because the lieutenant is so angry he doesn't care if we both get shot?

He shakes his fist in the direction of the jungle. He yells, "Serves you right, you dumb asshole."

I realize he's yelling at Jeff as if he's still out there somewhere.

Some of the other men come out of their hooches to see what's going on. One of them turns a flashlight on us, making us a perfect target for snipers. "Cut that damn light," yells the lieutenant.

The light goes off.

The lieutenant continues to yell out into the darkness: "Dumb pricks like you deserve what they get. Falling asleep on road duty. Serves you right, you dumb little Alabama prick."

The lieutenant must think Jeff was from Alabama, but he wasn't. He was from Georgia. It makes me wonder where the lieutenant is from. He doesn't have an accent, so he's probably not from the South.

He keeps on yelling at Jeff. His voice echoes in the night. Some of the other men come out with their helmets on and their rifles in their hands. They take up defensive positions behind the sandbag walls. They must all be thinking the same thing I am, that the snipers are about to open up on us. But they don't. After a few more shouted curses at poor Jeff, the lieutenant turns to me and says, "Come with me, philosopher. He leads us back to his office and goes behind his desk.

I'm not sure what I'm supposed to do, so I just stand there.

He waves for me to sit down, so I do.

He opens one of his desk drawers and takes out a bottle of whiskey. He takes a long pull at it and hands it to me.

I hesitate. Am I supposed to just take a drink? Is it appropriate for a lowly private to drink out of the same bottle as an officer?

"Go ahead," he says. "Have a drink."

I take a small swallow. It's whisky and it burns my throat, but I manage to keep a straight face as I hand the bottle back to him.

"Well, you'll be happy to know I'm not going to put you on report. You were too dumb to know the danger. First time out there. I figure Jeff must have been asleep too, so it's his fault as much as yours. You'll never sleep on guard duty again, will you?"

I shake my head no.

He takes several gulps of whiskey, and turns to stare at the doorway. "He wasn't a bad kid, that Jeff. Not too bright, but not a bad kid."

I wonder if I should tell him Jeff wanted to be in a rock and roll band, and that he was worried that some Jody had made off with his girl. I decide against it. No point in talking about things like that now.

The lieutenant hands the bottle to me again, and this time I take a couple of drinks before I hand it back to him. "Ah hell, kid. No use blaming yourself." He pauses, staring at me. "You know, Scotty, it's pretty funny you spend your time reading a philosophy textbook. Most of the others in this unit can barely read. All they ever read is letters from home, and maybe, at best, a comic book or a girlie magazine."

I don't know what to say to that, so I just keep my mouth shut.

"I went to college like you did, but I never took any philosophy classes. Not that I have anything against philosophy, but . . . well, I'll leave that kind of stuff to you brainy types."

I start to say I don't consider myself a brainy type, but he's still talking. He says he barely made it through Michigan State University. "Wasn't all that great a student in high school, so I couldn't get a scholarship. Signed up for the ROTC scholarship program. They give you free tuition and books. Course when you finish college, you have to go into the Army. You know, to pay back the scholarship. They make you a second-Louie." He laughs after he says that thing about being made a second-Louie, but then he gets quiet.

I suspect he's thinking back, remembering. I wonder if he's having regrets about the choices he made.

But then he takes another slug of whiskey, and that seems to cheer him up. "You know what? When I get back home to Michigan, I'm gonna get me a job in the auto industry. Good wages. Good benefits."

I can't think what to say about that, so I ask, "You're not going to stay in the Army?"

He laughs an especially harsh laugh at my question and holds up the bottle. "Here's to the gaddam Army. May we make it out of here alive and not remember too much of it."

He takes another drink and hands the bottle to me. I take a small nip. I'm starting to relax, and I'm actually enjoying being with him. Maybe it's the whiskey, but I think it's mostly just having somebody to talk to.

The bottle goes back and forth between us as he tells me about the town in Michigan where he grew up. He says his father had been a career Army officer until a heart condition forced him to retire. "Came back to Michigan. Got into golf with his buddies. My mother started going to church. Catholic. Went every week. And to midnight masses."

He takes another drink and stares off into the distance.

He's acting more and more tipsy, and I'm wondering if it's time for me to leave. The whiskey is making me very sleepy.

He leans across the desk and points at my face. "How about you, mister philosopher, you a believer?"

That wakes me up, but I'm not sure how I should respond. If his mother is a regular churchgoer, does that mean he is too? In the past, I've generally found ways to avoid getting into discussions about religion, but I can tell he really wants an answer. "Well," I say, "I don't really know much about religion. When I was little, my mother used to drag me to a Baptist church. About all I remember about it is the booming voice of that preacher telling us we were all sinners, and we were all doomed to suffer eternal damnation and burn in hell."

I stop talking. I wonder if I've already said too much.

"Baptist, eh? Your family is Baptist?"

"Well, my father never went to church, and when he got killed, my mother stopped going too."

"How?"

I'm not sure what the lieutenant is asking. "Uh, how what?"

"How did he get killed? In the war?"

"Oh. No, he was in the war. Navy. Shore patrol. But when he got back, he became a motorcycle cop. Got hit by a car."

The lieutenant nods thoughtfully. "My old man was in the war too. One of the first into Germany."

All I can think of to say is, "Oh."

The lieutenant frowns. "Hey, you avoided my question, didn't you? What do *you* believe?"

I try to think how to tell him about my mother turning away from God after my father died. But after thinking about it, I decide against telling him about that. Instead, I say, "My high school history teacher told our class that when an American sailor named Commodore Perry sailed his ship into Japan's Tokyo harbor, he was shocked to learn there was not one single Christian in all of Japan."

The lieutenant looks at me. He seems puzzled. "So?"

"So, I guess everybody just believes the religion they learned as kids. You know, whatever religion is in the country they grew up in."

"That's probably true, but don't think I'm gonna let you off the hook with some philosopher's answer. Do you believe in God, or not?"

I shrug and say, "I'm not sure. I guess I'm confused about it."

He laughs at that. "Good answer, philosopher. I guess I'm confused about it too." He laughs again. "In fact, I'm confused about a lot of things." He raises the bottle and says, "Here's to confusion." He takes another big drink and tries to hand the bottle to me.

I wave it off, but I do like his response. It's as if he's trying to say we're a lot alike. I decide to try to keep him on the subject. I scoot forward on my chair and say, "You want to know something I was just reading my philosophy text book? There's this group of philosophers known as Existentialists. They say everybody creates their own beliefs. Maybe that's the way it is. Do you think? Maybe we all make up our own version of God."

He smiles as if he thinks that's a funny way to look at it, Then, he asks, "Do you really want to go out on patrol?"

His question startles me. Without hardly even thinking about it, I say, "I'm ready." And now that I've said it, I realize I should have thought about it a little more because now there's no backing out. If he decides he wants to send me out, I'm committed.

He takes another long drink and stares at the bottle as if there might be answers in there.

He looks up at me and shakes his head. "I don't think so, Scotty. I don't think you'll ever be ready. But I guess it's up to you."

I don't know quite how to take his words. Won't ever be ready? It's probably an insult, but it could also be some kind of backhanded compliment, because he goes on to say, "Ah hell, Scotty, war is crazy. Both sides always lose."

I don't know what he means by that, but I don't get a chance to ask because he changes the subject. He tells me about how his elementary school class went on a field trip through the Ford factory. "They had some great old black and white pictures of the world's first auto assembly line there. Good jobs in the auto industry. I'm gonna get a job there. Maybe work my way up to management."

As he rambles on, I sit there feeling more and more sleepy and wondering why I blurted out that I was ready to go on patrol. What I was trying to prove? Did I think I owed it to Jeff? Or was I just trying to prove I was just as much of a man as the others, ready to go out and face death like the rest of them? I can't even imagine being out on patrol. I imagine enemy soldiers hiding in the jungle, watching our patrols go out, waiting to spring their trap and kill everybody. But maybe that's the way the other guys in this unit felt too until they went out there for the first time. If they did it, I guess I can do it too.

He finally winds down and sends me back to my own hooch. My three hoochmates are playing poker, as usual. They won't even look at me. Nobody asks me what happened. Those two drivers must have already been telling everybody. News travels like lightning around this firebase. I feel so tired, I can't even find the strength to take my clothes off. I fall into bed and stare up into the darkness. My mind wants to play it all over again; it wants to think through how it could have happened, how they could have shot Jeff and then come back to cut his head off, and I didn't hear a thing. But none of it makes sense. I'm too tired to think straight. All I can think about is that little turtle and how its little shiny eyes looked at me from inside its shell. The whole thing seems all foggy and strange now, like a dream. I can't seem to bring my thoughts together; all I get are vague images: that porn magazine, the yokels on the road, a B52 can-opener bomber overhead, a dead baby in a sack that wasn't really dead. and that damn elephant. A real live elephant that smelled like a wild animal. And that young girl that walked by with no top on. Jeff whistled at her. Is that why they killed him? Or was it the snake? I took the turtle to water. I prayed to my storyteller girl to save me. Did she?

It's still dark when the lieutenant wakes me up. "Wake up philosopher. They brought Jeff back. You want to go out and see?"

I sit up and shake my head no. He's standing above my bed, staring down at me. "Oh, and they found his head too. I thought you'd be happy to hear that. On the way back, they saw it stuck on a bamboo stake next to the road. Oh, it was Jeff's head all right, eyes wide open, ears missing, stuck on a pole right there next to the road for everybody to see." He glances toward the door. "You sure you don't want to go out and look? The others are out there, standing around, gawking. I'm letting them look at it for a while so they'll learn a lesson from it." He looks at me for what seems like a long time, and then he leaves.

I realize my hoochmates are gone. They must have gone out to look.

I turn over to stare at the wall. I feel terribly sleepy, but I keep seeing Jeff out there curled up in his hole with no head on his body. I know there's no way I'm going to be able to get any more sleep this night. I decide what I need is some pot. It might make my brain turn off, at least for a little while. I light up a joint and hold the smoke down hard. When I finally exhale, nothing much comes out. Good. This is Brent's extra strong weed. If it won't stop the thinking, nothing will. I keep taking hits, hardly even pausing to breathe, until the roach burns my fingers. I pinch it out and swallow it. I wait, but it isn't working. It's not stopping the thinking. The lieutenant said they found Jeff's head on a stake next to the road. Why did they cut off his head? It's just like those bodies Brent and I saw back in Saigon. They found their heads stuck on a stake out on a road too. The enemy must think of it like a Vietnamese roadside warning sign: "Beware, American, you are not wanted here. Leave before you end up like this." Did they kill Jeff because I pointed my rifle at that woman? In Indoctrination Training, they told us that even Vietnamese women and kids might be out to do us harm. They told us a story about some soldier who had gotten himself killed by a naked girl who had a hand grenade hidden in her cunt. They want us to be afraid of these people. I didn't believe the story, but now I don't know what to believe. I'm confused and tired and strangely numb, like it doesn't matter what I believe because Jeff will still be dead. I can't stop thinking that they didn't kill me because I saved that silly little turtle. I have to stop thinking about it, or it'll drive me crazy. Maybe I've already gone over the edge. None of seems real, but I know it is. I remember how strange and distant the war seemed when I was back in Arizona. In the Phoenix newspaper, just about every day there was another story about another dead local hero being shipped home. I'll bet when Jeff gets back home to Georgia, his local newspaper will have a tiny little obituary about a young guy named Jeff who died heroically in Vietnam. It won't say he wanted to learn to play the electric guitar. In fact, I may be the only one who knows that. His mother will be proud of him. In fact, everyone will be proud of him for dying while protecting his country. His girl will be proud of him too. She'll come to his funeral and stand there by the graveside crying her eyes out. She'll look nice in black. It will be a closed-casket affair, of course. I wonder if they'll they try to sew his head back on. More likely they'll just toss it into the casket with his body and close the thing up.

13

The Jungle Awaits

Something wakes me up. I realize it was the sound of a mortar being launched. Then comes the explosion. Here we go again. Another night of lying awake calculating my death odds. But this time, our howitzers start responding very quickly. It means I've managed to survive another night's dance with death. But I can't get back to sleep. I'm staring up at our flimsy tent roof, being thankful that our howitzer team was on the ball tonight, when the lieutenant comes hurrying into our hooch to ask for volunteers to chase after the mortar shooters.

I sit up and raise my hand. This time he points at me. My hoochmates all turn to stare. I ignore them and hurry to get dressed and pack up my stuff. This time I remember to put on my flak jacket. I put on my helmet and pick up my rifle, but the lieutenant says, "Leave it."

I'm not sure I heard right. "Leave it?"

"Leave it. You're packing today, not shooting."

All three of my hoochmates laugh loud and long at that.

Why are they laughing? What does packing mean?

Outside, I find out. The lieutenant points at a big, sort of Italian-looking spec-4 who's holding a machine gun. "You'll be carrying that."

The guy hands the gun to me. It's so heavy, I almost drop it.

"Plus this." With a grin, the guy hands me the ammo belt.

I get why he's grinning: the ammo belt is heavy as hell too.

The lieutenant nods toward the big spec-4. "He's the gunner. You're the AG, the packer." He shows me how to carry the gun on my shoulder and drape the ammo belt over my other shoulder. The line forms, and the lieutenant puts me in behind the gunner. As the line moves toward the gate, the lieutenant walks next to me. "Listen, Scotty, you do whatever the squad leader tells you. You hear me?"

I say, "Yes, sir."

He says, "I'm not kidding. If he says to do something, just do it. Don't think about it."

I say, "Yes, sir. I get it, sir."

As the line moves out through the gate, I look back. The lieutenant has a worried look on his face. Does he always look that way when the morning patrol goes out, or is it just me he's worried about?

The line moves fast. We make it across the clearing and into the jungle. It's still so dark I can't imagine how the squad leader can find the path, if there is a path. Because of the weight, it's a lot of work keeping up, but I'm actually feeling pretty good, a kind of excited high. I'm not all that unhappy about being out on an actual patrol, but there's a worried feeling wandering around the back of my mind, not exactly fear, more like a sort of lurking anxiety at being out in the dreaded jungle, the zoo, where the enemy hides. I try to stop thinking about that and just focus on what the jungle looks like. Mostly it's just heavy underbrush and bamboo thickets. There are a few palm trees, and there are also some tall trees with root-like projections that spread out from their bases like the fat toes of giants. And nearly every tree of that type is wrapped with tangled vines, some of them hanging down loose like the vines that Tarzan used to swing on in those old movies.

The line moves on in silence. It's quiet in the jungle, except for a few birds high in the trees that are making sounds I've never heard birds make before—not tweets, but clacks and rattles and drawn-out whistles. Their strange sounds echo through the jungle, giving me an eerie feeling. Our line of soldiers moves deeper into the damp dimness of the jungle. We push through tall grasses and low-lying ferns, glistening wet from the night's dew. As I take it all in, it hits me that this *is not* my first time in the jungle. I went through some jungle that day I took the turtle to water, the day Jeff was killed. But it was not as thick as this jungle; this jungle feels completely different, darker, more closed in. That thought makes me realize I haven't been thinking much about Jeff or what happened out there on road security that day. Have I been trying to pretend it never happened, that it was only a dream? But it wasn't a dream. Jeff really was killed. His head really was cut off and put on a bamboo stake by the side of the road. I wonder why I have so much trouble remembering that day. It's almost like some part of me was also killed out there on that road; maybe there's something in my brain trying to keep me from remembering. Maybe my brain hasn't been working quite right since that day. I push that thought away. There's nothing wrong with my brain. I'm just nervous about being out here on my first patrol. I need to stop thinking about bad things and just do my job, which is carrying this damn heavy machine gun. As we go along, the sky gradually gets a little lighter. I try to see deeper into the forest, but there's nothing to see except vegetation and more vegetation. It's like a dark green wall on both sides. Despite my trying to focus on the beauty of it all, my mind keeps telling me there might very well be enemies hiding behind the green walls of vegetation, real enemies with weapons. No, stop that. I don't want to think about things like that. These patrols go out all the time, and they never see a sign of the enemy. No reason to think today will be any different. But the jungle sure is thick. And I keep hearing rustling in the bushes. But nobody else seems to be noticing, so I must be imagining things.

When the first rays of the sun start to light up the tops of the tallest trees, I can see well enough ahead to realize we actually *are* on a path. It snakes through the trees, but it's so narrow and indistinct I wonder if we're following an animal trail, like the ones I used to follow in the Arizona desert. In the desert, I always enjoyed following the narrow, hollowed out trails made by the sharp hooves of the wild burros, the modern-day descendants of the burros let loose by the old-time gold prospectors. But this is no desert. Everything here is wet, as if it just stopped raining. But as far as I know, there was no rain last night. We go on and on, pushing through wet vegetation. It's getting my pants soaking wet. I look up, wondering if the sun is ever going to get high enough in the sky to overcome the darkness of this place. Above us, there are thick vines crossing back and forth. It reminds me of the tangle of electrical wires that crossed back and forth above the streets back in Saigon. No way Tarzan could get anywhere swinging on these vines. They're all tangled up with other vines; in fact, there are so many vines up there they're almost woven together, like thick brown threads running through dark green fabric. As we keep on going with no stopping and no slowing, I start to wonder how far we're going to go. How far is it to the Cambodian border? The lieutenant said not to go across the border. Now I can see why the squad leader complained about how he was supposed to know where the border is. There are no landmarks in this jungle; everything looks alike. Everything is green, a lot darker green than it looked from behind the perimeter wire back inside the base. The tall grass is green, the bushes are green, even the trunks of the trees are covered in green moss. It's like a painting where the artist only had shades of green to work with. The only thing that isn't green are the flowers. They're the best part of the jungle. There are flowers all over the place: big flowers, little flowers, most of them unlike any flowers I've ever seen before. Some of the big ones are so big and bright they look fake, like the kind of plastic flowers somebody might string overhead at a fancy party. There's one type of large red flower that almost seems like some kind of joke because of their fat petals that look like dark red tongues sticking out at us as we pass by. Another big white flower looks like a fancy hanging-down trumpet. and there are lots and lots of tiny little light purple flowers on vines that have invaded some of the bushes. Those flowers are so tiny you wouldn't even notice them if you didn't look close. And the bushes have their own flowers too. One type of large-leafed bush has white spindly flowers with thin petals that reach upward; they look like the legs of a white spider lying on its back. As we go on, I start trying to see how many different kinds of flowers I can spot.

My flower gazing is interrupted when I notice the big spec-4 gunner I'm supposed to be following is impatiently waving at me. I catch up and anticipate he's going to be put out with me for lagging behind, but he's acting friendly. He tells me his name.

It sounds something like "Vo-cha-ee-yo-how-ski." So he must not be Italian like I thought.

He notices my trying to silently pronounce his name, and with a laugh he tells me it's a Polish name. He says, "Don't bother learnin' how to pronounce it. Everybody just calls me the Polack."

"Polack?"

"Yeah. I don't mind. They don't mean it in a bad way."

"Okay. I'm Scotty."

"Right. Scotty, the philosopher."

I want to tell him I'm not really any kind of philosopher, that I only took one philosophy class at the university, but before I can say anything, the squad leader looks back and shushes us."

The Polack grins at me and puts his finger to his lips. He seems like a jolly fellow, and that's damn unusual at our firebase.

As we go on, I try to stay close behind the Polack's bobbing backpack. Not only is his backpack stuffed full, but he's got a hell of a lot of other things hanging from it: several grenades and ammo bags, a couple of worn-looking oilcloth bags containing who knows what, a red Swiss Army pocket knife, two canteens, a gas mask (why a gas mask?), and a silver cross on a silver chain. I figure he must be Catholic; but isn't he worried that the flashing of that silver cross in the sunlight might attract the enemy's attention?

The line starts to move faster, and with the heavy load I'm carrying, I have to work hard to keep up. I have to watch my step because there are vines and roots running across the trail that seem determined to trip me. But the deeper we go into the jungle, the less worried I feel. Maybe it just took me some time to get used to how dark and closed in it feels. Now I'm thinking it's kind of restful to be in the cool darkness. And it's nice to listen to the variety of birds that are now making quite a racket high above us. I can't see any of the birds up there, but I'm really enjoying hearing their weird chatters and clicks and clacks.

We go on and on: this is definitely not turning out to be the short morning hike I was expecting. The border must be farther away than everybody has been telling me. And the heavy machine gun I'm carrying is a tricky balancing act, especially when the slippery trail goes downhill. I can tell it's going to create a blister on my sweaty shoulder, but I tell myself not to complain; I've always liked hiking out in nature, so I should just enjoy this hike and quit thinking about how heavy and clumsy the damn thing is. To take my mind off the soreness of my shoulder, I think back to the time I hiked all the way across the Grand Canyon, all by myself, from the south rim to the north rim, carrying a thirty-five pound pack on my back. My shoulders got sore that time too, but it was worth it. I camped out in the north rim forest that night, and man, were the stars bright up there. My body ached, but I felt proud to have done it, especially because the park rangers had advised against me trying it. I figure if I could do that, I can do this. No problem.

We head up a hill, and for about the hundredth time, I wonder where the squad leader is taking us. But I'm pretty sure he wouldn't take kindly to a FNG asking him that kind of question. Saint Louee filled me in about this particular squad leader. His name is Carl. Saint Louee told me Carl is the no-nonsense, hard-core type, and I should be sure never to cross him. I've heard my other hoochmates refer to him as Carl The Older, or Old Sergeant Carl, apparently because he's quite a bit older than the rest of us. My impression is that maybe he's been out here just about since the war began. I wonder why he didn't put in this time and head back to the states like everybody else does.

The line stops. I look ahead and see that Squad Leader Carl has raised his hand to hold us up. He's got a map open, and he's looking at something in his hand—maybe a compass.

The Polack looks back at me and shrugs. Then, he moves off the trail and leans over to look at something on the ground. He waves me forward and says, "Hey, Scotty, come look at this."

Before I can move, there's a pop, and I only have time to think, What was that? when there's a loud explosion.

Time must have passed without me knowing it because the other guys are gathered around, looking down at me. Did I get knocked out?

Somebody says, "Jesus, he's just about blown in half."

But how can I be blown in half? I'm awake and seeing and hearing things, aren't I? I'm feeling some pain, but not enough to be blown in half. I have the sudden thought that maybe this is how it is when you're dead. Maybe things just go on like they would if you weren't dead.

All I know for sure is that I'm lying flat on my back and my leg hurts like hell. But at least I feel the pain, so maybe whoever said I was blown in half was exaggerating and it's only that my leg is blown off. I don't want to look down because I don't think I could stand the sight of seeing my leg gone and thinking about limping around on one leg for the rest of my life. And that's even assuming I don't bleed to death right here on the spot which seems pretty likely if your leg is blown off. I try to read the faces of the guys looking down at me to see how bad it is. They all look worried, so I decide this is it, this is where I'm going to die, lying on the ground feeling the wetness of the grass against my back. Or is it blood? Maybe blood is leaking out of my back. Maybe I really am just about blown in half, and I really am going to die. My mind is saying to me, now isn't this ridiculous, your first time out on patrol and you get killed. One minute you were looking at the pretty jungle flowers and listening to the funny Vietnamese birds, and the next minute you're dead.

Somebody says something, and the looks on their faces change. Now they seem pissed off at me. But why? It wasn't me that set off whatever it was that blew up; it was the Polack.

Then Doc Eric is there, kneeling beside me, saying, "Take it easy, Scotty. You're gonna be all right."

It's a nice thing for him to say, except I can't really believe him because that's probably what he would say to any wounded soldier, even if he was absolutely sure you were about to die. He does something to my thigh, and that causes it to hurt enough to make me lift my head to see what he's doing. I see that I *do* still have a leg. In fact I have two, and only one of them seems to be hurt. So what did they mean about me being just about blown in half? Doc Eric wraps something tight around my thigh, which tells me I do have a thigh, and then he does something, and almost immediately, I feel woozy. Must have been morphine. I think I like morphine.

Time may be messed up now because I thought I heard a helicopter, but I must have imagined it because somebody says, "We got to get him back," and somebody else says, "Oh yeah, how?" and somebody else says, "You'll have to carry him," and somebody else says, "Bullshit. I'm not carrying this pussy kid all the way back cause it shoulda been him that got it, not the Polack. But then somebody else with a deep gruff voice says, "Can it, all of you. Get busy and rig up something."

I'm not sure what's going on. My brain is off in la-la land and people are moving around me for what seems like a very long time, and then some hands grab my arms and legs and lift me up and put me down again on top of something that feels damn uncomfortable against my back. It feels like rough sticks jabbing into me. Then, things are moving past me, and I'm being jostled back and forth so much I have to hold on to the sides of whatever it is I'm lying on. Bushes slap against me. I'm seeing trees and sky and occasionally sweating faces that still seem to be mad at me. Their grumbling voices are filtering into my brain, but I can't quite make out what they're saying.

I think time is passing. There's moving and bouncing and hurting, and then they put me down. I open my eyes and see a tent roof. It must mean I'm back at the firebase, or at least my mind wants very much to believe that. I have the foggy thought that maybe I can just wake up now and all this will have been a dream, and hopefully not the kind of dream I'm going to die at the end of.

Doc Eric is hovering over me, and I'm lying on my back on a table that feels cold right through my clothes, so it must be metal. I guess I'm in Doc Eric's infirmary. and he's doing something to my leg. It means I have a leg. Whatever he's doing, it hurts a lot. There's a bright electric light shining in my eyes. I hear the sound of a generator outside. The light brightens and dims as the generator's motor surges and slows. Doc Eric is probing at my leg and mumbling something about how easy it is to get wounded out here: mortars, snipers, grenades, artillery, booby traps, mines. He notices I'm awake and says, "Your method of getting wounded was a bit unusual. A booby-trap mine they call a Bouncing Betty. Jumps up in the air about waist high before it goes off. Gives you just enough time to know you're about to be dead." He chuckles.

Why did he laugh? And if he's right, why aren't I dead?

I feel him probe deeper into my leg.

I half sit up and say, "Hey, that hurts."

He pushes me back down and says, "Almost done."

"Can I have a little more of that stuff you gave me out there?"

"Morphine?"

"Yeah."

"You don't need it."

He continues probing, and that makes me even more sure I do need it. I clamp my teeth together and try to think about something else beside the pain. So it was a mine, a booby-trapped mine. Booby traps have to be sprung. I know that, but I didn't spring it. It must have been the Polack. He must have stepped on something. All I remember is the bang—no, actually first there was a sound, a pop, followed by a really loud bang. Then, I was down on the ground looking up at a confusing sky of partly blue and partly gray clouds. "I think I must have got knocked out, Doc. I remember waking up."

"That's pretty common. You shouldn't move around too much for the next few days. Something coulda got knocked loose in your head."

Knocked loose? Inside my head? I can move around? Does that mean I'm not going to get an early helicopter ride out of here. The other guys talk about getting a 24-carat wound, one bad enough to get you out of Vietnam, but not so bad you won't eventually recover from it. I'm hoping I've got one of those. I try to ignore the pain of Doc Eric's probing by thinking about hiking out in the desert, sleeping on the ground, looking up at the stars. "Will I still be able to walk?"

"Sure. No problem."

What does that mean? No problem? Does he mean eventually? I say, "Somebody said it just about blew me in half. But if it's only my leg that's hurt, why did they say that?"

He gives me a strange look. "You don't know?"

Don't know what? Why is he looking at me like that?

"The Polack took most of the blast. It did just about cut him in half."

So that's what they meant. It wasn't me they were talking about getting blown in half; it was the Polack. Knowing the Polack is dead makes me feel very sad. He was about the only person who's ever been friendly to me here, except for the lieutenant.

But how did I get here? "Did they come with a helicopter?"

The doc shakes his head. "I had the radio guy call out to see if there was an angel track nearby, but we got no answer, so I called in a Medivac chopper. We heard it coming, but they radioed they were taking small arms fire and had to turn back."

Small arms fire? The enemy was that close to us?

"Damn thing was wobbling as it went away. Barely got up high enough to make it out over the trees. Squad Leader Carl said if that chopper was taking hits, we had to get the hell out of there quick."

"I think somebody carried me."

"Yeah. Carl told 'em to hop to and make something to carry you out."

"Did they think about maybe leaving me out there?"

Doc Eric is focusing on his probing, and it seems like he doesn't want to answer that question, so I don't push it. I wonder if most of the guys did want to leave the worthless FNG out there. I vaguely remember somebody saying I should have got it instead of the Polack. "I heard somebody say something about the Polack and Kool-Aid."

Doc Eric chuckles.

"Is it funny?"

He shrugs. "What is funny is all the terms they make up to avoid just saying somebody got killed. Kool-Aid is like KIA. Dead. But they'll say lit-up, greased, zapped, blown away, or bought the farm. And more. I've heard 'em all. The Army does it too. The term I'm going to have to put in my report about the Polack tonight is LHA, lost to hostile action. Anything to avoid saying the truth, that the guy is just plain dead."

Doc Eric seems to be saying all this to my leg. He doesn't seem to want to look at me. Seeing so much damage to human bodies must be getting to him. He seems like the kind of guy I wouldn't mind talking to sometime.

He does something to my leg, and I yell, "Ouch!"

He still doesn't look up. He just keeps on probing.

"Damn, doc, what're you doing down there?"

"Shrapnel. Got to get it all out. Otherwise, infection."

He again does something, and again it hurts like hell. It's like he's mad at me. Are they all pissed off at me because the FNG survived while an old hand like the Polack died?

"Looks like the bone isn't broken. Lucky."

I don't feel very lucky right now, but I guess he's right. I say, "So, is my leg going to be all right?"

"Sure. You only got a few shrapnel wounds and a little tear in your thigh. It's like a little plowed furrow in a field. Only a few inches long."

"I have a headache too," I say.

"I'll get you some pain pills in a minute."

He continues to probe, and then, "Aha!"

I say, "Aha what?"

"I got it." He holds up some bloody thing clamped in his forceps.

"Is that the shrapnel?"

He studies it over the top of his glasses. "It's what tore into your leg, but it doesn't look like metal."

He brings it closer so I can look at it too. It looks white, like bone. "I thought you said my leg bone wasn't broken."

He says, "It doesn't look broke. The tear doesn't seem deep enough. But you never can tell. Depends how much stuff they put in 'em." He drops the shrapnel into a metal dish, and goes back to probing.

"Jesus, doc. That hurts like hell. Can't you give me something?"

"I deadened the wound area. Otherwise you'd be jumping off the table. Your leg has been traumatized. It's gonna hurt for a few days."

Only a few days? Is he saying my leg wound isn't a 24-carat wound? Does it mean I'm not going to get to go home? I ask, or maybe more accurately, plead, "Only a few days?"

"Maybe a few weeks."

That's encouraging. Maybe my wound isn't bad enough to get me sent back to the states to the Walter Reed Army hospital—the "Wonderful Walter," as the old hands call it—but I might at least get sent to a hospital back in Saigon. I'll have to figure out a way to get word to Brent. Maybe he can find my storyteller girl and get her to come visit me in the hospital. She'd see me laid up and feel sorry for me. She might even stay with me for a while, tell me stories, nurse me back to health.

"Ow!" I look down to see what the doc is doing now. He's stitching me up, using a curved needle that's clamped to his forceps. It doesn't hurt all that much when he runs the needle through my skin, so I guess he really did deaden the area, but it still hurts like hell when he pulls the thread tight.

He finishes sewing and ties off the stitches. He wraps my leg up in a tight bandage. But instead of going to get me my pain pills, he goes back to puzzling over the piece of whatever it was he dug out of my leg. He grabs it with his forceps and holds it up to the light. "By damn, it *is* a piece of bone."

"So the mine knocked a chunk of my thigh bone out? Will it make it so I can't walk?"

He brings the piece of bone closer for me to look at. "It's not from your leg. Like I said, your wound isn't deep enough. I think it's a piece of bone from the Polack."

14

Gunny Sacks

It's been raining all night, and it's so noisy on our tent roof, I can't get to sleep. They tell me it's the start of the long-awaited rainy season. I'm learning Vietnamese rain is a tap-wide-open rain that never lets up.

I'm still recovering from my leg wound, but at least now I can make it to the mess tent and back. My hoochmates are still giving me no end of shit about what happened on my first patrol out. The Farmer makes smart-ass jokes about how the Polack gave his all for me, even his bones. Oh-Lee's favorite is "Hey, Philosopher, I got a bone to pick with you." They laugh about it like my getting wounded by a piece of the Polack is the funniest thing that ever happened. The Polack is dead and I'm wounded, and everybody thinks it's a big joke. The other day, when Doc Eric came in to change my bandage, I complained about all the jokes at my expense. He said they make jokes to relieve the tension. Maybe. More likely they've just gotten mean from being here too long.

I lie awake listening to the rain patter on our tent roof and worry. My leg wound is getting better, so why do I worry so much? Is there something wrong with my brain? I keep thinking about how the Polack got killed. Doc Eric told me it was the first time anybody got killed out on patrol since this firebase was built, the first time anybody here tripped a booby-trap. Does it mean the enemy is moving into this area?

An explosion. Not all that close. Probably out beyond the wire. It didn't sound like a mortar, and in fact, the enemy mortar shooters haven't been coming around lately. Guess they don't like the rain.

Two more explosions. Definitely not mortar explosions. Is it the enemy? Are we finally under attack? Should I grab my rifle and go out? I wait and listen. No more explosions come. If it was an attack, it was a short one. I feel for my flashlight and click it on. The hooch is empty. Where are my hoochmates? How did they slip out without waking me up? Maybe I'm taking too many of the pain pills Doc Eric gave me.

I hear voices outside. But they're not yelling, just excited talking. It must have been a false alarm. I decide to stay put and wait to see if anything else happens. I turn off my flashlight and listen to my own breathing in the darkness.

Soon, my hoochmates come clomping into the hooch. Flashlight beams are bouncing all over the place.

I say, "What's going on?"

A flashlight shines in my eyes.

"Nothing. A probing." It's Saint Louee's voice. "Go back to sleep."

A probing? What does that mean?

Their flashlights go out, and I hear a lot of mumbled cuss words as they crawl into their bunks.

I lie still and listen to see if they're going to say anything else. But they don't. Soon I hear the usual snoring.

So, what did he mean, a probing? And how can they go back to sleep so quickly? They don't seem to be too worried about it.

I stare up into the darkness and listen. But there's nothing to listen to except snoring. Why is it only me that lies awake thinking about the enemy out there. What if this "probing" means the enemy is going to start attacking this base now?

I open my eyes. Somebody is whispering. Did I sleep? A little light is coming in through the open doorway. It must be morning.

I turn over. It's the lieutenant. He's trying to wake Oh-Lee up. "Wake up," he whispers. "Gunny sack detail."

But Oh-Lee turns away from him. "No way. I hardly got any sleep."

The lieutenant heads for The Farmer's bunk, but The Farmer hears him coming. "Not me. Let Scotty do it. He slept through the whole damn thing."

The lieutenant whispers, "No, he's not ready. Get up."

I sit up. "I'm willing, as long as I don't have to walk far."

The Farmer laughs. Why did he laugh?

I say, "I mean, Doc Eric told me I should start moving around a little more. To help my leg heal."

The lieutenant shrugs. "Okay, get dressed." He goes out.

I chew up two of the pain pills Doc Eric gave me and get dressed as fast as I can. I grab my poncho and my rifle and go out.

When I get outside, I discover it's muddy, but the rain has slowed to a drizzle. Well, thank goodness for that at least. Through the drizzling mist, I see some guys lined up by the gate. The lieutenant is telling them something, pointing to the west.

Are we going out past the wire? Only two of the guys are carrying rifles. Three others have shovels over their shoulders. A stack of gunny sacks is on the ground near them.

I go to join the others, limping a little to show them my leg still hurts.

The lieutenant turns to me. "You won't need that rifle." He takes it.

A few of the other guys chuckle. What's so funny?

He says, "Pick up those gunny sacks and get to it."

I pick up the sacks. Get to what? We're going out with shovels and gunny sacks? What the hell?

The men file out through the gate. I fall in at the back of the line. I can't imagine what this detail is all about.

As soon as we're outside the gate, the two guys with rifles fan out on both sides, their rifles ready.

The group heads straight for the tree line, and that makes me nervous. Are we going into the jungle? With shovels?

Then I see them, near the trees, naked men lying on the ground. There's no way to tell how many they used to be because their bodies are not whole anymore. It's as if some evil giant has torn them apart and scattered the pieces around. Are these destroyed bodies the enemy?

The others go closer to look, but I stay back. I'm glad I haven't had anything to eat yet today. I'm sure I wouldn't be able to keep it down. There are bloody, flesh-smeared pieces of black cloth tangled up in the flattened weeds. I see what I think are two torsos, but it's hard to tell; maybe it's only one person torn in two.

The two men with shovels start digging. Now I know why we're here. We're here to bury these bodies.

One of the shovel guys, a big fellow with a wide face and a broken-looking nose says, "Beehive rounds got 'em good. Good shootin'."

The guy he's talking to, a tall spec-5 that I've never seen before, just shrugs and says, "Yeah, did a number on 'em. The lieutenant said to get 'em buried fast and get back inside, so let's move it."

Now I know what a beehive round is. Some kind of explosive shell that tears the shit out of human bodies. So this is the result of those explosions last night.

The others come to me to get gunny sacks. I hand them out, and they go to work picking up body parts and stuffing them into the sacks.

All I can do is stand there and stare. I keep thinking these pieces of flesh and bone were once humans. They were alive. I watch the others pick up the bloody and broken pieces of bodies and stuff them into the gunny sacks. They're doing it with their bare hands, acting like it doesn't bother them at all. It's like they're just out picking up trash.

The big guy with the broken nose stuffs what's left of a leg into his gunny sack. He notices me watching him. He says, "Well? Get to it."

Does he think I'm supposed to help? The lieutenant had me pick up the gunny sacks. He must have known I wouldn't be able to do the picking up part. I just want to turn around and hurry back to the base as fast as I can. This sloppy wet fleshy stuff that used to be humans is not something anybody should have to see, let alone touch.

Broken nose nudges the spec-5 and points at me. "Check out the FNG. Betcha a buck he's gonna throw up."

The spec-5 says, "Let him be."

But broken nose is not about to leave me alone. He holds out some kind of blob of flesh that's all squishy and dripping blood. He says, "Here, man. How about some breakfast?"

I tell myself I *will not* throw up. No matter what this asshole says or does. The spec-5 takes pity on me and leads me away from the big joker who's now laughing even harder and holding up his blob of flesh for everybody to see. He yells, "Breakfast anybody?"

The spec-5 leads me to a severed arm that seems to be somehow attached to the wooden stock of a bent rifle. The arm is full of what looks like silvery nails, like an arm-shaped pin cushion. Those beehive rounds must be packed a lot of nail-like pieces of metal. It not only tore this guys arm off, but it nailed his arm to the stock of his rifle.

The spec-5 says, "Just grab the rifle and stuff it in your bag along with the arm. Then he'll leave you alone."

I do what he says, trying to think of it as only a piece of meat nailed to a piece of wood.

He says, "Good," and then he turns to one of the guys who's digging the hole. "Hey, let this guy spell you."

The digger is happy to bring me his shovel and take my bag. I guess he thinks picking up body parts is easier duty than digging. I focus on digging, shoveling hard and fast, trying not to think about anything but getting the damn hole dug and getting the hell out of here.

The others bring their gunny sacks and toss them into the hole. Me and the other digger guys bury the sacks as fast as we can.

As we head back to the camp, one of the guys behind me in the line says, "Notice no good weapons or boots? They musta come back to get whatever was useful. Left their buddies just lyin' there."

Nobody comments or even grunts to acknowledge the truth of it.

We file back in through the gate, and I head for my hooch. My stomach feels like it's all tied up in knots. All I want to do is get back into my bunk, pull the blanket over my head, and go to sleep.

Broken nose calls after me: "Hey, buddy, not ready for breakfast?"

I ignore his loud laughing and keep going. When I get back to my hooch, I'm glad to see the others are still asleep. I tear off my clothes and crawl under the blanket. I don't want to think about anything. I just want to sleep, but I keep on seeing that arm nailed to that rifle stock. The sergeant said to think of it as only a piece of meat. And in fact, that's really all it was. War kills us, tears us apart, and then we are no longer human. It's like it says in my philosophy book: we live and then we die, and then we're only a piece of meat.

15

Noble Savages

Tonight, for a change, I'm alone in our hooch because with the rain-caused lull in the mortar attacks my hoochmates have been spending their time over at the mess tent playing in a big poker game. From their talk, it sounds like some serious money is being won and lost. It reminds me of the big money betting that went on at the dice table at Wong's bar. I wonder if that's still going on at Wong's. Sometimes I think about that young soldier who got stabbed and ended up under that dice table. Poor kid. Comes all the way from Iowa, or wherever, and then gets it in a bar fight. I sent Brent a letter, addressed to the warehouse, to ask him what's going on back there and if he'd seen my storyteller girl. But he hasn't written back. Maybe he never got the letter. Maybe Fart-Ass Farkas intercepted it. That would be just like him.

Without my hoochmates' distracting poker chatter, I can get some serious reading done. So far tonight, I've covered a chapter on John Locke who believed people are born without innate concepts, like a blank slate, a "tabula rasa." That idea went against Christian philosophy, and it got him into trouble with the religious authorities. Another guy my book talks about is Jean-Jacques Rousseau, a Swiss philosopher who contended that man is essentially good, a "noble savage," while he was in the state of nature, before the creation of civilized society. He believed good people are made bad, and therefore unhappy, when they are corrupted by society. He said the quest to acquire material things is the big problem. He also said that when a state fails to act morally, it ceases to function properly, and therefore it should cease to exert authority over the individual. After reading that part, I turn down the lantern and put down the book. Old Rousseau's statement has me asking the question, what if a government starts a bad war, an immoral war? Should it lose its authority over individuals? A lot of the young men back on campus were burning their draft cards and refusing to submit to the government. Is that the kind of thing Rousseau would have advocated? Is that what I should have done? But I know there's no use going down that conceptual road. The state, in this case, the United States government, has the power to put you in prison if you don't do what they tell you to do. I'm starting to realize that's the problem with philosophy: there are some great ideas in it, but how do you actually live according to those ideas? Brent would tell me it's dumb to waste time reading about things you can't change, but being here in Vietnam, it seems even more important to try to figure it out. I light up a joint and stare up at our tent roof thinking about it. It's not easy to make sense of it all. As soon as one philosopher says something, the next one says that's not the right way to look at it. But there seems to be one thread that's runs through all their theories: it's how an individual human thinks that creates that human's reality. That's a really interesting idea.

I hear somebody coming. A flashlight shines in my eyes. I hold up my hand to ward off the light, and see it's the lieutenant. He's rocking forward and backwards on his heels, which means he's been hitting his bottle a bit too hard again. He points his flashlight at my book. "At that book again, are ya, philosopher? And gettin' stoned too, I see."

He tosses some little thing at me. It hits me in the chest, bounces off, and falls onto my cot. I pick it up and hold it up into the beam of his flashlight. It's a medal. A purple heart. I've never really looked close at one before. The damn thing really is heart-shaped, a little gold heart-shaped medal hanging from a purple ribbon. My first thought is a stupid one, that when I get back home (if I get back home), it'll prove I got wounded. At least I'll have something to show for all this madness, something to remind myself that all this really did happen.

The lieutenant is still standing over me, still scowling, still rocking back on his heels. "Got bad news for ya, Private. Your loafin' days are over. Put that thing somewhere safe, and get your ass over to the infirmary. The doc needs ya."

I'm still looking at my purple heart. It's got a bust of George Washington on it. It's kind of pretty, but I wonder why it's got old George on it. Was he the first one to get wounded in a war?

"Move, soldier!" says the lieutenant. His hoarse, booze-colored voice is harsh, but I can tell he's not really all that pissed off at me. "And don't try to feed me any of that wounded bullshit. Your little cut is about all healed up, and you know it. We got real wounded coming in. Litters full of 'em. They're being hand carried in from the jungle because the choppers can't get up in this weather. Something's going on out there, and we must be the closest outpost. So move it. The doc asked for you."

I say, "All right, all right. I'm coming."

The lieutenant leaves, and while I get dressed, I'm wondering why Eric asked for me. It surprises me, and I feel kind of flattered by it. He must think more of me than the rest of them do.

I go out and slosh over to the infirmary, holding my poncho over my head. I go down the tunnel into Doc Eric's partly-underground, sandbag-protected infirmary tent. It's dark inside except for one fairly bright light above the metal examination table. Eric has his back to me. He's working on a big guy, and I can see from what's left of the guy's uniform that he's a Marine. What would a Marine be doing around here? The guy's chest looks all torn up. His eyes are closed, and he's groaning, throwing his head back and forth. It looks like he's only semi-conscious. His face is covered by what looks like a mixture of blood and mud, and the doc hasn't bothered to wipe it off. The raw meat look of the Marine's chest and all the blood pooling up on the metal examination table makes me feel like throwing up. I have the strong urge to turn around and get the hell out of here.

Doc Eric doesn't look at me, but he says, "Get over here and help me. I can't get this guy's damn clutch belt off."

I edge around to the other side of the examination table, trying not to think about the bloody mess I'm seeing; it's hard to believe that mess used to be this Marine's chest. I see the problem with the belt right away: the marine's belt clasp has been bent all to hell by whatever hit him. The metal of the clasp is partly embedded in his stomach.

Eric nods toward a metal cabinet. "Go over there and get some scissors or something. See if you can pry it loose."

I do as he says and in the top drawer, among a mess of silver instruments, I find a fairly strong-looking pair of scissors with rounded tips. I bring the scissors back and say, "This?"

"Whatever. Just see if you can get it loose. Hurry up."

Eric cuts away the rest of the Marine's shirt. There are ragged little holes all over his chest and stomach, and blood is oozing out of every one of them. He must have taken a direct hit by shrapnel. I wonder if the guy walked into the same kind of booby-trap the Polack did.

The doc is probing at the Marine's chest with a pointed metal instrument. Using a magnifying glass, he's digging out ragged little pieces of metal. I saw those torn-up enemy bodies we had to bury, but this is worse because this is a real, still-alive person. But how can this guy still be alive? His chest looks like extra-bloody raw hamburger, with thick white noodles mixed in. I have the horrifying thought that those white noodles might be some of his intestines coming out. I have to look away. It's too much to see a real human body all torn up like that. What if the Polack hadn't been in front of me when that booby-trap went off? I would probably look like this.

The doc looks up at me for the first time. "You're not gonna faint, are you? We don't have time for fainting. Get that damn belt loose."

I take a deep breath and start trying to get the belt clasp undone. I can't pry too hard because every time I push down, the sharp edge of the torn-up metal just digs deeper into the guy's stomach. Blood oozes out around it, and I do start to feel woozy. I grab the edge of the table.

"Sit down in that chair," says Eric, pointing with his bloody instrument. "Put your head down between your knees."

I do as he says, and pretty soon the wooziness fades. To keep from looking at the torn-up Marine, I look at the floor.

Eric gets impatient with me. "Come on, come on. Suck it up."

I get up and go back to work on the buckle, this time trying to focus on the metal and not on the flesh it's digging into. But my hands are so bloody they're all slippery, and I can't keep a good grip on the scissors.

"Aw, forget it," says Eric. "This guy's D-O-W anyhow."

"D-O-W? What does that mean?"

Eric shrugs. "Dead of wounds. Or dying of wounds. Take your pick. Help me move him." He nods toward a dark corner of the room.

"You're giving up on him?"

"He's all but gone. Help me put him on the floor over there."

I hesitate. The Marine doesn't look dead. He's still moving his jaw, like he's talking in his sleep. So why is Eric giving up on him? I say, "Do we have to? I mean, it feels like we're just, I don't know, dumping him."

Eric looks toward the doorway. "They've got others laid out in the lieutenant's office. They're doing tourniquets and such over there. We need to bring in the next one. Grab this guy's feet."

I grab the Marine's feet, and Eric gets ahold under his armpits. We lift him off the table, but he's such a big guy, Eric loses his grip and lets the guy fall. It's his head that hits the dirt floor first. The Marine doesn't react. Maybe he really is dead.

"Shit," says Eric. "Let's just drag him."

We get ahold of his feet and drag him off into a corner.

Then, Eric runs out the door. Where is he going? What am I supposed to do now? I'm left kneeling next to the Marine. I wish we hadn't put the guy down on this dirt floor. It just doesn't seem right. But the doc said he was D-O-W, so maybe it doesn't matter. He really does look dead now. I notice my hands are covered in blood, this guy's blood. Not very long ago, he was alive, and this blood on my hands was inside him, doing its job, going around in his veins. I wonder why he was in this area. Was he on some kind of special ops mission? From the looks of this guy, there must be some heavy shit going on out there in the jungle tonight. Does it mean Charlie is moving into this area? Is that why those enemy soldiers we buried were scouting out this base? Is our so-called "peaceful" period over?

I sit down on the floor next to the Marine and wait for Eric to come back. The only sound is the rain outside. Otherwise, it's quiet and dark with only the one light over the bloody examination table. For the first time, I notice how dirty the place is. Somebody has painted the words "EXTRA MEDICAL CRAP" in white spray paint on the front of a rusty gray metal cabinet, but the paint was sprayed on too thick and some of it ran down under every letter. There's a lot of junk piled in the corner next to that cabinet. My mind is telling me a person shouldn't have to die in such a dirty place. I look toward the doorway. I wish Eric would come back. It's very quiet in the infirmary, and I keep hearing a strange little sound. It almost seems to be coming from the Marine. I lean closer to him. There it is again, a soft little whistle. It comes, then stops, then comes again. The sound seems to be coming out of his chest. I hold my hand out over his chest and feel something cool against the damp blood on my hands. There's air coming out of the Marine's chest. It means he's still alive! I stand up. Should I run to get Eric? Air coming out of the Marine's chest means he's not dead Or does it? Maybe air coming out is some kind of involuntary thing people do after they die. Eric said he was dead, or about to be, and Eric should know. I kneel back down next to the Marine again and hold my hand close to his chest. I can feel it very clearly, a slight puff of air, so faint I probably wouldn't even have noticed it if my hands weren't wet with his blood.

Eric comes back in leading two big GIs who are carrying another wounded man. They drop the new patient on the table and go out.

I call to Eric, "He's still alive. There's air coming out of his chest."

But Eric has already gone to work on the new guy. "Leave him alone. We gotta try to save this one."

"But there's air coming out of his chest. In puffs. I can feel it."

Eric still won't look at me. I can't believe it. The Marine is still alive, and Doc Eric is telling me to leave him lying here in the dirt. I can't do that. "Eric, help me. What should I do?"

Eric won't answer me. He won't even look at me. He's doing something to the new wounded guy who's groaning and trying to push Eric's hands away.

"What does it mean, Eric? At least tell me that. What does air coming out of his chest mean?"

"It means his lungs have been punctured. It means he won't last long. Now come over here and help me."

I stare at the Marine. If Eric is right, shouldn't I at least stay with him so he doesn't have to die all by himself? Maybe he knows I'm here with him. I've heard that people who are unconscious can actually hear some of what is going on in the room around them. I try to brush away some of the blackened stuff that's stuck to his chest. But it won't go away. It's not dirt; it must be flesh, or shirt material that's been burned right into his flesh. My mind is still having trouble comprehending such horrible damage to a human being. I lean down close to him. I can still hear the soft whistle. And there's something else: a little bubble of blood, so small you'd hardly notice it if you weren't looking close.

"There's a little bubble!" I yell. "On his chest. A bubble. It means he's still trying to breathe. Can't we do something for him? Maybe you should make the hole bigger so he can breath better."

"Won't work," says Eric. "You can't breath through a hole in your chest. Not for long anyhow. A lot of the shrapnel penetrated his lungs."

"But what if I plug up the holes with my fingers? Then won't he be able to breathe through his mouth?"

Eric won't look at me. He says, "Give it up, Scotty. He's gone. We have to focus on the ones we might be able to save."

"Can't you at least give him a shot of morphine?"

Eric glances back at me and frowns. "Give him some if you want to, but didn't you see what was on his forehead?"

I look down at the Marine's face and see some smears of blood just above his right eye. It looks like finger painting. "What is it?"

"It's an M," says Eric. "Or supposed to be." He turns toward me and draws an M in the air with his finger. "Somebody used his blood to draw an M on his forehead. It's to warn us they already put at least one syrette into him. Look in his pants pocket. I saw a pack in there."

I do as he says and find a torn-open pack of tube-like things. "It's been opened, but there are still four in there."

"It was a six-pack. Means he's probably already had two."

"Jesus, do they let these guys carry their own morphine?"

"Special forces guys do. In case they get separated."

I realize what it means: it means these guys know there's a good chance they'll get wounded, and there will be no medic there to help them. I stare at the Marine's face. He looks calm now. I guess Eric is right; he's going to die. But you can tell he was a real warrior when he was alive. I wonder how men like this Marine can go so willingly into combat when they know there's a good chance they'll be wounded, and maybe even killed. Maybe they don't think about it. Maybe they just think it's their job, so they do it. They just saddle up and go out into the jungle, remembering to put a good supply of morphine in their pockets. As I look at this dying Marine, I'm hit with the absolute awareness that I'm nothing like him, and never will be.

I glance over at Eric. He's working on the new guy.

"So I can't give him any more?"

"He's a goner anyhow. You can pop him another one if you want."

"It won't be too much for his system to take?"

Eric finally turns to face me. "Listen, Scotty, like I said, it won't matter. Nothing is ever gonna matter to that guy again."

I can't stop looking at the Marine's chest. The little bubble of blood is fascinating: it rises, hesitates, then goes back down again.

"If you're gonna do it, just do it," yells Eric. "I need you over here."

I remember when Eric injected morphine into me, it made me less afraid. Maybe it will do the same for this guy, if he's still even a little bit aware of himself. I decide to do it. I pop open one of the syrettes. It looks like a small tube of toothpaste. I pull off the cap. There's a hypodermic type needle sticking out of one end. I take a deep breath and jab the needle into the Marine's arm. He doesn't react at all. Now, I guess I'm supposed to squeeze the tube to get the morphine into him. Do I really want to do this? In my wildest dreams, I would never have imagined myself squeezing morphine into a person. I squeeze the tube. There, it's done. It wasn't hard, almost too easy. I look at the Marine's face. It hasn't changed. His eyes are still closed, and he didn't react at all. Maybe I didn't do it right. I look at his chest and wait for the little bubble to appear. It does. It grows, shrinks back down, and is gone. I hope the morphine helped him. Maybe he *will* make it, no matter what Doc Eric says. I wait for the bubble to appear again, but it seems to be taking too long this time. I hold my breath, waiting for it. The bubble doesn't come. Oh no, did that morphine do something to keep him from breathing? I keep watching, hoping the little bubble will come back. I desperately want it to come again; it was the only indication I had that he was still alive. It was like a silent message to me: I'm alive, help me. But the bubble doesn't come. Frantically, I push down on his chest. It's so torn up, his chest feels all soft and squishy, not solid at all like a big man's chest should be. But I keep pushing. My pushing is squeezing a lot of blood out of his chest, and my hands are getting entirely covered in his blood. But that doesn't matter. I have to keep trying. I really, really want to see that bubble again. I let up and then push down again, but no bubble comes. It's not working. Does it mean he's dead? Did I kill him by giving him too much morphine? I have a sudden memory of pushing down on the chest of that kid under the dice table. I couldn't save that kid, and I'm starting to realize I can't save this Marine either. It makes me feel weak, powerless. People die, and I can't do a damn thing about it. I put my head down on the bloody hamburger mess that used to be his chest to listen for breathing, or a heartbeat—anything that might indicate a live human being is inside there. But there's nothing. I sit up and look at his face. His eyes are open now, staring at nothing.

I turn to Eric. "Damn, Doc, I don't think I should have given him that morphine. I think I killed him."

"Fine," says Eric. "Now get over here before we lose this one too."

I stand up and take one last look at the dead Marine. Would he have made it through the night if I hadn't given him too much morphine? Why did it have to be me that gave him the morphine? I'm not a medic. It's not my job to save people. I never even wanted to be a soldier in the first place. All I wanted to do was to go to college and take one lousy philosophy class. I wanted to learn about things. A part of me that's hidden way down deep wants to blame Brent for this. He's the one who talked me into signing up. But I shake off that thought. I know it's my own damn fault. I knew I was about to get drafted, but I didn't know what to do about it. So I went along with Brent's crazy plan and signed up. Why do I keep thinking about it? Waste of time. I go to help Eric.

He's got the guy's shirt cut away, and he's probing at his abdomen.

I go to the other side of the table. "What do you want me to do?"

"Use the cotton. Clean up some of the blood so I can see."

There's so much blood on the guy's stomach, I can't even tell what kind of wounds he has. I pull a big wad of cotton out of the box and use it to mop as much of the blood away as I can. Turns out, there's only one wound, a neat little hole in the lower part of the guy's stomach. He seems to be unconscious now. This one is also a Marine, but very young. He doesn't even look old enough to be a soldier. He's got a tattoo on his upper arm. It's a red heart, with the name Carla on one side of the heart and the name Bill on the other. So this is Bill, I think to myself, combat soldier Bill, lying with a bullet hole in his gut on a bloody metal table in a tiny remote outpost in the western part of Vietnam. What will Carla think when she hears what happened?

The boy opens his eyes and looks at me, then closes them again. It happens so fast I'm not sure I really saw it. They stay shut for only a few seconds, and then they fly open and stay that way. It happens so suddenly, it startles me. I step back. I look at Eric, but he doesn't seem surprised. I say, "His eyes are open. Does it mean he's dead?"

"Not yet," says Eric. He glances at me. "Hey, you've got blood on your face. What were you doing over there?"

I touch my face. "I had my ear down on his chest. I was listening to see if he was breathing." I look back toward the Marine, and again I feel bad that he has to lie there alone on the dirt floor. Why couldn't they have at least put down some wood, or a tarp, or something?

Eric glances at the dead Marine. "You did your best, Scotty, but he's dead, so now it's time for us to try to help this one. Pay attention."

I look at poor Bill. His eyes are still wide open. I say, "He looks deader than the Marine."

"Yeah, but he's not. When they're in really deep shock, they sometimes look like this."

With his eyes open, it feels like Bill is looking at me, like he's judging me for what I did to that Marine. I wish Eric would at least try to push the kid's eyelids closed, but I guess there wouldn't be any point to that.

Eric uses the hemostat he's holding to point at the guy's wound. "It's a T-and-T. Right in the middle of his gut."

"T and T?"

"Yeah. Through and through. Bullet went in the front and right out the back. So far, I've only found two holes in him, a little teeny one in the front and a bigger one in the back. He might make it."

"Really?"

"Yeah. Sometimes they survive a T-and-T. If he's lucky. Not much important stuff to hit in there, as long as it misses his spine. And as long as it's below his lungs and kidneys and such. Better in the gut than the head, eh?" He laughs a short sharp-edged laugh.

I've never heard Doc Eric make a joke before. At least it's sort of a joke. His laugh seemed bitter, even angry. I watch him work. I wonder where he's from. He's not an officer, so he can't be a doctor. Maybe he was a medical student or something before he got sent to Vietnam. He's working so hard on the guy, I feel like he's all but forgotten me. But then he hands me the scissors. "Cut off his pants and his underpants," he says. Let's see if we can find any more wounds. Never know what else we'll find once we start looking."

I try to cut away the GI's pants, but it's not easy. The thick blood-soaked material doesn't want to cut. I finally get a cut in the cloth and find it's easier to just tear away the rest. When I cut off the guy's underpants, I discover he's got another rose tattoo on his upper thigh, close to his crotch. The name Bill again, on one side, but a different name, Molly, on the other side. I wonder if Carla knows about Molly.

Eric says, "Get me some more cotton."

I go to the cabinet and find a box of cotton balls. I bring it back to Eric. He reaches in with his forceps and pulls out a big gob of them. He starts dabbing at the blood coming out of the soldier's stomach wound. The guy's eyes are closed now.

"Are you sure he's not dead?"

Eric shakes his head. "Naw, he's still with us, but his body's shut down. When the trauma to the body is bad enough, it just shuts down."

"But you think he might make it?"

"It's possible." He stares at the kid's face. "But not likely. He's probably bleeding inside."

"Are you sure?" I ask, and then I realize it probably sounds like I'm pleading. "I mean, how can you be sure?"

Eric shrugs. "I've seen 'em pull through with T-and-T stomach wounds like this, especially if the bullet goes through clean. This kid's wound is low enough it might have missed his lungs." He stops dabbing at the blood long enough to look up at me. "If you ever plan to get shot, get it right there. He uses the wad of bloody cotton at the end of the forceps to point at Bill's wound. Maybe it was supposed to be another one of his grim jokes, but he's not smiling, so I'm not sure.

"I'll try to do that," I say. "Are you going to operate on him?"

He looks up at me. He seems surprised at my question. "Me? I'm no surgeon. Do you see any bars on my collar? If I was a surgeon, do you think I'd be in a shithole place like this? Naw, I'm just a corpsman. All I can do is try to hold 'em together until they chopper them out to somebody who knows what he's doing."

"Can't you stitch up the bullet holes or something?"

"No time. We got others waiting. Besides, it wouldn't do any good. He'll still be bleeding inside. Might as well stitch up his asshole."

"Oh. Uh, is that where the blood will come out?"

"Sooner or later."

"So there's nothing else we can do for him?"

"Here's what I do. Watch this." He unwraps a couple of little bullet-shaped things and sticks them into Bill's two wound holes.

"What are those things?"

He grins at me. "Tampons."

"Tampons?"

"Yeah, women's tampons. They'll expand and fill up the holes. Stop the external bleeding until we can get him choppered back to a real hospital. Learned it from another medic who'd seen a lot of combat."

"Weird."

Eric shrugs. "Whatever works, man. He nods toward where the dead Marine is lying on the dirt floor. "Help me put this guy down over there. If he hangs on, we'll try to get a Medivac in to fly him out."

"And if he dies?"

"Then they'll fly 'em both directly to Bien Hoa.

"Bien Hoa? So it's true. There really is a hanger X there?"

He looks up at me. "Hanger X? So you've heard that one too." He shakes his head. "It's not a hanger, but there is a building at Bien Hoa where they get cleaned up before they ship 'em out. It's also used for training purposes. It's where I did my final training when I got here."

Training? Do they use the dead bodies to practice on?

We try to lift Bill off the table, but he's almost as heavy as the Marine. Eric decides to go out and get help.

He hurries out the door, leaving me to stare at poor Bill. His face looks dead, but he does seem to be breathing, a little.

Doc Eric is back quick with a big, dull-eyed fellow I recognize. He's one of the poker players in the mess tent poker game. He has a big lump of something inside his cheek, probably tobacco.

Eric puts down a stained blanket next to the Marine and tells the guy to help me put Bill on it. After we do it, Eric wraps the blanket around Bill and tells me to go with the guy to carry in the next one.

"Ain't no more," says the carrier. His teeth are the color of tobacco. He shifts the wad of tobacco over to the other side of his cheek and stares at Bill's naked body. Is he looking at Bill's tattoos?

Eric points toward the doorway. "There were two more in the lieutenant's hooch. I saw 'em."

"Died," says the carrier, shifting his tobacco back to it's original place. He turns to look toward the door, as if he wants to get out of there as quick as he can. It makes me wonder if the big poker game is still going on in the mess tent.

"Both of them?" asks Eric.

"Yeah," says the guy. He's still keeping his eyes on the doorway.

Eric waves him away, and the guy leaves quickly.

"How 'bout that," says Eric. "We get a break. Won't last long though. I bet they'll be bringing in more soon. You hungry? Let's go get something to eat while we can."

I shake my head. I can't even imagine eating right now.

"You sure? This may be your only chance tonight."

I shake my head again.

"Okay. You baby sit gut-shot Billy boy over there. I'll bring you back something you can eat later."

"What do I do for him?"

"Just make sure if he starts spittin' up blood, he doesn't choke on it."

"How do I stop that?"

"You don't. Just roll him up on his side, so the blood will run out."

"Shouldn't we put him back on the table?"

"Naw, if he wakes up he might start floppin' around and fall off. He's better off on the floor where he is."

He puts on his poncho and goes out, leaving me alone with the dead Marine and double-tattooed Bill.

I sit down on the ground between them. The Marine does look completely dead now. I stare at him wondering why people look like that after they're dead. It's not just that his eyes are open, as if he's staring up at the ceiling, there's also something very dead about his face now, like the caring has gone out of it, like the flesh of his face itself has given up. Right after he died, he didn't look much different than when he was alive, but now that he's been dead for a while, his face seems to have lost something. It's humanness, I guess. There's something about the deadness of his face that scares me. A tough guy like that, a guy who fought so hard to stay alive, and now he looks like a useless sack of bones and flesh, empty of whatever made him who he was. It reminds me of something I read in my philosophy book. A philosopher named Sartre described death as only another witness to the absurdity of human existence. When I read that, I wasn't sure what he meant, but now, seeing this dead Marine, I think I understand. This man must have wanted to be alive, like anybody else, but he put himself in a situation where he knew he might die. Did he think about death? If so, did he think his death would be absurd? I stare at the M-shaped smear of blood on his forehead. Who knows how much morphine he had in him. I shouldn't have given him that extra shot. He was a tough guy. Maybe he would have made it through 'til morning if I hadn't done that. Now I'm going to have to live with that for the rest of my life. I have to turn away from the Marine. I look at Bill. At least this one is still breathing. Maybe death *is* absurd, like that Sartre guy said, but some can get shot and not die. Bill got shot T and T, but he's still alive, at least for now.

Suddenly, there's a loud explosion outside, very close. I involuntarily duck, but then I feel dumb for doing it. Ducking isn't going to save me. It was a mortar. The damn mortar shooters have come back, rain or no rain. I wonder if it has anything to do with the wounded men they're bringing in from the jungle. Maybe this is the start of the "real" attack everybody has been waiting for.

Eric comes sprinting back in and slides down the muddy tunnel like a surfer. "Man, that was close!" he yells. "Did you hear that one? It was right over on the other side of the next hooch. If the sandbags hadn't taken most of the blast, I mighta bought the farm."

"Did anybody get hit?"

"Don't know. But we'll know soon enough if they start dragging 'em in here." He hangs up his wet poncho and comes to sit on the floor next to me. I'm glad he does that because maybe it means he thinks the floor is the safest place to be during a mortar attack.

Another explosion, farther down the hill this time, then another. I bet the poker players are sprinting out of that mess tent and getting themselves back to their hooches. Or maybe not. Maybe they're so caught up in the gambling they won't stop, like those gamblers at Wong's wouldn't stop to help that hurt kid under the dice table. More explosions, all farther down the hill. The mortar shooters are firing faster than normal tonight. Or maybe it's more than one mortar team. Now I'm sure something *is* going on out there tonight. I hope the guys on perimeter guard duty are watching. And I hope the Claymores are still functional, despite all the rain. Eric and I are both silent, both staring up at the tent roof. I know what he's thinking: what are the odds of one of those mortars hitting our particular roof? But the next explosion is even farther down the hill. The mortar shooters are not honing in very well tonight. Maybe it's because of the rain.

Eric looks at me and shrugs. He reaches into his pocket and pulls out a handful of uncooked wieners. He hands me a couple. I take them without thinking about how blood-covered my hands are. I'm hungry, but looking at them, I decide against it. I'd pretty sure I'd throw up if I tried to eat cold raw hot dogs right now. I stick them in my jacket pocket. Maybe later.

Eric munches away on his own handful of wieners. "All they had left," he mumbles, his mouth full. "Bunch of poker players over there eating up everything."

I look at the dead Marine and say, "I wonder if maybe guys like him know when they're going to die."

Eric glances at the dead Marine. "He must have known there was a good chance. On a lurp, I bet. Wonder what he was doing in this area."

"What's a lurp?" I ask.

He stuffs another hot dog in his mouth. "Longrange reconis patrol."

His mouth is so full of hot dogs, it just about merges into one word, but I assume he meant long range reconnaissance patrol.

He somehow swallows the whole mouthful of wieners, puts a hand to his chest, burps, and says, "Small groups. They go out into the jungle to ferret out enemy activity." He shakes his head. "Can you imagine it? Bein' out there at night in the jungle? In this rain? Spooky guys, those lurps. Adrenaline junkies, I bet." He hesitates, and then adds, "But I shouldn't say that. Who knows?" He goes back to eating wieners.

I'm getting new respect for Doc Eric. With his wide gap between his two front teeth and ears that stick out too far to the sides, he may look like a baby-faced kid fresh out of school, but he seems to know more about what's going on in this war than anybody else I've met so far. "Have you been out there with them? Lurp groups like that?"

Eric laughs his short little laugh again, and shoves the last wiener into his mouth. "You kidding? I've been out on lots of patrols, every patrol the LT sends out, but not with those types." He nods toward the dead Marine. "These guys are in a whole different world. They live for combat. When they come in here with wounds, sometimes they've doped themselves up so much on morphine they get to talking. In fact, they often talk quite a bit while I'm patching 'em up. I guess as long as I'm the one patching them up, I get to be their shrink too. Or as close as they're gonna get to something like a shrink out here. I listen to 'em and try to imagine if the things they're telling me could really be true. If you didn't see the tired looks on their faces and hear the flat way they tell it, you'd think it was all bullshit, like they're sayin' look at me, I'm a hero. But a lot of it is not bullshit. They think the risk of getting hurt is part of their job, what they were trained to do."

Eric stops talking, but I want to know more. "Do they talk about . . . like, killing people?"

"Sure. They talk about all the people they've killed like it's just another day's work. They talk about the number of times they've been wounded as if they're talking about somebody else, about somebody else's body. I pay attention enough to learn their lingo so I can impress newbies like you." Eric grins at me.

"Okay," I say. "I'm impressed."

Eric waves my comment off. He looks away and stares at the doorway. I wonder what he's thinking about. I look down at the dead Marine, trying to imagine him out there in the jungle killing people. How does somebody become like that? I say, "Back in Basic, they didn't tell us hardly anything about Vietnam."

Eric gets a chuckle out of that. "Well, at least they weren't lying to you. Me, I'm not even supposed to be here."

"You didn't want to be a medic?"

He starts to answer, but then he hesitates and looks away.

"Did I say something wrong? Shouldn't I have asked?"

Eric shrugs. "It's okay. No point talking about it though. Doesn't matter anymore. We're here now, aren't we? Whether we like it or not."

I wish he'd say more, but Bill starts moaning, and Eric reaches over to take the morphine syrettes out of the Marine's pocket. He pulls the cap off of one of them and shoots Bill up.

The young soldier's eyes fly open as if he's scared. Eric pushes them closed, and I'm happy to see that this time they stay closed.

Eric sits back against the wall and yawns. I wonder how longs it's been since he slept.

I ask, "What does it take to become a medic?"

He shrugs and seems to be thinking about it. I'm learning that his shrug is one of his main ways to communicate. "Not much. Just the willingness to do it. In other words, being dumb enough to do it." He laughs his short little laugh again. I'm getting to know that laugh as well as his shrug. That little laugh means he's thinking about something ironic. "After Basic Training, they sent me to medic training in Texas. Ten weeks. We listened to a lot of lectures, watched movies, and gave each other shots of saline. We learned to stick IVs in each other. That sucked. Some of 'em never did learn to do it right. Hurt like hell when they couldn't find a vein. But we never saw a real patient, not one. Just pictures of wounds and such. Told us what to do about bullet wounds, but we never saw a real wound. Only pictures."

He goes quiet, so I ask, "That's it?"

"Yep. Pictures and practicing on each other. Oh, and lectures about things like seizures. Lot of good that did us."

"You took care of my leg wound pretty good."

He grins. "What you might call on-the-job training. I've actually learned quite a bit since I got here." He shrugs again. "Pretty basic stuff. Cuts and scrapes. Stitches and salve. Try to get 'em to take their quinine pills so they don't get malaria, even if it does give 'em the runs. But if somebody gets seriously wounded, not much I can do for him out here. Swab out the wounds, pick out the shrapnel, wait for the choppers to come haul him away. But if a guy comes in here with something serious, like advanced trench foot? Nothin' I do is gonna help him."

"I've heard a lot of talk about trench foot, but I haven't seen any."

He nods, a grim look on his face. "Well, you will, now that the rainy season has started. Immersion foot is the official name. Bad news, that. Once that shit gets going in the tissues of your foot, you can lose toes. They'll send you out to a hospital ship off the coast while you recover, and then you might even get a month's leave in Japan before you go limping home. Been a problem for soldiers in just about every war. Just about wiped out Napoleon's army during their retreat from Russia."

His comment about Napoleon makes me realize how much I'm enjoying talking to him. Even though I've been crammed into a hooch with three other GIs, I guess I've been feeling lonely. They hardly every talk to me, and the lieutenant is usually too busy to bother with me.

"But I'm not about to cut off a guy's toes. They didn't teach us anything like that. Hell, I only learned how to suture after I got to Bien Hoa. They had me stitching up wounds on dead guys before they sent 'em home. Got to do a few practice tracheotomies there too, but the guys were already dead, so I'm not sure I even did it right."

We sit there in silence for a while until I ask, "So, did you want to be a doctor? Were you a medical student or something?"

Eric laughs his short bitter laugh again. "A medical student? That's a laugh. I didn't want to be anything special, not really. I was just a kid who went to college because I didn't know what else to do. Majored in psych because I didn't understand people. Didn't even understand myself. Then I got drafted, like everybody else."

The howitzers at the upper end of the camp start going off. I hadn't even realized the mortar shooters had stopped. We sit there staring up at the ceiling as the howitzers continue to blast away into the night. We remain silent, listening, knowing it won't last long. Sure enough, they soon stop. The artillery crew probably didn't like being out there in the rain. Besides, everybody knows there's no point to it: the mortar shooters are long gone.

Eric looks down at poor Bill. Then, he turns to me. "Well, if we're gonna sit around here jawboning, how about we have a smoke? I hear you came in with a stash of some really good stuff. Give me a joint, and I'll tell you my whole damn story."

I fish two joints out of my pocket and hand one of them to him. I take out the counterfeit Zippo lighter I bought in Saigon and light us both up. While he sucks in the smoke, I say, "You don't have to tell me."

He holds the smoke in for as long as he can, then lets out a little as he whispers, "I don't mind. I haven't told anybody else, but what the hell." He lets out the rest of the smoke. "It's in my record, so maybe the lieutenant already knows. Truth is, I had just finished my second year of college when I got drafted. I tried to appeal. Tried to get a college deferment. But they said, no way. So I told 'em I wouldn't go. They said, why not? I said I didn't want to shoot anybody. They said, fine, you'll go to prison. I said, okay, better prison than killing people. That's when they took me into a back room and offered me a deal. You already got two years of college done, they said. We can make you a medic. Smart kid like you. You can stay right here in the good old USA and be a medic. Train others maybe. Help people. That sounded pretty good to me, so I signed on the dotted line. They hustled me through that rinky-dink medic's training program down there in Texas, and whoops, next thing I knew they were telling me it was time to pack up and head for Vietnam. The war is heating up, they said. More and more Americans are getting wounded. We need medics. No way, I said. I'm not goin' over there. You'll be working in a nice safe hospital, they said. You'll be helping wounded fellows your own age. Like a fool, I believed them."

He stops talking long enough to take another drag off of the joint. "So here I am, smack in the middle of the jungle. They suckered me, but I guess it turned out okay. I'm not sorry about it now. Once I got here, I saw maybe I really *could* help. It was either help out being a medic, or go to prison where I wouldn't be any help to anybody."

I say, "You are needed here, Doc. You're all these men have." I nod toward Bill. "Bill there would probably be dead if it wasn't for you."

Eric grunts and looks away. "I can't do anything for him. He probably won't make it through the night." He concentrates on smoking his joint. Finally, he glances over at me. "If you don't mind, I'd rather you didn't mention any of this to anybody else."

I quickly say, "I won't. Who would I tell? Nobody talks to me."

He squints, blinks, and waves away some of the smoke. "Even so, maybe I shouldn't have told you."

"You can trust me."

"I figured I could. Otherwise, I wouldn't have said anything. It's just that some of the guys here are kind of . . . you know, gung-ho. They wouldn't understand me refusing the draft. I really do want to be of some help here if I can, so it's important that they trust me."

I can't think of anything to say to that so we just sit there. Then, he starts telling me about his hometown, Bloomington, Indiana. The strong marijuana seems to have loosened up his tongue even more. He rambles on about what a shitty town Bloomington, Indiana is. "But they got some really cute girls there," he says. "Problem is, they're so damn religious in southern Indiana it's hard to talk any of them into bed."

We both get a good laugh out of that, and I decide to tell him a little bit about growing up in Illinois, about how my mother moved us to Arizona after my father got killed. I even tell him about the frozen river, about how I fell through the ice, and how Brent and I had to work together to survive. "Brent and I have been pals ever since," I say. "He kind of . . . you know, watches over me. Thinks he has to protect me. Blood brothers, kind of."

"Because you saved him from dying in that river. Makes sense."

"No, it's . . . more than that. His little brother had been run over by a car not long before that day at the frozen river. Brent was supposed to be watching him. He's been guilty about it his whole life."

"So you became the little brother?"

He's staring at me, and I start to feel like I'm giving away too much information, like I'm betraying secrets that should only be known to Brent and me. I duplicate Eric's type of quick shrug and say, "Well, he was always the tough guy, and I . . . wasn't. So he did sort of act like my big brother."

"Makes sense, what with your father getting killed when you were just a little kid. Sounds like you both needed each other."

Was he right? I'd never thought about my friendship with Brent having something to do with my not having a father while I was growing up. I'm not feeling very comfortable with where this conversation is going, but it's been so long since I've had anybody to talk to, I go on. "I guess. The truth is after my father got killed, I didn't have much of a mother either. She turned . . . kind of . . . inward. Pretty much ignored me, so I got to do whatever I wanted. And Brent wasn't the type to let his parents tell him anything, so most of the time, we were on our own. We mostly hung out in a big old auto junkyard his father owned. It was out at the edge of town. Nobody else around."

"Sounds like he really was like a brother. Wish I would have had a brother. All I had was two older sisters. They either ignored me or teased me to make me cry."

"It was Brent that talked me into joining up. To avoid the draft. He had this big idea that if we joined up we could avoid getting sent here. You should have heard his stories. He claimed we'd get sent to someplace nice. Like Florida. He talked about girls in bikinis. Lying on the beach. Stuff like that." I do another one of Eric's shrugs. "As you can see, it didn't exactly work out like that."

Eric chuckles. "I'd like to meet this Brent character sometime."

I say, "Maybe you will. If you ever get leave to go down to Saigon, go to a place called Wong's Bar. Ask anybody where it is. It's in the off-limits zone. Tell Brent I sent you, and he'll fix you up with whatever you want. Beautiful girls. All the pot you want. Just tell him I said so."

Eric grins and slaps me on the back. "Damn. That sounds good. Wong's Bar, eh. Don't you wish we were there right now?"

I think about my storyteller girl and admit that I do.

We hear a chopper coming in, and I notice for the first time it's starting to get light outside.

Eric jumps up. "They're here. Medivac. Rain must have let up." He kneels down next to Bill and feels the side of his throat. "A pulse. Damn, this kid is still kickin'. How about that? Might make it after all. I'll go get a couple of guys to carry him to the chopper." He runs out.

I look down at poor Bill. He's still unconscious, and he looks kind of gray. Maybe that's what they look like when they're losing blood inside themselves. I hope Eric is right about him having a chance. Maybe if they get Bill back to Saigon in time, they'll do surgery on his insides and he'll pull through. Maybe he'll even eventually make it back to the states. If he does, I bet Carla and Molly will be really happy to see him.

16

Even If God Exists

The rain hardly ever stops, and I can tell you one thing: you notice rain a lot more when you're out in it, humping along, hour after hour, getting soaked by it. The reason I'm out in the rain is because Doc Eric did the worst thing he could do to me: he told the lieutenant I did a great job helping him with that batch of wounded troops that came in. The next morning, the lieutenant called me in to his office and gave me a rah-rah, good-going-son talk. Said he was reassigning me. From now on, I'm assigned to stay with Eric and help him. So even though I'm supposed to be laid up and am officially—I emphasize, officially—designated as "on profile" (wounded), I've been spending all my time at the infirmary helping Doc Eric. And then yesterday, I found out I'd have to go out as the medic's assistant whenever Eric goes out on patrol. So here I am, out in the rain, with a big heavy medical supply pack on my back, on my first patrol as a medic's assistant. We're chasing after the mortar shooters who once again came to throw a few miss-aimed mortars at us during the night.

We're trudging through the jungle, the rain beating down loud on the hood of my poncho, chasing an enemy who I sure hope we don't find. It's fairly cool in the jungle, but I'm carrying the heavy M5 pack, and with the hood of my poncho up, it makes it so hot inside I'm soaked with sweat. The grasses and weeds underfoot are so thick I can't tell what I might be stepping on, and remembering what happened to the Polack, that makes me very nervous. Eric said not to step on anything that looks "unusual," but how am I supposed to know what is unusual? He also said to watch out for the dreaded deadly Krait snake because the rain brings them out. "They call it the two-step snake 'cause if it bites you, you'll be lucky to make it two more steps before you fall down dead." I hope he was just trying to scare me.

Squad Leader Carl is up ahead, pushing the pace. Before we left camp, he put Eric and me in the middle of the long line. Eric gave me a thumbs up and said, "Middle position. Safest place to be. You never want to be up front. If we make contact, the ones up front will be the first to get it. And don't lag behind either. The enemy might be following us. I've heard stories about the last guy in line just disappearing."

I plan on staying right where I am, in the middle position.

As we start up a hill, the guy behind me says, "You're Scotty, the philosopher, right?"

I look back. It's a light skinned black guy, a spec-4 rifleman I've never talked to directly, but we've been on sandbagging duty together.

"Yeah, that's me."

"Hey, put it there, Scotty. I'm the Monday Man." He reaches forward to shake my hand.

"Why do they call you that?" I ask, but then I wonder if maybe I'm not supposed to ask a black man about things like that. There wasn't a single black person in the school I went to back in Illinois because we lived on the south side of town and black people were not allowed to live in that area. And when we moved to Arizona, the few blacks that were in my school pretty much kept to themselves.

But the Monday Man doesn't seem to mind my question. He says, "Oh, it goes back a long ways. Chicago. We all had nicknames."

I say, "Chicago? When I was a kid, I lived down in Springfield."

He claps me on the back. "So we're both Illinoisers. Hey, I drove through Springfield one time on my way to St. Louis. Looked like a nice town. Bet it wasn't like Chicago, was it?"

"Uh, I've never been to Chicago."

"Never been to Shy? Man, you haven't lived. Cool town. Cool music. But plenty tough, though. Ever heard of Englewood?"

I shake my head.

"Tough neighborhood. Damn tough. So tough the cops take out their guns and put 'em on the seat when they drive through there."

I say, "Really?"

"Damn right. I'm not shitin' ya. Damn tough place to grow up in."

I don't know what to say to that, so I just say, "Jeez."

"Jeez, is right. You had to watch your ass all the time, man. Couple of kids I grew up with got offed. Shot. Right in the street. Shot dead before they even made it to high school. Me, I did all right. Kept my head down. Made it clear through high school. Just about the only kid on my block that did. Yeah, I made out. Dealt a little weed for spendin' money. Hey, I heard you're into weed too. Got any on you?"

I look ahead to see if Squad Leader Carl is looking our way. He isn't, so I fish out a joint and hand it over.

The Monday Man sniffs it and grins. "Hey' thanks, man. I'll give this shit a try when we get back to base. And I'll give you some of mine. We can compare."

I say, "I'd like that." I wonder if he'll invite me over to the black soldiers area. Ever since Phil got killed on road security and those two black guys wanted to leave me out there, I've been cautious about trying to be friendly with any of them. Like most of the other white guys, I just stay away from them.

"Hey, if you're passing out cigs, I'd take one." It's Arturo. He hurries to catch up to us. He must think I was giving the Monday Man a cigarette out of my sundries pack. Arturo is a big Mexican guy who hits me up for the cigarettes in my SP pack every time we happen to work next to each other on sandbag duty. He told me he grew up in Tijuana, Mexico, and joined the U.S. Army even though he's not really a legal U.S. citizen. He's a pretty cool guy. He lives a few hooches away from ours. On quiet nights, I hear him softly singing Mexican songs.

I give him a cigarette, but of course, that also means Naturally is going to want one too. He hurries to catch up with me before I can put the pack away. He holds up two fingers, like everybody in camp does when they want to bum a cigarette. Naturally is a moody guy who brags that he knows all the words to every single Beatles song. I think that has something to do with why they call him Naturally. I give him a cig, and he and Arturo hurry to drop back to their places in line before Squad Leader Carl notices.

We push on through the grasses and weeds and pretty soon, the rain picks up again. This time it's a hard coming-in-sideways rain that sends water inside my poncho's hood to trickle down the back of my neck. It actually doesn't feel too bad, because a hot, very white sun keeps on popping out from behind the thick clouds. I look up at what little sky I can see through the tall trees above us, hoping to catch sight of a rainbow. But there isn't one. Now that I think about it, despite all the rain, I've never seen a rainbow here. Maybe they don't have rainbows in this brokenhearted country.

Unfortunately, the heavy clouds soon roll back in and the rain intensifies. The moisture has worked its way down my spine to the crack in my butt, and the constant wetness down there in my underwear is starting to chaff my butt.

I catch up to Eric and complain about it.

He just laughs.

I'm surprised he'd laugh at my distress. Eric is usually a pretty kind person. But then he stops laughing and gets serious. "Take off your underwear and throw 'em away," he says. "I should have told you."

I think about pulling off to the side and doing as he says, but I'm damned sure not going to make myself the butt of the other men's jokes by standing there with my bare butt hanging out. I think about pulling over and letting them all go past before I do it, but after what Eric said about not falling behind, I don't much like that option either.

As we trudge on, over his shoulder, Eric says, "Ants. Pass it on."

I ask, "Ants? What about them?"

He just says, "Button up."

I don't know what he means by button up. I'm thinking, here we are in the jungle, in the enemy's territory, maybe about to get shot or blown to shit at any minute, and he's worried about little bitty ants? But then, I feel the first bite on my ankle, sharp as hell, and then another. I smack at them, and then again. I figure I must have nailed 'em because they've stopped biting. I have a sudden memory of the stories my storyteller girl told me that night at Wong's, stories about being kind to the lesser creatures. And now, I've just killed a jungle insect. I have the weird thought that maybe I'll get punished for it, like Jeff was punished for killing the snake. I try to tell myself I shouldn't be punished because my reaction was involuntary, a quick slap in response to pain. I didn't really mean to kill it. But then I have to laugh at myself. Thinking about not hurting insects because you might get punished is pretty silly, like I'm starting to believe in some kind of insect God. Still, as I feel the continuing sting of that ant bite, I do silently apologize to my storyteller girl for killing the poor little thing. I hope in Vietnamese Buddhist belief there's a difference between killing a turtle and killing a biting ant. If I ever see her again, I'll ask her. I wondering where she is right now. A part of me hopes she's not still working at Wong's. I hope she went back home, wherever that is.

I slog along behind Eric, often hopping on one foot to scratch at the ant-bite welts on my ankles. This slogging through a wet jungle can be damn uncomfortable. Not only am I getting bit and chafed, the big pack full of medical shit I have to carry for Eric feels like it's actually getting heavier. The shoulder straps are cutting into my shoulders, and they're starting to chafe too.

Eric looks back at me and sees me shifting the pack around. He says, "Shoulders getting sore?"

"Yeah," I say. "Damn sore."

He says, "Here, get in front of me."

I do as he says, and as we continue to walk, I can feel him digging around inside my pack.

He hands me a couple of thick square bandages. "Here, try these."

I get it. I put the bandages under my shirt where the shoulder straps have been rubbing.

"Better?"

"Yeah. Thanks."

He gets back in front of me, and we push on. I stare at the bouncing motion of the little pack on Eric's back. He only has to carry the little M3 medical bag with the emergency stuff, while I have to carry the much larger M5 bag that has the not-so-emergency stuff. There's no one thing in my M5 bag that's very heavy, but it adds up. Last night, when Eric found out I would be going along as his assistant, he made me take out everything that was in the M5 pack so he could tell me what each thing was for. We laid it all out on his metal examination table, and he said I should try to memorize what everything was and where each item was stored in case he needed something in a hurry. I tried to concentrate as he went over each item:

- Three scalpels in a folding canvas pouch. Eric took each of the scalpels out. One was big enough to be a weapon (if necessary, he said), a medium-sized one that he warned me to be careful of because it's really sharp, and a little one so small it looked like a child's toy. I asked him what that one was for, but he only said, "Little stuff."

- A huge number of hemostats, cool shiny chrome tools that looked really useful for grabbing things and holding on. I used one of them to grab onto Eric's sleeve, but he unhooked it and told me to get serious. He said I should get familiar with hemostats because my main job in an emergency might well be pinching off veins and arteries that get cut. I asked, "What's the difference between a vein and an artery?" He said, "Veins in, arteries out. If the blood is bright red, it means it's on its way out, but it doesn't matter. If you see blood leaking out, clip on a hemostat. A lot of blood, use a tourniquet." I nodded to show I understood. There were also some assorted scissors and probes and forceps and tweezers in that pouch, which Eric didn't seem to think needed any explanation.

- Several suturing kits with assorted pre-threaded needles. He took one of them out and pretended like he was going to put a stitch in my forearm. When I pulled away, he laughed and made clucking sounds like a chicken. I said I didn't need a demonstration because I assumed he would be doing all the stitching, but he said stitching was easy, even a girl could do it. He grinned to make sure I got the joke.

- One field eye dressing kit, that Eric didn't want me to open for fear of contaminating whatever was inside. Like most of the other stuff, I tried to imagine using it in an emergency situation, but I couldn't picture it. What did I know about injuries? The more Eric pointed out his medical tools and described what we would do with them, the more I knew I was getting in way over my head. I was ready to tell him to stop, that I could never learn all this stuff in one night. I wanted to run to the lieutenant and tell him it would be a big mistake to send me out as an assistant medic, because I would probably do something wrong and make things worse. Eric seemed to sense that I was getting cold feet, so he stopped describing medical tools long enough to pat me on the arm and say, "Don't look so worried. When it's time to act, you'll find that it's all pretty straightforward. You'll do fine."

- Two big boxes of cotton swabs on little wooden sticks that seemed hopelessly fragile, a tool for dabbing, not for saving someone's life.

- Two sizes of tourniquets, a bunch of them. He said it was obvious how to use them, but it got me to wondering if I would be able to remain calm enough to put one of those things on a person?

- One packet of tongue depressors. I silently wondered why he would want to be depressing anybody's tongue in a combat situation.

- One package labeled Jackson Tracheotomy Cannula, which Eric said was the tube you stuck into the hole in a guy's throat after you'd done an emergency tracheotomy. I asked if we would be doing any emergency tracheotomies, but he only shrugged and wouldn't make eye contact with me. I knew what that meant: let's hope we never need it.

- A tin of Rexall surgical powder. When I asked him what it does, he said, "Nothing, but shake it all over the wound. It makes the guy think you're doing something to help him." Eric opened the top and shook some of the powder out, "See," he said, "it hangs in the air. Magic curing powder." He laughed his quick sarcastic laugh that I was starting to get used to, and went on to the next item.

- Three boxes of merthiolate swabs. "More magic?" I asked. He said, "No, it really does help avoid infections. If you have to use it, use a lot."

- Two tins of sunburn cream. Eric held them both up, one in each hand, and grinned. "Suntan oil. Can you believe the stuff they give me? Of all the crap." Thinking those tins looked pretty heavy, I suggested we should leave them out. But he said no, we should leave it all in. He gave me a wink. "Besides, you never know when you might meet a too-tight girl out there in the jungle." I thought it was a pretty crass joke, particularly for a gentle guy like Eric. Eric caught my look and shrugged. "It's a joke, Scotty. Something I heard from a guy in a lurp unit who came in here to have me treat his trench foot. He liked to talk about all the young native girls his unit had raped." When I asked if things like that really happened, he said, "Aw, hell, Scotty who knows? That guy also bragged that he was the first in his unit to get a "daily double," raping a girl and then killing her." Eric's words shocked me, not only because of what he'd said, but the matter-of-fact way he'd said it. I couldn't help but think about those young girls back there at Wong's. I imagined them getting raped and killed by the asshole Eric was talking about. Eric looked up at me, and I must have looked upset, because he said, "You can't believe everything you hear, Scotty. Some of the younger jerks use that kind of talk to put on a brave act." But I wouldn't leave it alone. I asked him it could be true, what that guy said. He looked toward the door like he was afraid somebody might come in and hear what we were talking about. He quietly said, "Aw shit, Scotty, everything happens in war. You know, like that spec-5 shooting those people over a damn pig. Missed his mamma's home cooking, he said. Wanted pork, he said, like back home." Eric shook his head. "Can you imagine shooting somebody for a pig? Damn." He picked up the next item, a package of bandages, and stared at it. I pretended like I knew what he was talking about and just nodded. So that was "the trouble" with the villagers everybody in camp had been talking about. Now I understood: apparently some sergeant had shot a whole family because he wanted their pig. I could tell Eric didn't want to talk about it, but I couldn't hold my tongue. I asked if the guy got prosecuted. Eric said, "Prosecuted? Have you ever heard of anybody getting prosecuted just because they killed a Vietnamese? The lieutenant transferred him out to another unit. Now, come on, Scotty, we've got to get through all this stuff and try to get some shuteye." He went back to explaining the different types of bandages, but I couldn't stop thinking about that sergeant killing innocent people and then nothing happening to him. If I had known what all the whispering was about back then, I would have gone right in and asked the lieutenant what he was going to do about it. No wonder nobody wanted to tell me what had happened. Eric brought me back from my thoughts by counting out all the various types of bandages. There were a hell of a lot of them: rolls and rolls of elastic bandages, and a lot of packages of triangular bandages. I half listened but I couldn't stop thinking about an American soldier, a sergeant in my own unit, shooting an innocent family just because he wanted their pig. Eric saw I wasn't paying attention, and said, "The crazy thing is after all that, the cook wouldn't even touch the damn pig. He said it was full of worms and told the guy to get the fucking thing out of his kitchen. I wanted to ask Eric more questions, like how often things like that happened, and why the Army was so willing to cover it up, but Eric was already onto the next item.

- One rubberized emergency surgical sheet. I lifted it. Also heavy.

- A bunch of assorted Band-Aids in paper packages, plus several tins of Rexall Quik-Bands. I suggested we could get rid of the tins and just stuff the quick-Bands in with the Band-Aids, but Eric nixed that idea.

- One bottle of water purification tablets. I asked Eric if they worked. He said he had no idea, but if he had to drink any stream water out there in the jungle, he would probably use the tablets. I asked him what would happen if you drank water from a stream or river in this country. He said you'd probably just get the runs. I told myself to remember to fill my canteen before I went to bed.

- Some pre-medicated petrolatum gauze dressings. Eric said if a guy gets wounded, use them first. "And these." He pulled out a handful of sealed women's tampons. "Well, you already know how to use these."

- One box of ammonia inhalants, to be used if you have to get a man up and walking quick.

- A bunch of tubes of various salves, tannic acid jelly for burns, and tubes of ophthalmic ointment that Eric said I should squeeze into any man's eyes who complained about eye irritation. "Dust, pollen, gunpowder smoke. Whatever. It works pretty good. And this." He showed me a tube of petroline bacitracin ointment. "Good antibiotic stuff. I use it on everything from chafed toes to wounds."

- One little mirror and a magnifying glass. Eric said he had never used the mirror, but it might come in handy. He told me to take good care of the magnifying glass because it's the only one he had, and it's how you find what's in frag wounds.

- One pen light with two extra batteries. Eric shined it in my eyes. "Be damn careful using this at night. Makes you a perfect target."

Then, he showed me how to pack all the stuff up again. He did it carefully, putting the least likely to be used things on the bottom, the more likely to be used things nearer the top. He told me to memorize the order where everything was in case he needed it fast. But the more I thought about it, the more unsure I was about how I'd react if I actually had to grope around in that big old bag in a real emergency. And now that I'm actually out here as his assistant, the memory of how careful he was to explain everything gives me an eerie feeling. Did he have a premonition that something was going to happen? But why would something happen this time? Doesn't the enemy always just run back across the Cambodian border where we can't follow.

The rain lets up a little, but the ground is so wet I sink in a bit with every step. I feel like the heavy M5 medical bag on my back is trying to push me down into the earth. The line speeds up, and I look ahead to see why. Squad leader Carl is off to the side of the trail impatiently waving everybody forward. He always wants the line to move faster. I remember him from the last time I was out on patrol, the time the Polack got blown up, and I remember he was never satisfied with the pace. He's a sour guy. Never smiles. Gruff. No other word for it: he gives orders in a gruff way and answers questions in a gruff way. It's like he's impatient with everybody, never satisfied with what anybody does. As we go past him, he waves us forward with an abrupt wave of his hand. From just that wave of his hand, I can tell he's fed up with all of us, like he thinks we're a bunch of wimps that just don't measure up.

As soon as he gets the line moving faster, he jogs back up to the front. He always takes the point, which as I understand it, is not necessarily SOP (standard operating procedure) for a squad leader. I figure he must have been out here a long time because his uniform has the old-style black-on-white name tape. I've only seen that type of name tape on the older top sergeants that gave us our Indoctrination Training back in Saigon. But I don't need clues like that to tell me he's been out here a long time: he has a grim-set jaw and wary eyes that say he's seen it all. Actually, to look at the way he dresses, you wouldn't know he was a sergeant. He's dressed like a regular rifleman, and he's loaded down with ammo pouches and grenades. He keeps a bottle of bug juice tucked under his helmet strap on one side, and a pack of smokes on the other side in a plastic case to keep them dry. His sleeves are rolled up, and he's not wearing a flak jacket, even though our orders are to wear them at all times when we're out in the field. This morning, before we headed out, Eric told me Carl knows what he's doing, so we'd be in good hands. It seems surprising that he's not a top sergeant if he's been in country a long time. It makes me wonder if he got into trouble some time in the past, maybe for losing men. Maybe he got busted down, and that's why he's only a staff sergeant now. For some reason, he doesn't even wear his stripes. I hurry up next to Eric and whisper, "Why doesn't Carl wear his stripes?"

Eric whispers back, "Thinks it makes him too much of a target."

"Makes him a target? So he thinks the enemy is watching us?"

"They are."

I drop back in line. They are? If the enemy is always watching us, what makes them decide when it's time to stop watching and attack us? I try to peer deeper into the jungle, but it's so dense, there's nothing to see in there but darkness. There could be any number of enemy hiding in there, and we'd never see them. I look ahead at Carl. The only indication that he might be a non-com is that he carries a CAR-15 instead of the M16s most riflemen carry. I guess he doesn't think the enemy is smart enough to notice that. I think Squad Leader Carl has the right idea: dress and act unimportant. I hope it's clear to the enemy that I'm the least important of anybody in this line.

The line stops. I look ahead and see that Carl has stopped us. He's holding up one hand while he looks ahead. Is he worried about something? Did he see something?

I move up next to Eric again. "What's going on?"

Eric shrugs. "Maybe he's found a spider hole. The lieutenant somehow got it into his head that Charlie could be hiding underground in tunnels. He thinks maybe that's how they disappear so fast."

"Why does he call them spider holes?"

"Beats me."

Carl calls forward Little Billy, the smallest guy in the unit. We all crowd forward to look, and sure enough, there *is* a hole in the ground. The entrance was covered by brush, but it's been kicked away. Carl is sending Little Billy down into the hole with a flashlight.

After only a short time, Billy pops his head back out. "Nothin' down there, Sarge. I couldn't get back very far. It's too tight."

Squad Leader Carl shakes his head like he's disgusted with Little Billy. He tells us to mount up, and we go on, keeping our heads down against the spitting rain. I'm thinking about the possibility that the Viet Cong really could be hiding in holes like that. But if that hole was too small for Little Billy, how could Charlie get down into it?

We haven't gone much farther before Squad Leader Carl stops us again. I ask Eric why we keep stopping.

Eric does his usual shrug. "Maybe he's jumpy because of that lurp patrol that got all shot up near here."

I think of the lurp Marine. Did he buy it near here? I again try to see into the forest, but the driving rain is obscuring everything.

I put down the M5 bag and rub my shoulders. They're a lot more sore than I thought. I can't even imagine how sore they're going to get on the way back. It seems like we've come a long ways from camp. I pull up my pant leg to see how bad the ant bites are, but as soon as I see what's on my ankle, I forget about ant bites. It's worse. Leeches, two of the little bastards. I get Eric's attention and show him.

"Oh yeah. You got to keep your pant legs tight."

I know they're just little leeches, but seeing them there happily sucking away at my blood gives me a creepy feeling. I try to keep my voice calm as I ask Eric how to get them off.

Arturo comes over holding out a lit cigarette. "I'll get 'em."

But Eric holds him back. "No, don't do that. That could shock 'em and make 'em regurgitate back into the wound. Could get infected."

Arturo shrugs. "Always works for me." He heads back to his place.

Eric squats down and carefully picks them off. He puts them down on a bare patch of ground. "You want me to step on them? Or do you want to do it? It's your blood." I shake my head, and he quickly stomps on them. Blood squirts out from under the side of his shoe. Eric turns away, and I'm left staring at two splotches of my blood on the ground.

We're still not moving, so I take time to loosen my belt and look down inside my pants to make sure there aren't any more leeches in there. I can't see any, and I don't feel anything except the usual chafing, but then I didn't feel those two on my ankles either, so who knows.

I hear Squad Leader Carl call out to Benny the RTO to get on the line. He tells him to make sure he can raise somebody. That seems to surprise Benny. He's only been out here a couple of weeks so he's even more of a FNG than I am, but Saint Louee told me he actually had the benefit of some real radio-telephone operator training back in the states. To look at him, you wouldn't think he was a FNG. Unlike me, he's learned real quick how to mimic the old hands by putting on a pretty good stone face to act like he isn't scared of anything.

He says, "Sure, Sarge," like it's no big deal, but I still wonder if Carl's order is unusual, like maybe he's never before told Benny to make sure we are in radio contact. I may be misreading it, but it makes me nervous. Does Carl know something he isn't telling us?

Benny gets on the radio, and right away we can all hear that he's talking to somebody on the other end of the line. He gives a thumbs-up to Carl who nods and heads up toward the clearing. We're all watching him as he hesitates before going out of the trees. He gestures for us to stay back. He takes a last drag off his cigarette, tosses it away, and walks out into the clearing. I see sun on the side of his face so there must be a tiny little break in the clouds up where he is. That cheers me up. If the sun really is coming out, that would be great. It might dry out my clothes, and it might even start to dry out my chaffing underpants.

Carl stands out there near the edge of the clearing for a long time, looking around. He's got his rifle in the ready position, but not quite up to his shoulder. Finally, he lowers it and waves us forward.

I pick up the M5 bag and we move out. As soon we're all out into the clearing, Carl begins barking at us to hurry it up. He still seems nervous. I suppose he wants us to get out of the clearing as fast as possible, but there really is a little bit of sun, and I feel more like slowing down to try to take advantage of it while I can.

Carl is impatient, yelling, "Move it! Move it!"

What is he so uptight about?

As I go past him, he yells, "Keep the line straight, damn it. I want —"

He never finishes saying whatever he was going to say because I hear the crack of a rifle, and at the same instant, I see him get hit square in the chest. The bullet makes a thud sound when it hits him, like a wet baseball being hit by a bat. Carl stumbles backwards, trying hard to stay on his feet. He has a surprised look on his face, as if he's been sucker-punched. He looks down at his chest and touches it gingerly with one finger. But then another shot hits him right in the cheek. It spins him around and he goes down hard. He doesn't move, and I can't seem to decide what to do about it. Should I try to help him? There's more shooting, and I start to think maybe I should run. My brain doesn't seem to be working right: somebody is shooting at us, at me, from all around, but I'm not sure what I should do about that either. I'm seeing muzzle flashes from deep within the wet greenness of the jungle. The guys around me have hit the ground and some of them are shooting into the jungle. But what can I do? I don't have a gun. The RTO is screaming, "Fire support! Fire support!" but my heart is thumping so loud inside my helmet I'm not sure I'm really hearing anything that's real. Some of the others are scrambling back toward the jungle we just came out of, but I'm not hearing any orders, so I don't know what I'm supposed to do. The lieutenant told me to do whatever Squad Leader Carl says to do, but Carl is lying on the ground, not moving. Some of the other guys that were lying down, jump up and start pushing me back the way we came from. My feet are moving, even though I'm not sure I'm in control of them. We're almost out of the clearing when somebody starts shooting at us from that direction too. The guys in front of me turn back and knock me down. I try to get up, but they're stepping on me and pushing me down. I can't seem to get my feet under me. Somebody falls on top of me, then another and another. I feel like I'm getting pushed down into the wet earth. Every time I try to get up, somebody else falls on top of me. I stop trying and close my eyes. I put my hands over my face and pull my legs up to my chest. Another person falls on top of me and doesn't move. It feels like a big guy, and I wonder who it is. I feel like I'm being buried alive in soldiers. Are they all dead? Is everybody dead? There's so much shooting, I can't tell who's doing it, the enemy or our side. Then, there's a close-by explosion. My brain says, Grenade! It means I'm about to die. But is it possible your brain can really know when you're about to die? I feel somebody in my pile squirming. He must be trying to swim out of our jumble of bodies. I fend off his kicking feet until he stops doing it and lies still. He must be dead now. The shooting continues. Maybe it will never stop. Maybe it will go on forever, and I'll be forever trapped under a pile of dead men. My mind tells me if they are dead, then I should play dead too. I lie still and listen. I hear shooting. I hear explosions. I hear shouting and screaming. I don't think I'm shot. At least I don't think I'm feeling any pain. All I feel is the weight of the guys on top of me. Their weight convinces me that I should just stay where I am. If I tried to crawl out from under this pile of men, I'd get shot. My brain is saying, better to not move. Do nothing. My brain is right. Smartest brain in my high school, that's what that counselor said. He'd tell me staying still is the best thing to do. But the guys on top of me are so heavy, I can barely get a breath. That brings a sudden memory of not being able to breathe when I was under the ice, and I feel a wave of panic. I push at the bodies that are on top of me, trying to reach the sky that was on the other side of that ice window. But my brain says, Stop that! Just lie still. Play dead. There's another close-by explosion, and a guy in my pile frantically squirms right up next to me and starts clawing at my chest, like he's desperate to get inside of me. He starts murmuring something. Is he praying? I pat his arm and whisper, "There, there." He doesn't move. Is he dead now too? Maybe I should be praying too. Should I ask God to help me? But if the others are dying, why should He care about me? Besides, I don't know how to pray, even if I wanted to. Praying is for churches. Back in Illinois, my mother made me go to church with her every Sunday. The preacher was a short, squat man, and he yelled a lot. His sermons made me afraid, so I tried to think about other things. I would pretend I was not there listening to an angry man rant on and on about how all sinners would get theirs in the end. Instead of listening to him, I would pretend I was doing one of my favorite things, fishing for crawdads in the mossy pond near our house. I'd use a string and a piece of raw bacon I'd stolen from the refrigerator. The crawdads would grab the bacon and wouldn't let go. You could pull them right out of the water, and they still wouldn't let go of that piece of bacon. It was fun. But then I didn't know what to do with them. I killed the first one I caught by hitting it with a rock. But that made me feel so bad I cried. I hated to see the poor thing all squashed and messy. So after that, I didn't hurt them. I just played with them. I'd try to get the crawdad to let go of the piece of bacon by showing it another piece. When it let go, I'd pull both pieces of bacon away quick and laugh like crazy. Ha, ha, tricked you. Then, I'd throw the crawdad back into the water and try it again. Silly crawdads. Sometimes the same crawdad would go for the same trick again. So maybe that's why I never learned how to pray; I was thinking about crawdads instead of listening to that preacher and learning how to pray. And after my father died, my mother stopped going to church. She turned away from God. She said if God wasn't willing to save her husband, then to hell with God. I was happy I didn't have to go listen to that angry preacher anymore. I got to spend Sundays at the pond, all by myself, catching crawdads with pieces of bacon tied to a string. The shooting goes one and on. It's like those enemy shooters have gone mad and are just shooting and shooting and shooting. I swear I can hear bullets going by, like angry gnats, moving fast, on their way to somewhere important. I hear, or maybe I feel, a thud, and then another. Are they shooting at my pile? Will one of those angry gnat bullets get through the pile to kill me sooner or later? I keep my eyes closed. I don't move. Maybe I can't move. Maybe I'm paralyzed. That thought makes my stomach clench, and I feel like I'm going to throw up. I tell myself to calm down and use my brain. My philosophy textbook said that compared to the other animals, thinking is really the only thing we humans are especially good at. It's our ability to think that sets us apart from other animals. It said only we humans think about who we are and why we exist. So I should use my human brain. I should use it to think through this problem. If you want to know if you're paralyzed, try to wiggle your toes. I wiggle my toes. I can feel them inside my boots. They feel sore and chaffed. It means I'm not paralyzed. See there, all you had to do was think. Thinking is what sets us apart from the animals, so just keep thinking. The shooting stops. Is everybody dead now? It seems so quiet, it feels like a dream. Did the enemy run away? Why would they do that? There can't be many of us left. Why don't they just come out of hiding and finish us off? Maybe they will. Maybe they will come soon and kill me. I keep my eyes closed and wait.

In the quiet, I hear whispering: "Tell her. Tell her . . ."

I whisper back, "Tell who?"

There's no answer. Maybe he died. Maybe those were his last words, whoever it was. Who did he want to tell? His girl? His mother? What did he want me to say? If I knew I was going to die, would I want to tell somebody something? My mother? What would I want to tell her? I haven't had a sit-down serious talk with her for years. She has her mother to talk to, so she doesn't talk to me. Even if I knew it was going to be my last words, I wouldn't know what to say to her.

Everything is so quiet now I can hear the birds again. In the distance, I hear a strange bird call, like a low whistle, but it ends abruptly. Did it get shot? I'm surprised there are any birds brave enough to be this close after all the shooting and explosions. Maybe the war has been going on so long the birds have gotten used to it.

Somebody is yelling. It's almost like somebody is yelling my name, yelling, "Help me, Scotty."

It sounds like my father. He's pinned under his motorcycle and needs me to get it off of him. I can't help you, father. I can't help you because it's raining, and I'm stuck under a pile of dead soldiers. You shouldn't have gone out on such a rainy night, father. It's too dangerous. You could die.

"Help me, Scotty. Damn it, where are you?"

Wait, that's not my father. Why are you thinking weird thoughts like that? Your father is dead. A long time ago. That's somebody nearby yelling my name. Why? What do they think I can do? I can't help anybody. I'm stuck right where I am, buried under dead people. I can't even help myself, let alone anybody else.

"Scotty. Where are you?"

That voice. It's not my father, it's Eric. He's alive. All the others are dead, but Eric is alive. I'm very glad to hear his voice. I squirm forward until I can see him. He's out in the middle of the clearing. He keeps sitting up and looking around, and then he hunkers down again behind something. I push my arm out and wave, but then I pull my arm back in. Why did I do that? The enemy might have seen that. My brain says, Do not move. They will shoot you. But another voice inside of me says Eric is calling, and you should go help him. Maybe I should at least try to see what Eric wants. I take a chance and peek out again. Eric is doing something over there behind that thing. What is that thing he's hiding behind? It looks almost like a cow. A big fat cow. In fact, I'm sure it's a cow. A dead cow. Was that what Squad Leader Carl was worried about, a dead cow in the middle of a clearing? I can tell the cow has been dead for a long time: it's all bloated up. I saw a dead cow like that one time, lying on its side out in a field, its legs sticking straight out. Where was that? It must have been back in Illinois. When I was a child. I was in the back seat. My father was driving. A dead cow was out in the middle of a green field, all blown up like a cow balloon. My father said something about it. What was it he said? Something like, I wonder if the farmer knows about that? Why do I remember what he said? Why do I remember that cow? I can hardly even remember my father. And now here is another dead cow all blown up. Am I dreaming this? Am I back in Illinois? Maybe I never grew up. Maybe I'm still a little boy, and I'm in bed dreaming about a dead cow in Vietnam. But why would there be a cow in the Vietnamese jungle? I squirm out a little more and lift my head up to get a closer look. It's not a cow. It's a water buffalo, a damned dead bloated-up water buffalo. What's it doing here?

"Scotty, where the hell are you? I need the M5."

I feel the weight of the M5 pack on my back. I'd completely forgotten about it. Now that I feel its weight on me, added to the weight of whoever is lying on top me, it's no wonder I can't move. With all that weight on me, there's no way I can go to help Eric. I wish I could, but I can't. All that weight is pushing me down into the wet earth, all but crushing me. Nobody will be able to blame me for not going to help him. They'll see that I was held down by the weight of the M5 pack and all those other soldiers lying on top of me. Nobody could say I even heard Eric calling my name, not with all that shooting going on.

"Scotty, God damn it. I need the trach kit."

I try not to hear him. I try to focus on the guy who's next to me. I have to stay here and help him because he's scared. Who is he anyhow? He's lost his helmet. He has long dark hair. Who has hair like that? I get ahold of his hair and pull his head back It's Naturally. The guy who loves the Beatles. His eyes are open, staring right through me. I carefully let his head rest against my chest." I pat him on top of his head and say, "There, there, Naturally. Everything is going to be all right"

"Scotty, if you can hear me, get me the trach kit. I need it quick."

Why does Eric have to keep on yelling like that? What makes him think I'm even still alive? Everybody else is dead, so why should I be alive? Or are they? Maybe I should look. I push up against the people who are on top of me, and one of them rolls off. oh no, it's Arturo. He has to be dead because part of his face is gone. I'm not even sure how I knew it was Arturo with half his face gone like that. His one remaining eye stares at me. I have to turn away. It's very quiet. A frog croaks in the distance. Must be water nearby. It makes me think about the turtle I saved. I carried it to water. That turtle saved me. Maybe that turtle is still watching over me. Maybe that's why I'm still alive. But that makes no sense. Why am I thinking about turtles? Am I going crazy? Do you have thoughts like that when you're going crazy?

I again feel the weight of the M5 bag. Eric needs stuff out of it. I crawl forward a little and cup my hand like a megaphone. "I'm over here."

Why did I do that? Now the enemy knows where I am. Now they will shoot me.

Eric's head pops up from behind the dead water buffalo. "Where? I can't see you."

I whisper again, "I'm under here. Under these guys."

He looks in my direction. "What the hell are you doing? Come here."

"They fell on me. " I can't move. I'm stuck under here."

"You're not stuck. I need the trach kit. Get over here. Now!"

"I . . . I don't think I can move. There's somebody on my legs."

"Bullshit. Just crawl out and get over here."

The enemy is not shooting anymore, but I know they're still around. They're waiting, watching for any movement, and there's nothing but open space between where I am and where Eric is. I wouldn't have a chance out there. They'd pick me off for sure. There are already two dead guys lying out there, and there's no way I'm going to go out there to join them. One of them is face down in the grass, the other next to him, is lying on his side, his knees drawn up with his arms wrapped around them. He must have had time to get himself in that position before he died. He has mud all over his face, but there's something familiar about him. Then, I realize it's one of my hoochmates. It's the Farmer, the farmer's son from Nebraska who didn't want to be a farmer. He said he was going to go home to be a carpenter. How could I have not recognized him? Something must be wrong with my brain. Poor dead Farmer. He only had a few weeks to go. He was all excited about going home. He said he was going to get rich building houses for all the returning GIs. Always talking about joists and footers and double-pane windows. He could get more excited about wood and tools than the other guys got about girls. He won't be building those houses. Too bad.

"Scotty! God damn it, get over here. I'm losing Carl."

"All right, all right. I'm coming."

Why did you say that? You know you aren't going out there. You may not get out of this alive, but you damned sure don't want to die over there with Eric behind a damn dead water buffalo. I squirm out from under the pile and start crawling toward Eric. I wonder if I'll hear the shot that kills me. I make it to the dead water buffalo, but the smell of the thing is so bad, it just about makes me throw up. I stop, but Eric reaches out and drags me right over the top of the dead thing. Oh shit, now I've got the stink of it all over me. Eric doesn't even say hello, or thank me for risking my life just to bring the damn M5 pack. He just roughly flips me over onto my stomach and rips the pack off my back.

I sit up, but Eric pushes me back down again and whispers, "Keep your head down. They may not be shooting, but they're still out there."

I keep my head down and watch what Eric is doing. He must have dragged Squad Leader Carl behind this old dead water buffalo, and now he's got him laid out on his back. Carl has a hole in the side of his face, and there's a tampon stuffed into the hole. He looks dead. But his eyes are not open and staring, so maybe he isn't. Eric takes off his helmet and starts madly digging through the M5 bag. He finds what he's looking for, the medium-sized scalpel. He digs through the pack some more until he finds the package labeled "Jackson Tracheotomy Cannula." He's going to try to save Sergeant Carl by doing an emergency tracheotomy? Is there really a chance that will help him? I whisper, "What should I do?"

"Get out the hemostats. All of them."

I dig into the bag and find them right away. I feel proud of myself: I knew exactly where they were.

Eric cuts through the skin in the upper part of Carl's neck. I hand the trach kit to him, but he waves it off. "Not yet."

I hear a sound, but far away. Could it be a chopper? Maybe that's what scared the enemy away. I look at Squad Leader Carl's face. He looks pretty much already dead, but what do I know? Maybe Eric is going to do a tracheotomy even if Carl dead. Why not? I'm ready with a hemostat in each hand, but when he cuts through Carl's throat, I'm not ready for the amount of blood that comes out. I quickly clip on two hemostats and dig in the M5 pack for cotton swabs. But the blood is filling up the hole in Carl's throat faster than I can swab it out.

"Come on, come on," says Eric.

At first, I think he's unhappy with me, impatient that I'm not stopping the blood, but then I realize he's talking to himself: he's struggling to cut a little trapdoor-like flap out of Carl's throat. More blood comes out. I clip on more hemostats and go back to swabbing. I'm using up almost all of the cotton just to try to keep the blood out of Eric's way, but it's no use; I can't keep up with it.

The sound gets louder. Now I'm sure it's helicopters, coming closer. I begin to have the tiniest bit of hope we might get out of this alive.

And then, a Huey gunships sails in just over the tops of the trees. It hovers right above us, incredibly loud, the wind from its rotors flattening the tall grasses of the clearing. I can smell the heavy burned-oil smell of its exhausts. He drops down so low above us, I can see the pilot. He looks right at me, and then pulls up and swings his chopper sideways. It stalls over the trees at the edge of the clearing, and the door gunner begins firing his machine gun into the jungle. The chopper rises and sinks slightly in response to the bursts of machine-gun fire that the gunner is laying down. The gunner is swinging his machine gun back and forth, constantly firing, raining down a curtain of ferocious fire that snaps off an entire row of small trees. Those trees going down so neat like that strikes me as funny, and I laugh out loud. It's silly, like some kind of knock-down-the-trees game at the county fair.

Eric glances up at me, and I stop laughing. This is serious business. We have to try to save Squad Leader Carl.

Another chopper comes. It hovers over the jungle, farther away, also laying down fire from its 50-caliber. In between the machine gun bursts from the two choppers, I hear some rifle shots coming from the jungle. It means the enemy *has not* run away. They're firing at the choppers.

I turn back to our patient and see Eric has already got a stitch in the doorflap to hold it open. Damn, he's fast. He said he practiced doing tracheotomies on dead guys back at Bien Hoa. He learned it well.

Eric says something, but the closest Huey is so loud I can't hear him. I assume he must be asking for the cannula tube, so I let loose of one of the hemostats to hand it to him. He takes it, and I go back to my job of swabbing the blood away.

I think I hear a pop from the tree-line, and I look in that direction, but there's nothing there. I look up at the choppers. They're still firing at the jungle. So much noise. Makes it hard to think.

I look back down at our patient, but Eric hasn't inserted the cannula. Why hasn't he put it in? Is he waiting for me to do it? I look at him. He still has the tube in his hands, but he has the strangest tight grin on his face, almost as if he's forcing a smile. Does he think something is funny? Does he think my futile efforts are funny? I'm doing the best I can.

He slowly begins to lean forward toward me until he ends up with his head resting in my lap. What the hell? Did he pass out? But then I see he has a hole in the back of his head. Why is there a hole there? My mind doesn't want to believe what I'm seeing. Maybe it's not a hole, maybe it's only a dark spot. But when I lean forward to look closer, I see it *is* a hole, oozing blood and some white goo. I feel strangely outside of myself, as if I'm watching this happen. The part of me that's outside of myself is saying I should do something, but I don't know what I'm supposed to do. I shake my head to make the weird feeling go away, but it won't: I say, "Eric, are you all right?" But then I feel stupid for saying that. Of course he's not all right; he has a hole in the back of his head. It means he's been shot. I try to think what I'm supposed to do. I have to concentrate. Eric said if a man is wounded, first put on a pre-medicated petrolatum gauze dressing. I dig through the M5 bag until I find it. I start to put the gauze dressing over that little oozing hole in his head, but then I stop. What good is that little bit of gauze going to do? Maybe I should clip on a hemostat to stop the bleeding. I pinch up the skin around the hole and clip a hemostat on. But then I look at the hemostat and realize it's not going to help him. How could it? He's been shot in the head. But hemostats are the only tools I've got, and clipping them on is the only thing I know how to do. I stare at the useless little hemostat dangling from the back of Eric's head. If only I was smart like Eric, maybe I'd know what to do.

I look toward the jungle and wonder why they shot him. Of all people, Eric shouldn't have been shot. He was a medic, for Christ's sake. He didn't even have a gun. He was a kind person. A good person. All he was trying to do was save Squad Leader Carl's life.

I look at the helicopters. I wish they would stop all that shooting and come down here and tell me what to do. Everything seems to be slowing down. The Huey is still up there, hovering, but it's rising and falling too slowly. The chopper stops firing, and the sudden quiet snaps me back inside of myself. I look up. The helicopters are getting smaller. Are they going away? I yell, "Wait! Don't go! I don't know what to do." But it doesn't come back. It banks off and flies low over the jungle, firing its machine gun as it disappears behind the trees. It must be chasing the enemy. But what about me? What about Eric?

The choppers are gone, and in the quiet that follows, I imagine somebody is calling my name. I look down at Eric. Was he speaking to me, telling me what to do? But Eric is not moving. He's still lying in my lap, a hole in the back of his head. There's one silly little hemostat clipped over the hole, dangling, useless. I don't know what to do. I stroke his hair. I say, "There, there, Eric. Everything is going to be all right." I like the feel of his head in my lap. It has the weight of reality to it, even if nothing else in this insane world of people dying does.

I hear that voice yelling my name again. I wish whoever is doing that yelling would stop it. I look in the direction of the yelling. It's the Monday Man. He's yelling at me and waving his arms. What does he want? That shouting is so irritating. But then I remember, the Monday Man is a good guy, one of the few guys who actually talked to me in a friendly way. The Monday Man is from Chicago, from a tough neighborhood. A neighborhood so tough the cops took out their guns before going in there. What was the name of that tough neighborhood? Why can't you remember? But the Monday doesn't stop still yelling. He's kneeling over somebody and yelling at me. Is that guy dead? There are bodies all around the Monday Man. Strangely, almost all of them are touching each other in one way or another: hands reaching out to touch feet, arms thrown over shoulders. Two of the bodies are holding hands, like little kids do when they're scared. There's something about the way they're grouped together that makes it seem not real. Like it's only a kid's game, that all fall-down-and-don't-move game. You have to lie still in whatever position you fell in. Anyone one who moves is the loser until somebody yells, "Olly olly ox in free."

Monday yells, "Scotty, come help me. I don't know what to do."

He's asking *me* to help. Why me? What can I do? I can't even help my friend Eric who has blood and white stuff leaking out of his head. A least I think we were friends. We talked like friends. He told me about his life back home. How he ended up in the Army.

"Scotty, for Christ's sake. Come here and help me."

I look at Squad Leader Carl. Did he move? He might have. His face looks so old, so gray. Carl the Older; that's what some of the guys call him, even though he probably isn't really all that old. He's just old in terms of experience, an old hand at this war-fighting thing. He shouldn't have stayed in this damned country so long. He should have known his string was running out. Why didn't he go home when his hitch was up? He probably has a wife back home. Probably kids too. Boy, they're really going to miss him.

I watch the blood from Eric's incision disappear down into the hole in Carl's throat. It's like a drain, or a toilet, swirling blood, round and round, down and down into him. I can't take my eyes off of it. All that blood has to be going somewhere. But where? Into his throat? Down into his lungs? That's not good. Eric would say that's not good. Eric would tell me to do something to stop it. I clip on a couple more hemostats along the edge of the incision. That seems to help, but only a little. I clip on more, and more, but the damn blood just won't stop. I wish I knew what I was doing. I'm just clipping on hemostats and the damn blood still won't stop. Eric would know what to do. I wish he could help me. He still has the cannula tube in his hand. He must have been about to stick it into Carl's throat. Maybe I should do it for him. Maybe doing something would be better than not doing anything. I gently try to take the tube out of Eric's hand. But he doesn't want to let go of it. I try to pry his fingers back, but they don't want me to have it. I whisper, "I'm only taking the tube, Eric. It's for Carl." I finally get the tube out of Eric's hand. I lean toward Carl, being careful not to let Eric's head fall off my lap. I plunge the tube into the hole in Carl's throat. The blood gathers around it. Is that good? He doesn't seem to be breathing, so I probably didn't do it right. I stare at the tube. I don't know what else I'm supposed to do. I watch the blood drip down the side of his neck. I'm not doing him any good. I'm not doing anybody any good. He's going to die, just like that Marine died when I gave him that last shot of morphine. Why do they all have to die?

Now that damn irritating Monday Man is yelling at me again. "Come help me, Scotty. Hurry."

He's not going to stop yelling until I go over there and see what he wants. I carefully roll Eric onto his side, and gently lay his head onto a tuft of grass, using it as a nice soft pillow for him. He stares at me with sad unblinking eyes. I want to do more for him, but I don't know what else I can do. I stand up and stumble toward the Monday Man, being careful not to step on any of the dead people. It seems to take me a long time to get to him; it's like in a dream where you want to go somewhere, but you can't get your legs to work right.

When I do finally get there, the Monday man says, "Help me, Scotty. I can't stop their bleeding."

Bleeding. If arms or legs are bleeding, it requires a tourniquet. Eric told me that. But the tourniquets are in M5 bag. Where is the M5 bag? I'd better go find it. I turn away and start walking back toward the dead water buffalo. It again feels like I'm watching myself walk away. What a strange feeling to be outside of yourself, watching yourself.

The Monday Man calls after me, "Hey, stop. Don't go away, Scotty. I don't know what the fuck I'm doing here. Help me."

I want to tell him I've got to go find the M5 bag, but for some reason I can't make my mouth talk. Besides, what is there to say anymore? The important thing is to go find the M5 medical bag.

When I get back to where Eric and Carl are lying, I try not to look down at Eric, but I can't help myself. He looks pale and lifeless. How can a nice person like Eric be alive one minute and then dead the next? It makes no sense. If things like that can happen, then the world makes no sense. Is there a reason why this sort of thing happens? If there really is a God, why would He let this kind of thing happen? I remember my mother leaning forward in that church pew, her eyes closed, her head against the back of the pew in front of her. She was praying. Was she asking God to protect her husband? If so, He must not have been listening that day either. Most of the old philosophers in my book say there is no God. They say man made up God, not the other way around. They say there is no reason for anything, things just are. Now I see they are absolutely right. Eric is dead, and Squad Leader Carl is dead, and the others are dead too, and none of it means anything. I stare at Eric, and that's when I know for certain the same thing is going to happen to me. But I also know it doesn't matter. It's just like it says in my book, things just are. People are alive, and then they're dead, and it doesn't matter to anybody. Sooner or later, a bullet like that will make a little hole in my head, and then I'll be dead too, and nobody will care. I look over at the trees where the enemy was hiding. Is the sniper that shot Eric still there? Is he going to shoot me now? Or did the choppers scare him off. Maybe he has his rifle aimed at me right now. Maybe he'll shoot me, and then I'll be dead like Eric. I stand up. I yell, "Go ahead, shoot me! I don't give a shit." I wait, but I don't get shot. Maybe the enemy know I'm not important enough to shoot.

The Monday Man is yelling at me again. "Scotty, damn it. Come back here and help me ."

I pick up the M5 medical bag and take it over to where Monday is. He's still kneeling over the same guy. Who is that guy? Oh, it's Charles from Lake Charles. Why would somebody give their son the same name as the town they live in?

The Monday Man is telling me about Charles's leg. He says Charles has been shot in the leg. He says the bone is sticking out.

I look. Sharp looking, that splintered bone. Lot's of blood coming out. I know what to do about blood coming out. Eric said if an arm or leg is bleeding, put on a tourniquet. I dig a tourniquet out of the M5 bag and put it on the guy's upper leg.

Monday helps me up and leads me to the next one. It's the new kid. Only been at the firebase for a few days. What is his name? FNG Joey. Or FNG Jerry. Something like that. He was fussy about his hair. Always combing it. His hair doesn't look so good now. Got mud caked in it. Monday shows me where the kid has been shot in the side of his chest. Blood is leaking out fast. I do what Eric taught me and check for a pulse. I find one, faint. It means he's still alive. Next, see if he's breathing. I put my ear down next to his mouth. No air coming out. Means he's been shot through the lungs. Means he will die. Eric taught me what to do when they're going to die: nothing. I look at the kid, knowing he will soon be dead. The kid's face is all muddy, but there are clean streaks down his cheeks. It means he's been crying. His hair is all messed up. I use my fingers to try to comb it for him, but it's too caked with mud. I look at Monday and shake my head.

Monday shrugs, and leads me to the next one. I don't know him. Must be a brand new guy. Wounded before he could even get to know anybody. I pull up his shirt. He's also been shot in the chest. There's lots of blood, but he's awake, blinking rapidly. Does he even know we're here? As I check his pulse, he says something. I lean closer to hear what it was. He whispers it again, "I'm sorry."

Why did he say that? Is he sorry to be dying?

I stare at the wound in his chest. From a bullet maybe. Or from grenade shrapnel. I don't have any idea what to do about a wound in the chest. What would Eric do? I look at the Monday Man for help, but he just shrugs again and helps me up.

He leads me to the next one. Wounded in the leg. Tourniquet.

Monday leads me to the next one. Arm wound. Tourniquet.

Will it ever end? Will there always be a next one? I let the Monday Man lead me around. I go through the motions. I clip on hemostats. I put on tourniquets and bandages. I remember the can of Rexall surgical powder in the M5 bag. If there's nothing I can do for them, I shake some of the powder over their wounds. It hangs in the air, and I say, "There, there. Everything is going to be all right."

I soon run out of tourniquets. I use their shoestrings instead. I run out of the large bandages, so I use the small ones, side-by-side. They don't work very well. It dawns on me that I'll have to put in a medical supply order when we get back. Tourniquets. A new trach kit. Lots and lots of bandages. It'll be a big order.

I'm putting a shoestring tourniquet on a guy's shot-up arm when I hear a loud noise. It takes me a minute to realize the loud noise is above me. I look up. A helicopter. It's got a red cross on the front of it. A medevac chopper. It hovers up there, blurry through the rain. When did it start to rain? The medevac chopper starts to descend. It gets louder and louder.

17

T and T

I wake up in my own hooch. I'm hungry as hell. How long did I sleep? I sit up. I'm stiff and sore, but I don't seem to be wounded. That makes me feel guilty. Others were wounded. Or dead. Dead soldiers were on top of me. Or was that a dream? No, it couldn't have been a dream. Men were killed. People get killed in war. Eric got killed, and after that . . . what happened after that? The Monday Man led me around. Tourniquets. Bandages. Sprinkling Rexall surgical powder. A helicopter came. A lieutenant I've never seen before was giving orders. More helicopters came. Wounded men were being lined up on the ground next to the helicopters. They were being treated by medics, real medics who knew what they were doing. I wanted to tell them they were leaving too much space between the men. Before, those men were touching each other, holding hands. Now they pulled them apart. Too lonely. Why couldn't they at least let them touch each other? Somewhere in the midst of all the soldiers moving around, yelling, too-loud helicopters taking off and landing, I seem to remember the Monday Man pulling me into a helicopter. It seemed like only an instant later when we landed inside our firebase. The lieutenant was there waiting. His eyes were red like he'd been crying, but I knew that couldn't be true. Lieutenants don't cry. He touched my shoulder, and his eyes were wet. He told me to go get some shuteye. I wanted to talk tell him Eric had been killed. I wanted to tell him I didn't know what to do, but he wouldn't let me talk. He said go to bed. Talk later.

I did what he said. I slept. Now I'm awake and my hooch is empty. Where is everybody. Did they all die? No, the Farmer was the only one with us. Now his mattresses has been rolled up. His stuff is gone. Somebody came in and took his stuff. How did I sleep through that? He's probably already in that Army mortuary place back at the Bien Hoa Air Base, getting prettied up before his long trip home to Nebraska.

I notice I'm still dressed. My clothes are damp and caked with mud. Something has stained the front of my pants. I swipe at it to try to get it off. It won't come off. Oh, I get it; it's blood. Not my blood, other men's blood. How did their blood get on me? Oh, wait, weren't some of the others on top of me? I'm almost sure of it, but my brain is not thinking very clearly. I must be too hungry. How long since I had anything to eat? I have to get out of this bed and go get something to eat.

I change my uniform and put my boots on and go outside. It's raining, but only a little. I forgot my poncho. Doesn't matter. I start in that direction of the mess tent, but there is no mess tent. I stop. What happened to the mess tent? Could I have gone in the wrong direction? No, everything else is where it's supposed to be. The mess tent couldn't have disappeared, could it? I have the weird feeling that maybe I've been away for a long time. But wasn't it only yesterday when Squad Leader Carl led us into that clearing? Or was it the day before? I stare up at the sky and try to remember. Men were killed. Eric was killed. And Carl too. All gone. All dead. Did it somehow make the mess tent go away too? Maybe I'm still asleep. Maybe this is only a dream. Maybe it was all a dream. But I'm hungry, so I wish there was still a mess tent. I keep walking toward where it should be, because I don't know what else to do. When I get there, I see a large lighter-colored square on the ground. That's where the mess tent used to be. It's like it up and flew away. The square outline in the dirt brings a sudden memory of a picture I once saw. The picture was taken from an airplane. The aftermath of a tornado. There was a square concrete slab showing where a house used to be. A white pickup truck was still sitting in the driveway. The house was completely gone, but the truck didn't look damaged at all. Is that what happened to the mess tent? Did a tornado come and take it away? No, couldn't be. Not logical. I have to be logical.

A PFC is passing by carrying a shovel on his shoulder. He's a new guy that I don't recognize. Have the people here all changed too?

I ask him where the mess tent went. He looks at me funny, and then points down the hill. He heads that way. I follow him because I don't know what else to do. And then I see it: the same old mess tent, but it's been moved. Why did they move it? Soldiers are swarming all around it, making sandbags walls all around it. A bunch of ants swarming around an anthill. Seeing that it still exists makes me feel better. Less crazy. The lieutenant is there, directing the work. I head toward him. He sees me coming and hurries to meet me. He puts his hand on my shoulder and says, "Well, how're you feeling, soldier? All rested?"

"I'm hungry."

He glances back at the being-buried-in-sandbags mess tent. "They'll have it ready to go by supper time." He pats me on the shoulder again. I wish he'd stop doing that. It makes me feel like a little kid, and he's the parent saying, There, there. Everything's going to be all right.

He says, "Hey, I got some grub in my hooch. Let's go over there." We head that way, and he keeps me moving with a hand on my shoulder, gently urging me. It's almost as if he's afraid I'm going to bolt and run back to my bed, which is exactly what I do feel like doing.

"I hear you did a hell of a job out there, Private. We'll have to see about getting you a medal or something."

I have no idea what he's talking about. I say, "I was scared."

He goes back to patting me on the shoulder. "Of course, you were scared. Who wouldn't be? Taking fire from all sides like that. But you did your job. That's all I can ask of you, all we can ask of any soldier."

"Eric died."

The lieutenant nods thoughtfully. "Yes, damn shame. A good man."

"I didn't know what to do. He had a hole in the back of his head."

The lieutenant gives me another reassuring pat on my shoulder. "Yes, that's what I heard. I'm having Jones write up a report."

"Who?

"Monday."

"Oh, right. He was the brave one. He should get the medal."

"Well, that's not the way I heard it. He said you did all the medical work. You saved men's lives out there, son. You should be proud."

Proud? What is he talking about? I say, "Eric risked his life. He went out there to get Squad Leader Carl. There was a dead water buffalo."

"Right, right. And I'll see about getting Eric a posthumous medal. But you're our poster boy, Scotty, the one everybody's gonna be talking about. You risked your life to save the others, and that's what I'm going to tell them. Why, when I tell them what you did to save—"

"It's a lie."

He stops to stare at me, his mouth open. But then he recovers: "Now, no need to be modest, Private. You did your job, under fire, assisting the medic, heedless of your own safety. Then, when he got hit, you took over. Courageous. Why if you hadn't acted when you did, your squad leader would be dead now instead of recovering in the hospital in Saigon. He owes his life to you."

"Carl is alive?"

"You bet he's alive. One of the medevac guys said that trach job was one of the best he'd ever seen."

"Eric did it."

"Well, of course he did the directing, but Monday said Eric was already dead and you had to finish the trach job on Carl before you could get to the others." We arrive at the lieutenant's office, and he leads me inside. He sits behind his desk and begins to open drawers.

What's he looking for? As I watch him, I'm wondering why the Monday Man is trying to make a big deal of what I did out there. I can hardly remember any of it. I think I put on some tourniquets, some bandages. But there wasn't much I could do. Most of them were already dead, or about to be dead. They were lying all over the place. Some were holding hands, like it was a kid's game. All fall down and freeze. You can't move until somebody says, Olly olly—

"Here it is. I knew I had one in here somewhere." The lieutenant slides a Baby Ruth candy bar across the desk to me. I quickly open it and start eating it. Why am I so hungry?

"First thing I'm gonna do is get you a field promotion. You're a specialist now. What do you think of that?"

I wonder what he's talking about. Can you be a specialist without specialized training? I get the weird feeling again I'm outside of myself watching this happen. My mouth says, "Uh, a specialized what?"

The lieutenant looks surprised. "Why a medic, of course. Based on what you did out there, I can tell Eric did a hell of a job training you. You're our new medic. The new *bac-si*. Do you know that Vietnamese word? It's a term of respect, and it should be. You deserve it."

I shake my head. "I'm no medic, Lieutenant. Eric did everything. I just . . . held stuff. He made me carry the M5 bag on my back. It was heavy. When he wanted something, I was just supposed to—"

The lieutenant raises his hand to stop me. He gets a serious look on his face and leans across the desk toward me. "Listen, son, I'd like you not to say anything like that in front of the men. If you're going to be the new medic, they need to have confidence in you. Understand?"

"But I . . . I can't do it, Lieutenant. You have to believe me. I wouldn't know what to do. I mean, without Doc Eric there."

The lieutenant puts his hands flat on the top of the desk and looks me in the eyes. "You got no choice, soldier. There is no one else. While you were over there in your hooch sleepin' like a baby, I been trying to get us a new medic. I said I'd take anything, even a kid right off the boat. They told me there's nobody available. Said medics are droppin' like flies. Gettin' killed or shot up. So, like it or not, son, you're it. Now get to it. Pack up your stuff and move over to the medic's quarters."

I stand up and walk out of his office like I'm in a trance. I go to my hooch and sit on my bunk. It's a sad little place now, lonely with nobody in it. The ones that are still alive must all be over working on the new mess tent. I gather up my stuff and lug it over to the medic's quarters. I drop my stuff on the floor and look around. I know right off the bat there is no way I should be here. This is Eric's place, not mine. Nobody has even thought to clean out his stuff. The place is just like he left it. His extra clothes are neatly folded and stacked on top of an upside-down cardboard box. To try to keep them dry, I guess. His alarm clock is still where he left it, on a stool next to his bed, still set for five AM. An early riser. On top of his foot locker, in a silver frame, is a picture of a thin man in a dark suit. The suit is too big for the man. The man is standing in front of a shiny black car. The car is tall with rounded off fenders, an old car, from back in the forties maybe. Is the man Eric's father? Who will tell him about Eric?

I sit down on the cot, Eric's cot, to think about what I should do. I can't be the unit's medic, no matter what the lieutenant says; I don't know anything about being a medic. But here I am, in Eric's quarters. If somebody gets wounded, they'll expect me to help them. It makes me want to just get stoned and go to sleep again. The whole damn thing is so stupid it makes me feel like crying. Why did they all die and not me? I didn't even get hurt. My neck is stiff and my back aches, but I don't feel any other kind of hurt. So why do I feel so . . . down? I've felt sad before, but never this bad. Shouldn't I be happy I survived? But I'm not. Just the opposite. I'm sad and depressed, and it's worse than ever. I feel down, very far down, and I can't see any way I'm ever going to be not down from now on. I look around at the empty hooch. And now, I'll be even more alone than before. It would have been better if that sniper would have picked me out as his target instead of Eric, better for everybody. I would be dead, and Eric would still be alive to help if others get hurt. If somebody comes in hurt, what can I do for them? Nothing.

I notice a stack of books on a board that's set across two empty paint cans. Medical procedures books. Eric said he only got a little training back in the states, but he must have wanted to keep on learning about medicine once he got here. He didn't want to be in a war, didn't want to be a soldier, but when he got roped into it, he did his best to do it right. He was a real medic; not like me, a know-nothing fake medic. I pick up the book that's on top of the stack. *Treatment of Blunt Abdominal Trauma.* I should at least try to learn a little. I get undressed and take the book to Eric's cot. I get out my pencil and my notebook and lie down. I open the book to page one. It says care of the blunt force trauma patient requires speed and efficiency. No need to write that down—that's obvious. It goes on to say evaluating patients who've sustained blunt abdominal trauma remains one of the most challenging and resource-intensive aspects of emergency care. It lists all the possible internal things that might have been injured. I write them all down. The next page lists symptoms that can indicate types of internal injuries. Gastrointestinal hemorrhage. Pain. Tenderness. I'm getting sleepy. Why am I so sleepy?

I'm awakened by the thump sound of a mortar being launched. The explosion is close: blown-up-into-the-air dirt rains noisily onto my tent roof. *My* roof. Did it only take one night for Eric's place to become mine? More explosions, every one of them pretty close. Maybe I won't have to worry about trying to be the medic. Those falling mortars don't know the difference between a medic's tent and a combat soldier's tent. Maybe my first day as a medic will be my last. But I hardly have that thought when the howitzers start blasting away. It means the mortar attack is over. Odd. I realize I wasn't scared. Not at all. In the past, I would have been scared shitless, expecting the next mortar shell to come down and kill me. This time I wasn't the slightest bit scared, just impatient for it to be over. Has something changed inside of me? Did something happen to me out there to make it so now I don't care if I die? I try to assess how I feel, but I don't feel anything. I feel sad, but other than that, I just feel numb, as if none of it matters anymore.

I decide to go back to reading. I'd rather think about blunt abdominal trauma. But I'm hardly started reading again when the lieutenant comes hurrying in, out of breath. "Saddle up, Medic," he says. "We're going out after 'em."

I just stare at him. I don't like him calling me the medic. I'm not ready yet. I've hardly started reading Eric's books. I show him the book.

He looks at me, puzzled, but then he comes and takes the book out of my hands. He puts it back on top of the other books and grabs my arm to help me up. "Don't worry about that right now, Scotty. We gotta move fast before they get away."

"We? You're going out with the patrol?"

"After what they did to my men on that last patrol? You bet your ass I'm going. If we move fast, I think we can catch 'em. We'll cut 'em off before they can sneak back over the border. Hurry!"

He heads for the door.

"I'm hungry," I call after him. "I still haven't had anything to eat."

He's already out the door, but he says something back over his shoulder. I hope it was that he'd get me something to eat. I hurry and put my helmet and flak jacket on. I pick up the M5 bag, but it's so light I realize I just about emptied it after we got ambushed. I rush into the infirmary and start pulling stuff out of the medical cabinet. What do I need? Tourniquets. Bandages. Hemostats.

The lieutenant comes back and yells, "Let's go!"

"Yeah, I'm coming. I have to get some medical stuff."

He goes away, and I stare at the stuff in the medical cabinet. What else will I need? Not much left in there. Morphine. I might need morphine. I dig through the cabinet, but there's no morphine. I pick up the M5 bag and head for the door. But then I stop. Why am I carrying the M5 bag? I'm not the assistant medic anymore. I should be carrying the M3 bag, the bag with the emergency stuff in it. But where is it? Eric was wearing it when he died. Did anybody remember to bring it back? I look around and find it behind the examination table. Somebody must have thrown it behind there when they brought his stuff in. I pick the bag up. It's almost empty too. I look inside. A few small bandages and that little pair of scissors Eric liked. I paw though the bandages and find one morphine syrette. I stand there looking at it. The label on the box says "Solution of Morphine Tartrate - WARNING: May be habit forming." For some reason, that stern warning strikes me as funny. This one syrette won't be enough to even stop the pain for one person, let alone enough to get anybody addicted to it.

The lieutenant is back. "Didn't I say to hurry it up?"

I show him the syrette of morphine. "We only have one."

"Fine. Let's go. Now!"

I transfer everything from the M5 pack to the M3 pack. I look around. Is there anything else I might need? A weird thought jumps into my head: I should take my book. Why did I think that? Do I think I'll need to look up some philosophy when I'm out on patrol? A dumb thought. But what if I don't make it back? But that's a dumb thought too. What good would my book do me if I'm dead? But what if I get wounded and they chopper me out? See there, that's a logical thought. I'd want to have my book with me, wouldn't I? I grab it and stuff it into the M3 pack along with the medical stuff.

Outside, the men are already in line waiting for me. I fall in, and we head for the front gate. There's just a bit of light in the sky to the east, but the sun won't be up for a while. The ground is soggy, so it must have rained hard in the night. Odd, I don't remember hearing any rain. As we go out through the gate, the guards glare at me. Why are they looking at me like that? Are they mad at me because I survived and so many others died? I think about the last time I went out through that same gate. Eric and the others were still alive. When was that? Yesterday? No, you slept. How long did you sleep?

Monday catches up to me. "You okay, man?"

Why is he asking me that? Do I look sick? I don't feel sick. I just feel numb. I say. "I guess so."

He grins and holds out his fist to start the complicated handshaking thing he and the other black guys like to do, but I've never figured it out, so we just bump fists. He chuckles and gets back in line. I fall in behind him, but the lieutenant waves me forward. I'm the medic now, and he wants me in the middle of the line, the safest place.

We cross the wide field of grass that surrounds the base and the bottoms of my pant legs are already getting wet. It must mean it did rain hard last night, but now, for a change, it's only misting. The clouds overhead seem thick and unbroken, but behind us, in the east, the sun is starting to make streaks of gold inside the moody dark clouds. It might turn out to be a nice day after all. We go into the jungle and the mist turns into a fog that hides the tops of the trees. I look at the other soldiers to see if I know any of them. I've seen some of them around the camp, but I can't say I really know any of them.

I look back at the Monday Man. He's dropped back to bring up the rear. I wave at him, and in return, he gives me an odd little salute. He has a grim look on his face. That's not surprising: after what happened the last time we went out, he must be worried. But for some reason, I'm not. I try not to think about why that is and just focus on where I'm putting my feet on the slippery sidehill we're crossing. The lieutenant has us moving fast. He must really think this time we're going to catch those mortar shooters. As far as I know, he's never gone out with a patrol before. It's not SOP to have the camp's highest ranking officer leave the base, so I wonder why he's doing it. Maybe he's trying to make up for losing so many men on the last patrol. I remember how upset he got after Jeff was killed. He must really be going through hell now after losing so many. With Benny dead, the lieutenant has got one of the FNGs carrying the radio. I wonder if he even knows how to work the thing. The FNG is sporting a blondish, peach-fuzz beard. I bet he hasn't even started shaving yet.

One of the black guys up near the front of the line, a big guy, keeps looking back at me. He looks like he's pissed off at me for some reason. Why? Does he think he knows me? He spits into the grass, and then turns away. What did that spit mean? Has he got something against me? But now I remember him: he was the driver of the truck that night Jeff got killed. He was the one who was going to leave me out there alone. So why should he be mad at me? I should be mad at him for wanting to leave me out there. I look back at the Monday Man. Should I ask him why that guy is giving me the evil eye? Or is it not cool to ask a black guy about another black guy? But the Monday Man and I went through that ambush together; almost got killed together. That should count for something. I drop back next to the Monday Man. "Uh, Monday, can I ask you something? Why is that guy up there staring me down like that? Does he have something against me?"

Monday hesitates and scratches the back of his neck. Finally, he says, "Problem is, man, the dudes over in darktown think you've got the jinx on ya."

"The jinx? Me?"

"Can you blame 'em, man? That guy said he had to go out and save your ass when that Jeff dude got wasted. And then you go out as a gun packer, first time out, and the Polack gets blown to shit right in front of ya. Then you go out as assistant medic, and . . . well, we both know what happened that time."

I don't know what to say. He's right. I hadn't thought about it, but bad things do seem to happen every time I go out. I walk along next to Monday for a while before I ask, "Do you think I'm a jinx, Monday?"

He waves the idea off. "Aw, who knows about that kind of shit, man? Don't let it get to ya. Things just happen."

I nod to let him know I appreciate what he said and head back up to my place in the line. But I can't stop thinking about it. Does everybody in this line think I'm a jinx? It must seem to them like all the bad shit at this firebase started happening when I got here. But that's not logical. They told me when I got here that the enemy would come get us, sooner or later. So why should they all be blaming me? Maybe it's because I don't believe in luck like they do. For luck, a lot of them carry one of the company's challenge coins, or else a bullet they dug out of a tree, or a fragment from an enemy mine — anything to show the enemy can miss.

I decide it doesn't matter what they think of me. I still don't believe in luck. When it's time to die, we die. It says so in my philosophy textbook. It says we are born, we live our lives, and then we die and there's no rhyme or reason to it.

The lieutenant has got us moving even faster now, and everybody is watching their feet as we go up yet another muddy and slippery hill. At least they aren't looking at me anymore. They're all just trudging along, grim faced, probably all of them pretty nervous after what happened to the last patrol that went out. The lieutenant is leading us to the west. He'd said he was going to try to head Charlie off before he could make it back across the Cambodian border. Does he really think the mortar shooters are going to follow this path? I bet they have their own paths, secret paths. Or maybe they hide underground like Carl thought, and that's why they've never been caught.

The lieutenant continues straight on west, following a clear path. I idly wonder if he knows what he's doing. Doesn't the enemy also know where this path leads? But for some reason, that thought doesn't bother me much. I'm hungry as hell, but that doesn't matter either; back in Arizona, I sometimes hiked all day in the desert without anything to eat. I look back at the Monday Man. We make eye contact, and he shrugs. I think that shrug, and worried look on his face, means he's still jumpy from the last time we went out. I wonder why I'm not.

He comes up next to me. He pulls me off the trail and lets the others squeeze past us. He whispers, "Hold up a minute."

I start to ask him what's wrong, but he squeezes my arm hard and puts his finger up to his lips to shush me.

The rest of the squad goes on past us. Most of them are looking gloomy, shuffling along, heads down, shoulders humped forward. They hardly seem to notice us.

When they've all gone past, Monday whispers, "Do you hear it?"

I listen. The jungle is very quiet. "I don't hear anything."

"Right," he says. "Too quiet. No birds. Just like when Sergeant Carl knew it was too quiet before he led us into that clearing."

I look ahead. There's no clearing as far as I can see. And I don't remember the birds being especially quiet when Carl led us into —

Two quick pops. Was that rifle fire?

There's a burst of noise that I know all too well: a machine gun. Somebody ahead of us yells something, but I can't make out what it was. Everybody in the line hits the ground. The Monday Man also dives to the ground, and I stare down at him. He looks up at me and gestures urgently for me to get down. I know he's right, I should get down, but I can't seem to move. It seems odd to see him lying there in the wet grass.

The chattering of that machine gun starts up again. I turn to see where it's coming from. It sounds ridiculous, like some dumb machine that's gone out of control. I wonder what the Monday Man thinks about it. I look down, but he isn't there anymore. Then I see him. He's squirming his way under some bushes. He's wiggling forward like a snake, and that strikes me as funny: the Monday Man, usually so cool, is on the ground wiggling like a snake.

The sound of rifle fire joins the sound of the machine gun, and I begin to hear something like bees going past me. Very fast bees. Invisible bees, buzzing past me. Actually, it's more like a whizzing sound. Whizzing past, then gone. I have the strangest feeling I've heard that very fast sound before. Little pieces of the bushes right next to me are being clipped off, as if by an invisible gardener. I'm fascinated by it. I lean closer to try to figure it out. Some of the pieces of the bushes start jumping right up into the air; it's as if they have a life of their own. It's so funny, I want to laugh, but I can't laugh because something tells me it's very sad. But why should it be sad? Something seems to be making my brain feel sad, and I don't know why. The shooting goes on and on. I have the strangest feeling that none of this is real. Either that, or I'm invisible. Maybe they can't see me because I'm not moving. Maybe if I stay very, very still, the enemy will go right past me like I'm not even here. I look down at the Monday Man. He's half under a bush. Only his legs are sticking out. He's holding onto his helmet with both hands.

A very loud explosion knocks me over. Now I'm down on the ground too. That's odd. My ears are ringing, and I'm staring up at a cloudy sky. One of my legs seems to be hurting. I try to figure out which leg it is, but for some reason I can't quite remember which is left and which is right. I guess it doesn't matter. I try to sit up, but I can't because one of my legs is sticking out the wrong way.

The big black guy who thought I was a jinx comes running toward me. Where is he going in such a hurry? He looks scared. He doesn't have his rifle. I wonder what happened to his rifle. The sound of a shot comes, and he goes right down on his face. Man, he went down hard. It was like he had a rope tied to the front of him and somebody gave it a hell of a jerk. I'm amazed: he didn't even put out his arms to try to break his fall. I feel bad for him. Big guy like that. Must have really hurt.

I look up at the sky and try to figure out why the sky is not blue. In Arizona, the sky is always blue. I'm taking really fast breaths. Why am I doing that? None of this is real, so why should I be scared? I tell myself to slow my breathing down, but it doesn't seem to want to. It's as if my breathing is a little animal inside of me that has a mind of it's own. Odd.

My brain says I should do something. But what? I don't have a gun, so I can't shoot anybody. I don't have a gun because I'm the medic. Am I supposed to be doing medic things? But I don't hear anybody calling for the medic. What about that big black guy? He fell down on his face. Does he need the medic's help? I flip over onto my stomach and crawl to where he is. Crawling hurts my leg. What the hell is the matter with my leg? Never mind. You're the medic. Do your job. I make it to the guy and do what Eric taught me: first, feel for a pulse. I put my fingers against the side of his neck. No pulse. I lie next to him, facing him. I reach out and pat him on the back and say, "There, there." He doesn't respond. He doesn't move at all. I roll over onto my back. I guess there's nothing the medic can do for him.

Another explosion, not so close this time, but it stirs Monday into action. He scrambles out from under his bush and tries to run, but he must not be seeing so good because he steps right in the middle of my chest and falls down. He gets up on all fours and stares at me like he doesn't know who I am. His eyes are all wild, like he's an animal caught in some kind of trap.

The shooting has stopped. No explosions either. How long since the shooting stopped? Why didn't I notice?

The Monday Man jumps up and runs in the direction we came from. I turn onto my side and watch him go. So long, Monday Man. Hope you make it. But he doesn't get far: a little guy in black pajamas steps out of the bushes right in front of him. Is that the enemy? Is that Charlie? I've never seen the enemy before. But how can the enemy be so small? He's pointing a rifle at Monday. It's a big rifle, too big for such a little guy. I have the passing thought that maybe I should do something. But what can I do? I'm lying on the ground, and my leg is not working right, and I don't have a gun. But still, if that little guy is the enemy, shouldn't I try to do something about it? But maybe he's not the enemy. He's not shooting Monday. He's just standing there, pointing his too-big rifle at Monday's chest. I have the strange thought that I'm glad I don't have a weapon. If I did, I might try to shoot that little guy. To save the Monday Man. But wait, if that little guy is the enemy, shouldn't I want to kill him? My brain is all confused. It's telling me not to do anything. It's telling me there's nothing you can do because you don't have a gun and you can't sit up because your leg is hurt and sticking out the wrong way. It's telling me to just watch and see what happens. You are the watcher; therefore, you are only supposed to watch.

The little Charlie guy and the Monday Man seem to be frozen in place. The little Charlie guy has his eyes locked on Monday, and Monday has his eyes locked on the little Charlie guy. I don't think the little Charlie guy sees me down here on the ground. Maybe I really am invisible. Maybe I don't exist anymore. Maybe I never existed. Maybe I'm only that brain in a vat, dreaming this.

Monday has his hands up. He's backing up, backing toward me. His rifle is slung across his back, just like Squad Leader Carl always said we were never supposed to do. Squad Leader Carl was right: that rifle won't do him any good that way. The little Charlie guy doesn't seem to want to shoot Monday. Maybe he doesn't know what kind of human Monday is. Maybe he's never seen a light-skinned black from Chicago before. Maybe he won't ever shoot. I hope he doesn't. But then, as if my thought makes it happen, the little Charlie guy pulls the trigger, and the back of the Monday Man's flak jacket puffs out. That's odd.

Monday looks down at his chest. He turns to look at me. He looks like he's about to ask me a question, but then he falls down.

He needs the medic's help. Eric would want me to help him. I crawl over to help Monday. He's lying on his back. His eyes are blinking rapidly. Why are his eyes blinking so fast like that? He opens his mouth, but no words come out.

I say, "What is it, Monday? What do you want me to do?"

He stares at me. He says, "Maybe you are . . ." He seems to be trying to swallow but can't. "Bad . . . luck." He keeps trying to swallow, and his mouth keeps opening like he wants to say something else, but he never gets to say it because the little Charlie guy shoots him again.

My face is instantly all wet. At first, I wonder how it could have started raining so fast. But it's not raining. I realize it must be Monday's blood that's on my face. I don't try to wipe it off. I don't mind. It's Monday's blood, and Monday was a good guy.

Now, the little Charlie guy is standing over me, staring down at me. He has his too-big rifle pointed at my chest now, just like he pointed it at Monday's chest. Now that he's closer, I see that he's just a kid. A kid wearing old worn-out black pajamas. I'm amazed to see how young he is. He can't be more than thirteen or fourteen. Can this boy really be a soldier? He's not wearing a uniform of any kind, not even a helmet. Shouldn't they at least give him a helmet? He has his rifle pointed at my chest, but he's not shooting me. Maybe he's not going to shoot me. Maybe he knows I'm the medic. But how would he know that? I stare at the kid, and he stares at me. He doesn't look much older than those kids who were begging in the street of Saigon. I smile at him, but he doesn't smile back. I wish I knew his language. I'd tell him he shouldn't be out here in the jungle shooting people. I'd tell him he should be home with his parents. Suddenly, the whole situation seems ridiculous. This is the enemy? This young boy? How could he be anybody's enemy? Is this who we're fighting? Little kids? That must be why I'm not scared. How can you be scared of a little boy, even if he does have a rifle? I hold up both of my hands and smile at him. I say, "See? No gun." I try to smile even wider to make sure he understands. I wonder if I should try to stand up. Show him some respect. But I decide against it. With my leg all messed up, I'm not sure I could do it, and besides, he's so short I might seem more threatening standing up. I keep smiling, but no matter how much I smile at him, he won't crack even a little bit of a smile back at me. He seems nervous. That's understandable. He's just a kid. He thinks I'm the enemy. I have the sudden thought that he looks a lot like that boy who was riding on that elephant when Jeff and I were on that road security detail. Is this that same boy? No, couldn't be. That was a long ways from here. At least, I think it was a long ways from here. I keep smiling. Maybe it's working. Maybe he's not going to shoot me. He can see I have no gun, so he must understand that I'm no threat to him. I'm only the medic. Squad Leader Carl always said these Cong guys were smart. He said they watch us, know everything about us. To make sure he understands, I say, "I'm a medic. See," I turn slightly to show him the M3 medical bag on my back. I reach back to take out some bandages to show him, but that wasn't a very good idea because now he looks even more scared, and he uses the barrel of his rifle to push me back down. "Whoa, hold on," I say, holding up both hands again. "I wasn't reaching for a weapon or anything. Just bandages. To show you I'm a medic. *Bac-si*? Understand? *Bac-si*. But I can tell from his eyes he doesn't understand, or doesn't care. From behind me, there's a single shot. Did somebody else get shot in the head? The Cong kid looks in that direction. Is he thinking he should be over there helping his friends instead of wasting his time with a worthless, no gun, medic like me? He looks back down at me, and this time, I can tell from the look in his eyes he's going to do it; he's going to shoot and be done with me. I can almost feel the increasing pressure of his finger on the trigger. It's odd that I don't feel scared. All I feel is . . . disappointed, disappointed that it has to end like this. It seems a shame to die in a war that I didn't want to be part of in the first place. And it's especially disappointing that I'm going to die before I can go back to Saigon to find my storyteller girl. And I wish I could have finished reading my philosophy textbook. I should have read faster. My mind wants to think about what will happen after I'm dead. They'll come and find me. Maybe they'll take me back and dump me onto a metal examination table like they did when they brought in that tough dying Marine. They also brought in poor Bill with his two different heart tattoos for his two different girls. The Marine died, but Bill didn't because he was shot through and through. T and T. That's what Eric called it. Bullet goes in the front and comes out the back. Not so many things to hit right there, Eric said, only intestines. Eric said if you ever get shot, get shot T and T. I wish this Cong kid would shoot me T and T. Then I might still get a chance to find my storyteller girl and get the chance to finish reading my book. A Vietnamese word comes into my mind. It's a word I learned back in Saigon, at Wong's Bar. Sometimes the guys would be really drunk and get so excited by Wong's beautiful young girls, they would try to screw them right there in the bar, on top of a table, right in front of everybody.

The girl would always say a word. What was it? Something that sounded like, "dan-tu." It must mean wait, or stop, or something like that. The girl would then lead the guy to the back room, the guy pawing at the back of her fine white silk dress as they went. I try it: "*Dan-tu.*"

The Cong kid hesitates. Did he understand?

I put on my most friendly smile, and slowly reach up to touch the barrel of his gun. I say it again, "*Dan-tu.* Not in the chest, please. Shoot here." Still smiling, I slowly, cautiously push the barrel of his gun down until it's pointed below my stomach, not quite in the middle. Eric said Bill was lucky that the bullet didn't hit his spine. He also said Bill was lucky because the bullet went in below his lungs. "There," I say, smiling a calm and friendly smile. "Shoot there."

He must understand because he pulls the trigger. The sound is unbelievably loud, and I actually feel the bullet go right through me. An amazingly unreal feeling. I want the world to stop while I think about that weird feeling. But it doesn't stop, and now pain is all inside of me, and I can't seem to get a breath. Did I choose the wrong place? Did his bullet hit my lungs? Was Eric wrong? Is the whole T and T thing wrong, a myth, a medic's old wives' tale? Is everything wrong? The sky is wrong, that's for sure: it's very, very white. And why do I feel so hot?

And now it's dark? How could the sun go down so fast?

No, dummy, it's dark because your eyes are closed. It's always dark when your eyes are closed. So open them.

I do it. Bight. Too bright. You blink your eyes. Daytime, but not clear. Something is wrong with your eyes. Something is making them blink. Oh, it's rain. You're getting wet. Damn. That's funny: here you are, probably dead, or about to be dead, and you're worrying about getting wet. Something else wants your attention. It's that damn pain again. It hurts. Well, of course it hurts, dummy. You got shot. The Charlie kid shot you in the gut. T and T. Why do they give young boys like that a gun? Don't they know they might shoot somebody?

Book Two
The Puppet Master

1

The Mind of the Beholder

What a weird thing to feel like you're outside of yourself, watching yourself. It's like you're floating up above, looking down at a young man who's lying on his back in a jungle. If that's you, how can you be up above, seeing yourself? Does it mean you're dead? Think. Figure this out. You were the smartest kid in school. And then you were the watcher. You're watching a young man lying in a jungle. Who is he? By his uniform, you can tell he's a soldier in the Army of the United States of America. He is known by many as Scotty the Philosopher. What's wrong with him? He has been wounded. That's sad. He must be in great pain. Yes, but mercifully, he thinks it's only a dream. He asks out loud, "In this dream, am I dead?" A voice from within his head says,

"You are not dead. I order you not to be dead."

The young man known as Scotty the Philosopher thinks it's very odd to have a voice inside his head. He wonders who, or what, the voice is. He decides it's not important. What is important is knowing if you are dead. But how can you tell? You might only be a brain in a vat dreaming you are alive. After you are dead, a new dream starts. Like in that movie back at the university where the puppet was dead, but he couldn't really be dead because he was only a wooden puppet. The movie was about a puppet in black pajamas. The puppet shot him. Then, he was in his coffin. A big nail came down at his face. Scotty feels sad. Why did the little puppet in black pajamas have to kill him?

" It was an order."

That's it! He was a puppet. A puppet has no choice. He was being controlled by a puppet master hiding somewhere up above in the darkness, pulling the strings. So it was the puppet master that made the cute little puppet get that old rifle and shoot poor little Scotty in the stomach. Then, the puppet master made the killer puppet put the dead puppet into a casket and made him drive a huge nail down through the casket lid, right at his face. Now Scotty understands. We all think we're in control, but we're not; we're all puppets in a puppet play. Someone high above us pulls the strings, and we puppets must act out the story. In this story, we're in a war in some far-away country, and the puppet master says we have to shoot each other. But isn't killing wrong?

"It is your duty. You must follow orders."

Scotty has a memory of a sign on a wall. Where was that? He tries to remember. He was wet, dripping water. He was standing on a concrete floor in his bare feet. He must have just come out of the showers; therefore, it must have been that first day back at Basic Training Camp. He was looking up at huge block letters that were painted on the wall:

> DON'T ASK.
> DON'T WONDER.
> DON'T THINK.
> FOLLOW ORDERS.

As he stared at the sign, the brand-new soldier known as Scotty was thinking, I'm doing what the sign says I'm not supposed to do, I'm thinking about if it's really possible to not think. Even though he knows he's not supposed to think, Scotty thinks about that sign on the wall. A soldier is told to kill, so he kills. He is only following orders. It must mean a soldier is not being bad when he kills because he's only following orders. It all makes sense. It was just a matter of applying logic. A soldier is not accountable for his acts, not really, because all soldiers are controlled by the puppet masters that are far above them. The puppet masters know best. If the puppet masters say kill, we have to kill. We should not ask why. We should not wonder why. We should not think at all. Our task is only to follow orders. And if the puppet masters say die, we have to die. Which brings up the same question again. Is he dead? If he is, will his mother come to his funeral? Maybe she'll want to stay in that dark old room at the end of the hall with her own mother, the two of them in there day and night, whispering together, not paying any attention to poor little Scotty who has to make his own lunch, a hot dog, a piece of Wonder Bread, a bag of potato chips. She doesn't care about poor little Scotty. Maybe she won't even care that he's dead. Maybe nobody will care.

But wait, God will care, won't he? They told us in Sunday School that God cares when even the smallest of his creatures dies, that he knows when every sparrow falls. But what if mother has already killed God by turning away from Him? What then? Oh well, maybe it's too late for questions anyhow. When you're dead, it's too late for anything. You said, shoot here, T and T. The puppet master manipulated the strings and made the puppet boy shoot. You remember how the bullet felt as it went through you.

"That's remembering. It is not your duty to remember."

The memory of the young puppet boy begins to drift away until it's only a vague and whispery shadow. But there's something important about that memory. Scotty is not sure he wants it to go away.

"An order is an order. You are not to remember."

The memory begins to dissolve. Scotty wishes he could hold onto it, but it's becoming delicate and fragile, like his grandmother's precious old lace shawl that she keeps wrapped around herself at all times. That stupid old lace shawl is so old and fine it's in danger of melting away. And then the memory is gone. Scotty can't even remember what it was about. Something about an old lace shawl. An old woman down at the end of a dark hallway. She hides in that room, wrapped in her precious old shawl that's full of memories. Scotty thinks maybe he should go down the hall to that room and try to get his memories back, but before he can make it to that door, more memories come toward him, kicking up dust on a dirt road. They are old, these memories, old farmer memories, old women running away afraid because Jeff shot the snake memories and then an elephant came and then he saved the turtle and—

"Stop! It is not your duty to remember."

Those memories also begin to fade, melting into the darkness of Scotty's mind. They are barely shadows now, and that makes Scotty sad. They were precious, those memories, so he tries to call them back. But they're swimming away, mysterious and delicate little fishes, going down and down into the darkness of the deeper water. Although he knows it's not his duty to remember, Scotty is sorry to see them go. He reaches out for them—with curiosity, rather than apprehension, for he knows this is only a dream. But although these swimming memories are impossibly slow swimmers, for some reason, he can never quite grasp them: they slip out of his fingers and slowly disappear into the depths. Scotty wants to follow them down there, but something is holding him back. Is it the puppet master?

Then, suddenly, startlingly, a new memory comes whether Scotty wants it to or not. It's a noisy memory, a memory of marching soldiers, a whole gaggle of noisy marching soldier memories all in a line, marching past Scotty in perfect formation, every one of them buzz-cut identical, every one of them looking straight ahead. Then, simultaneously, as if on an unheard command, they all turn to look at him. They yell out:

"They say that in the Army the pay is just fine
They give you a hundred and take back ninety-nine
Sound off one two. Sound off three four."

Scotty enjoys watching these memories march by. He calls back to them, "Sound off one two. Sound off three four." He waves to them. They look so fine in their fancy military uniforms. He smiles at them to let them know he's no threat to them, no threat to anybody. He doesn't even have a gun. But then, as if his thought about a gun makes it happen, the uniforms change: they become all torn and bloody. Scotty doesn't like that memory. One more soldier comes, shuffling along, all alone, unable to keep up with the others. It's Doc Eric. Scotty is happy to see him. As he marches by, Eric smiles and waves. He calls out:

"They say that in the Army the shoes are just fine
You ask for size eleven they give you size nine
Sound off one two. Sound off three four."

A joke. It makes Scotty laugh. Good old Doc Eric. Always ready with a joke, even if he's dead.

"I order you to stop remembering."

Oh, right. Not supposed to remember. Too painful. With all his memories marched away, Scotty feels empty. He worries that without his memories, he might not exist. Maybe he's not real, like that puppet, in that puppet movie. Not real. Being manipulated.

The strings are manipulated and Scotty's eyes snap open. Scotty sees that it's still daylight, but he thinks it might get dark soon because he sees ribbons of dark clouds reaching across the sky. They start in the distance and grow toward him, thick bands of clouds, dark and roiling, like huge dark fingers reaching out for him. Is it the hand of God coming to take him up to heaven? No, wait, his mother killed God. Therefore, this cannot be the hand of God. This must be an evil hand. It must be the hand of the puppet master. Maybe he's coming to take him up to puppet heaven. Of course, that must be it. Only logical. Scotty remembers that he used to be very good at being logical. He was the watcher, wasn't he?

But now Scotty feels pain. He wants to be logical and not feel this terrible pain. He tries to ignore the pain by thinking about why his face is getting wet. If his face is getting wet, it must be raining. Only logical. Scotty feels proud he applied logic and figured it out. But that leads to another thought: rain falling on your face and getting into your eyes might mean you are not dead. That's also logical, isn't it? But he still feels pain. Logically, if his brain doesn't recognize the pain, there will be no pain. He closes his eyes and concentrates on using logic to not feel pain. But it doesn't seem to be working. He feels pain in his gut. He feels pain in his knee. And he feels something uncomfortable under his back. What is it? M3 comes into his mind. What is M3? It comes to him. M3 pack attached to my back. Now that the mystery of the thing on his back has been solved, he begins to think there's something important about that M3 pack. He tries to be logical. An M3 pack has medical stuff in it. Bandages. Hemostats. Medicine. What kind of medicine? Medicine for pain. Morphine! That's it. The M3 pack has morphine in it. It stops pain. But can he reach it? It hurts too much to move. Maybe the puppet master can help. Like magic, the strings are manipulated, and Scotty is on his side. Now Scotty's hand is inside the bag. His fingers touch things: bandages, metal things, scissors, a book. Why would there be a book in an M3 pack? Got to stay focused. A book does not stop the pain. Morphine is what stops the pain. Keep feeling for it. He feels more metal things, more bandages, a small tube of toothpaste, more metal things. No wait, go back. That's it. That's not toothpaste, that's the morphine. Scotty takes the tube out. The correct strings are pulled to make him take off the cap and stick the needle into his arm. He squeezes the tube like he did with that big Marine.

The sky is strange, clouds like thick dark fingers are reaching, reaching. Did time pass? Does time exist anymore? Is it still the same day? Something is wrong with his gut. He should find out what it is. Be logical. He realizes what he's feeling is pain, very intense pain. He reaches down to touch where the pain is. It feels wet down there. Why is it wet? It must be blood. Only logical. Blood was leaking out of a big Marine. Had blood on his forehead too. An M. An M written in his own blood. M for morphine. Scotty thinks maybe it would be good to have an M on his forehead like that big Marine did. He dips one finger into his own blood. His hand moves slowly up to his forehead, as if controlled by strings. He watches his own hand move. He has no control over it. He is only the watcher. His finger draws an M in blood on his forehead. But was it an M? Maybe the puppet master made my finger draw it upside down. Then it would be a W. What does W stand for? Wounded? Worried? Weary, so weary. Wishing? If he had one wish, he would wish not to be dead. But his father always said if wishes were horses, even beggars would ride. Scotty wishes his father wouldn't have died in the rain that night. He should have stopped. Waited for the rain to let up. But no, he wanted to get home to his wife and young son. A good man. A good soldier. Followed orders. Died on a dark and slippery road on a cold rainy night. Left his young son alone with no one to guide him.

2

Comes the Chopper

Scotty is outside of himself, watching himself. He is the watcher.

Now, he's hearing a loud sound. Too loud. Coming closer. The sound of it, the rhythm of it, chop, chop, chop. It's like that old rhyme: comes a candle to light you to bed, comes a chopper to chop off your head. Jeff's head got chopped off. Men on the street, no heads on any of them. Chop, chop, chop. Sorry, can't get into heaven without a head.

"Here's one. This one's still alive."

Yelling. Who's yelling?

"Medic! Medic! Over here. This one's alive."

Too loud. Shh.

Somebody has ahold of his arm. Pain, too much pain.

He opens his eyes. Did time pass? How are you supposed to keep track of a thing like time? Is it night? How did it get to be night?

People are talking. Vague shadows are moving. Is this what happens when you're dead? Does the puppet master just cut the strings and your body falls down into a puddle of worthless nothing, a pile of dead puppet parts, no longer of any use to anyone? But he thinks, I'm thinking, aren't I? My brain is thinking. If your brain is thinking, therefore you are. Somebody said that. In a book. Thinking proves you are alive. Or does it? Maybe you are only dreaming that you're thinking, a brain in a vat dreaming about thinking. The book said that. It said, how can we prove we're not just a brain in vat dreaming about being alive? A brain in a vat can't die. You just dream you're dead and the dream of life goes on.

His eyes are seeing something up there. A vague, blurry thing, moving, going round and round. Chop, chop, chop, the chopper coming to chop off your head. He thinks, have I had that thought before? Does having thoughts mean I'm alive?

He tries to concentrate. He wants to be logical. A white ceiling up there. Is that possible? What happened to the dark sky? What happened to the rain? That thing is going round and round up there. Round and round it goes, where it stops nobody knows. There has to be an explanation for it. Be logical. Looks like . . . a fan. That's it! A fan going round and round on a white ceiling. Only logical. But how did he get here? Wasn't he in a jungle? And where did he see that fan before?

There was a man in a white suit. Siting at a desk under a fan. It was a wobbly fan. Dangerous. Dangling down on its wire, twisting, twisting, ready to break and come down to chop off everybody's head.

A face appears in front of the fan. A woman's face. Is it *her*? Is it his storyteller girl? Has she come back? The face smiles at him. Her mouth is saying something, but Scotty doesn't know what the words mean. Her voice is soft, sweet, but coming from far away. Must be a dream. Time to dream.

"By God, Scotty, you *are* alive. They reported you as MIA, probably dead. Whole squad wiped out. I'm not shittin' you, that's what they said."

That voice. Scotty is almost sure he knows that voice. He keeps his eyes closed while he tries to figure it out.

"Alive and kickin', by God. And right here in Saigon. I'm telling you the damn straight truth, old buddy. You were dead and gone. That's what they said. But I didn't believe it. Not my buddy. Too smart to get himself killed. Smartest kid in the whole damn school. That's what I told 'em. And I knew I'd find you. I got my contacts. Put out the word. Look for my buddy, I told 'em. And sure enough, they found you. Right here in this damn hospital. How're ya feelin', Scotty old lad?"

So many words. What do they mean? MIA? Alive and kickin'? Scotty's eyes snap open. He sees a blurry face. Fan blades behind the face, going round and round. Chop, chop, chop, comes a chopper to chop off your—

"Hey, Scotty, you in there? Wake up. It's me, Brent. Still with us?"

Somebody touches his shoulder. Is it the lieutenant? Scotty wishes the lieutenant wouldn't keep on doing that. Too fatherly. But the father never did that. Didn't ever touch little Scotty. The lieutenant is not the father. The lieutenant wants to lead us where we shouldn't go. No, Lieutenant, you're taking us too close to the border.

It's dark. Somebody nearby is sobbing. Why are they sobbing? Scotty turns his head. A lighted hallway. People moving past, all in white.

One of the white people comes closer. "Time for your shot, soldier. How are we feeling tonight?"

He should answer. It is his duty to answer. "Am I . . . dead?" But maybe he doesn't really want to know. Doesn't matter anyhow. She's gone.

Scotty hears sounds and opens his eyes. Bright, too bright. People are moving around, lots of people. Wasn't it just night? How is he supposed to keep track of whether it's day or night when it keeps changing? Purple haze all round. Wasn't that a song? Hard to remember. Long time ago. Men yelling. Arguing. Fighting. Wasn't he the watcher? A kid was under the dice table. Blood leaking out. How's the corn crop this year, kid? He will say, Not bad, but I'm hurt. Blood leaking out. Dying now, I think.

Too bad. Two nice kids from the Great Midwest. Both got shipped back home in boxes. American flags on top. Medals pinned on. Two girlfriends standing at the graveside, crying their eyes out. Beautiful in black, but so sad. One of them is a storyteller. She steps forward and begins to whisper a story. The one inside the casket will listen to her story. It will be a story about a turtle. She will say, save turtle, and turtle save you. The inside the casket, in the dark, will say, Yes, I did it, my love. I saved the turtle. I did it for you. I believe in you. I trust you.

Daylight. He's looking down at the young soldier known as Scotty the Philosopher. Scotty is lying in a very white bed. A woman in white appears. She may be a dream, but he decides to try speaking to her anyhow. He whispers, "Where . . . am . . . ?" Then, he thinks, did I say that out loud? Maybe not, because she isn't there anymore. But what *is* here is pain. Pain in his gut. He tries to think why there would be so much pain. A memory comes: a bad little puppet with an old rifle.

"Your duty is to not remember."

That voice again. Duty. Not his duty to remember. But that bad little puppet with a rifle keeps coming back. Must be hiding somewhere. Far back in his mind. Too young, that puppet, too young to be playing with guns. Bad boy. Put on black pajamas. Go to bed without any supper.

"Hey, Scotty. Can you hear me? Wake up."

It's an order. He must open his eyes. Scotty opens his eyes. He sees a face. He thinks, I know this person. It's Brent. From Arizona. Kids. Pals. Under the ice together. Always together after that.

"Hi." Scotty is not even sure that sound came from him. Sounded too hoarse. Like a frog. Frogs live in water. Turtles too. In water. You saved the turtle. Took him to water. Did the turtle save you again?

"So, you're talking now. That's good, old buddy. They told me you wouldn't talk to anybody 'cept yourself. They say you shoulda been snappin' out of it by now. The docs around here were beginnin' to think you'd gone off your nut. But I told 'em no way. Not my buddy. I told 'em you were the smartest kid in the whole damn school. No way my little buddy is gonna be one of those nut cases."

The face comes closer. Is the face trying to look inside his mind?

"You're not, are you? Not one of them nut cases, I mean."

He wants you to talk. He's your buddy. You should talk to him. "What . . . should . . . I say?"

"Hey, that's my boy. I knew you were in there."

The face smiles. One of the eyes winks. "No need to talk anymore, old buddy. I get it. You're just layin' low. Good idea. Play it cool. Let those pretty nurses take care of ya. They say you're not supposed to move a muscle, so don't. Not' 'til you heal up inside"

Nurses. Hospital. Remember that. You are in a hospital.

"They said you'd lost so much blood you were more dead than alive when they found ya. When they put you in that chopper, they didn't think you'd make it back to Saigon. But you did, didn't you? That's my pal. Tougher'n they thought."

"T . . . and T."

"Tea? What does that mean? Never mind, they'll give you somethin' to drink later. For now, they're feedin' you through that tube stuck in your arm. Some kind of white stuff. But they say you're gonna make it now, no problem. Just lay low. Let everything inside ya heal up."

"Hungry."

"I bet, after goin' so long without eatin'. But you can't eat yet. Not 'til those holes in your guts heal up. Doctor told me. Bullet went in the front and out the back. Lucky it missed your spine. That's what the doc said. Another inch toward the middle, youda been paralyzed for life. And good thing your intestines were mostly empty. Less danger of infection. They cut out some of your gut, but you'll be good as new."

The face comes closer. The mouth whispers, "You got to hurry up and snap out of it, Scotty. You got to come back and be with the living."

Why is he whispering?

"Listen, business is red hot right now. I worked out some new deals. Big stuff. You won't believe it."

He puts both of his hands behind his head and yawns. "Oh man, I gotta get more sleep." He laughs. "No time for sleepin' anymore, old buddy. Busy as a hound in tick season."

Scotty tries to imagine being busy as a hound.

"Well, better get goin', Scotty. But I'll come back and see ya. Soon as I get a minute. I'll make sure you're getting the best. You can count on that. Got connections now. Big time. Wait 'til you hear."

That's Brent. Likes the big time.

Brent is gone. Where did he go? Scotty thinks about the big time. Big time Brent. Busy Brent. Brent the mover and shaker. Makes things happen. The self-realized type. Said so in book. Where is that book? Must be gone. Everything gone. Everybody gone.

Something is wrong with his nose. It feels like . . . like a tube. He wonders why he has a tube going into his nose. It feels like it goes down through his throat. Scotty doesn't want to have a tube in his nose. He tries to pull it out, but it's stuck. Tape. He tears away the tape and pulls on the tube. It starts to come out. He feels it coming up through his throat. A weird feeling. Makes him want to throw up, but he keeps pulling on it, and it finally comes out. He stares at it, trying to figure out why he would have such a thing in his nose.

"Hey, what are you doing?"

A woman in white. Where did she come from? She looks angry.

She goes away, but soon comes back with a man in white. They both look angry. They try to put the tube back in Scotty's nose, but he doesn't want it in there. He fights them.

"You have to let us put it in," says the woman in white. It's to pump out your stomach. You can't have anything in your stomach, not even saliva."

Another man comes. They're holding him down. Scotty doesn't like to be held down. It's like being under a pile of men.

"Stop fighting us. We're doing this for your own good. Let the tube go down. Don't fight it. Pretend you're swallowing it."

Scotty is unable to resist them. The tube goes back in.

"And don't try to pull it out, or we'll just come and put it back in again. You hear me?"

The people in white go away.

They hurt his throat. And his gut hurts. And his knee hurts. He feels very sorry for himself. He asks the puppet master, "Why do you hate me so much? Why won't you just let me go home? I don't want to be here anymore. I want to be in the desert, looking up at the stars."

Somebody in white comes. "So, you want to make trouble, do you? I heard what you did. We know how to deal with the likes of you." The person in white grabs Scotty's arm and does something to it. A vague cloud gathers around him. It makes it hard to think, hard to be logical.

Morning. Things seem a bit clearer this morning. He turns his head. Other men in beds. Beds lined up against the walls of the long narrow room. He turns his head to look in the other direction. More beds. A man in each bed. Some are moaning. Somebody down the way is screaming. Past the last bed in the row, he sees a wide doorway. People going past the doorway, out in a hallway. Busy people. Across the room, sunlight angles in through a big window. Shaft of too-yellow light, fine dust hanging in the air. A world outside that window. Sunlight bright, dims, then bright again. Something outside that window interrupting the sunlight. A tree? He imagines leaves dancing in a breeze, sometimes blocking the sun. Only logical. Scotty likes being logical. He tests his brain. Women in white. Nurses. Men in beds. A hospital. Good. Brain is working better now. How long here? Don't know. Doesn't matter. Time doesn't matter. Time is morning light, then dark and the long night of trying not to remember. Not your duty to remember.

3

Heroes

Scotty opens his eyes. Sunlight is angling in through the big window. He thinks he had a dream about flowers. Weren't there flowers in that jungle? Didn't people die in that jungle?

"Stop. It is not your duty to remember."

Scotty decides he doesn't want to remember. So what should he think about? Names. In a book. That's right. Philosophers. Schopenhauer. A German. A pessimist. Said the world can't be understood. Boy, that's for sure. That Schopenhauer guy was right on. He should have come to this crazy country. Then he'd know how right on he was. If that guy ever saw so many people getting killed, and people all over the place with no heads on them—

"Stop! That's remembering."

Oh, right. Got to stop remembering. Got to be logical. No such thing as remembering. Not rational. The Rationalists. They were rational. Talked about doubt and existence. Mind and body. Knowledge through experience. Does it mean dreams are real, and reality is not? A rational person should doubt truth because the only real truth is doubt. Said so in book. Where is that book? And the father's bent-up police badge? Is that gone too? Gone in the rain. Gone on a rain-slicked highway.

The morning nurse comes with the morning shot.

"My book?" he says. "My father's badge?"

"Oh, so you've decided to talk to us. Good. I'll tell the doctor."

"My book. Will they . . . bring it?"

"Oh, you mean will they bring your possessions. Not likely. Things get lost. The Army way, you know."

As she gives him his shot, it evokes a fart. Scotty didn't mean to let it make a noise, but it did.

She looks surprised. "Did you just pass gas?"

"I'm sorry."

"No, no, it's a good thing. I'll tell the doctor."

She leaves, but soon she's back with a doctor who says, "The nurse tells me you've been passing gas. It's a good sign, son. It means your digestive system is starting to work again." The doctor turns to the nurse. "You can remove the tube." He stands at the foot of the bed and watches while the nurse slowly pulls the hateful tube out of Scotty's nose. What a weird feeling: the tube snaking its way up, ticking his throat, until finally, out it comes. Scotty feels happy to have that damn thing out of him, but now he can feel how sore his throat is.

The doctors says, "Clear liquids," and leaves.

She cranks the bed up a little and leaves.

Scotty is happy to be at least partly sitting up. Now he can see how big the ward is. Very big. Lots of hurt men in lots of beds.

Soon, a young girl dressed in a pink uniform brings something in a cup. Is it food? Scotty is really looking forward to eating. Strange that the simple act of eating, something that was so . . . regular, now seems like such a wonderful thing, a thing everybody should be grateful for. It turns out the stuff in the cup is something red. She puts a spoonful of the stuff into his mouth. It tastes very, very good, like maybe the best thing he's ever eaten in his life. The girl says it's Jell-O. She explains that Jell-O is actually a type of clear liquid, but in solid form. Very informative that Jello-O girl. She puts another spoonful of it into his mouth. Wonderful stuff. He savors every bite. Scotty tries to remember when he last had Jell-O. Probably not since he was a kid, Thanksgiving dinner maybe. The girl feeds him slowly, pausing between each spoonful. Scotty wonders if she's timing the pauses between spoonfuls. Is she counting in her head: one thousand one, one thousand two. She gives him a spoonful, then looks away while she waits. He wonders why she doesn't want to look at him.

The pretty young nurse, the one with the damp eyes, comes to watch. "Take it slow, soldier. Don't want to tax your intestines, do we?" She smiles, and he wonders if that smile means she's trying to make him believe he's going to be all right. Should he ask her? Should he say, Am I going to be all right? But she would just say, There, there, everything is going to be all right. Didn't he once says that to somebody?

"Your orders are to don't remember. And not to feel. Not your duty."

Scotty agrees with the voice. Not good to remember anything. Not good to feel anything.

Morning comes again. The damp-eyed nurse comes with his morning shot. She says he's recovering just fine. She says, "You're very lucky. You could have died." She looks around. "Everybody on this ward is lucky. They all had serious wounds. Had surgery, like you."

After she's gone, Scotty tries to memorize her words. You were wounded. You had surgery. Everybody on this ward was wounded and everybody had surgery. He looks around. It's a big room with lots and lots of beds. Some of the men are able to get out of their beds and sit in a chair while their sheets are changed. Some of the pulled-off sheets have blood on them. That doesn't look good. Why would they still be bleeding after their surgery is over and done with? Is it coming from inside them? Scotty worries that blood might still be coming out from inside him too. Are his sheets bloody? How would he know? His sheets don't get changed very often. It takes a nurse and an orderly to tip him up onto his side while the nurse rolls the sheets out from under him. It hurts him, so they don't do it very often. But if he has blood coming out, wouldn't the nurse notice it? Therefore, there must not be any blood. Only logical. Sometimes the mean night nurse washes him with a sour-smelling rag. She does it quick and not very well. Maybe she wouldn't care if there was blood. She's always so impatient. She scolds him for not talking, but he doesn't want to talk. Why should he?

The ward gradually becomes noisy. The morning nurse makes her way down the row with the bedpans cart for those who can't get up, or who, like Scotty, aren't supposed to. Those that can get up, do. They limp out of the room, probably happy to get out of the stink of this big ward. Too many men. Too many stinking men. A new patient is brought in. He's missing a leg. He's barely conscious. Scotty thinks he must have just come out of surgery. One of the men, about halfway down the row, is lifted out of bed and put on a cart with wheels. Is he going in for more surgery? Scotty looks across the way at the big window. Sunshine comes in through that window. Is the rainy season over? How long has he been in the hospital? He wonders why he doesn't know. He does know he's on a big ward. Lots of beds, a man in every bed. That's real. There's a big window across the way that's partly open, and he can hear birds outside. He heard birds in the jungle too.

No, no. Not supposed to remember. There were no birds. No jungle. None of that was real. The bird that made those strange chatters and rasps—not real. That bird that sounded like a falling missile, starting out high-pitched and then getting lower and lower until it ended in a deep-throated clicking—not real. Such a sound could not be made by a bird. Therefore, not real. Only logical. Nothing is real, except . . . what is real? Pain. That is real. Scotty wishes he didn't have to remember the pain in his gut. He reaches down to touch where the pain is. His fingers feel a scar. It starts next to his navel and goes down from there. It's a long scar. The scar is the pain and the pain is the scar. Scotty decides he doesn't want to think about pain either. He decides to watch the ceiling fan go round and round and not see or hear or feel anything. He's doing pretty well at not seeing or hearing until a doctor comes to stand at the foot of his bed. The doctor looks at his chart. He asks Scotty how he is feeling. Except for the pain, Scotty is not feeling all that bad. But he doesn't feel like telling the doctor that.

The doctor frowns and stares at him.

There's something about the way the doctor is looking at him that makes Scotty realize he's outside of himself, watching himself. It's like this is all a dream, and he's floating up above watching the dream happen. In this dream, there's a doctor standing at the foot of the bed. He's wearing a white coat. He's holding a chart. Somebody is lying in a white bed staring up at a fan going round and round. Scotty thinks, that person in the bed must be me. And that doctor must be thinking, why won't this soldier talk? Good question. Why doesn't he talk? Well, why should he? What is there to talk about? None of this is real. A brain in a vat can't talk. When you die, you just go on like you didn't die. The brain in the vat starts dreaming a new reality. That would explain a lot. It would explain why a person would feel like he was both inside of himself and outside of himself.

Scotty opens his eyes. Morning again. Men are moving around. Somebody is screaming. Scotty hardly notices the screamers anymore. Just part of the sound of the ward. Those screamers must be remembering bad things. The puppet master should tell that man not to remember. Not good to remember.

Scotty doesn't want to end up like those screamers, remembering bad things. Instead of remembering, Scotty watches. He's good at watching. He used to be the watcher. He watches the ones in wheelchairs. They get around fine. They may not have any legs, but they have two good arms, and they use them to spin the wheels and make their chairs go. Scotty is learning that humans adapt. Like the two across the aisle. Both of them are missing a foot. Scotty hears them talking about how it happened. Neither of them knows what it was they stepped on, but whatever it was, it blew their foot off. One of them lost his right foot, the other lost his left foot. They're always together, those two. They have their own little lost-foot club. They ignore the rest of the men on the ward and sit on the missing-right-foot guy's bed playing cards. Scotty reasons that they must sit on that bed because it's next to the open window. It must not smell as bad there. Only logical. Scotty has been watching them, and has figured out they are playing gin rummy. Being a good watcher; Scotty observes that the missing-right-foot guy, the one with the red-hair and freckles, is always laughing, even though he seems to be way behind in the ongoing gin game. He keeps on saying that someday, when he's "in the chips," he'll cover his gin losses. That makes Scotty realize they must be playing for real money, and the dark-haired, Italian-looking missing-left-foot guy, is way ahead. Scotty can see he's cheating, but the missing-right-foot guy doesn't seem to notice. Or maybe he doesn't want to notice; you don't accuse a guy of cheating when he's your only friend, the only other person in your missing-foot club.

Scotty has also been watching the guy in the bed next to him. One side of his face is all covered up with bandages. The guy mumbles a lot, so it's hard for Scotty to be sure what he's saying. He may be praying.

By being a good watcher, Scotty has learned that on this ward, hand wounds are as common as dirt. So are foot wounds. Squad Leader Carl said never step on dried grass. Could be a booby-trap. But in the jungle, you stepped on dried grass all the time, at least before the rainy season.

"Stop. That's memory."

Scotty stops remembering and goes back to being a good watcher. One guy on the ward, a guy who's lost both of his legs, is always talking very loud, like he's lecturing. He makes himself out to be an expert on strange enemy booby traps. He likes to sit in the middle of his bed and repeat his lecture about booby traps and the resulting wounds. He says there are hidden metal spikes that the enemy has doctored up with human shit to create infections. He says if you step on one of those you're in deep shit. Then he laughs. It's a joke. He says he has seen almost-invisible fishing lines rigged with grenades. If you feel a fishing line against your ankle, bingo, you're dead. Says a guy in his detail once got shot through with a bow and arrow setup. A springy tree branch strung with fishing line. Hand-carved wooden arrow. Right in the front of his throat and out the back of his neck. He says the medic told them not to pull the arrow out because it was plugging up the hole, keeping the blood in. Every morning, the booby-trap expert wakes up and starts telling the same stories all over again. Scotty tries not to listen. He stares up at the ceiling and wonders if they had booby traps in World War Two. Did his father have to worry about booby-traps in that war? Probably not. Humans have gotten a lot meaner since then.

Now another loud-mouth expert starts going on about shrapnel. Is he trying to drown out the booby-trap expert? "Bet half you guys got shrapnel wounds, right? Me, I got it in the legs. Buncha times." The doctors told Scotty it was shrapnel that wiped out his knee. Flying metal, they said, probably from a grenade. Knocked the shit out of your knee. They did some surgery on it, picked out as much of the metal as they could, but they said it would need more surgery when he gets back to the states.

The shrapnel guy is getting louder. "Shrapnel. Amazing invention. Get yourself some high explosives. Pack it inside a metal casing. Put in a bunch of sharp metal bits, and you got yourself a thing that tears the shit out of human bodies. Scotty wonders who first thought of shrapnel. It must have been a very mean person.

Now, some of the other guys on the ward have joined in. They all want to tell their own stories. One guy says, "Let me tell you about luck. If I hadn't bent down at that moment to pick up my canteen, I'd of been shot dead instead of only shot in the butt." Another guy says, "If I hadn't just walked behind that tree when the grenade went off, it'd be my head gone instead of only my arm. Just lucky, I guess." Another guy says, "Oh yeah, what about the other kind of luck, the bad kind? If I wouldn't have been the one who had to ride in the back of the jeep, I wouldn't have got a scratch. Shit. Why did the LT have to pick me to sit back there?" Another guy says, "Eight in a line, and I'm the only one who gets hit. Talk about bad luck." That makes Scotty remember something. Some of the guys in his unit thought he was bad luck. A jinx.

"Stop. That's a memory."

It may be a memory, but Scotty wonders if it could be true. Bad things did happen when he was out on patrol with them. Could they have been right? Is he bad luck? Is it his fault everyone is dead?

"I order you to stop remembering."

Right, Scotty doesn't want to remember about being bad luck. So, what should he think about? How about the memory of *her*, his beautiful storyteller girl? That's not a bad memory. Even if all of his other memories go away, he wants to hold onto the memory of her. Where is she right now? What is she doing? But that leads to a bad thought: what if she's still back there at Wong's doing what all those other young girls do? Scotty doesn't like that thought. He tries to think about something else, maybe something he read in his book. But it's hard to think about his book when his gut hurts so much. And his knee hurts too. His book said things aren't real, but pain is real. Maybe it's the only thing that is real.

An officer, a captain, comes to stand at the foot of his bed. Scotty wonders if this officer could be some kind of doctor. All the other doctors are officers. But this one isn't wearing a white coat like the other doctor's do. The officer is looking at Scotty's chart. It must mean he *is* a doctor. He makes a note on a large pad of paper, and then he sits down on a chair next to his bed. The officer says, "How are you feeling, son?"

Scotty stares at him. Why do they always ask that question? Don't they know by now he's not going to answer? He never answers questions like that because he knows it's not a real question; it's just what doctors say. The officer writes something down on his pad of paper. Scotty begins to worry about who this man might be. He doesn't like the man's dark watchful eyes. Those eyes make him feel like he's outside of himself watching himself. He's seeing an officer staring at a patient in a bed. The officer is asking the patient a question. The patient doesn't answer. The patient can't even remember the question. The officer writes something down on his paper. The patient in the bed wonders what the man wrote down. Did he write, Patient won't answer? Something tells the patient he'd better say something. The question was about how he was feeling. The patient says, "Better."

The officer nods and says, "Good, good." He again writes something down on his pad of paper. Then he leans forward and says, "I'd like to ask you a few questions, son. Is that all right?"

The patient in the bed shrugs.

"Are you feeling nervous? Or afraid?"

Uh oh, Scotty doesn't like that kind of question. No doctor has asked that kind of questions before. Scotty doesn't feel like he's outside of himself anymore. He's inside of himself, and he's feeling anxious. He decides he'd better say no. He says, "No."

The officer is staring at the patient in the bed. He says, "Well, that question took you away, didn't it? What were you thinking?"

Scotty shrugs.

The officer smiles. "My questions seem to be making you think. Would you describe yourself as a thoughtful person?"

Scotty would like to answer him, but he's not sure how to. If he says he *is* thoughtful, the officer might be like Brent and say he thinks too much. But if he says he *isn't* a thoughtful person, the officer might think there's something wrong with his brain. While he's still trying to come up with a non-suspicious answer, the man says, "Well, let's go on." The officer says, "Do you often feel worried?"

This time Scotty tries not to let the question start him thinking about other things. He says, "No." Did that sound like the truth? Is it true? Is not remembering anything the same as not being worried?

"You don't mind these questions?"

Does he mind? Scotty looks at the officer, trying to figure out what he's after. He decides the man must be some kind of shrink. He must be asking these questions to see if Scotty is normal. So, Scotty should act normal. He should give normal answers. He says, "No problem."

The officer leans closer. "Tell me son, when you were in combat, did you see friends die?"

Scotty says, "Yes, I guess so." But he's not sure if they were his friends. Was the Monday Man a friend? Maybe. What about Doc Eric? He was a friend, wasn't he?

"You did. You actually saw it? Not just heard about it afterwards."

"A few."

"A few? You mean you saw more than one die?"

"Some of them were dead. Did they all die?"

"Who?"

"All the others."

"I don't know the details of your situation, son. I'm just here to see how you're feeling."

"I'm feeling okay. I got shot. They did surgery on my guts."

"Yes, I saw that on your chart. Is it very painful?"

Scotty is not sure how to answer that. Of course it's painful, but maybe a soldier is not supposed to admit that. Maybe only cowards admit that wounds hurt. But how do you tell if you are a coward? Scotty didn't run away, but maybe he was just too scared to run. "Not so bad now. If I don't move."

The officer nods. "All right, let's go back to that day. When you saw your friends die, how did you feel?"

Back to that day? But he's not supposed to remember. Scotty knows he has to act normal, but he's not sure he wants to tell this man he wasn't scared. He used to be scared all the time, but he wasn't scared that day. It didn't seem real, so why should he be scared? But maybe it's normal to be scared. Now he's stuck: if he says he was scared, maybe it means he wasn't a good soldier, but if he says he wasn't scared it might mean he's not normal.

"Do you understand the question, son? I'm asking about how you felt at the time. How much fear you felt."

"I guess so."

"You guess you were scared? You don't know?"

"I guess I was scared. Who wouldn't be?"

The officer writes something on his paper, and that makes Scotty wonder if he said the wrong thing. He tries to make his mind work better. He used to be scared, scared of going into the Army, scared of getting sent to Vietnam. He was scared that day he went into that dark movie auditorium and saw the puppet master make the sweet young puppet with rosy cheeks kill his little friend, made him shoot a whole family just because he wanted their pig, made the puppets fly way up into the sky in a big can-opener airplane and drop bombs to kill cute little babies who were sleeping in their cribs and—

"Son, are you all right? Can you hear me?"

There's a man standing too close, asking questions. Scotty wants to cry out, No, of course I'm not all right. I'm being controlled by the puppet master. He won't let me remember things. I'm not supposed to remember seeing my friends get shot, or blown to shit, but now this officer is trying to *make me* remember. He wants me to remember seeing Eric get shot in the back of the head, and make me remember the Monday Man who was—

"Son, if you can hear me, squeeze my hand."

The officer's face is too close. He's squeezing Scotty's sweaty hand, trying to make him remember, trying to trick him.

"Look at me, son. I'm not going to hurt you, but I have to ask you these questions. I'm trying to help you. Do you understand?"

Scotty pulls his hand away. "Uh, understand . . . what?"

"Were you remembering it, son? Is that what took you away?"

"Remembering?"

"You went away for a few minutes there. Were you remembering that day you were wounded?"

The day you were wounded. It was raining. The Monday Man said the birds got quiet, too quiet. But wait, wasn't there a question Scotty says, "Uh, what was the question?"

The officer sits back down and writes something on his pad of paper. Then he looks back up. "Now it would be perfectly understandable if such memories frighten you. Is that how you're feeling now? Frightened? Is that why you don't want to talk about it?"

There it is again, the fear question.

Scotty says, "Uh, they give you a lot of morphine here. I also got hit in the knee." Scotty points down toward his knee. "By shrapnel."

"Yes, I saw that on your chart."

"I can't figure out how it happened. My knee, I mean. There were some explosions. The RTO kid went flying."

"You describe him as just a kid. Do you think of yourself as older?"

Scotty does feel old, but he doesn't know why. Maybe it's because he's lost track of time. Maybe so much time has passed that —

"You often don't answer my questions. Is it because you're thinking? Are you remembering how it was to be in battle?"

Scotty isn't sure if he's supposed to say he's remembering, or that he isn't. Maybe it would be better to say he doesn't think about it. The man is asking questions too fast.

"Uh, I was just thinking about . . . uh, if I feel older now."

"Do you?"

"I guess so. I'm not sure why."

"That's not an unusual feeling, not after what you've been through."

Scotty wonders how the man could know what he's been through. Could there have been somebody left alive to write a report? But who? The lieutenant was up at the front of the line, so he was probably the first one to get it. Maybe one of the old hands survived. Maybe the old hands have tricks that make them know how to survive.

"That's a memory."

"No it's not. It's just —"

"What's that? It's just what?"

Uh oh. Did he just say something out loud?

"Are you remembering now?"

"Yeah. I guess so."

The officer writes something down on his paper.

Scotty wishes the man would stop writing things down. What is he writing? Is it some kind of trick?

"And those memories worry you?"

"You'd think I'd remember something like that."

The officer nods thoughtfully. "Are you referring to your knee?"

"Uh, isn't that what we were talking about?"

The officer writes something else down on his paper. "Let's get back to your personal experience. You said you saw friends die. How did that made you feel?"

Scotty knows he should say bad. He says, "Bad."

The man writes that down on his paper too.

Scotty watches him write. Did he write down, Patient felt bad? Wouldn't anybody say bad? Maybe some guys would say, No, I didn't give a shit that they died. Scotty worries that maybe that really is how he feels. Maybe feeling numb and not remembering is not caring.

The officer is staring at Scotty, but Scotty is again seeing it from outside of himself. It's strange to feel like you're in two places at once, seeing yourself as if you aren't really yourself. It's like you're somebody else watching yourself do things. Does it mean he really is going crazy?

"Let me ask you another question, son. Do you have bad dreams?"

For just a moment, Scotty thinks about telling him about the wonderful dreams he had when he was back at Wong's with the storyteller girl, magical dreams about her being a beautiful young princess who led him through a peaceful deep green forest filled with kind and gentle animals instead of a jungle full of enemies with guns.

The officer is watching Scotty closely.

Scotty quickly says, "No. Not having dreams. Wish I was."

"But you were remembering something, weren't you?"

Scotty wonders if he should tell this officer about those dreams? Isn't dreaming normal? "Well, I was thinking back to dreams I used to have."

"Do you want to talk about them?"

Scotty is tempted to tell him. What would this officer-doctor think of the dreams the storyteller girl gave him. Does having wonderful dreams about beautiful young girls and magic forests mean you're crazy? Maybe it does, if the girl is too young. That reminds him of the question he wanted to ask someone. "Uh, are you a doctor?"

"Yes, I am. I'm a psychiatrist."

"That means you went through medical school, right?"

"Yes."

"The reason I asked is, uh . . . I have a medical question."

"Of course, son. You can ask me anything."

"Anything?"

"Go right ahead."

"Well, I used to dream about this one girl. She was, uh, young. That's what I wanted to ask about. How do you tell how old a girl is?"

"In a dream?"

"Uh . . . yeah, in this dream I had."

That makes the man smile. "You dreamed about a girl, but you weren't sure how old she was?"

"Yes. How do you tell?"

"I suspect this is not a dream girl you're referring to. I see you were stationed here in Saigon before you were sent to the front. Did you happen to visit what they refer to as the red-light district?"

Scotty tells himself he should have known the man would figure that out. But didn't just about every soldier in Saigon go to those places? So it must be fairly normal. Scotty says, "Well, there was this one girl. I didn't do anything to her. But I did see her without any clothes on. She didn't have much hair. You know, down there."

"Well, that would be one way to tell her age. I've, uh, heard these Asian girls have a fair amount of pubic hair. Dark, so it's noticeable."

"So how old are they before they get their pubic hair?"

The officer sits back and crosses his legs. He smiles. "Well, it's been a while since I studied human anatomy, but as I recall, most girls start getting at least a little pubic hair by the time they're twelve or so."

Twelve? The officer's words shock Scotty. Twelve? Was he in bed naked with a twelve-year-old girl? She couldn't have been that young, could she? "Uh, twelve? Really?"

"About then. It varies, Some girls start menstruating at age twelve. Which means they can get pregnant. You haven't got yourself involved in something like that, have you?"

Scotty is still thinking about the age of twelve. Too young. Way too young. "Uh, you said it varies. Is there any other way to tell?"

"Not without a physical exam. If a doctor wanted to determine a girl's age, he would probably look at her breast development, and maybe examine her *mons pubis*."

"Her what?"

"It's a lump down . . . there. Under the pubic hair. A rounded fatty mass that lies over the pubic bone. Girls begin to develop it when they reach child-bearing age. It protects them during sexual intercourse. It's evolution. Probably goes back to our cave man days. Pretty rough guys, I bet, those cave men." He smiles broadly to show he's making a joke.

But Scotty isn't thinking about the officer's joke. He's thinking back to that night. He remembers that part of her so clearly. He couldn't take his eyes off of that delicate crevice under what little pubic hair she had, a crevice that led down to her magic place. But did she have a lump? He can't remember. What about the other girls at Wong's? He's seen a few of them naked when the drunken soldiers get so excited they pull up the girl's dresses to see what they're about to pay for. But Scotty can't remember if they had a lump down there or not. If the storyteller girl didn't have one, it means she really is still a child. Thank goodness he didn't do anything to her. But what would a child be doing in a place like Wong's? She was dressed exactly like the other girls, in a white silk dress. And when she took off that dress, she was so beautiful, so perfect, she must have known that any normal American soldier would immediately try to have sex with her.

"That got you thinking, didn't it, son? What are you thinking?"

"Uh, I was just trying to remember. So, if she was like, uh, maybe at least sixteen, she would have that lump?"

"Yes, at least the beginning of one. Unless she was malnourished. The *mons pubis* is made up of fat cells."

Maybe that was it. Sure, she could have been malnourished. That could be why she was at Wong's. Maybe she was hungry. And that's why she needed money. To get some food. So maybe she really wasn't all that young, just malnourished.

"Would you like to talk about it? Does that memory bother you?"

"It's kind of hard to remember that night. I was pretty . . . drunk."

"I bet. That's what those kinds of places exist for, to get you drunk and relieve you of your money. Tell me, son, there's reported to be a lot of drug use in those kinds of places. Have you used drugs?"

"Drugs?"

"Yes. There are reports that drug use is becoming rampant among the troops. Even reports that men in combat situations are using drugs."

"Uh, like what kind of drugs?"

"Hallucinogenic drugs. Marijuana, especially."

Scotty shakes his head. "Not me."

The officer stares at him for a long moment.

The man makes a note on his paper, and then he says, "Let's forget that question. Let me ask it another way. If you did use drugs, do you think it might have had anything to do with how you got wounded?"

"I'm not sure what you mean, sir. The kid who shot me didn't pick out only the drug users."

"No, what I mean is—"

"But now that I think about it, the Viet Cong boy who shot me might have been stoned. He looked kind of stoned, almost . . . hypnotized."

"That's not what I meant either, but never mind. One last question. Do you think you could function well enough to carry out your duties? When your wounds are completely healed, that is?"

Scotty knows for sure how to answer that question. "No, sir. I don't think so. The doctors here told me I'll need more surgery on my knee. They say I'll have to undergo rehabilitation after that surgery."

"Yes, but if your knee could be completely healed."

"It can't be."

"Yes, but just for the moment, let's pretend that it could be. Do you think you would be willing to go back into combat?"

Scotty says, "No. sir, I don't think so."

"You wouldn't be able to go back into combat?"

"No, sir."

"Why not? Would you be too afraid?"

Scotty is not sure he would feel afraid. He's not even sure he knows what fear is anymore. Maybe fear is not real. That day, when . . . things started to happen, it felt . . . not real. Like it was happening to somebody else. The loud explosions were like somebody else was hearing them. And what about that kid . . . T and T. Was he afraid then? No, more like . . . disappointed. And sad, sad that it all had to end like that, sad and disappointed that there wouldn't be anything more. When his mother used to make him go to church, the preacher talked about what it would be like after you are dead. He said you would rise up to heaven, and it would be very nice, not a bad thing at all. You would get to sit up there on a cloud. That was the part Scotty the child didn't believe. It would be too silly, sitting up there on a cloud. He had learned in science class that clouds were just made of water vapor. So you couldn't actually sit on one. No way. But if you don't go off to sit on a cloud, what does happen? Does it all just end? Or maybe you just go on like you didn't die. You could think you were in a bed in a hospital, but you really wouldn't be, you'd actually be—

"Son, are you listening to me?"

Scotty tries to get his eyes to focus. The man is standing by the bed again. How did he get there? How does he move so fast?

"You went away again, didn't you, son? Is it because you're not sure how to answer the question?"

"It's all kind of confusing. I was trying to remember."

"I'm sure it was confusing. But how would you feel if you had to go back into combat now. After what you've been through."

"I'm not sure I would feel anything."

The officer looks surprised.

Scotty worries that he might have said something wrong. But would he feel anything?

"You wouldn't feel anything? You mean you wouldn't be afraid. It's normal to be afraid in combat."

Scotty feels like he's being twisted around. Does the officer want him to say he would be afraid, or that he wouldn't?

"The truth is . . . I don't care anymore. I'm wounded, and I'm going home. I'm never going back out there."

"Not even if you were ordered to?"

Scotty tries to focus, but it's like he's got too many voices in his head, confusing him. And he's not sure what this officer is up to. Is this some kind of experiment? Is the man trying to get a reaction out of me? He feels shaky all over. He laces his fingers together and squeezes hard, really hard, to keep his hands from shaking.

The man is writing something down. Is he writing down that the patient's hands were shaking? Scotty tries to think of something to say that will make the man stop writing. "No! I'm never going back out there. No matter what they do to me. You can't make me. Nobody can make me. I have to go back to the states and get my knee fixed. That's what they told me. I'm hurt, and they're supposed to fix me up. It's not my fault. I can't help if I . . ." He struggles to hold back the tears.

The man stops writing and pats Scotty on the arm. "Calm down, son. I wasn't saying you'll ever have to go back. It was just a question."

Scotty looks away. He's drenched with sweat. When he glances back, he sees that the man is again sitting in the chair. He's busily writing something down on his stupid pad of paper. What is he writing now? Patient is shaking? Patient is sweating? Patient can't control himself?

The man finishes writing and stands up. "All right, son. Good luck with that knee. I'm sure they'll be able to help you back at Walter Reed. It's a good hospital. I did my internship there."

The officer leaves. Scotty is feeling all jittery and nervous. Why was that officer asking all those questions, trying to make him remember? He doesn't want to remember.

"Wha . . . ee . . . say?" asks the half-a-face guy in the next bed. "Couldna . . . hear . . . all."

Scotty doesn't want to think about the psychiatrist's questions. He doesn't want to think about anything. "Nothing. He was just asking me some dumb questions."

"Who . . . wha he?"

"I don't know." Scotty won't look at him.

"I know," comes a shrill voice from across the aisle.

Scotty looks over. It's one of the missing-foot guys.

"I know too," says the other missing-foot guy.

They quickly abandon their gin game and slide off the bed. They put their arms over each other's shoulders and head across the aisle toward Scotty's bed. They move pretty well that way, swaying a bit from side to side, but making steady forward progress, each taking his turn at providing his good foot for the next step. Scotty has the funny thought that they look like two locked-together drunken Greek dancers. It makes him laugh, but he covers it with his hand. He doesn't want them to think he's laughing at their sad condition. He's never spoken a word to either of them before, but now he feels really appreciative of them for making him laugh for the very first time since . . . since he can't remember when, maybe for the first time since he got to this country.

The two guys arrive at the foot of his bed. The missing-left-foot guy says, "I'll tell you who he is. He's a ga-dam shrink, that's what he is."

"Yeah, a ga-dam shrink," says missing-right-foot. "You got to watch out what you say to those guys."

Scotty says, "I was pretty careful. I said normal things."

"Are you nuts?" says missing-left-foot. "You got to make them think you *are* crazy."

"Yeah, crazy as a loon," adds missing right-foot.

"Why would I want to do that?"

"Because otherwise, they'll say you're fit for duty," says missing-left-foot. "That's what they're tryin' to do."

Scotty says, "Not me. They told me I'm going to need more surgery on my knee. They said as soon as my gut heals up, they're sending me back to the states for more surgery."

"That don't matter," says missing-left-foot. "We're being sent back too. What matters is for you to get permanent disability. You got to be traumatized. That's what they call it. If you aren't traumatized, when you get back to the states, they'll just patch you up a little and put you on desk duty or somethin'. Not only that, but when you finally do get out for real, you won't get on disability. You won't get nuthin'."

"Do I need disability?"

"Damn right you do," they both say in unison.

"Soon as this war is over, they'll forget about you damn quick," says missing-left-foot. "They'll send you home and pretend like nothin' ever happened to you. You'll be on your own."

"On your own," adds missing-right-foot.

Scotty feels very ready to be on his own. He's ready to forget about the Army, forget about Vietnam, forget about it all.

"Oh, I know what you're thinkin'," says missing-left-foot. "You're thinkin'. You're willin' to be on your own. I know your type. But what if they don't do so good at getting your knee fixed up? Or what if your gut doesn't get better? Huh, what then? That's why you got to have full disability. So you stay in the system."

Scotty doesn't want to talk anymore. He shrugs, hoping they'll get the idea and leave him alone.

"And what if you need a prosthetic thing, like we do?" says missing-left-foot. "Those things need follow-up. The trick is to get battle fatigued. If you aren't battle fatigued, you'll get nothin'. I'm tellin' ya, ya got to get yourself outta the regular line and into the disability line."

"Yeah, you got to get in the nut case line," adds missing-right-foot.

The face-half-shot-off guy in the next bed mumbles, "Ree-lee?"

Missing-left-foot turns to him. "Damn right. You got to stay in the system to get anything out of it. We know. We got it all scoped out."

"Scoped out," adds missing-right-foot.

"Shl-shukd," says missing-half-a-face.

In unison, the missing foot guys turn to him and say, "What?"

"Shll . . . shked," says missing-half-a-face, carefully sounding out the words as best he can.

"Right," says missing-left-foot. "Shell shocked. You got to tell 'em you got that."

"And you got to tell them you won't ever get over it," adds missing-right-foot, shaking a finger. "Scared shitless. Nerves all shot to hell. You got to tell 'em that."

Scotty turns away. He doesn't want to be crazy, or even act crazy.

When he looks back, they're doing their funny linked-together Greek dance back to their bed. Then, they resume their gin game.

The face-half-shot-off guy turns away and starts mumbling to himself. Scotty wonders if he's practicing acting crazy.

Scotty stares up at the ceiling, grateful to them for warning him to act crazy so he can do the opposite. If that shrink comes back, he will be sure to not act crazy. The last thing he wants is to stay in the system. For better or for worse, he's ready to be done with the Army. Even if he is a little bit battle-fatigued, or shell-shocked, or whatever they want to call it, he doesn't want them deciding what to do with him. All he wants to do is go back to Arizona and walk in the desert and try to forget any of this ever happened.

Somebody touches his shoulder. He opens his eyes, but what he sees tells him he must still be asleep and dreaming. It looks like Lieutenant Dasen standing next to the bed. Scotty wonders how the lieutenant got into his dream. Scotty blinks his eyes to try to make the dream go away, but this time it won't go. The dream lieutenant is still standing there, staring down at him. Something is wrong with this dream: it seems too real. It scares Scotty to have such real dreams about people who are dead. He closes his eyes and tries to dream about something else, but somebody touches his shoulder again. He wishes they would stop doing that. He doesn't want to remember.

"Wake up, Scotty."

Scotty opens his eyes. The dream lieutenant is still there. It sure does look like the lieutenant, and he doesn't seem dead at all. He doesn't even seem to be wounded. But he doesn't look very happy.

The lieutenant drops a duffel bag on the bed. "Here, philosopher. I brought your stuff."

Scotty is beginning to think this dream might really be real after all. He asks, "Are you . . . alive?"

The lieutenant scratches the back of his neck and looks down at the floor. "Yeah, unfortunately I am."

Scotty tries to figure out why the lieutenant would say something like that. Would he rather be dead?

The lieutenant reaches out to touch the duffel bag. "Your book is in there, Scotty. It was in your hands when they found you. The rest of your stuff was at collections. They thought you were dead, but I knew you weren't because I helped them load you into the medevac chopper. And I kept track of where they took you."

Scotty eagerly digs into the bag. The first thing his fingers feel is his father's bent up police badge. He takes it out, but he doesn't know what to do with it, so he just pins it to the front of his smock to make sure he doesn't lose it again. He looks up at the lieutenant." It was my father's."

"He was a cop?"

"Yes, sir. He was killed. On his police motorcycle."

"Sorry to hear that."

Scotty shrugs. "It was a long time ago."

Next, Scotty takes out his philosophy textbook. He's very happy to see it, very, very happy to hold the precious book in his hands again. He closes his eyes and holds it tight against his chest. But the book smells odd. He opens his eyes and looks at it. What's that smell? He sniffs the cover and the sides, and that's when it hits him: it's the smell of the jungle. He holds the book away from his face. He doesn't want to smell the jungle. The jungle is where—

"Stop that!"

"Oh, that's right, I'm not supposed to remember."

The lieutenant says, "What? Not supposed to remember what?"

Scotty shrugs. "Uh, oh nothing. Just thinking out loud."

Scotty opens the book and tries to act very normal. He leafs through the book, pretending to read, but he's actually only thinking about how happy he is to see the wonderful words on the pages again. But then, when he turns another page, it's stained red. He quickly turns more pages. A lot of them are colored red.

He holds it up to show the lieutenant.

"Yeah, blood."

"Blood?"

"Yeah, your blood. Like I said, you were holding it."

Scotty touches the blood stain, almost afraid it might still be wet. Thankfully, it isn't. The words are still readable despite the stain, but he worries that now every time he reads his book he will be reading through his own blood, remembering how it got on there. He doesn't want to remember.

The lieutenant says, "I figured you'd be wanting that book."

Scotty looks up at him. It really does seem to be the lieutenant, but his eyes look sad, and very tired. "Is it really you, Lieutenant?"

He scowls. "Don't call me lieutenant. I'm not a lieutenant anymore. I'm nothing now."

"You're not?"

"No. I resigned my commission. And there's nothing they can do about it. I have the right to resign. I'm just a regular soldier now."

That confuses Scotty. The lieutenant once told him he'd let the Army pay for his college education. And that meant he had to become an officer in the Army. Now he doesn't want to be one anymore? "Uh, I don't get it, sir. Why did you—"

"And don't call me sir. Nobody will ever call me that again. I don't deserve to be an officer. I led my men into mortal danger like a complete idiot. I was under direct orders to stay away from the Cambodian border, but did I? No. I led you right into a trap. I deserve to be court-marshaled, but they won't do it. They say they need officers now even more than ever. Too many officers getting killed, they say. So you know what I did? I told 'em to stick it where the sun don't shine. They couldn't stop me from resigning my commission. So from now on, I'm just like you, philosopher. A regular soldier. Let somebody else give the orders. Somebody who knows what the hell they're doing."

Scotty doesn't know what to say. Was the lieutenant really a bad officer? Scotty isn't sure how you tell. The lieutenant was the only commanding officer he ever had. Scotty remembers that the lieutenant got upset when Jeff got killed, so at least that meant he was concerned about his men. And a couple of times the lieutenant shared his whiskey with Scotty. They had talked together like two regular human beings. Scotty doubts other officers would talk to a lowly private like that. Scotty says, "I think you were a good officer. You shouldn't resign."

The lieutenant looks angry. "You don't know a damn thing about it, philosopher. You have no idea what makes a good officer, and I don't either. I wasn't trained to be responsible for an entire unit. I hardly got any training at all. If you don't know what you're doing, people are going to get killed. Because of me, good men died."

He stops talking and stares at the wall. It's like he's forgotten Scotty is even there. Scotty wonders if maybe he's drunk, like he often was back at the firebase. But he doesn't act drunk. He just acts . . . upset.

He looks back at Scotty, still looking angry. "Besides, who would want to follow me into combat? Who wants to follow a coward?"

"You're not a coward, sir. Why would you say that?"

"Because it's true. When the shooting started, I ran. I ran away like a scared little child and hid in the bushes."

Scotty tries to think what to say to make him feel better. "You . . . probably did the right thing. We should have all . . . uh, retreated."

"Retreated?" shouts the lieutenant "What a bunch of horseshit. I didn't retreat, I ran. That's what I did. I was scared, and I ran. My first time under fire, and I turn out to be nothing but a damn coward. That's what I wrote in my report. I wrote that every one of my men responded with bravery and heroism, but not me. Instead, I ran away. I wrote in my report that they all deserve posthumous medals while I only deserve to be court marshaled and shot. I wrote, The commanding officer failed in his duty and should be stood up against a wall and shot. That's what I wrote, and that's the real God damn truth of it." He's getting louder and louder.

Scotty says, "Please quiet down, sir. The others will hear."

"I don't give a shit if they hear." He turns and yells, "That's right, God damn it. I ran. And I don't give a shit who hears." Several of the other men look up, but then he yells, "What the hell are you looking at? He turns back to Scotty. "What does it matter to me now what anybody thinks? It's all gone to hell. That's what my father will say. You should have seen him when he came to see me off. He cried with pride when he saw me in my brand new officer's uniform. He retired from the Army as a God damn major. Got wounded in Germany and kept right on fighting. The day I left for Vietnam, he hugged me for the first time in maybe twenty years. He stood back with tears in his eyes and saluted me. He was so damn proud of me. What will he say now?"

"He will understand, sir."

The lieutenant's face gets all twisted up. "Quit calling me sir, damn it! They taught us that word was a sign of respect. Do I deserve respect now? No. And I don't respect my superior officers either. You know what they did when I filed my report? Said they were going to tear it up. Said it was my men that made mistakes, not me. Said my men were the ones who walked into a trap. Can you believe it? They were going to blame it on my men. They said I did the right thing, finding a way out, and now I needed a rest. They were going to reassign me. Keep me here in Saigon. Make me a rear echelon motherfucker. Hide me away somewhere. Know what I said? I said, fuck you. That's what I said. Said it to a full-bird colonel. Right to his face. Told him if he tore up my report, I'd just write it again. I told him I wanted to be sent to wherever the action was the hottest. As a regular rifleman. He said fine, have it your way. They're sending me out tomorrow, but I knew I had to come here to apologize to you before they send me up there to get killed."

Scotty wishes he could think of the right thing to say. Is the lieutenant a coward? What is a coward? Who can say? "You didn't leave us to die, sir. It's not your fault. It just happened."

He looks at Scotty, his eyes full of tears. "No, no, it didn't just happen, Scotty. They died because of me. They won't lock me up, and they won't shoot me, so the least I can do is try and make it up to you. I'll be an ordinary rifleman. I'll learn how to be brave like you."

Brave like me? That really confuses Scotty. The one thing he knows for sure is that he wasn't brave. He knows he's not allowed to remember, but he thinks he just stood there and did nothing.

The lieutenant seems to be lost inside his own head. Scotty stares at him, thinking, he should say something.

Finally, Scotty says, "I wasn't brave, sir. All I did was—"

The lieutenant grabs Scotty's hand. "No, you were brave. You did your duty, and you got wounded. They tell me you were shot right in the gut. Painful as hell, I bet. Said you were lucky to be alive. While you were being brave and getting wounded, what was I doing? Hiding in the damn bushes. Hiding while my men were cut down."

"Please sir."

"It's all right, Scotty. I know what I have to do. But I didn't forget you. The last thing I did before I resigned my commission was to put you in for that medal I promised you. And another promotion too. You're going to be a sergeant when you get out of here. What do you think of that?"

Scotty can't believe what he's hearing. The lieutenant's crazy words about being brave are making Scotty have that weird feeling of being outside of himself again. A medal? A sergeant? Brave? It's not true. "The truth is, lieutenant, I don't deserve a medal. And I don't want to be a sergeant. I was never a real soldier. All I ever did was carry things for the real soldiers."

"Well, you're getting the medal anyhow. I already put you in for it. And you're gonna be a sergeant too. That'll put you in a higher pay grade until you get your discharge. It's the least I can do for you. You won't see me again, soldier, but I'm proud to have known you."

Scotty tries to think what to say, but all he can come up with is, "I . . . I'm proud to have known you too, sir. I hope you, uh . . ."

"Survive?" The lieutenant shakes his head. "Not likely. If Charlie doesn't shoot me, maybe I'll shoot myself." He takes out his pistol and holds it out toward Scotty.

Scotty glances across the aisle at the two missing-foot guys. They've stopped their gin game and are watching.

"See this automatic? They gave it to me when they made me an officer. But did I use it to shoot the enemy? No, I just hid in the damn bushes until the choppers came. It's brand new. Hardly ever been fired. I could have at least used it to shoot a few of them, but did I? No. I just hid, crouched down behind a bunch of bushes, pointing it at nothing. My whole arm was shaking like a scared little kid. Yesterday, I took it out and put it against the side of my head, like this." The lieutenant holds the gun up against the side of his head.

Scotty sees that more of the men on the ward have noticed what the lieutenant is doing. The ward gets very quiet. One guy down at the far end slips out of his bed and tiptoes out the door. One of the nighttime screamers, puts his pillow over his head, and the pillow begins to shake. Scotty suspects the guy is sobbing under there. Remembering, probably. Not good to remember.

The lieutenant cocks the gun. "I sat there for a long time with this gun at my head thinking about what it would be like to die. Ever thought about that, philosopher? Of course, you have. All you ever do is think. But not me. I just stumble through life like the idiot I am. Of course I didn't pull the trigger. It would take a real man to do that."

The pretty nurse and a big orderly come through the door down at the end of the ward.

Scotty holds up his hand to tell them to stay back.

The lieutenant doesn't even notice. He's still got the gun against the side of his head, and he's staring up at the ceiling. Scotty suspects that even now he's thinking about pulling the trigger. Scotty tries to think of something to say quick to make him not do that. "Uh, you know, Lieutenant, if you're going to shoot yourself, this wouldn't be a very good place to do it. They'd take you right into surgery and probably save your life." Scotty smiles to show him it's a joke.

The lieutenant makes a half-hearted laugh. "Good point, philosopher. I'd probably screw that up too. Here you take it. I won't be needing it anymore." He drops the pistol on the bed.

The nurse and the orderly hurry to the lieutenant's side. The nurse says, "You'll have to come with me, sir. The MPs have been called."

Scotty quickly says, "No, no, it's all right. This is Lieutenant Dasen. My commanding officer. He just came by to show me his new pistol." Scotty picks it up and holds it against the side of his head which causes the pretty nurse to take in a sudden breath. "It's not loaded. He was just showing me how one of the men shot himself. Right in the side of the head. Like this. Very sad case. Isn't that right, sir?" Scotty carefully releases the pistol's hammer and holds the gun out to the lieutenant.

He takes it and glumly puts it back into its holster.

The nurse frowns at him. "Well, sir, you'll have to leave this ward this instant. It was not very smart to bring a weapon here."

"Good point," Scotty says. "He won't do it again, I promise."

The lieutenant looks into Scotty's eyes for a long moment, then turns away and heads for the door.

Scotty calls after him, "Good luck, sir."

The lieutenant waves one hand, but doesn't look back.

The orderly follows him out, but the pretty nurse stays to stare at Scotty. "What was that all about?" she asks.

"He's been through a rough time. He was with me when I . . ."

She frowns at Scotty, but then she turns and leaves. The two missing-foot guys go back to their endless gin game.

As the ward settles down, Scotty lies back to think about what the lieutenant said. Was it cowardice to hide instead of getting killed? Wouldn't a sane person run away? It seems more crazy to let yourself be killed. The lieutenant said he was a coward, so he doesn't want to be an officer anymore. He'd rather be dead. To Scotty, that seems crazy too, but he knows it's not because in his textbook it says that each person makes up his own reality. That means everybody has their own version of what is crazy and what isn't. But the lieutenant seemed mostly concerned about what other people would think, what his father would think. So maybe it's other people who create our reality, the puppet masters. Maybe everybody has their own puppet master to make up reality. Scotty stares up at the ceiling imagining the lieutenant hiding while—

"Stop! Memory is not allowed."

"I know, I know." Scotty looks around to see if anybody heard. Nobody is looking at him.

He discovers he's still holding his book in his hands. He missed his book, and he's very happy to have it back. He opens the book and turns pages until he finds a passage that's underlined. It says Kant believed in the *concept* of God. It says he moved God out of the realm of ontology and into the realm of epistemology. What does that mean? Scotty reads through more of the pages, trying to find more about why humans believe in God. He comes to pages that are stained red. The lieutenant said that red stuff was blood. But Scotty doesn't want to think about blood; he only wants to find out if God is real. He searches on through the red pages until he sees the name Schopenhauer. That's a name he remembers. He sees another underlined sentence. It says, The world is not a rational place. Scotty rereads that sentence. It almost seems like Schopenhauer is saying everybody who doesn't think the world is crazy, is crazy. Maybe the ones in this hospital that get labeled as crazy, the shell-shocked ones, the screamers, are really the sane ones because they know the world is crazy. They only get labeled as crazy because they believe something different from everybody else. What would Schopenhauer say about what we are doing here in Vietnam? The puppet masters tell us it's good to die for the honor, good to kill the local people because they live here and we don't, good to drop bombs on babies in their cribs because they live in a city up north we don't like. But isn't that crazy? Scotty feels like the world has turned upside down. Everything that's supposed to be right now seems wrong. He wants to understand, wants to be logical, but it feels like he's starting to believe things that nobody else believes. Does that make him crazy? He rereads the underlined words one last time. The world is not a rational place. Schopenhauer is right, the world is definitely not a rational place.

4

Saved From Being Saved

Scotty feels like somebody is shaking him. Maybe it's the lieutenant come back. No, that can't be: the lieutenant was going away to try to get himself killed. So maybe it's the storyteller girl, come back to tell him another story.

"Scotty, wake up."

No, that's not her sweet voice. Too bad. So who is whispering?

"Scotty, snap out of it." Is it the missing-foot guys again? He decides he should just tell them he's not going to act crazy and that's final. Scotty opens his eyes. It's still dark. There's somebody standing next to his bed.

"Come on, old pal. We got to move quick."

That voice. He knows that voice. It's Brent. Old pal Brent. What's he doing here in the middle of the night? Scotty can barely see him in the dim light of the nighttime ward. Why isn't Brent wearing his Army uniform? Farkas used to dress everybody down for not keeping their uniforms in "proppa military dee-core-um." What would he think if he saw Brent not wearing his uniform?

"Help me get you up. Let's get you out of here."

Brent is trying to lift him out of bed. Scotty feels pain. Not supposed to be moving around. "Ow, Brent. That hurts."

"Shh. Not so loud. Swing your legs over the edge of the bed."

What is Brent up to? Scotty realizes he hasn't tried to sit up since . . . how long has it been? A long time. He tries to help, but his muscles are so weak, it feel's like he's become part of the bed. Every movement makes his stomach muscles clench. "I can't do it, Brent. It hurts."

"Here, try this. Brent hands him a little red straw. Scotty wonders where Brent could have found a little red straw like that in Vietnam. Brent holds out a small glass jar and unscrews the lid. "Here, snort up some of this shit."

Scotty tries to focus. The jar looks like an old-fashioned fruit jar, only smaller. It's full of some kind of tan-colored powder. He looks at Brent. "What is it?"

"Magic pixie dust. Good shit. Stops the pain. Hurry. Snort some up."

Thinking about pain makes Scotty remember there are stitches inside of his gut. "But, Brent, they said I'm not supposed to move."

"No time to worry about that. Do up some of that stuff. Quick."

Scotty remembers this part. Brent used to give him coke powder to snort. Good stuff. Made everything bright and sharp. Scotty uses the little red straw to snort some of the powder. It burns the inside of his nose, but it's not a bad burn. He snorts up a little more. Interesting. It leaves an odd taste in the back of his throat. It starts out as kind of a chemically taste, sharp and irritating, but then there's another taste underneath, like some kind of plant, maybe . . . flowers? Whatever it is, it works fast: the pain in Scotty's gut immediately starts to fade. Scotty has the pleasant thought that maybe it will make the pain go away forever. That would be nice. Maybe all the hurting will soon be nothing but an old memory, something unpleasant that happened in the past.

Scotty finds himself sitting on the edge of the bed. He feels woozy, and the room is spinning around. Scotty wants to wait until it stops, but Brent is still hurrying him. He feels his bare feet touch the cold floor, but then something goes wrong, and he's sitting on the floor.

"Damn," whispers Brent. "Sorry, Scotty. Lost my grip. Here, better have some more of this shit."

He sticks the straw into Scotty's nose. Scotty is happy to snort up a bunch more of the magic powder. It instantly sets off that same strange taste in the back of his throat. He's still trying to figure out what it tastes like when he sees a bright flash of light. He looks around. Did somebody turn on the lights? No, the ward is still dark. Everybody is asleep except for the screamers, and Scotty can't even hear them very well because there's a ringing inside his ears. He finds himself sitting in a chair. What a feeling! To be sitting up in a chair after such a long time. The chair begins to move, and that brings the dizziness back again. Scotty tries to focus. What's happening? He's moving between the rows of beds. In the dim light, they look like rectangular white blocks, evenly spaced, precise. It's great to be out of that bed and moving. But then he remembers his book. "Stop! I need my book."

Brent urgently whispers in his ear: "Shh. Pipe down, damn it."

"But I need my book. It's under my pillow."

Brent goes away, but soon he's back. "All right, here's your damn book. Now keep quiet."

Scotty clings to his book. Whatever is going to happen, he knows he must keep a tight hold on his book as if his life depends on it.

The rows of beds start going by again. Scotty can hardly keep himself from yelling out, Look at me! I'm out of bed. I'm in a chair that's moving. But then they're in a dimly lit hallway. There are no people. Did Brent somehow make them all go away? The ride gets bumpy as they go out through a door. A white car is parked outside. Scotty tries to think where he's seen that car before. It looks French. Is it the Frenchman's car? Another person appears and gets ahold of his arm, and then he's inside the car. Scotty is amazed to think that a moment ago he was in a bed, and now he's in the back seat of a car. He feels happy to be in a car, moving through the night. Buildings go flying past. A car horn sounds over and over. People are running out of the way. Loaded-down bicycles go wobbling away.

"Hey, man, *"ça va?*

Scotty tries to figure out who is talking.

The person says, *"Ça fait un bail."*

Been a long time? French? The driver is speaking French.

"Hey, man. No remember me, eh?"

A memory comes into Scotty's head. The Frenchman's car. It must be Mar-lon, the fancy-dressed Frenchman's driver. He's talking over his shoulder as he drives, saying some of his words in French.

Brent says, "Shut up and drive."

They go fast down narrow streets, tearing through the night like somebody is chasing them. Scotty likes seeing everything go by so fast. He's enjoying a new feeling inside of his head. What's in that powder? It makes him see swirling colors out there.

The car stops. Too fast. It makes Scotty's gut hurt. He looks out the window and sees a square box of a building. Young girls are standing out in front of the building. Soldiers are talking to the girls, touching them, trying to kiss their necks. A familiar place. A memory. Is it Wong's? Is this Wong's Bar? How can it still be here? It's like nothing has changed, like no time has passed at all. Can such things still exist? Is this a dream?

"Let's go, Scotty. Time to get out now. Help me."

Scotty tries to get out of the car, but his legs feel like wet noodles. "It hurts." He thinks maybe he said that out loud, but then, he's moving, swaying, like he's riding a horse. He figures it out. The horse is Brent, playing horsey. Scotty is riding piggyback, just like they used to do back in the junkyard. Brent always got to be the horsey, and Scotty always had to ride piggyback, had to play the part of the little brother, being carried.

Nobody in the barroom seems to notice, or care, that Scotty is riding through the bar piggyback. Men are shouting, laughing, arguing.

The horsey is moving fast now, and Scotty has to hold on tight. They go down a hallway. A door opens. They go into a room. Scotty knows this room. It's the dream room, the room where the storyteller girl told him those wonderful stories. Is this another dream? He's been back in this room so many times, in so many dreams.

5

Better Dreams

Dreams are better than when you're awake. In this dream, Scotty is dreaming that his beautiful storyteller girl is right there next to him, sitting on the edge of his bed, looking down at him. This dream is so real he can even smell her strange scent, like magical jungle flowers. She's touching his forehead with her cool hand.

"You wake now, Sca-tee? That good. I go tell Brent."

She gets up and leaves. The dream must have ended. Too bad. That's the trouble with dreams—they end. Oh, why did you have to go, my wonderful storyteller girl? Why couldn't you stay and tell me a story?

The door opens. Someone enters. Tall. Blurry.

"So, you're finally awake. You plannin' to sleep your life away?"

A face, hovering way up there. Who is it?

"Well, old buddy, how does it feel to be free?"

Scotty's eyes come into focus, and he sees who it is. It's Brent. He's standing up there so tall, and he's grinning. He's drinking from a bottle. Tiger beer. Memories. Bad tasting local beer. Makes your piss smell bad. But Brent likes it. Says it tastes like Vietnam. Says since we're here now, might as well eat, drink, and smell like Vietnam.

"I . . ." Scotty's throat feels numb, but he wants to talk. He wants to know. "Was she . . . here?"

"You mean Kim-Li? Yeah, but she had to go back out front."

Did he say Kim-Li? Is that her name? Does it mean she's real?

"She said you were awake. Damn, man, you know how long you been sleepin'?"

Sleeping? Scotty does feel sleepy. Maybe he should go back to sleep. He closes his eyes.

"Hey, don't go back to sleep. We got to get you eatin'. Got to get you strong again."

Scotty opens his eyes. Is her name really Kim-Li? "She never told me . . . name. That night. Wasn't even sure . . . she was . . . real."

"Yeah, she said you two spent a little time together before you went off to war. She's somethin', isn't she? Cute little chick."

"Kim-Li? Real?"

"You bet. Really somethin. What a body. But hey, she said you need to eat, and she's right. I'll have her get you somethin'."

"She really is . . . real?"

"You're askin' funny questions, old buddy. Maybe you've been doin' up a bit too much of that good old Cambodian magic pixie dust. Helps the pain though, doesn't it?"

"I . . . guess so. Can I have . . . more?"

"Sure. Much as you want. But first you got to eat somethin'. You've got so skinny your pants'll fall right off ya. If you ever decide to get up and put on pants, that is. How long you plannin' on layin' there?"

"How long . . . been here?"

"Few days. You don't remember?"

Scotty thinks about Brent's words. Days? That can't be right. Is time moving on without me?

"So how're ya feelin'? Better?"

"Hungry."

"That's good. A good sign."

Is it a good sign to be hungry? Scotty puts his hand on his stomach to feel where the hunger is. It feels like there's a scar there. He runs his fingers along it. It makes him think about luck. Is he lucky to be alive with a scar like that? "I . . . have to pee."

Brent grins. "Yeah? Well, that's probably a good thing too. Means everything inside of you is workin' okay. Here use this." He drains the rest of his beer and holds out the bottle. It says, *Biere Larue*, and there's a picture of a tiger on the bottle. Do they have tigers in this country?

"Well, don't you want it?"

Scotty reaches for the bottle, but misses.

Brent takes his reaching hand and puts the bottle into it.

"What happened to . . . bedpan?"

"No bedpans here, old buddy."

"Here? Where is here?"

"You don't remember? You're back at Wong's. In one of the old rooms. Wong expanded since you went off to war. Some new rooms."

"New rooms? What about . . . hospital? Don't I have to . . . go back?"

Brent laughs again. "The hospital? Why the hell would you want to go back to that damned place? You're free now, free as a bird."

Free? Scotty tries to think what that could mean. His mind doesn't seem to be working right. Free as a bird? Free as those strange Vietnamese birds? "In . . . night?"

"That's right. Had to get you out of there at night. Paid off the night guy to look the other way and out you went. Slick, eh? You're safe here, that's what counts. Just rest. We can talk later."

He turns to go.

"No, wait." Scotty reaches out toward him. "Why am I not in . . . that place? Hospital?"

Brent sits down on the edge of the bed. "Listen, Scotty, I had to get you out of there. And fast. My spies were tellin' me they were about to send you back to the states."

"You saved me from . . . being . . . sent back?"

"Right. I couldn't let you miss out. Wait 'til I tell ya."

Scotty tries to sort it out. Saved me? From going home?

"Scotty, you won't believe the sweet deal I got goin' here. We're gonna be rich, my man, real rich."

Scotty is not sure he wants to be rich. Wasn't he supposed to go to the Wonderful Walter hospital to get his knee fixed up? He points down at his knee. "But Brent, what about my—"

"Don't you worry a thing about that," says Brent. "I took your sheets and threw em away. I rolled up your mattress like they do when somebody gets transferred out. I know the Army. The day shift'll come in and find your bed empty. They'll think you're on your way back to the states. They'll just make up the bed and bring in the next poor sap. Far as they're concerned, you'll be gone as a gone goose."

A gone goose? Why is a goose gone? Maybe better to be gone.

"Don't look so glum, my friend. Don't you get it? You're free as a bird now. No more playing soldier for you. No more jerks like Fart-Ass Farkas tellin' ya what to do. No more getting your guts shot all to hell off there in the jungle. All you got to do now is lay right here and rest up 'til you're all better. Then I'll show ya. Wait 'til you see." He pats Scotty's shoulder. "I got it all figured out. You're French now. You took those French classes in high school, right? Well, now's your chance to use some of that book learnin'. Anybody comes in, you talk French to 'em."

"French?"

"Right. You're not a soldier anymore. Just some French guy. Got it?"

"French guy."

"Right. Not American. A French guy with stomach trouble. Right?"

"If you say so."

"Okay, got to go now. Business to take care of. How's the pain? Want some more magic pixie dust?"

"I . . . guess so. Starving."

"I'll have her bring you something. Here, have a snort."

There it is again. A little jar full of powder. A little red straw. Scotty sucks. Burning inside his nose, but a good burning. A magical burning. A strong taste of dried plants. Pain fades. Then Brent is gone. Scotty is left alone in the little room. He's dizzy and confused. The magic pixie dust is running through his brain, making things all weird. But it's a pleasant weird. Scotty stares up at the ceiling. Strange rusty face up there. Why is that face up there? Is it the face of the puppet master? "Tell me what to do. Help me." There is no answer. Might as well go to sleep.

Somebody is stroking his hair, whispering to him. Such a beautiful dream, Scotty doesn't want to wake up, but he opens his eyes, just a little. Darkness, but a little bit of flickering light. Candles? They have candles in church. Is this a church? Is somebody praying? Should he be praying? Does he still know how to pray? A face appears, a beautiful Vietnamese face. Is it her? Has his storyteller girl come back? Scotty hopes this is not just a dream.

"You eat now, Sca-tee?"

That voice. It really is her! His beautiful storyteller girl is right there beside him, holding a spoon out toward him. This dream is so real he can even smell the food: fruit maybe, probably the most wondrous sweet fruit in the world. Does he dare talk to her? Or would that make her disappear? He decides to ask her the most important question you can ask in a dream: "Are you . . . real?" His voice doesn't seem to be working so good. Only a whisper, but maybe that's what happens in dreams.

"Real? What you mean, Sca-tee?"

"I mean, are you . . . really here?"

She smiles. "Silly, yes, I here. Why you say?"

"But are you . . . really? I mean, you won't go away?"

"Not go away. Not 'til eat. You eat now."

She puts the spoon close to his mouth. He takes a chance and touches her hand. It's cool, just as it always has been in his dreams.

She smiles again and pats his hand. So far, she hasn't disappeared, but just to make sure, he catches hold of her wrist. She tries to pry his hand off, but he's determined not to let go. No way, not now that he's found her again. He's been dreaming about this moment for so long there's no way he's going to let her slip away again.

She laughs a quiet little laugh and stops trying to pry his hand off. With her other hand, she continues to hold the spoon out to him.

"Must eat, Sca-tee."

"I thought you were . . . a . . . dream."

She doesn't answer, but she smiles again.

It's a wonderful smile, and Scotty understands what it means: it means she is real, and she wants to be with him. It means he's safe, finally safe. He's no longer going to be lost and alone. "I thought I . . . dreamed you."

She frowns as she holds out the spoon. "Must eat now. Get strong."

Scotty avoids the spoon and pulls her hand to his chest. "Stay with me. Please. Are you going to stay with me?"

She pulls her hand away. She's frowning, and her frown scares Scotty. Has he broken the spell? Will she disappear now?

She touches his cheek. "I go. I leave food. You eat."

He reaches for her and tries to sit up, but his stomach clenches, and he has to lie back. He whispers, "Please don't go. I'm afraid."

She puts a gentle hand against his chest. Her eyes are steady and watchful, as if she's trying to see inside his mind. He wishes she really could see inside him. Then she would see how much he cares for her. She would see how afraid he has been, how lost and lonely.

She picks up the little jar of magic pixie dust. "You hurt. You want?"

Scotty hasn't been thinking about the pain, but if she wants him to take more of the magic powder, he will. She must understand how much pain he is in. Even if no one else understands, she does.

She holds the straw for him, and he snorts up quite a bit of the stuff. It tastes so strange, so sharp and strong. It feels so strong, he worries a bit about what it might be doing to his brain. But he doesn't want to think about that; it's precious and irresistible, like her.

Some of it trickles down his throat. He coughs.

She quickly gives him a drink of water.

So helpful. So caring. And such intense eyes. Dark, deep and mysterious, but at the same time, tired, and maybe wary. Not the eyes of a young girl. Has he had that thought before?

She strokes his cheek with the back of her hand. "Sleep, my Sca-tee."

The feel of her cool hand against his cheek is good, so good. He closes his eyes and feels the magic powder going to work inside of him. It seems to be settling deep inside his brain, maybe far back in some hidden place. He feels the coolness of her hand against his cheek. Now there is no such thing as pain, no such thing as war and guns and people dying. Mortars do not fall on your tent roof in the middle of the night and kill you. Little boys in black pajamas don't play with real guns instead of toy guns. It was all a bad dream, but this is real. In this reality, there is only the touch of her hand and the strange warmth deep inside his mind. It is enough, but he wants her to understand how much he has been thinking about her since that night they spent together in this room. "Do you . . . remember? You and me? In this room? Before they sent me away."

She's still holding the spoon close to his mouth. "Open. Must eat."

He opens, swallows, and says, "But do you? Do you remember?"

"Open."

Scotty opens his mouth, and she feeds him another spoonful.

"Please tell me you remember."

She looks at him. Such dark eyes. What is she thinking?

"You shy."

Does she mean now, or back then? "You told me stories."

"Story? You like story?"

"Yes, I like your stories. Very much. You told me a story about a magic horse. And a story about a turtle. About saving a turtle. Do you remember?"

"You eat." She puts more of whatever it is into his mouth.

He's feeling more and more full, but he swallows whatever she puts into his mouth. She's helping him, feeding him to make him stronger. To make him well. "But don't you remember? You told me to save the turtle. I did. I did what you said. I saved the turtle."

She shows him the bowl. It's empty.

"Good. You eat all. I go tell Brent."

She starts to stand up, but Scotty catches hold of her wrist. "No, don't go. Stay here with me. Please. Tell me why you told me that story. Why did you tell me I had to save that turtle?"

She smiles and lightly touches his lips with one finger. "You like story? Want story?"

"Yes, please tell me another story. That would be wonderful."

She sits back down on the edge of the bed. She leans close and begins to whisper into his ear.

One night father mother go out in boat. Catch fish to eat. Storm come. Mother and father drown. Leave two brother alone. They have nothing. Only old house. Older brother greedy. He not want share house. He say, I oldest. House belong me. He drive young brother away. Young brother have no money. No food. He go into dark forest. Hope to find food. He get lost. Almost starve. Come to star fruit tree. Fruit look good. At last he have food to eat. He try get fruit but giant bird fly down out of tree. Bird say no eat. This my tree. But I starve, say young brother. Need only one little star fruit. No, say bird. This my tree. I need. I have shiny metal men want. You take shiny metal. No eat star fruit. Young brother agree. Giant bird say get on back. I show. Young brother afraid, but know Buddha say trust all animal. He climb on back of bird. Bird fly way up in sky. Fly far far out over sea. Young brother very afraid. Hang on tight. Bird land on island. Show young brother mountain of gold. You take shiny metal, say bird. Not eat star fruit. Young brother begin dig gold. Bird say not take too much. Too heavy fly. Young brother believe bird. Only take what pockets hold. He climb on bird. Bird fly back to land. Young brother use gold buy house. Marry best girl. Older brother come visit. He jealous of fine house. Say where you get money? Young brother trust older brother. Tell truth. Tell about star fruit tree. Tell about giant bird. Tell about fly to island. Tell about gold mountain. Older brother run to forest. Find star fruit tree. Giant bird fly down. Say go away, this my tree. Older brother say take me to gold or I chop down tree. Older brother get on bird. Bird fly to island. Older brother dig up much gold. No, say bird. Too much. No can fly. Older brother say I take all gold. You fly my gold or I kill you. Bird try fly back to land with

older brother on back. Too much gold. Too heavy. Fall into sea.
They die.

The story is over. Scotty opens his eyes and discovers she's staring at him. What does she want him to say? Does she want him to say it was a nice story? He whispers, "Good story. Shows what greed can do."

She continues to stare at him, her eyes cool and watchful.

Why isn't she saying anything? Scotty worries that he said the wrong thing. He wants to tell her how much he liked her story, but the more he thinks about it, the more he begins to wonder if it was such a nice story after all. Maybe it was like the story about the turtle. Maybe there was a warning hidden in the story. Maybe she's trying to say there is danger. Scotty tries hard to make his brain focus. Thinking logically, he decides this story wasn't as gentle as the others. This one had a sharper edge to it. The younger brother was rewarded for being cooperative and for trusting the bird, but there was also the threat of death for anyone who might do otherwise. Scotty wonders if that's what the Buddha teaches in this country. Maybe they have a special Vietnamese version of Buddha, a Buddha for a war-torn country, a Buddha that says they have to obey his rules or die. And unlike her earlier stories, this one wasn't saying gentleness is its own reward. This one seemed to be saying we have to trust the animals, that we must do as they tell us because it's the only way to stay alive. In that way, it's like the turtle story: rescue the turtle or you will die. You will end up with your head cut off, like Jeff. And this story is not like the story of the magic horse. That story was funny. The horse was supposed to poop gold, not phân bón. The man was tricked. But wait, the man in that story did get badly beaten, and in the end he was left destitute, still unable to feed his family. And all because he threatened to chop down a tree. Maybe that story was also supposed to teach him something. Did he miss the point of that story too? Maybe all her stories have something to do with punishment for those who break some kind of sacred trust? Are Americans the ones who are breaking the trust, the ones who are going to be punished by their God for our transgressions? He's sweating, and he doesn't know why. He can't seem to think clearly. "I'm sorry," he whispers. "I'm trying to understand."

She touches his cheek. "You sleep now, Sca-tee. You tired."

6

To Be Clean and Pure

Scotty opens his eyes and sees a face up on the ceiling. It's staring down at him. The face is trying to tell him something. It's saying she's gone and will never come back The thought of her being gone starts a panic growing inside of him. It grows and grows until he cries out, "No, she can't be gone. I need her."

The face stares at him, cold, unsympathetic.

He cries out, "No, please. Don't make her be gone."

The face just stares. It makes him remember the eyes of the Monday Man. Staring. Accusing. You caused this You are a jinx.

"Memories are not allowed."

Scotty knows it's not good to remember, but his brain is not cooperating. It wants to remember bad things. Shooting. Explosions. Men dying. Men staring at nothing.

"Stop remembering! I order you to stop."

That's right. He has to stop remembering. Not good to remember. The magic pixie dust must be messing up his brain, trying to make him remember bad things.

He tries to sit up to make the face stop staring, but that hurts his gut, and he has to lie back again. Why does it still hurt so much? He worries that something has gone wrong inside of himself. He thinks about going out to try to find Kim-Li. Maybe she can help. But what if she really is gone? That would be logical. There's no reason why she would want to be with a sick person in a grimy little back room. Scotty knows he's of not value to her, of no value to anybody. Nobody knows him, and nobody cares about him. Something is wrong inside his gut, and it hurts and no one cares. Maybe he hasn't been using enough magic powder. Where is it? He turns over onto his side and reaches down to the floor. He feels for the little jar, but it's not there. Where did it go? Did she take it away? No, she wouldn't do that. She cares about me. Doesn't she? He walks his finger like a spider across the floor, feeling for the little jar. But his fingers don't feel anything except the old wooden floor. His magic powder is gone. Panic is growing in the middle of him, making his gut hurt even more. He frantically keeps his fingers walking, scurrying left and right, forward and back, searching everywhere. But he feel nothing.

He cries out, "Help me." But of course, there is no response. He's alone. No one will help him. Even the puppet master has abandoned him. He reaches out as far as he can and finally his fingers touch something. Is that it? A small jar. That is it! His hand feels so sweaty and slippery, he's almost afraid to try to pick up the smooth glass jar. What if he spills it? But the pain is getting worse. He needs it, right now! He grabs hold of the jar, gripping it tightly. Careful now, careful. He almost gets it up to the bed, but then it slips out of his sweaty fingers. He hears it hit the floor and roll away. Oh no, now you've done it. You lost it. He leans out of the bed and peers into the dimness. He can't see it. He puts his hand down again and frantically feels around for it on the wood floor. But his fingers feel nothing except the warmth of the floor. How can wood be so warm? It's like there's fire under the wood, in the ground. Maybe hell is just beneath the surface of this doomed country, always there, always reaching up for more souls to pull down. Maybe that's why there have always been wars in this country. Occupiers. First it was the Japanese, then the French, and now us. With hell so close just under the surface, the wars in this poor country will never end. The leaning out is making him dizzy. He lies back and takes fast breaths. He's sweating, and he feels all shaky. He feels like he's going to throw up. He doesn't want it to happen, but he can't stop it. He leans over the edge of the bed and lets it go. He stares at the floor. Nothing much came out, but for some reason, it looks red. But why should it be red? Think. Be logical. It must be because he hasn't had any magic powder. He was trying to find it. It has to be down there on the floor somewhere. He leans way out again. Ow. Damn it. Now he's on the floor and all is pain. But at least now he's down on the floor where the magic powder is. He looks around, and spots it: the jar rolled up against the wall. All he has to do is crawl over there and get it. Then the magic powder will stop the pain. Even though it hurts like hell, he manages to get turned over onto his stomach. He will crawl like a snake and get his magic powder, and then the pain will go away. He becomes the kind of rattlesnake he used to see in the desert: secretive, dangerous. The jar is getting closer. He reaches for it. Being very, very careful, he wraps his fingers around the jar and cautiously picks it up. But there's no lid. And part of the top of the jar is broken off. He looks inside the jar. It's empty. How can that be? Where did his magic powder go? Hoping there might be a little bit left inside the jar, he puts his tongue inside and turns the jar around. It hurts his tongue, but it's working: he tastes a little bit of the powder. He tries again. He has to get every bit of it. When he's sure he got it all, he stops and waits for it to take effect. But nothing happens. Why isn't it working? It must not have been enough. But there was more in the jar. He puts his eye down close to the floor and sees some whiteness all along the wall. Is that it, is that his magic powder? He sticks out his

tongue and licks at the white stuff. It tastes like . . . yes, that's it, the
familiar, sharp, chemically taste. He pushes his face closer to the wall as
and runs his tongue along the crack where the wall meets the floor. It
tastes mostly like dirt, but he's getting some powder too. But now, he
can't see anymore whiteness. Just to be sure, he licks the floor all around
the area, even in the cracks between the boards. It tastes icky, but it's
worth it if there might be a little bit of magic powder mixed in with the
dirt. When he's finished, he's out of breath, but he's proud he found a
way to get it all. He waits, and soon the signal comes, the bright flash of
light inside his brain. Scotty knows the light is not real light; that
wouldn't be logical. It just means the powder is going to work inside his
head. The familiar feel of it is in there in the middle of his brain. He
loves that feeling. Now that his powder is working, he lies still on the
floor, staring up into the darkness. He thinks about how good it was for
Brent to find him the magic powder. Good old Brent. Always taking
care of him. He should remember to thank him for that, for finding him
the best drug of them all. And then, he wonders what makes it work so
good. It must be because it wanders through my body looking for the
real me, the essence of me. But what is the essence of me? Scotty thinks
about that question for a while, and the answer comes to him: sadness.
The real essence of me is sadness, so that must be what the magic
powder likes best. It's comfortable in that part of me, the sad part of me.
It is my friend, my very best friend. No, more than a friend: it is my
savior, my lover, my only real hope in this terribly sad world.

For some reason, his tongue hurts. He sticks out his tongue and
touches it with his finger. It feels rough. It feels like . . . splinters. He
tries to think how he could have gotten splinters in his tongue. He looks
at his finger. It's red. Is he bleeding inside his mouth? He thinks about
spitting the blood out, but no, that would be wasting the powder. He
should swallow the blood and the dirt from the floor. Only logical. He
swallows it all, satisfied that he found the right answer.

Now he's content to just lie still on the floor and let his magic
powder work. There's nothing wrong with lying on a floor. The warm
wood feels good against his naked body.

The door opens. A slight breeze. It cools the sweat on Scotty's naked
body. He hadn't realized he was sweating so much.

Feet come in through the door: small feet, wearing the little black
slippers all Wong's girls wear. Ankles. Nice ankles. The feet hurry
toward him. Something touches the back of his neck. "Why on floor,
Sca-tee? You hurt?" It's Kim-Li. She's come back! Such a sweet voice, a
caring voice. "What you do, Sca-tee? Why not in bed?"

"I . . . I lost my powder."

"Powder? I find."

She goes away, but soon is back. She shows him the little jar. It's still empty. How sad.

"It all gone You go back bed now?"

She takes his arm to help him up, but Scotty doesn't want to get back in that bed. He hates that damn bed. That bed stinks. Besides, the floor is not so bad. It's warm.

"Pain. Need more . . . powder."

"You want more? You wait. I get more."

She's gone. Why did she have to go? But then she's back. How could she go away and then be back again so fast? Time is not working right.

"You sit up now, Sca-tee."

She helps him to sit up, but it makes him dizzy. Things are going round and round. She's holding something up in front of his eyes. It's his jar. Except now it has a little bit of magic powder in it. She did it. She found more. What a wonderful girl. She holds the little red straw for him, and he snorts as hard as he can. Instantly, he feels the burn at the back of his throat. It's a good burn, a familiar, friendly burn. She tries to take the straw away, but he wants more. He catches her hand and looks into her eyes. He silently begs: just a little more, please. She allows it, and he sucks in most of it before she can take the straw away.

She looks worried. Don't be worried, lovely Kim-Li. The magic powder will fix everything.

She puts her cool hand on his shoulder. "You wait. I fix bed."

She helps him lie back. The floor is warm. Comfortable. He feels the powder begin to work. This time it seems to be hitting him hard. He has the vague idea that maybe he has never taken in that much before. But more is good. More will fix whatever is wrong inside of me.

She's back. She's helping him sit up again.

"You want go bathroom? I take?"

Yes. Scotty thinks it might be a good idea to go to the bathroom. How long has it been? Does he need to pee? He's not sure. Wasn't there a bottle to pee in? Tiger beer?

"I help. We go now."

She tries to help him up, but he feels very dizzy, and he sinks back down to his knees. She gets ahold of his arm and somehow is able to get him standing up. How strong she is. How can such a sweet little thing be so strong? She puts her arm around his waist and leads him toward the door. Scotty keeps his feet out wide, sure he's about to fall down. But he doesn't. The powder is beginning to work. It's making his brain pay attention to the world. It's making anything possible, even walking. But he has to plan each step. Put one foot out, get your balance, then do it again. Uh oh, he seems to be leaning a little too far to one side. Going down again. But no, she catches him and straightens him up. So strong. So dependable. With her help, he's almost sure he can make it all way to the bathroom. He feels her strength. He will draw strength from her, and she will make everything right again. The magic powder is wandering through him, and his mind seems to be working a bit better now. He looks at her and sees again how beautiful she is. He looks at her pretty white dress and thinks about the beautiful body that's hidden away under that pretty dress. Under that dress, he knows she's thin, fragile. But so alluring. But then he wishes he hadn't come up with that word. It brings a worrisome thought: if she is alluring, all the other soldiers will want to see what's under that pretty dress. Sometimes she goes away. What does she do when she goes away? Do other solders get to see what's under that pretty dress? He doesn't like to think about that. If they see, they would want. And that can't be allowed. It would be better if she would just stay with him all the time. If she would do that, he's sure he would get better. The pain would go away, and the dizziness would go away, and he would be happy.

Her arm is around him, and his arm is over her shoulders. He's moving. Once they are out of the little room, he sees two young girls in white dresses go past. They stare at him, and he realizes he has no clothes on. Doesn't matter. Kim-Li is with him. That's all that matters.

When they make it to the bathroom, he sees somebody else is already there. It's another one of Wong's beautiful little girls, and she's got her dress hiked up around her waist. She's straddling a pan of water. She's splashing up inside of herself. Why is she doing that? Scotty tries hard to make his brain focus. She's splashing herself to make herself clean after being with a soldier. She wants to get that soldier's stuff out of herself. Good idea. Logical. Scotty is proud that his brain is working again. He watches the girl. It occurs to him that this is his opportunity to see if she has one of those lumps that doctor described, that *mons pubis* thing. That doctor said it was the way to tell how old a girl really is. He gets his eyes to focus. She doesn't have much hair down there, but that doctor said the important thing was to see if she has a lump. Scotty analyzes that part of her carefully. Yes, she does have a bit of a lump down there. Not all that big, but noticeable. It might mean she's not as young as she looks.

The girl looks up and sees him staring at that part of her.

He smiles and shrugs.

She frowns and stares right back at that part of him.

He looks down. He'd forgotten again that he's completely naked. But he knows she probably doesn't care. Wong's girls are used to seeing naked Americans.

She takes her time finishing splashing herself, and then she pulls her dress down, nods at Kim-Li, and leaves the room.

Scotty looks at Kim-Li. She's been watching him. Is she mad at him, mad that he was looking at that part of the girl? He was only trying to see how old she was. He does his shrug again as he tries to think how to explain what he was looking at.

But she doesn't seem to care. She leads him to the hole in the floor that serves as a toilet in this country. She holds his arms to help him squat down, but his hurt knee doesn't seem to want to bend like that, so he just leans against the wall. He hopes he can hit the hole in the floor leaning like this. He doesn't want to make a mess.

Kim-Li is watching, and that makes it hard for him to concentrate. He waves for her to turn around.

She hesitates, but then turns away.

As soon as she turns away, some almost liquid stuff comes out of him. He hopes that's not a bad sign. When he's done, he looks down between his legs. There's a lot of shit down there in that hole, and man, does it stink. It reminds him of Kim-Li's story about the magic horse. When the innkeeper wanted to be paid, the horse gave him nothing but a really smelly big pile of *phân bón*. Funny story. That pile of horse poop must have smelled a lot like all that human poop down there. He wonders if all that *phân bón* stays down there forever. But wouldn't it pile up too high? Somebody must come to take it away. He imagines them taking it away and using it on their crops. Maybe they're using American shit to fertilize their vegetables. Wouldn't that be funny? They use whore-house shit from American soldiers to grow their vegetables, then they sell the vegetables back to us American soldiers who eat the vegetables to produce more shit. A very nice system. Clever. And logical, completely logical. Scotty sees something move down there. Tiny little eyes look up at him. It's a rat. Then, he sees more of them. There are a whole lot of rats moving around down there among the torn strips of newspaper, rooting through the pile of *phân bón*. What are they looking for? Do they eat the *phân bón*?

Kim-Li gets ahold of his arm and helps him straighten up. She hands him a strip of newspaper. He wipes his butt, but it feels all wet. He looks at the piece of newspaper. It's soaked with something red. Is it blood? He tries to make his brain think about why blood would be coming out of him. It could mean something bad.

He holds the red piece of newspaper out to show it to Kim-Li.

She frowns. "That bad. You bleed inside."

Now he knows he has to make his brain think. He has to be logical. He must be bleeding inside. But how could that happen? Did the stitches they put inside come loose? Maybe that's why he's been feeling so hot and so dizzy. Maybe that's why the pain has been getting worse.

Another girl comes in. She looks even younger than the girl who was there before. She hardly seems to notice him, but she does turn away as she straddles the washbasin and splashes herself.

Kim-Li grabs the piece of newspaper out of Scotty's hand and throws it down the hole.

Watch out you rats down there. Incoming.

When the other girl has finished splashing herself, Kim-Li says something to her in their language. The girl comes and they get on each side of him. They take ahold of his arms and lead him toward the bathroom's back wall. Scotty doesn't know what they're going to do to him, but he's not worried. He trusts Kim-Li. She wouldn't hurt him.

They guide him to the wall, and he puts his hands out and leans against it. It feels smooth and cool. Large square tiles. Yellowed. Old.

Scotty notices a rusty pipe coming out of the wall up near the ceiling. There's a faucet handle in the middle of the wall. Is it a shower? A shower would be nice. How long has it been since he had a shower? He can't remember, but he's sure it's been a long time. Scotty wonders if water would come out of the pipe if he turned that handle. But before he can try it, Kim-Li reaches out and turns it. Nothing happens for a few seconds, then a dribble of brown water comes out and splashes on Scotty's feet. It's cold.

Kim-Li says, "Shit."

So she does knows the English word for *phân bón*. Of course she does. That's one of the first American words the girls learn out in the bar. Scotty remembers when he was the watcher. He would sit at the bar and listen to the soldiers try to teach those kinds of words to the girls. They thought it was funny to hear such cute little Asian girls say American cuss words. Scotty tries to remember what else those American soldiers said. It all seems vague and hazy, as if it was a long time ago. Football. Something about trying to teach the girls about high school Friday night football games. The girls didn't understand, so the boys told them it was like soccer except it's okay to use your hands. The girls sort of understood that. And they tried explain about drive-in restaurants and car hops and how cool it is when you take the hood ornament off your car and fill the holes in with melted lead and lower your car down close to the ground and put on dual exhausts with glass-pack mufflers so your car not only looks cool but makes exactly the right cool sound when it takes off fast. Scotty tries to remember that sound. He tries blowing out some air while he vibrates his tongue. "Thrrruppp."

"What you say, Sca-tee?"

He tries to think how to explain it, but then he realizes none of that matters anymore. Besides, it's better not to think about back home.

"You okay, Sca-tee?" She turns him around and looks into his eyes.

Such dark eyes. And yet there's a mystery in them. What are those eyes saying?

"Sca-tee?"

Did she say something he missed? And where did the other girl go?

He looks toward the door, then back at Kim-Li. She's naked. She must have taken her pretty white dress off to keep it from getting wet. He sees it hanging from a nail in the wall. When did she do that? Was he off in his head dreaming?

Kim-Li cranks the faucet back and forth. Nothing happens. She bangs on it with her little fist, and amazingly, a bit more water starts to dribble out.

She turns Scotty around and pushes him against the wall. He rests his cheek against it. It feels cool. He feels the cold water running down his back. It feels good, very cold against his hot back.

Kim-Li uses her hand to wash the blood off of his butt.

What a sweet girl. So kind. So gentle.

She turns him back around to face her, and again she looks into his eyes. She seems like she's about to say something, but she doesn't. Scotty thinks, Those deep dark eyes look worried. Is she worried about me? Or is it something else?

She begins to wash his chest. Scotty looks down. She's found a tiny sliver of soap somewhere, and she's using it to carefully wash him. He watches her hand move across his chest. He tries to get his mind to think clearly. She's washing my chest. It must mean she really does care about me. That thought makes him very happy. It's the first time in a very long time he's felt anything except pain and loneliness. Watching her carefully wash him, he wonders if in Vietnam it's the wife's duty to wash her husband. He likes the idea that she's taking care of him like a wife would. He holds onto that pleasant thought as she washes his arms. Could it come true? Would she be willing to come to Arizona and be a wife? He could show her the desert. She would like the desert. He watches her naked body move as she does the washing. So thin. So graceful. But then Scotty remembers he's missing his chance to look at her *mons pubis*. That doctor said it would show how old she really is. He looks down at that part of her and sees that she does have a little bit of a lump down there. It's even more pronounced than that other girl who was splashing herself at the wash basin. Seeing it makes Scotty's mind come to a very clear conclusion: she is not a child. She doesn't have much of a lump down there, but that doctor said she might not have much of one if she had been malnourished. And she really is very thin. Scotty decides she must have been malnourished when she was little. The important thing is now he knows she's definitely not a child. Therefore, she really *could* become his wife. He imagines walking down the street with her. He would be so proud of her. Everyone would be staring.

Kim-Li glances up and catches him looking at that part of her. Her face asks a question.

Scotty tries to decide how to tell her why he was looking down there. He wants her to know he wasn't looking for any bad reason; he just wanted to know how old she is. Maybe he should just ask her. But he hesitates. She might be old enough to be a wife in this country, but what about back home? What if there are laws in the U.S. about how old you have to be before you can get married? He has to know for sure. He has to make his mind really focus on this. It's important.

"I, uh, Kim-Li, can I . . ." His mouth doesn't seem to be working very well. How long since he talked? He can't remember. He clears his throat and tries again. "Can I ask . . . how old?"

She just continues to wash him, working her way down to his stomach. She's being very gentle around his long scar down there.

"Kim-Li, uh, how old are you?"

She doesn't answer. She turns him around and begins to scrub his back.

He turns his head to the side and says, "I mean, I was just wondering."

She quietly says, "Not know."

She's scrubbing the backs of his legs. She seems to be focusing extra hard on the task. Is she lying? But maybe she really doesn't know. Maybe in this country they don't keep track of girl's ages.

"Well, I mean, about how old?"

She just continues to wash him.

Scotty can tell she doesn't want to answer. Maybe in this country age isn't so important. Maybe in this country parents don't even bother to tell their children how old they are. But what about at school? Wouldn't there be a certain age when you went to school? Maybe she's never been to school. Or maybe she's an orphan. There must be some reason why she doesn't know her age. He says, "I mean, it doesn't really matter. I was just . . . curious." He smiles to show it's all right. Now that he knows she's not really a child, her actual age doesn't really matter at all.

She squats down and begins washing around his crotch area. She gets plenty of soap on her hands and begins washing that area as if it's no different than washing any other part of him. He tries not to think about what she's doing. He tells himself she's only washing him. She wants him to be clean. She wants him to feel better. She wants him to be happy. And he is happy. He's happy to be with her and that's enough. He keeps on repeating it to himself. It is enough, it is enough. She seems to know about washing boys. It might mean she has little brothers. He reaches down to touch her damp hair. He whispers, "Do you have brothers? A little brother?"

At first, she doesn't answer. She focuses on her washing task. But then she quietly says, "Gone now."

"Gone? You mean . . . ?"

She doesn't look up. "He die."

Does she mean he was killed in battle? As young as she is, it doesn't seem possible she could have a younger brother old enough to be a soldier. He strokes her hair and whispers, "I'm so sorry, Kim-Li. Will you tell me what happened?"

She stops the washing and looks up at him. "Plane come. Bomb fall. He die. Many die."

It means an American bomber killed her brother. It brings a memory. Wasn't there a big bomber that flew over him very low once? His mind wants to think about a can opener. A can opener in the jungle. Bombs.

"No! There is no jungle. There is no can opener."

Scotty doesn't want to remember. He doesn't want to think about jungles and airplanes and can openers. She must blame the American invaders for her brother's death. She might even blame him. He desperately pushes that thought away. No, she's being so kind to him, she must know he's not like the others. She must know he would never fly in a big airplane and drop bombs on her little brother. He says, "I . . . I'm not like that, Kim-Li. I mean, like the others. I would never—"

She stands up and puts her fingers to his lips. "No talk."

He does as he is told. She's right. There's no need to talk. She understands. She understands everything.

She pulls on his shoulders.

What is she doing? Oh, she wants him to lean forward so she can reach his head. He leans forward, and she begins to wash his hair. She's no longer being gentle; she's really scrubbing. Ws his hair really that dirty? Maybe he has bugs.

Kim-Li is still washing his hair when another girl comes in and squats over the hole in the floor. She stares straight ahead as she does her peeing, not paying the slightest bit of attention to them.

The girl finishes peeing, shakes herself, pulls her white dress down, and leaves without even glancing in their direction.

Kim-Li finishes washing his hair and pushes him back under the water to rinse him off. The water is cold, but Scotty doesn't care. He will do whatever she wants him to do. She stands back to inspect him. Now Scotty is worried that he said too much, asked too many questions. Maybe now she regrets telling him about her dead brother. Maybe she doesn't want him to know too much about her. He really doesn't know anything about her. He doesn't know how old she is, or where she came from. All of a sudden, he's not even sure Kim-Li is her real name. It doesn't even sound like a Vietnamese name. He wishes she would tell him more about herself. He wishes she would trust him. Most of all, he wishes he could make her understand how much he cares for her. If only he could make her understand how he feels, make her understand that he would protect her, protect her family, take care of her. "Kim-Li, I . . . think I'm . . . I mean . . ." Should he say it? Why not? It's true, isn't it? He decides to whisper it. "Kim-Li, I think I . . . love you."

She smiles at him, but it's a sad smile. She again puts her fingers against his lips.

Why did she do that? Does it mean she doesn't want him to say things like that? Maybe she doesn't believe him. Maybe other soldiers have told her that before. Maybe a lot of them tell her that.

"No, I really mean it. I really care about you. I'm so sorry your little brother had to die. I wish . . ." He can't think how to go on. He wishes he was better at saying important things. He wants so much to make her believe he really would do anything for her. Most of all, he wishes she would let him just hold her.

As if she understands what he's thinking, she moves closer and lightly touches his chest.

He carefully puts his arms around her. He wants her to know he's not holding her like somebody who wants to make love to her, even though they are both naked. He holds her gently, cautiously. He wants so much for her to understand.

The cold water runs over the two of them, but Scotty doesn't care how cold it is. All he can think about is that she's with him, that she gently washed him, like a wife might wash her husband. And she told him a little about herself, about the death of her little brother. He wants to console her. He wants to hold her in a way that lets her know that he is only trying to comfort her, that and nothing more.

"Well this is a pretty picture."

They both turn. It's Brent.

"Getting a little wash up, are we? And with the special Asian naked washie-washie thrown in?"

Kim-Li frowns and turns away. She turns the water off, and goes to get her dress. It bothers Scotty that she doesn't seem to be in much of a hurry to put it on. Has Brent seen her naked before? Scotty tries to push that thought away. He doesn't like that thought.

Brent is watching him, grinning. "I wish I had a camera, old buddy. You're quite the picture there. Naked as a jaybird, with your flagpole hangin' out at half mast."

Scotty looks down. Brent is right. He's disappointed in himself.

Kim-Li frowns at Brent and comes to take Scotty's arm. "Come. We go back bed now."

Brent takes his other arm and they slowly make their way back to the little room. Scotty feels very tired, but he doesn't want to go back to that room. It feels like he's being taken back to prison. The last thing he wants to do is get back into that damn bed, but his knee is killing him and the pain in his gut gets worse with every step, so he knows he has no choice. He needs more magic powder. He can feel it wearing off.

They make it to the bed, and Kim-Li lends a supporting arm under his back to help him lie down. The pain is really intense now, and he closes his eyes to fight it. But it's no use; he needs his magic powder. He blindly reaches out for the jar.

Kim-Li takes his hand. "What you want, Sca-tee?"

"Powder. I need . . . please."

Her hand goes away.

Scotty opens his eyes. She's showing the jar to Brent.

"Almost empty, eh? Has our boy been hitting the magic pixie dust a little hard? So what? Get him some more."

He hands her something. Was it a key?

"Our boy here deserves a little reward for making it to the bathroom and back. It's about time he got out of that damn bed."

She shakes the jar at him, frowning. "He have blood."

Brent turns to look at Scotty. "Blood? What blood?"

"Out of him."

"Blood? You mean in his shit?"

Kim-Li goes out the door without another word.

Brent comes to sit on the edge of the bed. "So what's this she's sayin'? You been shittin' blood?"

Scotty tries to make his mind stop thinking about the powder. He forces his mind to pay attention. "Guess so. Dizzy. And hot."

"Jesus, Scotty. What the hell happened? A few days ago you were feelin' better, and now look at you, for shit's sake."

"Sorry."

"You don't have to be sorry. But you have to let me know when somethin's goin' on. I said I'd take care of you, didn't I? I said that after we went through the ice, and I meant it. I have, haven't I? Ever since? You're my buddy, but you got to tell me these things."

"Don't know . . . what's wrong with me. Just feel . . . bad. Will I have to go back to . . . that hospital?"

"The hospital? You can't go back there. No way. They think you're gone. Left the country. You go back and they'll throw us in the brig."

"But . . . what should . . . I do?"

"Now don't go gettin' all upset. You know how you can get all upset about nothin'. I'll figure this out."

"But it's not right that I should be bleeding inside."

"Hell, I know that, but we don't know for sure what it is. It's probably only that you've been movin' around too much. Didn't they tell you not to move around?"

"Yes, but that was last week. Or has it been two weeks? How long have I . . . been here?"

"Not all that long."

"But I should be healing up . . . shouldn't I? I didn't bleed like that when I was in the hospital. And why do I feel so crappy?"

"Christ, Scotty, you got shot right in the gut. You coulda died. These things take time to get better. Hey, maybe you been humping Kim-Li too much. Is that it? I bet you two've been goin' at it like bunnies. Am I right, or am I right?"

"No."

"Ha, I bet. I know you, Scotty. You can't keep your hands off her, can you? I bet you been goin' at it like there's no tomorrow."

Scotty wishes Brent wouldn't talk about Kim-Li like that. But he doesn't want to admit that he hasn't made love with her. He'd probably laugh his ass off. Brent doesn't even know he's still a virgin. It's the one thing Scotty never shared with him. Luckily, Brent never came right out and asked. Scotty remembers those nights with girls out at the junkyard. He would look at the stars with his girl while Brent screwed the other girl in the back of the old junked van. Afterwards, Brent would ask how it went, and Scotty would just say fine, or okay.

Brent brings Scotty back with a pat on his shoulder. "Hell, what's done is done. You just lay off our little miss Kimmy for awhile, and you'll be gettin' better in no time. Tell you what, I'll tell her to just give you head from now on. That way, all you have to do is lie there and let her make you happy. Easier on your shot-up tummy that way, right?"

Scotty tries to comprehend what Brent is saying. Is he saying he can tell Kim-Li what to do? Well, he can't. That's up to her and me.

Kim-Li comes back with a brand new jar, and it's clear full. What a sweet girl. She hands the jar to Brent and gives him a look.

Scotty tries to figure out what that look meant. Does it mean she disapproves of how much of the powder Scotty has been using?

She goes back out the door.

Brent opens the jar and holds the little red straw for Scotty to snort some. Scotty only sucks up just a little bit of the magic stuff. He wishes Kim-Li would have stayed to see how little he took this time. He lies back and waits for it to start working.

Brent closes the jar and sticks it under Scotty's pillow. He's grinning, like he's thinking about some kind of joke Scotty is not in on.

"What?" says Scotty.

Brent chuckles. "Ya know, your little bathroom scrub-up scene reminds me of that time I tried to get you laid in that whorehouse in Nogales. Bought you a pretty little Mexican gal that most guys would go after like a hound goes after a runnin'-away gopher. But what did my pal Scotty do with her? Remember?"

"I remember. She was nice."

"Nice? Nice? You were supposed to get your rocks off and come back out quick so we could go see the Canal Street sex shows. You were in there with her so long it scared the shit out of me. I figured they'd cut your throat and took your money. I had to knock two guys down to get in there to save you, and what did I find?"

"She was showing me pictures. Of her kids."

"Right. There you were, both of you buck naked, sitting on the bed, looking at a bunch of damn pictures spread all over the place. I still don't know how you managed to talk to her. Far as I could tell, she didn't speak a word of English."

"My high school French is sort of like Spanish. We figured it out."

"Yeah, but what you didn't figure out was how to fuck her. That's what I paid good money for."

"We were getting to it."

"Getting to it? You don't have to talk these whores into the mood. They flop, you fuck. That's their job."

Scotty is beginning to get the feeling Brent is not happy about something. "Does this have something to do with Kim-Li?"

"Damn right it does. You're actin' like a lovesick puppy around her. She's a hooker, remember? She's your servant. You do what you want with her, not the other way around."

"Don't talk about her like that."

"See, there you go. It's like you have to protect her reputation. Wise up, my friend. She doesn't have a reputation to protect."

Scotty tries to fight down his anger. "Lay off, Brent. She's different from the others, and you know it."

"Yeah, she's different all right. More expensive, that's for sure."

"What does that mean? Are you paying her?"

"Everybody around here gets paid, old buddy. In this place, it's all about the money. Haven't you heard? It's why the girls are here. Or did you think those little girls just enjoy flopping down on their backs to get hammered on by sweaty Americans?"

The way he said "little girls" makes Scotty wonder if he knows how old they are. "Uh, when Wong recruits them . . . I mean, how old?"

"How old are they?" Brent thinks about it. "Now that you mention it, I don't think I've ever asked 'em. Does it matter?"

"Just curious."

"You wondering how old Kim-Li is?"

"She looks very young. But she doesn't . . . act young."

"Right. She looks young because that's how Wong picks 'em. The ones who look young are worth more, so that's what he recruits."

But how old do you think they are? Really?"

"Hell, I don't know. If I had to guess, I'd say they're mostly around sixteen, maybe a few are a little younger."

It's not what Scotty wants to hear, but now that he's started, he can't keep himself from asking more. "You think Kim-Li is only sixteen? Or maybe even younger?"

"I didn't say that. Actually, I think she might be a little older than the others. Acts older anyhow. If you want to know so damn bad, why don't you ask her?"

"I did. She says she doesn't know."

"Then she probably doesn't. She's a pretty honest little chick."

"But her body is like a little girl. A child. She doesn't have hardly any hair, you know, down there."

That gets another laugh out of Brent. "Shit, man, none of 'em do. Wong makes them trim their pussies. To make 'em look even younger. Like I said, it's all about the money, man."

That makes Scotty feel a little better. Maybe she's not all that young. But he doesn't like Brent's crack about money. "So are you saying Kim-Li is all about money too? Are you paying her to take care of me?"

That stops Brent. He scowls at Scotty. "Did she tell you that?"

"No, but are you?"

"Naw, but I'll tell you what I am payin' for. This room. It's costing me a damn fortune. Costing you, I should say, because I'm taking it out of your cut. You can be sure of that. You think Wong's going to let you tie up this money-making room for free?"

"So are you paying her or not?"

"Drop it, Scotty."

"Tell me."

He hesitates. Scotty suspects Brent is thinking up a good lie.

"Let's just say she's not going hungry. But if she's being nice to you, it's because she likes you. I try to help her out a little. You know, time is money. She loses money every time she's with you."

"So you are paying her."

"Lighten up, Scotty. Like I said, I just help her out from time to time. But whatever else she does with you is up to her."

Scotty wonders if Brent is telling the truth. To get what he wants, Brent will say whatever he has to.

Brent stands up. "Hey, buddy, I got to go. Important business to take care of. Your job, for right now, is to stay put and get better."

Scotty reaches out toward him. "Wait, Brent. What do you know about her? Tell me what you know."

Brent does his usual who-knows shrug.

"Does she come from the country? She doesn't seem like a city girl."

"Who knows? She doesn't hang out with the other girls. Like I said, nobody seems to know much about her, not even Wong. He says he didn't recruit her. Says she walked right in and said she wanted to go to work. He gave her a trial run, and pretty soon she was in demand."

"So she does . . ."

"Fuck for a living? What did you think? You think she's in a place like this for her health? But she doesn't go down for just anyone. She's not one of your volume humpers. She mostly waits for the officers."

"Have you?"

"Popped her?" Brent shakes his head. "I've thought about it. But since you seem to have a thing for her, I stay out of her panties and just keep it to business."

"Business? What business?"

"She sends quite a few good dope customers my way. Officers. When they pan out good, I pay her a commission."

Brent thinks he knows what Kim-Li does with those officers, but Scotty knows he's wrong. When she goes into those rooms with them, she just lets them look, same as she did with him. He doesn't like the thought of anybody else looking at her naked, but she must need the money. At least Brent is not doing anything with her. It's a relief to find that out. He points a finger at Brent and says, "Well, you'd better not be looking at her naked anymore."

Brent seems surprised. He shakes his head. "Christ, Scotty, you get your bowels in a uproar about the damndest things. Why are you so hot for her anyhow? You know as well as I do she's just a—"

"Don't say it."

Brent throws up his hands and heads for the door. "Fine. Have it your way. I got to go."

"Wait. So you really don't know anything about her?"

Brent stops with his hand on the doorknob, but won't look back. "All I know is she disappears from time to time. No one knows where to. Wong gets pissed off when one of her officer customers comes in and she's not here. But for some reason, he puts up with it."

Scotty starts to ask Brent how often she disappears, but Brent holds up his hand and opens the door. "Hey, I gotta go. Things happenin'. I'll be back tonight. We can talk then. See ya."

And then he's gone, leaving Scotty lying there thinking about what Brent said. He said Kim-Li disappears sometimes and nobody knows where she goes. Where could she go? Home? Somewhere outside the city? Maybe it's like he thought, she's from a farm. Maybe it takes her a while to get to her home, and that's why she's gone for a while. He likes to think about her home with her parents on that little farm.

7

God's Strange Medicine

Scotty opens his eyes. There are sounds coming through the wall. Music. Shouting. They're living their lives out there, having fun, while all he has is pain and heat and confusion. Nobody cares if he is too hot. Nobody cares if his throat is burning from throwing up too much. The face up there on the ceiling is laughing at him. It doesn't care either. Scotty discovers his face is wet. He must be crying. He asks himself, can I really have any tears left in me? Maybe that's all I have left in me. Tears. Maybe I'm only a hollow shell full of nothing but tears.

Somebody says, "Help me, Sca-tee." But Scotty doesn't know how to help. They are all dead, lying on the ground, waiting for somebody to yell, Olly olly ox in free.

But the voice won't stop: "Help me, Sca-tee. Turn on side."

Scotty opens his eyes. It's Kim-Li. So beautiful. So kind. She wants him to turn onto his side. He does it, and she puts something under him. It's a pan. It must be like that bedpan at the hospital. To catch the blood that's coming our of him. Blood and pain and tears. That's all he has in him. He can't understand why she even bothers. Better to just throw him down the hole with all the other *phân bón*.

She rolls him onto his back. Puts the pan down on the floor. Brings a cup up to his lips. "You drink, Sca-tee. Must drink."

He does as he is told. He drinks. Water. Why is she bothering to give him water? Waste of time. Waste of good water.

"More. Must drink more."

Is she trying to fill up the hollow shell? Can't be done. But he wants to do whatever she wants him to do. He drinks.

"That good. Drink all. I be back soon."

Her beautiful face comes close. Her lips touch his lips, just like in the dream. But this time it was real, wasn't it? How do you tell what is real and what is not real? Maybe it tells in his book. Maybe Mr. Nietzsche knows. The book said Mr. Nietzsche was a dour man, a pessimist, like Schopenhauer. Mr. Nietzsche wouldn't be surprised to see the state he's in. He'd say, So what if you're in pain? So what if you're dying? We're all in the process of dying anyhow, so what does it matter? He'd say even God had to die, so what's the big deal?

The door opens. It's Kim-Li. She's come back. But who is this dried up old Vietnamese woman with her? Her mother? No, too old to be anybody's mother. At least a thousand years old. Maybe this old woman is God. No, you forgot, God is dead. Mr. Nietzsche said so. But this old woman looks old enough to be God. Maybe this old God woman has come down to earth to check up on things. She won't be happy with how things turned out. She'll ask, What is this war thing all about? Why are all these people dying? Who started this nonsense?

The old God woman is looking down at him. It makes him realize he's naked. Scotty feels ashamed before the Lord. He thinks, Oh, my dear Kimmy, why would you let this old God woman see me like this? I am before God without clothes to hide myself, and I smell bad because my body rejects food. It even rejects me and makes me stand outside of myself, seeing myself as I am. I am ashamed of myself, ashamed to be nothing but a hollow shell filled only with tears and pain and sweat and piss and shit and blood that won't stay inside where it belongs.

The old woman probes at his stomach. Scotty wonders why the old God woman is probing at him as if she knows him. He is sure she doesn't know him. Scotty thinks, only Mr. Nietzsche knows me. He knows me because we are two brains in the same vat. We discuss why the world makes no sense. Mr. Nietzsche tells me stories.

When Scotty was only a boy, he left his home and went through the desert. He went up into the mountains. There, in the cave of his solitude, he enjoyed his loneliness. But then his heart changed. Lo, he became weary of wisdom, of knowing too much, of seeing too much. Therefore, he must descend into the deep. He must never again drink from that cup. Besides, the cup is now empty. Therefore, he must never again pretend to be a man. He must never again pretend to be alive.

"Is he bad sick? Is he die?"

The old God woman says Her magic words: *"Nuean mong deong."*

Lo, then Scotty went down the mountain alone and into the forest of the magic tree and the magic horse. There stood before him God in his white robes and long white beard. Thus spake God: Scotty, thou are no stranger to me, wanderer. Although thou hath been much altered, as a child alters to become a man, wildst thou now carry your ashes down to the valley, just as you carried your fire up into the mountains?

"You help now? You make him better?"

"Nuean mong deong."

God proclaims: This Scotty is as a child who hath finally awakened. And yet, he wants to go back to the land of the sleepers. But he may not. He must awake and follow orders. He must kill. But Scotty doesn't want to kill. God says, If you love me, you must kill. You must love me, not men. But Scotty decides if following orders means killing people, he doesn't want to follow orders anymore. He says, No, I will not kill. If you, God, truly want me to kill these men, then it is you that must die. I will kill you myself. I will kill you by not believing in you, just like my mother did. Then, you will be dead too, just like we are all dead. We are all dead because the lieutenant led us too close to the border. You *must* follow orders, says God. It is required. If I say fly over their cities and drop the bombs of death on their little babies in their cribs, you must do it. But why must I do it, God? Why must I kill innocent babies in their cribs even if they do live in the land of the devil? God says, Because it is an order. Because I, the puppet master order it. Scotty says, No, I will not. You are not a brain in this vat with me. You are not even in my book.

Scotty smells something. Plants. Am I in the jungle again?

"Drink, Sca-tee. You drink now."

Scotty thinks, Yes, I will drink. For you, my lovely sweet Kim-Li, I will drink from the magic spoon, be it poison or be it honey.

"That good, Sca-tee. You drink all. Get better." She touches his forehead with her cool little hand, and Scotty's brain registers pleasure. He's grateful that she's with him, grateful that she can make the confusion and loneliness go away, at least for a little while.

The spoon is in the air again, again wanting to go into his mouth. She speaks softly: "You drink now. Make you all better."

The spoon wants to go into his mouth, but Scotty's doesn't know what is in the spoon. It smells bad, very bad.

"Must drink, Sca-tee."

So what if it does smells bad? Kim-Li wouldn't make him drink anything that was bad. He leans forward and takes the wanting spoon into his mouth. Liquid. Some kind of tea maybe. The stuff does taste bad, but not as bad as his mind thought it would.

"You so quiet, Sca-tee."

Is that true? Has he been quiet? His mind has not been quiet, but maybe his mouth has been quiet.

She holds out the spoon again. "Take more now."

Scotty does as he is told. He focuses on the taste of it. Tastes like . . . herbs. Plants from the jungle, maybe. He's never tasted anything like it before. Should he ask her what it is? Maybe she doesn't know. The old God woman knows. She brought it. Who was that old woman? Such a strange smell. Actually, many smells: plants, flowers, dirt . . . insects?

She smiles. "You like? Not taste bad?"

"I like you."

She pretends to be disappointed. "Only like? Before you say love."

Love? Yes, it's true. He lets the idea of it settle over him. Of course he loves her. He has always loved her. "I do love you," he says. "I do."

8

What It Means to Be

Scotty wakes up, not sure where he is. But then he sees the face up on the ceiling and he remembers: You are in a back room at Wong's. I was sick, but now I'm getting better. That old God woman's brew must be magic. It cured the pain in my gut. That gives him an idea. Now that I'm feeling better, I should go back to reading my book. He used to read it a lot. But where is it? He leans out and looks all around the floor. No book. He sits up. That causes pain. Maybe he needs a little more magic powder. But only a little; otherwise, Kim-Li might not like it. He feels under his pillow, and the little jar is there. And he feels something else under there: his book! Kim-Li must have put it there.

He carefully opens the jar and dips the little red straw deep down into the magic powder. He sucks some in, but not too much. He closes the jar and puts it in it's special place under the pillow. He takes out the book and looks closely at it. The book has stains on it. And it has a smell. It smells like . . . the jungle? Why would it smell like the jungle?

"Memory. Not allowed."

Scotty decides he doesn't want to think about why the book smells like that. A book is for reading, not smelling. He opens the book, and sees that some of the pages are stained red. The lieutenant said it was his blood. He decides to skip the red pages. The first page that's not stained red is in the middle of a chapter about the existentialists. Scotty has heard about them. The professor in the class talked about the existentialists. He said they believed in the individual is a self-determining agent. But what does that mean? Scotty begins to read. It's about a man named Martin Heidegger. The book says he was a German philosopher who talked about the nature of being. The book says Heidegger asked whether we really know what it means *to be*? Scotty thinks about that. Doesn't everybody know what it means to be? We just are, aren't we? Or are we? Am I? The more he thinks about it, the more unsure he is. Maybe this Heidegger guy was onto something. Do we ever really stop to think about who, or what, we are? Scotty tries to think about who he is, but it keeps on getting mixed up with who he used to be, and that's remembering, and he's not supposed to remember. Scotty reads on and finds out Heidegger was famous for saying only a God can save us. But the book says nobody is quite sure what he meant by that. Nietzsche said people lived their lives as if God was dead. The book says, for that reason, Nietzsche was an outcast among philosophers. He said if nobody believed in God, then there is no God. But what if nobody believed in war. Would there be no war? If they held a war and nobody showed up to fight in it, wouldn't they have to give up having wars. Only logical. But wait, if Nietzsche said people lived their lives as if God was dead, they must have believed he wasn't dead at one time. Did He die? Can God die? Maybe it's better to believe He never existed in the first place. That would make more sense. Or maybe he was alive a long, long time ago, back when he was doing all those miracles. But then He died. Maybe now, with all the wars we're having, and all the killing that's going on, it means He isn't alive anymore to stop it. If he was alive, he wouldn't allow bombs to be dropped on babies in their cribs, like in Nagasaki and Hiroshima. But despite those things, some people still believe He is alive. Can they all be wrong? Maybe they are just *hoping* He's still alive and will start doing miracles again. If so, he'd better hurry up. Scotty decides to stop reading. He doesn't want to think about being. Most of all, he doesn't want to think about maybe not even having ever existed, because then he would have never found Kim-Li. He wants to only think about her. He closes his eyes to think about how beautiful she is. He hears the door open. He hears footsteps. Is it her?

"You read book, Sca-tee?"

Scotty opens his eyes. It is her. It's Kim-Li, looking more lovely than ever. She's holding his book. He watches her as she turns the pages. She comes to the part that's stained red and shows it to him. Her eyes are asking a question, but he doesn't want to answer. He shrugs.

She puts down the book and holds out a cup. "Time more. Okay?" She holds the spoon full of the awful-smelling herb mixture up to his lips. Scotty knows he's capable of feeding himself now, but he likes her doing it, likes the idea of her taking care of him.

After he drinks a few spoonfuls of the old God woman's brew, she puts down the cup and says, "I bring eat. You want?"

Scotty nods and watches while she unwraps what looks like a small round loaf of bread. He realizes he hasn't seen bread since he's been in this country, except for the soft and tasteless white Wonder Bread that's served by the U.S. military. She tears off a hunk of the bread and hands it to Scotty. The bread is light brown inside, and the sight of it makes him very hungry. Maybe he's been hungry for a very long time but didn't realize it. He starts to take a bite of the wonderful looking bread, but then he decides to wait for her so they can eat together. Humming softly to herself, she unwraps something else, a small piece of white cheese. Cheese is another thing Scotty has never seen before in this country, except for the overly-yellow thin slices of Velveeta cheese they put inside the lunch time splat sandwiches back at the warehouse. He wonders where she would get real cheese in this country. Do they have cows? He asks, "Is that cheese? Where did you get it?"

"From goat." She looks at him quizzically.

Does she think he doesn't know where cheese comes from, or is she making a joke? He decides she's not joking. He can't remember her ever making any kind of joke.

"From rich bastard."

Scotty has never heard her use a word like bastard before. Was she referring to American officers? He decides he doesn't want to ask. He's not sure he wants to eat any "rich bastard" goat cheese. He tries to think if he's ever had goat cheese before. It smells kind of strong, but he feels very hungry, and if Kim-Li brought it for him, he should eat it.

She hands him a piece of the cheese, and takes a nibble of her bread. That gives him permission to start eating also. He takes a bite of the bread and it tastes good. In fact, it tastes very good. He takes a nibble of the cheese. It's not as good as the bread, and it leaves an animally aftertaste in his mouth, but he's not about to say anything negative about it, not if she brought if for him. He says, "Good. Thank you."

She smiles a thin, kind of sad, smile. Then, she leans forward and kisses him on the forehead.

That little kiss makes Scotty very happy. It brings tears to his eyes. He wants to tell her so many things, about how much he cares for her, but also how lonely he is when she isn't there. He wants her to understand. "Kim-Li, I . . . want to tell you something."

She's focusing on eating her bread and cheese.

"I mean . . . something important."

She stops and looks at him with a question on her face.

"I want to thank you for taking care of me. While I was sick, I mean." She smiles. "You better now, yes?"

Scotty tries to think how to say it, how to make her understand. "But I think I've been sick in another way. I mean . . . besides inside my gut."

She puts down her bread and cheese and takes his hands in hers. "You sad, yes?"

"Yes, but more than that. I've been . . . hearing . . ." He hesitates. Maybe he shouldn't tell her. Maybe she'll think he's gone crazy. Maybe she won't want to have anything more to do with him. But if he can't tell her, then who will he ever be able to tell? He decides he has to tell her. "I mean another kind of sick. In my head."

She's gazing at him, waiting.

Scotty feels afraid to tell her, but he knows he must. He shakes his head to try to make his brain focus. He wants her to know everything, even about the puppet master. "I've been . . . hearing things."

Her eyes look confused. "Hear thing?"

"Yes. I keep thinking about this movie I saw. I mean, before I came here. It was about these two puppets and . . ." Scotty can tell she's not understanding. "Uh, it's hard to explain. But there's this . . . voice."

"Voice?"

"Yes. Inside my head." He touches the side of his head to show her. "It tells me not to remember. I think I have bad memories, but it won't let me remember them because . . ."

She looks into his eyes. So intense, those dark eyes.

"You have bad memory. I know. Many have bad memory. I had bad memory too. From when bombs fall. It okay. It go away soon." She reaches up to touch his cheek. "You tell voice go away. All done now."

He nods and smiles to show her he understands. He's glad he told her. He will do what she said. The next time the puppet master comes, he won't listen. With her here to help him, he doesn't need to have a voice in his head anymore. He looks into her eyes and sees the kindness there. And the wisdom. She understands. She knows what war is like and what happens to people in war. He remembers her telling about how her little brother died. An airplane. Bombs. It means she must have been there too. She might have been killed. He hopes someday she will trust him enough to tell him about it.

She goes back to eating her bread and cheese.

He watches her. He's amazed at how wise she is. Sometimes when he looks at her, she's a child, a beautiful innocent child, but at other times she seems very wise, wiser than anybody.

He takes her hand and kisses it. He holds it against his chest, and the feel of her cool hand makes him feel so grateful, he wants to cry. And then, even though he doesn't want to cry in front of her, he knows he's not going to be able to stop it. The tears begin

She puts down her bread and cheese and takes him in her arms. She holds him tight to let him cry against her shoulder. The tears are coming now, and Scotty can't stop them. They've been wanting to come out for a long time. She strokes his hair and lets him cry against her until the tears and the shaking finally begin to subside. Then, she holds him by the shoulders and looks into his eyes. "Okay now? Better now?"

He nods and wipes his eyes with the backs of his hand. He believes her. Things will get better now as long as she is with him.

She goes back to eating her bread and cheese, so he hurries to finish his too. As he watches her carefully folding up the paper wrapping, she looks so beautiful he wants to tell her how perfect she is. But he can't find the words. He cautiously reaches out and touches her wrist. She knows what he wants. She lies down next to him. He turns onto his side to face her. She looks at him, not smiling.

What is she thinking? What goes on inside that beautiful head?

She closes her eyes. She seems tired. Maybe she has had a hard day.

He stays very still, not wanting to break the spell. Maybe she'll go to sleep. That would be nice. He would love to just sleep next to her. He remembers lying with her that first night. She didn't have any clothes on that night, but he didn't try to do anything to her. Just being with her was enough. Now it is the same. It is enough.

She sits up and looks at him. So she wasn't asleep. She stares at him for a long moment, and then she stands up.

Oh no, did he do something wrong? Maybe he shouldn't have told her about the puppet master. Maybe she's going to go away now. He reaches out toward her. He wants to tell her he's sorry, but before he can get the words out, she takes off her pretty white dress and hangs it on the nail in the wall. He's afraid to breathe. It's just like that night so long ago: she's completely naked, standing right there in front of him. He stares at the wondrous beauty of her slender body. The memory of that night comes flooding back. It feels like it's happening all over again; he has the same feeling of wonder as he watches her, the same feeling of amazement that such an absolutely flawless body could exist in this terrible world. He holds his breath to see what she's going to do next.

She gets back into the bed, but unlike that night so long ago, she does not keep her distance. She snuggles up close to him.

He's afraid to move a muscle. It feels exactly like it always does in the dream. In the dream, she wants to be close to him, wants to make love to him. But this is not a dream. He won't let it be a dream. He knows he's not supposed to move. In the dream, he doesn't have to do anything. She does what she wants to him. All he has to do is lie still and allow it. He focuses on the feel of her against him. He's amazed by how cool her small breasts feel against his chest. How can that be in this heat? Has he felt that before, or was that in the dream?

She begins to move her hand down his chest.

Isn't that what happened in the dream too? His body wants to react, but he tries to hold it back: if this is real and she stops, it would be too sad to bear. He doesn't want to do anything to make this dream end.

Her little hand gently touches the surgery scar on his stomach.

"It hurt?"

He quickly whispers, "No. No hurt."

She partly turns away. "You want powder?"

How long has it been since he had any of his magic powder. He can't remember, but he's sure of one thing: he doesn't want any right now. He doesn't want anything to interfere with what he's feeling. He shakes his head and pulls her close against him.

She doesn't resist. She rests her head against his chest, and her gentle fingers begin to trace his long scar. The feel of her touching him is electric. It's bringing all of his focus to each place she touches, as if there was a magical connection between his skin and the tips of her delicate fingers. She's doing exactly what he wants her to do. It's almost as if he's guiding her movements with his mind, just like in the dream.

Her hand moves past his scar, lower now, still very gentle.

He doesn't dare react. The slightest movement might make her stop.

When her fingers reach the edge of his pubic hair, a warm surge flows from there all the way through to his spine. More and more, his body wants to react, but he's determined not to move.

She whispers in his ear, "No hurt?"

Afraid to speak, he shakes his head. He lies still and waits.

She shifts her position and for a terrible moment he's afraid she's going to go away. But she doesn't go away, she does exactly what he's dreamed about so many times: she slowly and carefully straddles his legs. "It okay? No hurt?"

He's barely able to get out a whisper, "No hurt."

She moves forward, and with one smooth motion, she reaches down and puts him inside of her.

Everything in him wants to push up into her, but he forces himself to remain still. In the dream, he always knew he was supposed to remain perfectly still, so that's what he does. He's determined to let it be just like in the dream: if he does nothing, she will do what he wants her to do. All he has to do is wait. He keeps his eyes closed, trying to feel every nuance of what is going on down there. Even though he's never felt anything like this before in his whole life, it feels natural, exactly the way it should be. He focuses on the warm wetness inside of her, and the surprisingly light weight of her on top of him. He wishes she would start to move, and if in response to that thought, she does. She moves against him, but only a little. It's as if she's teasing him, trying to see how he will react. He opens his eyes to look at her face, and he can tell right away that she's not teasing him; she's just being careful not to hurt him. She's being gentle. But she's moving too slow. His body wants her to move faster, but he knows he shouldn't force it to happen. There's a rhythm to what she's doing, an almost imperceptible cycle of repeated movement. And her eyes never leave his eyes. She's watching him closely, watching for the slightest reaction. He waits for the next part of the dream to begin, and it does: She begins to move a tiny bit faster. Scotty's whole body wants more of this feeling, wants to make her speed up, but he knows that's not how it's supposed to go. To make it be like in the dream, he has to hold back. He has to let her be in control. She maintains the same slow, dreamy motion, and her eyes never stop watching him. Scotty is drifting away with the feel of it, but then he feels something start to happen. He senses his body is ready for it to come to a conclusion. He tries to resist. He doesn't want the feeling to end, not yet, please not yet. In the dream, it never ends. She senses what's happening and stops. But that's not right either. He doesn't want her to stop. He wants it to go on and on and never end. She understands and begins to move again, but even slower. Scotty closes his eyes and tries to fight the feeling that's building down there. It's going to happen on its own, and there's nothing he can do about it. His body is taking control: it wants it to happen—now! It builds to the point where he can't stand it any longer: he grabs her narrow little hips and begins to pull her against him. Harder! Faster!

But she reaches down and pries his hands off of her hips. She's no longer moving. She leans down close to his ear and whispers, "Shh. Wait. Wait."

At first, he doesn't want to wait, but then he realizes she's right: why should he want make this wonderful feeling end? He leaves his hands down at his sides and lets her be in control again, the way it should be.

She murmurs something in her language, and goes back to an even slower rhythmic movement.

Scotty tries to move his focus away from what he's feeling down there. He concentrates on the light touch of her hands against his chest, but there's something about the feel of her hips moving against him that wants to bring his entire focus back down to that part of himself. He feels the warmth of her sweat as it runs down the front of her to mingle with his, and that's when he knows he's not going to be able to stop it from happening. He closes his eyes and waits for it.

She senses it too and begins to move faster. When it begins, she understands exactly what he wants her to do: he wants her to continue moving against him, slowly, but not stopping, making sure his body gets to completely finish doing what it needs to do.

But then it's over. Scotty opens his eyes and sees that she's still watching his face. What is she seeing? Does she know this was his first time? Can she somehow sense it? For some reason, the idea that she might know he was a virgin embarrasses him. He has to stop looking at those dark eyes. He looks up at the face on the ceiling. It's still there, still watching, watching them both. That face up there makes Scotty want to cry, not because he's sad, but because he's . . . What? What is he feeling? Grateful. Yes, he's grateful she was willing to make what he dreamed about so many times come true. And he's grateful she was the first, grateful that that he didn't do this with those girls Brent kept on finding for him in Arizona, and so very grateful that this didn't happen for the first time on that ratty old mattress in that smelly old van Brent kept out in the back part of the junkyard.

She slowly and carefully rolls off of him. She lies close, her gentle hand on his chest, waiting for their breathing to slow down. He feels her quick warm breaths against his neck, and he is happy. He feels no pain. He feels no sadness. He feels only her warm breath on his neck, and nothing else in the world matters.

9

The Reality of Money

Scotty wonders when you wake up how you can be sure you're really awake. Kim-Li made love to him, just like in his dreams. It makes it hard to be sure what is the dream and what is real.

Brent walks in. He's grinning. Why is he grinning? Did she tell him?

"Hey, sailor, already awake this mornin' are we? Glad to see it 'cause we got things to do."

Scotty wonders why Brent is so cheerful. And why isn't he in uniform? And what's in that plastic bag he's got tucked under his arm?

"I hear you're feelin' a lot better, old buddy. That true?"

"I am feeling better. My gut still hurts, but not as bad. My knee—"

"Well, sure, these things take time to heal. You can walk can't ya?"

"I guess so. But I can't walk very fast with my knee all messed up."

"Right, right. But our little miss Kimmy says you're able to make it to the pissing hole by yourself now. I guess it means you won't be needin' her to hold your dink for ya anymore."

Why is he grinning like that? Does that mean he's not going to let her help him anymore?

"I . . . need her. She . . . feeds me."

"Feeds you? Ha. Is that what they call it now?"

Scotty is about to protest, but before he can get the words out, Brent sits down on the edge of the bed and says, "Just kidding, old buddy. I'm not gonna take her away. I'm just happy she helped get you better. Good thing, because I need you now, my man. Big things in the works."

"What kind of big things?"

"*Real* big things. No more small-time shit for this boy. I tapped into the mother of all deals this time. You won't believe it, Scotty. I only gotta pull a few things together, and we're on easy street. For life."

Scotty knows Brent is waiting for him to ask what it's all about. Brent loves to lay on his big surprises. "What is it this time? You're about to take over the Vietnamese government?"

Brent chuckles. "Not as far off as you think. Wait 'til you hear. You remember me telling you about the officer who's in charge of supply?"

"No."

"Yeah, guess not. You've been pretty out of it. Let's just refer to him as the major. I got an in with him. Been supplyin' him."

"Supplying him?"

"Yep. With dope and girls."

"Uh, isn't that a little . . . I don't know, risky? Selling to an officer?"

"Hey, Scotty, you're not getting it. It's not for himself. I mean the girls are for him, but not the dope. He's reselling it to the troops."

"Selling pot? To his own troops?"

"Not *his* troops, *the* troops. All the troops. To everybody. Like I said, he's the head of supply." Brent winks. "How about that? I made contact with the guy whose in charge of the whole damn shootin' match."

"You're supplying the supply guy."

"Damn right. Sellin' him my best stuff. Talk about goin' right to the top. Been supplying him for weeks now. Fairly small amounts so far. I think he's testin' me out. Seein' if I'm reliable."

Scotty feels like Brent is telling a story from some other world. He tries to concentrate "How? I mean . . . you found the main guy?"

"Naw, he found me. How 'bout that? Somebody musta told him I knew where to get good dope."

Scotty tries to understand. "What about . . . the warehouse?"

"Not there anymore. You didn't know that? Man, you have been out of it. The major got me transferred to his headquarters."

"Old Fart-Ass must have been . . . pissed off . . . about that."

"Aw, who cares? The major is his boss, so what can he do about it? Anyhow, now I'm free to track down dope deals all day. That's all the major wants me to do. Wants me to become his expert on the stuff, his right-hand man when it comes to pot. That's why I needed you to get better quick. I need your help. We got big things to do, old pal."

Scotty is not sure he wants to hear about it. Brent's big deals haven't always worked out the way he thinks they will. "Uh, are you sure you know what you're getting yourself into? I mean, with an officer?"

Brent waves off the question. "Hey, man, you gotta go where the deals lead ya. I was gettin' tired of retail anyway. Been ready to step up to wholesale for a long time. That's where the real profits are. So far, I've only been gettin' him a few Ks at a time, but now the major has got a new deal lined up and things are gonna really start happenin'."

"Uh, is everybody making a profit off this war?"

Brent taps his own forehead. "You always get it real quick, don't you, Scotty? Aren't I always telling Wong you're the brains of this outfit? I tell him his being patient with you being sick and tyin' up a room will pay off for him in the long run. My buddy. Smart as a whip, that's what I tell him. That you've just been like . . . out of it, cause of bein' sick and all. But I told him you're gettin' better now, about ready to go back to bein' my partner again. Man, we're gonna be rich."

Scotty nods as if he's agreeing, but he can't stop thinking about what Brent said about everybody making money off of this war. Can that really be all this war is about, making money?

"I can tell you're thinking about it, aren't ya?' says Brent. "Always thinkin', that's my pal. Pretty damn good deal, eh? Like I said, big time. I told you we'd hit the big time sooner or later. Well, while you're thinking about that, think about this. Can you imagine how much demand there is for our product up there at the front? Hell, you've been through it up there. You know what it's like for those guys. They need what we got. Can you imagine how much of our dope those boys up there will smoke up once we get control of the whole supply system? Can you imagine it? We could end up with our own damn warehouse. Full of our weed. With us in charge. Can you dig it?"

Brent's mention of a warehouse brings back sudden intense memories of Farkas's warehouse. "Is Farkas still there?"

"Yeah, and from what I hear, he's still the same old asshole, still spying on everybody with his big old binoculars. But now when I run into him at supply headquarters, which isn't often, he steers clear of me. Just scowls when he sees me. Boy, if looks could kill. Hey, listen, I got to tell you about my last day at the warehouse. I'm slavin' away, hot as hell, loadin' up my cart like usual, when I see this spit-and-polish sergeant walk in lookin' cool as a cucumber. He goes right to Farkas's office and asks for me. Fart-Ass comes and finds me and says somebody wants to see me. Asks me what it's all about. I say, how the hell should I know? I follow that sergeant outside, and there's this major sitting in the back seat of a big ol Army staff car. I get in the back with him and feel the car's air conditioner blasting away. It was actually cold in there, if you can believe it. Then, the major lays it out for me. Says he's been hearing about me. About my dope dealin'. At first I think, oh shit, I'm in big trouble, but then he tells me I'm being transferred to his headquarters. The major tells the driver to go, and we drive away. I look back and there's Farkas, out on the loading dock watchin' us go."

Scotty tries to imagine Farkas watching that major drive away with one of his slaves. "Farkas must have been fuming. He was probably trying to figure out what his boss would want with a lowly private."

"Right, but private no more, old buddy. You ought to see me in my uniform. Bunch of fancy sergeant stripes on my shoulder now. Now, nobody 'cept the major can tell me what to do. Whatta ya think of that?"

Scotty tries to imagine Brent as a sergeant. But none of it makes sense. "You're the same rank as Farkas?"

"Yeah, but who cares about him? I'm way outta his league now."

Scotty has a bad feeling about it. He thinks Brent shouldn't forget about Farkas. Farkas is not likely to take that kind of slight laying down.

Brent jumps up and claps his hands. "Hey, old buddy, aren't you tired of lyin' around naked all the time? We got places to go. People to see. Check out the duds I brought for you." He holds out the plastic bag.

Scotty looks in. Clothes. "I'm supposed to wear these?"

"Yep. Get dressed. Can't have you going out naked, can we?"

Scotty thinks about what it would be like to actually go out of this room. Isn't there danger out there? What about the war?

"You must not remember war."

Scotty shakes his head to make the puppet master go away. He doesn't have to listen to the puppet master anymore. Kim-Li said so, and she's right. Besides, the voice isn't real. It's just his own brain. But being logical, maybe it's too soon to be going outside. "I don't know, Brent. My gut still hurts, and my knee is all messed up."

Brent sits down on the edge of the bed again. "I know you've been feeling like shit. But Kim-Li says you're doin' a lot better now. And I got a little task for you. It'll give you a chance to get out of this damn bed."

"I don't know, Brent. It's been—"

Brent taps Scotty on the arm. "I know, I know. It's been tough. Kim-Li told me. She said you were real sick. Coulda died. Some kind of infection inside you, she thinks. But that's all over now, and I need you with me. And it's got to be today. My spies tell me somethin' is gonna go down in the next few days."

"Something's going to happen? What?"

Brent shrugs and looks toward the door. "Not sure. Nobody seems to know, but they're all worried it's gonna be big. The Tet holiday starts tomorrow, so maybe there's gonna be more protests. Or maybe Johnson is comin' back. Somethin' big anyhow."

"President Johnson. Here?"

"Yeah, you didn't know that? Went to one of the big air bases up north. For Christmas. Bob Hope put on a show. With Raquel Welch."

"Christmas? Has Christmas gone by already?"

"Yep, come and gone while you were layin' low here. But you haven't missed much. The war goes on. Gettin' even worse, I hear."

"I thought it was supposed to be over by the end of the year."

"That's a laugh. Just the opposite. A lot more bodies gettin' shipped back home now. Anyhow, people are sayin' the local troublemakers might use the Tet holiday to do somethin'. Maybe another monk or two is gonna burn himself up. Who knows. It'd be just like those weirdoes to mess things up just when I get everything workin' good. Anyhow, it might not be safe for you to be here alone."

"I won't be alone. Kim-Li will be with me."

Brent stands up. "Aw, she's gone off and disappeared again. I wish the hell she'd stop doing that. She told me to look after you while she was gone. Said she'd be gone for a while this time. She could have at least told me where she was goin' in case I needed her."

Kim-Li gone? Scotty has a sinking feeling. Gone? Where? What if she doesn't come back? Scotty quickly pushes that thought away. She wouldn't do that. She wouldn't leave him now, not after they —

"Don't look so worried, Scotty. I got it all under control." He points at the clothes. "Just put those things on and lets go."

Scotty stares at the clothes. It would be great to get out of the room. "But won't somebody see me out there? The MPs?"

"No worry. We'll be in a car. French car. You're French, remember."

French? That's right. Brent said I was French now. "Okay, *Oui*."

"Hey, that's my boy. *Oui*. French talk. That's good. Put those clothes on. And as soon as we walk out that door, I don't want you sayin' one word of English. Get it? You're just some French guy."

"Sure. I mean, *oui*."

"Right. Hey, listen, did you learn enough in that French class of yours to say it's genuine. In French, I mean."

"I guess so. Il *est véritable*."

"Great. That's all you have to say. When I give you the nod, you say . . . that thing . . . whatever you said. That's your only job. Other than that, you keep your mouth shut. Got it?"

"You're taking me somewhere so I can say a few French words?"

"Yep. That's all you have to do. I'll take care of everything else."

Scotty decides it would be good to get out of this room, even though the idea kind of scares him. But if Brent needs him. And if Kim-Li is going to be gone for a while, and maybe there will be protests, it might be better not to be left alone. He sits up and puts on the shirt. It's an off-white French sort of thing, loose-hanging with a partly open front. It clings to him because of the damp heat. He pulls on the pants. They are very white, and he notices they have only one pocket, in back. The clothes are lightweight, but Scotty is startled at how uncomfortable they feel. He can't even remember the last time he had any clothes on.

Brent steps back to look at him. "Stand up," he says.

Scotty stands up. Brent looks at him and chuckles. "By God, you do look French in that getup. Like a damn queer Frenchy."

Scotty looks down at himself. "Really?"

"You bet. It's perfect. Nobody will ever mistake you for a soldier." He winks. "If they ever did." He takes a pair of lightweight leather sandals out of the bag and tosses them to Scotty. "Here, put these on."

Scotty sits back down and puts on the sandals. They are loose fitting, but even constraining his feet this much doesn't feel right after going barefoot for so long. "Maybe I should just go barefoot."

"No more going native, Scotty. Or I should say, Pierre. We got important business, and I need a French sidekick. It's important. I had to hurry and move everything forward because of the chance there's gonna be trouble with this Tet holiday thing coming. Ready?"

Scotty takes a few steps toward the door, but the pain in his leg reminds him he forgot his magic powder. "My powder."

Brent says, "Leave it. I've got a bagful in my pocket."

Scotty hesitates. "You're sure? I . . . need it."

Brent pats his pocket. "I'm sure. Let's go."

Brent leads the way out the door, but he doesn't go down the hall to the bar. Instead, he leads Scotty out the back door to the alley. Scotty's knee hurts, but he tries hard to keep up. It's the first time he's tried to walk anywhere farther than the bathroom. When they go out the back door, Scotty is almost bowled over by how big and wide open everything looks. He stops to try to take it all in.

"What's the matter?" says Brent. "You all right?"

Scotty can hardly speak. "It's so . . . big. The sky and . . . everything."

"Right, right," says Brent. "The sky is big. Very observant, old buddy. Let's keep it movin'."

Brent leads him down the alley to where the Frenchman's Citroen is waiting. Scotty thinks the car has quite a few new dents in it.

Brent helps Scotty into the back and gets into the front. Mar-lon is behind the wheel. He's still playing the teenage gangster, same beret, same very dark sunglasses. He touches the front of his beret in a kind of mock salute. "Hey, Scotty, you lookin' better. Last time, not so good."

Scotty tries to remember when the last time was. Was Mar-lon there the night Brent snuck him out of the hospital?

"Hey, no more of that Scotty shit," says Brent. "His name is Pierre." He turns to Scotty. "Say something to him in French, Pierre."

"Uh, let's see. How about . . . *comment ils accrocher*, kid?"

Mar-lon looks puzzled. He looks to Brent for an answer. "What that mean? How they hang?"

It gets a big laugh out of Brent. "That's the idea, Frenchy. So you do remember some of that crap. Maybe it wasn't a total waste after all."

Mar-lon starts the car and begins tearing through the streets at incredible speed. It's as if he's seeing how close he can come to every pedestrian he sees. He's driving so fast through the great big world, it makes Scotty dizzy. When they come to a screeching stop, Scotty looks out and sees a building he recognizes. It's the Frenchman's office.

"Just got to duck in here for a minute," says Brent. "You wait here." He gets out and runs into the building.

Mar-lon says, "*Poulet*. You say you know French. What it mean?"

Scotty wonders what kind of game Mar-Lon is playing. *Poulet* is the French word for chicken. Scotty ignore him and stares out the window.

Brent comes back out of the building. He has an Army pack slung over his shoulder, and he's walking so fast he's almost running. Scotty is sure Brent didn't have that pack when he went in. What's in it? Pot?

Brent gets back into the front seat, out of breath. "Tan Son," he says.

Mar-lon starts the car and takes off fast.

Tan Son. Scotty tries to remember if he's ever heard that name. He leans forward and grabs the back of Brent's seat. "What's Tan Son?"

"Air base," says Brent over his shoulder.

"Air base? I thought we were just going for a little car ride."

Brent says, "Little farther. Vietnamese air base. Not to worry."

Scotty knows what "not to worry" means: he should start worrying.

As Mar-lon squeals around corners, Scotty feels the old familiar ache in his gut. "Uh, Brent, I think I need some of that powder."

Brent hands Scotty a plastic bag.

Scotty says, "No little red straw?"

Brent digs out a big roll of bills held together with rubber bands. He pulls one off, hands it to Scotty, and goes back to his thinking. Scotty starts to roll the bill up to make a snorting straw, but then he discovers it's a U.S. one hundred-dollar bill. He glances at Brent. Are the rest of the bills in that roll also hundreds? The casual way he peeled off that hundred makes it seem like he's gotten very used to handling that much money. Just how much pot is Brent dealing these days?

Scotty rolls up the bill and uses it to snort up some of the powder. Ah, same old taste. Wonderful. He tries to hand the hundred-dollar bill and the bag of powder back to Brent, but he just says, "Keep it."

As they speed along the crowded streets, still coming as close to pedestrians as ever, Scotty sits back to wait for the magic to work.

They arrive at a guardhouse. Mar-lon rolls down his window and shows some kind of pass to the ARVN guard who waves them through. Scotty wonders why the guard didn't ask him or Brent for any kind of ID. But then, he doesn't have any identification. Nothing in his one French-pants pocket except the powder and a one-hundred-dollar bill.

Scotty can hardly believe what Mar-lon does next: he drives right out onto the runway, weaving the car between parked airplanes and helicopters. He pulls the car up next to a black helicopter and stops. The helicopter has absolutely no markings on it. And why is it black?

They get out of the car, and a skinny ARVN soldier with a few stripes on the sleeves of his uniform appears out of the shadows. He takes Brent aside and they talk in whispers. After a minute, the ARVN heads for the black helicopter, and Brent waves for Scotty to come. Brent hops up into the helicopter and reaches back down to help Scotty up. They're hardly inside when the blades begin to slowly turn. Brent goes to sit on the floor opposite the open doorway, so Scotty goes to sit next to him. Scotty notices there's no door on this helicopter, just a wide open doorway. If they wanted to, a person could get up and walk right out that big open doorway. He wonders if all helicopters are open like this. He doesn't remember ever being in a helicopter. But he knows he must have been in one after he got shot. It was loud and —

"You are not allowed to remember that."

Scotty ignores the puppet master's voice. Kim-Li said it's not real, and he doesn't have to listen. Besides, he doesn't want to remember.

He wonders where they're going, but oddly, he doesn't especially care. He's beginning to think this batch of Brent's magic powder is different, stronger, or is it him that's changed? He starts to get that odd feeling of being outside of himself watching himself, but he tries to make it stop by forcing his mind to get interested in the inside of the helicopter. There are no seats and no windows. Is that normal?

The chopper's blades go faster and faster until they lift off with a sideways jerk. The helicopter's engine and the spinning blades make it very loud inside Scotty's head. He puts his fingers in his ears. As they rise up, the chopper swings back and forth. It surprises Scotty because it feels like they're hanging by a string. It doesn't feel at all like being in an airplane. The ARVN soldier is standing up front behind the pilot. He's hanging onto a strap that's attached to the ceiling, and he must have pretty good balance because he doesn't seem very concerned as the chopper banks off toward the late-afternoon sun.

Scotty takes his fingers out of his ears and discovers it doesn't seem as loud now. He looks out through the big open doorway, and sees the streets and houses of Saigon below. He glances at Brent and sees that he's lost in his head, as usual. What is he thinking about?

Soon, Scotty can see that they are no longer over the city. There's nothing out there but jungle, and they're not very high above the trees. He wonders why they're flying so low. Isn't it dangerous to fly so low?

Brent taps Scotty on the knee. He yells something, but with the wind whipping around inside the empty chopper and the chopper's motor roaring, it's too loud for Scotty to quite hear what it was. It might have been something about how cool it is to have our own private chopper.

No sooner has Brent said whatever it was he said, when Scotty hears something hit the underside of the chopper. A ping of some kind. In response, the helicopter chopper banks hard and the engine gets louder. He looks at Brent and sees that he has a scared look on his face. That surprises Scotty. He can't remember ever seeing Brent look scared.

The ARVN looks back at them and yells, "Taking fire." He seems worried too. The chopper's engine labors, and Scotty can feel they are gaining altitude. Brent still looks scared, and Scotty thinks maybe he should explain to Brent that death is nothing to be afraid of. It just happens, and then things go on just like they were before.

The chopper levels out and heads straight for the setting sun. They must be going somewhere west. Scotty wonders if they're going to fly right over that firebase where he used to be. He wants to see if it's down there. He gets to his feet, but the rocking of the helicopter makes him feel very dizzy. Brent reaches out and grabs onto his pant leg. He yells for Scotty to sit down, but Scotty points at the open doorway. "Just going for a quick look."

Brent yells something about being careful.

Scotty tries to walk toward the open doorway, but the swaying of the helicopter turns his attempted straight path into a zigzag. The chopper banks a little to the left, and that sends Scotty careening toward that big open doorway. He has the funny thought that maybe he's going to go right on out, and then this will be his day to learn how to fly.

But the skinny ARVN soldier moves surprisingly fast and gets ahold of Scotty's arm. That stabilizes Scotty enough for him to get to the edge of the opening where he can hold onto the steel door frame.

The ARVN looks at him in an odd way, and Scotty suspects the guy thought he was going to jump out. Scotty says, "Just want to look."

The ARVN shrugs and goes back to his place behind the pilot.

Scotty leans out and feels the wind tear at him. He likes the feeling of that wind trying to grab him. It's trying to turn him into a bird and send him flying. There's a bit of coolness rising up from the jungle below. It feels good. For the first time in a long time, Scotty feels glad to be exactly where he is, glad to be out of that damn bed, glad to be flying along over the jungle. As he looks down at all that green, it seems oddly familiar, like a place he knows well. He holds onto the door frame with both hands as he leans way out. The wind makes his eyes water, so he closes them. That cooling wind feels good, very good.

The helicopter dips and rises so quickly it almost makes him lose his grip. He wonders what would happen if he decided to just let go. He leans out even farther and looks down at the dark green of tall trees blurring by. The color and the pattern of it is so consistent, so perfectly the way it should be, it seems like a place he might want to be, a place where his troubled mind might find peace. But then, he sees a slight change in the pattern of jungle. The unending pattern of disorganized green has somehow changed to become neat rows of a lighter green. They must be flying over some kind of farm. From up in the air, it looks like the endless rows of corn he used to see when he was a kid back in Illinois. Do the Vietnamese grow corn?

The helicopter abruptly noses down. The ARVN yells, "Hang on!"

Scotty starts back to his place next to Brent, but before he can get there, the chopper's nose goes way up, and he finds himself on his butt sliding backwards on the metal floor. He comes to a sudden stop against the back wall. The chopper touches down, and the chopper's blades begin to gradually wind down. Scotty accesses the damage. His gut hurts, but the pain is not too bad. He takes it as a sign that his insides are getting closer to being all healed up. That thought makes him think of Kim-Li and that weird old woman that made him drink that terrible tea stuff. He has the sudden worry that Kim-Li will come back to Wong's back room tonight and won't find him there. Will she think he's gone away? Will she wait for him to come back?

Brent picks up his backpack and helps Scotty stand up.

The ARVN says, "I told him to hang on."

Scotty says, "I'm all right. Where are we?"

The ARVN doesn't answer, and Brent gives Scotty a look that says don't ask. He leans closer to whisper in Scotty's ear, "From here on, you're a Frenchy, remember?"

Scotty nods and says, "*Bien sûr. Française.*"

They climb down from the helicopter, and Scotty sees that they landed in a cleared-off circle of dirt, but they're completely surrounded by jungle. The landing place is barely wider than the chopper's blades. Scotty stares at the dark green wall of vegetation. Didn't he used to be afraid of the jungle? Now, it seems very peaceful.

He turns back and sees that Brent and the ARVN have moved away from the helicopter and are whispering together, so he decides to take a look around. He walks a short distance away from the helicopter. It seems odd to Scotty that they haven't cleared away much of the surrounding jungle, and there is no rolled up razor-wire fencing. No protective sandbag-protected guard stations either.

Brent grabs his arm, "Damn it, Scotty. Don't go wandering off."

Scotty says, "I was just looking around."

Brent whispers, "French, damn it."

"*Ah, oui. No problème.*"

The ARVN leads them through neatly spaced rows of green tents. It's almost like a boy scout camp, a place where there's no war going on. The AVRN soldier stops in front of a small tent. He says, "Wait here."

Scotty is thinking he'd rather look around this strange place a bit more, but Brent grabs his arm and pulls him into the tent. Inside, there are two cots. A lantern is hanging from a rope. Scotty sits on one of the cots and realizes how tired he is. He lies down on his back and puts his arm over his eyes. He wonders why he feels so sleepy.

Brent puts the backpack down on the other cot and whispers to Scotty: "Listen, Scotty. Don't mess around with these guys. Just play it cool. And like I said, you only speak French."

Scotty opens his eyes. Brent is pacing. "What is this place, Brent? We flew over some kind of farm. Like rows and rows of corn."

Brent lowers the tent's door flap. Then, he turns back and grins. He whispers, "If it's corn, it's the most expensive corn in the world."

Scotty gets it. "Pot?"

"Damn right. Pot fields. Maybe the biggest pot farm in the world."

"You've been here before?"

"No, but I've been hearing about it. From the major."

"The major? Has he been here?"

"No way. He's too smart to take any risks. He sends his flunkies, like me. That way, his hands are clean."

Scotty grins. "So you've worked your way up to flunky?"

"Very funny. But I got my own plans You noticed my little trip to the Frenchman's on the way here?"

"Yeah. You came out with that pack. What's in it?"

"Supplies."

"What kind of supplies?"

Whatta ya think? Didn't I say I was ready to be the wholesaler?"

"Oh, you mean money."

"Right. In this business, money is the most important supply."

"So, you're here to buy pot."

"Yeah. Up to now, the Frenchman has been the one supplying me. Now I'm turnin' the tables. I'm gonna be supplyin' him."

Scotty thinks about it. "Weren't you making enough money before?"

Brent looks surprised. He chuckles and shakes his head. "In business, old buddy, there's no such thing as enough. When opportunity smacks you in the face, what you gonna do, walk away?"

Scotty thinks about getting smacked in the face by money. He has the strong feeling Brent is getting in over his head, like always. Brent the businessman. Brent the one who gets what he wants. But tonight he seems nervous. That's not like Brent. He remembers the scared look Brent had on his face in the helicopter when they were getting shot at. That memory makes Scotty realize that Brent has probably never been in the jungle before, and probably has never been shot at. Scotty now feels protective of Brent; now he's the one who knows about jungles and war and people shooting at you, and Brent is the inexperienced one. Scotty can't remember ever feeling this way about Brent before. Back home, he sometimes felt Brent was getting into things over his head, but that was a concerned feeling, not a protective one. Scotty knows Brent will never let him play the big brother, but maybe he should at least try to find out what's going on. "Brent, what aren't you telling me?"

Brent is still pacing. "Nothing to worry about. I got it covered."

"You wanted me along on this deal, but now you won't tell me what's really going on? Did the Frenchman give you that money?"

Brent sits down on the other cot. "Yeah, but he doesn't know where I'm gonna get the pot. I just told him I'd found a new supply."

"And he went along with that?"

"He had no choice. He's desperate. A while back, my spies told me where the Frenchman has been getting his dope supply. Turns out he has relatives over in Cambodia. They have a big farm over there. When we Americans started arriving in this country, they switched over from banana farming to growing pot. Up 'til now the Frenchman had things all his way. He was the biggest supplier in Vietnam, so the major and me had no choice but to buy from him. But last week, guess what happened. The Frenchman's family farm got wiped out. One night, they got hit by some kind of plant poison sprayed from the air. The Frenchman swears it was us that did it, the good old U.S. Air Force, and he's pretty pissed off about it. Thinks we did it intentional, that we sent those spray planes over there to wipe out his supplier."

"Did we?"

Brent grins. "Well, I can tell you this, the major laughed his ass off as he was telling me about it. Slapped me on the back and said, 'Now who do you think would do a mean thing like that? Now it'll be us supplying your Frenchy friend.'"

"The major has that much power? To send planes into Cambodia to spray plant poison on a pot farm?"

"Sure, he has the power. Him and his officer pals. They can do whatever the hell they want."

Scotty tries to get his brain around it. A high-ranking officer in the U.S. Army sending U.S. warplanes to wipe out a pot competitor's farm in Cambodia? What has Brent got himself involved in? And then Scotty remembers the unmarked black helicopter that brought them here. And the skinny ARVN that acted like some kind of guide. "So what do the ARVNs have to do with it?"

Brent shrugs. "All I know is they run this place. The scuttlebutt around the major's office is that some government big wigs set up this pot farm. Let me tell you, Scotty, those big wigs are makin' a fortune off this war. When we were back at the warehouse, didn't you ever notice how many cases of food were going out the door and into ARVN trucks? We weren't supposed to be supporting ARVN troops. They have their own supply warehouses. Those cases of food weren't going to ARVN troops. No way. All that shit was heading straight for the black market. I bet some of it even gets sold back to us."

Scotty tries to imagine who would do a thing like that. Brent says it was government big wigs. It's hard to believe. Is that what this war is all about? Making money? "But wait, why doesn't this place get wiped out by the enemy? There's no security."

"Good question. I wondered about that myself. Soon as we landed, I thought, Hey, no guards. So, what does that tell you?"

Scotty tries to think it through. An unprotected ARVN base in the middle of the jungle? Why hasn't the enemy attacked it?

"I'd bet there's no security because they don't expect any attacks"

"The enemy won't attack this place? Why not?"

"Well, it's for sure the Cong know it's here. So what does that tell you? Think about it. What is there to attack? A bunch of pot plants."

"But the pot must be worth a fortune."

"Yeah, to us. But you think the Cong wanna become dope dealers? You can damn sure bet they don't allow their soldiers to smoke the stuff. And that means?" Brent pauses to let it sink in, then answers his own question: "Maybe they don't mind what we're doin'."

"They don't? Why not?"

"I think they've been watching us. How can you tell a Cong? You can't. They could walk right down the middle of the street in Saigon and you wouldn't know it. These Vietnamese all look alike. What if they've been reporting back about all the dope smoking? Maybe they think dope smoking hurts morale. Makes us less capable as soldiers."

"Maybe it does."

Brent seems surprised at Scotty's words, but he shrugs it off. "Hey, everybody does what they want to do in life. That's the American way, right? If our guys want pot, they'll get it somewhere. If not from us, they'll get it from the locals. It's not up to us to say whether it's right or wrong. Besides, the way I hear it, none of our guys would be crazy enough to go out into that jungle if they weren't stoned."

Brent goes back to pacing as Scotty thinks about Brent and the major selling pot to soldiers. Could it be hurting the war effort? A major in the U.S. Army is making sure the soldiers get as much pot as they want? And what about the ARVN leaders? It's their country. Don't they care what happens to it? Are they letting the war go on and letting people get killed just so they can make money? Scotty knows this is something that needs to be thought about, but it's confusing. Maybe what he needs is a little more powder. He takes out the bag and uses the rolled-up hundred-dollar bill to snort up a goodly amount. He waits, but it seems slow to start working. His brain is still doing that damn thinking, thinking, thinking about war and business and money. He decides he must not have taken enough and takes another big hit. He lies back on the cot to wait for it to go to work. Finally, the ringing in his ears tells him the stuff is starting to work. No more thinking about people dying. No more thinking about bombers dropping bombs on babies in their cribs just so somebody can make money. None of it is real anyhow.

The tent flap opens and the same skinny ARVN soldier peeks in. He points at Brent and says, "Come with me."

Brent grabs his backpack and waves for Scotty to come too.

Scotty feels a little shaky, but he manages to make it to his feet.

The ARVN holds up his hand. "Not him. You only."

Brent steps in front of Scotty. "He has to go too. He's the Frenchman's representative."

The ARVN scoffs. "He not French."

"Sure he is," says Brent. He turns to Scotty. "Say something, Pierre."

Scotty tries to think of something to say in French that will impress the ARVN. He decides it doesn't matter because the ARVN probably doesn't even speak French. He says, "*Je suis Français. De Par-ee.*"

The ARVN shakes his head in disgust. "They wait. We go."

He leads quickly them through the rows of tents. Scotty tries to keep up despite his damn messed up knee. At least he's not feeling much pain. The night is warm, and there are millions of stars up in the sky so what more could he want? That reminds him; he hasn't once looked up to see Cassiopeia since he got to Vietnam. In Saigon, it was always hazy, and when he was on that firebase, you couldn't go out at night because of the enemy snipers. He stops and looks up toward the northern part of the sky. But Cassiopeia is not there. Can the stars be different here?

Brent comes back and grabs his arm. "Damn it, Scotty, keep up."

Scotty whispers, "Do you remember when I showed you the Cassiopeia stars? Remember? We went fishing."

"No time for that shit now, Scotty. This is serious. Can I count on you or not? Do you remember what you're supposed to say?"

Scotty says, "Sure, I remember. *Il est véritable.*"

Brent says, "Good. Don't say anything else." He pulls Scotty along.

Scotty tries to stay focused. He aims for a straight path between the tents. As they pass through, Scotty sees that one of the tents has the front flap pulled back. He glances inside. No soldiers in there, only two old men. Must be farmers. Maybe pot experts.

Scotty stumbles over a tent peg and almost goes down, but Brent grabs his arm and keeps him on his feet. "Damn it, Scotty, pay attention."

Brent's urgent whisper sounded pissed off. Scotty knows he should pay closer attention, but this new magic powder is too strong. It's making it hard to focus.

Their ARVN guide leads them to a tent that's much larger than the others. He pushes them inside. Armed guards are standing behind a table with three men sitting at it. It's surprisingly bright in the tent, with several lanterns hanging from a rope above the table. The men sitting at the table are wearing the old-style green ARVN uniforms, but without unit patches or ID strips. There's only one chair on this side of the table, and Brent moves quickly to sit in it. Scotty moves to the side, trying to stay out of the bright light. He will be the watcher.

The ARVN sitting directly in front of Brent is fatter than just about any other Vietnamese Scotty has ever seen. That man leans forward and points a stubby finger at Brent. "You have money?"

"I do," says Brent calmly, "and the major sends his regards."

The fat man uses his fat finger to point at the table. "Put here."

Without a word, Brent dumps the contents of the pack onto the table.

It takes Scotty a moment to realize what it is. It's money all right, bundles of money, but it's not American money, and it's not Vietnamese money; it's a huge pile of French Francs.

The fat man picks up one of the bundles. He shows it to the others.

"Genuine French Francs," says Brent. " Isn't that right, Pierre?" He turns to Scotty.

Scotty knows it's his cue, time for his one and only job, but he can't seem to remember what it was he was supposed to say. Brent didn't tell him it had anything to do with money. Brent's new magic powder seems to be making everything funny. It's telling him he should say something clever, and he tries to remember the funny phrases he learned in his French class. He remembers *Avoir le gueule de bois*, which translates to having a wooden face, but to the French it means having a hangover. He giggles at the memory, and all the men in the tent stare at him suspiciously. Brent's scowling face brings him back. He has to remember what Brent wants him to do. Brent needs his help. Genuine. He has to say genuine. Trying hard to maintain a serious expression, he raises one finger high in the air and says, "*Il est véritable.*"

The men at the table stare at him for a long moment until Brent jumps in. "Like he says, it's genuine French money. From now on, the French buyers prefer to deal in French francs. Take it or leave it."

The men at the table turn their attention back to the money. The fat man lays out the bundles of bills in a long row and counts them, whispering the count to himself.

Brent leans back in his chair, crosses his legs, and waits. He's looking up at the top of the tent as if he's not the slightest bit interested.

Scotty is impressed at how calm Brent seems to be. He was afraid in the helicopter, but now he seems very calm. Is he pretending? The armed men standing behind the table don't look very friendly, but Brent doesn't seem to notice. Scotty doesn't feel very calm, but on the other hand, he doesn't feel afraid. Not at all. He only feels numb. His brain is trying to tell him this is a dangerous situation, but he can't seem to make himself care. It's more like a movie that's playing out and he's only the watcher. Brent is playing the big time drug dealer, and the men with guns are pretending to be soldiers. None of it seems very real.

Finally, the fat man looks up at Brent and says, "Six hundred kilos."

Brent frowns and shakes his head. "No, I'm supposed to bring back no less than eight hundred kilos. He turns to look back at Scotty. That's what they said, didn't they, Pierre?"

Scotty knows he's supposed to say something in French, but his mind is still thinking about this being a strange movie. Didn't he once see a movie where they were speaking a foreign language. The wheel of a black hearse was stuck against the curb. It kept on hitting it until—

"Pierre! Isn't that what the major said? Eight hundred kilos?"

Scotty looks up and sees everyone is staring at him. Brent is looking at him in the way he used to when Scotty was supposed to back him up, no matter what. Scotty again raises his finger in the air and says in his deepest voice, "*C'est vrai. C'est vrai.*"

The three men go back to their excited whispers. Finally, the fat man turns back to Brent. "Seven."

Brent slowly shakes his head again. "Nope. Eight hundred. That's what the major said."

The fat man comes back quickly with, "Seven-fifty."

Brent hesitates for just a second and says, "Done." He leans forward to shake hands on it.

The man doesn't shake Brent's hand. Instead, he stands up.

Brent also stands up. "We'll be waiting for it in the helicopter."

Brent goes straight to Scotty and gets ahold of his arm. Scotty is trying to think of something else he can say in French, but Brent quickly leads him out of the tent. Brent keeps ahold of his arm and leads him through the rows of tents, moving fast. He whispers, "You did great, Scotty. Those assholes didn't know what hit 'em. Let's get the shit loaded and get the hell out of here before they figure out how much that pile of small French bills is really worth."

Despite Scotty's bad leg, they end up almost running the last part of the way to the helicopter. They find their ARVN guide waiting there, leaning up against the side of the chopper with his arms crossed.

Brent helps Scotty up into the helicopter, but he waits outside.

Scotty decides to sit down and celebrate whatever it was that made Brent so happy. He takes out the little bag of magic powder and discovers there isn't much left. He decides he might as well finish it off. When it's all been snorted up, he sits back to wait for the helicopter to take off. He wants to feel it rise up into the night sky again. He wants to be free of the earth, free of this reality, free to fly.

But they don't take off. Time keeps going by and nobody comes. Scotty wonders what the hold up is. He's not scared, but he can see Brent is acting worried again. Scotty is trying to make his brain concentrate. Why is Brent worried? Who were those men at that table? Secret Vietnamese people? He decides it's too complicated to figure out. He'd rather think about Kim-Li. He hopes it won't be too late when they get back to Wong's. Kim-Li will be worried.

Finally, an old man appears, bent over from the weight of a huge bale of pot he's carrying on his shoulder. Brent reaches down to take the bale off of the old man's shoulder, and then he slides it clear to the back of the helicopter. Other old men soon appear, each one carrying a bale of pot. One by one, they dump their loads into the helicopter and Brent starts arranging the bales in neat rows, mumbling to himself, counting, probably estimating weights and quality and values. As more and more bales are loaded, the inside of the chopper begins to smell more and more like fresh green pot. Scotty leans forward to pick up one of the buds that fell onto the floor. It smells like really good stuff. He nibbles on the bud as he watches them load.

Eventually, the loaders stop coming, and either Brent is satisfied that the count is right, or else he doesn't care. He signals the pilot to take off by spinning his forefinger around in the air, and as if by the power of that circling finger, the chopper's engine starts to whine.

With the combination of the magic powder already in his system and the mellow dreaminess of the marijuana bud going to work, Scotty is feeling pretty good. He's ready to feel the helicopter lift into the air, ready to have that hanging-from-a-string feeling again.

Brent is standing in the doorway looking out. He still looks nervous. Is he expecting trouble? Scotty starts to think if Brent is looking nervous like that, then maybe he should feel nervous too. But he doesn't feel at all nervous. He doesn't feel anything. In fact, he doesn't even feel like he's entirely here; he's outside of himself watching all this happen.

The chopper lifts off and quickly gains altitude.

Brent goes back to counting his bales of pot.

Scotty leans back against the chopper's metal wall and tries to imagine what they might seem like from the ground. An unmarked black helicopter zooming through the black night would be just about invisible, nothing but sound. The local villagers will hear us go over, but they won't be able to see us. We're nothing but a noisy ghost passing by overhead. Down there, maybe the farmers rush their children inside and hide until the noisy invisible ghost is gone. But what about the enemy? They'll also know we're up here. And they'll know we're not a ghost. They'll know it's some kind of helicopter going over. Will they shoot at us? He imagines what it would be like to be shot out of the sky, then falling, falling, falling down to the earth. Then, I would be dead, he thinks. No one would ever know what happened to me. Would it matter to anybody? Would my mother ever find out how I died? Probably not because I'm not even supposed to be in this country anymore. I no longer exist. But maybe it doesn't matter. Maybe nothing matters anymore. But then he thinks of Kim-Li. She matters. She'd care if I died. Better not die.

He decides he needs a little bit more pot to stop thinking bad thoughts about dying. He scoots forward and quickly grabs another stray bud from the floor. He pops it into his mouth, but then he feels like a little kid who might get caught with his hand in the cookie jar. He looks at Brent to see if he noticed. But Brent isn't noticing anything except his precious bales of pot. He's counting and sorting and calculating, a businessman in his counting house, counting his bales of amazingly-expensive weeds. He has a little notebook and he's writing something down in it. Probably numbers. He's the picture of concentration, so focused on his task he doesn't even seem to notice the constant swaying of the chopper. He's probably already adding up in his head exactly how rich he's going to be.

Scotty chews on the bud and watches Brent work, appreciating his

302   *E.E. "Doc" Murdock*

friend's talents. But at the same time, he wonders how he ever came to know a person like Brent. They've been best friends for so long it seems like they should know everything about each other, but as Scotty watches Brent focus on his sorting task, he could be a complete stranger. How could he have changed from the guy who was satisfied with rebuilding cars in his father's junkyard to this big-time businessman who negotiates with military officers in a foreign county and commands a mysterious unmarked helicopter that flies invisibly through the night? Maybe Kim-Li knows why Brent changed. But that thought makes Scotty wish the helicopter would go faster. He imagines being in bed with her again, her cool little breasts against his chest.

The lulling sound of the helicopter's engine changes, and he's forced back into a world that's inside a helicopter filled with bales and bales of pot. The helicopter lands and the engine begins to wind down. Brent goes to the open doorway, jumps down, and jogs away into the night.

Nobody told Scotty what to do, so he stays where he is. He's thinking he sure could use a little more magic powder, but when he takes the plastic bag out, he sees it's empty. How did that happen?

Soon, Brent is back, along with a bunch of young ARVN soldiers. He climbs back into the chopper and slides the first bale to the open doorway. A soldier takes it, balances it on his shoulder, and goes off into the night. Another soldier comes and Brent shoves the next bale to him. Scotty is impressed at how fast they're working. He sits back to watch them. They are very efficient, these ARVN fellows, not saying anything, just doing their job. Scotty suspects they probably snatch a few buds when they get into the darkness. Scotty realizes he is again being the watcher. Brent is the doer, and Scotty's role is to be the watcher. Will it always be that way?

As soon as they finish unloading, Brent hops down out of the helicopter and waves for Scotty to come. He helps Scotty down and keeps ahold of his arm as they go into the darkness. Scotty feels like he's floating, and it is only Brent's strength that's keeping him from drifting away into the dark sky like a kid's balloon. They come to the Frenchman's car, and Mar-lon is behind the wheel. Brent puts Scotty in the back seat and gets into the front. He tells Mar-lon to go, and they go out through the guard gate, moving fast. Soon they're back on crowded streets, and crazy Mar-lon is doing what he always does, driving fast, risking the lives and limbs of everybody. When the car stops, Scotty looks out and sees they're back at the Frenchman's building. He wishes they wouldn't keep on stopping. He wants to get back to Wong's to see if Kim-Li has returned.

Brent gets out and hurries into the building.

Mar-lon turns to look back at Scotty. "Big holiday come. Tet. New Year. Three day. Much party. *Vacances importantes.* You know?"

Scotty *comprenez,* but he doesn't feel like talking. But then he remembers that Brent was worried that something might happen during the Tet holiday. But what could happen?

Brent comes hurrying out of the building. He looks happy. Mar-lon starts the car, and they go back to careening down the too-narrow streets. Mar-lon said there was going to be a big celebration, but Scotty wonders what these people have to celebrate. People are still dying in the war. It's supposed to be some kind of religious holiday. Maybe they'll all be praying for an end to the war. Or maybe their God is like our God, telling them that war is good. He wonders if the holiday is the reason Kim-Li went away.

The car stops, and Scotty looks out. They're back at Wong's. Finally! As soon as Brent opens his door, Scotty jumps out and hurries into the bar. The place is crowded with soldiers, as usual, and all the girls are there, but no Kim-Li. Scotty feels very sad. Where could she be?

Brent strolls into the bar and yells, "Happy Tet, everybody! Drinks are on me!" He throws some money up into the air. Scotty sees the floating-down money is French francs. Everybody starts yelling, and all of the girls jump up from soldier laps and start trying to grab the floating francs out of the air. Many of the soldiers also try to grab some of the money, but the girls are quicker and get most of it. Two of the girls are hugging Brent. He stuffs French money down the tops of their dresses. Everybody is laughing. Everybody is happy. Everybody except Scotty. Kim-Li is gone, so how can he be happy? But then, he wonders if she might be waiting for him in his room. He hurries down the hallway and opens the door. No Kim-Li. Oh no, why isn't she here? What about last night? Didn't that mean anything to her?

He falls into the bed. The face up there on the ceiling is trying to tell him she's gone, gone for good. But he doesn't want to hear it. He just wants to sleep until Kim-Li comes back. He feels like crying. He turns onto his side and sees his little jar of magic powder. It's almost ready to roll off the bed. He grabs it and holds it tight with both hands. His magic powder will fix everything. It will make the sadness go away. Maybe if he takes enough of it, the terrible sadness will go away forever. He's about to open the jar when the door opens. Through blurry eyes, he sees a long white dress. Is it her? Has Kim-Li come back? But as she gets closer, he sees it's not her. It's another girl. He wants this girl to go away. He doesn't want to see anybody. He just wants to have enough of his magic powder to sleep for a long, long time. But she doesn't go away. She comes to sit on the edge of the bed. She touches his cheek and says, "How you do, soldier? Brent say you sad."

Scotty looks up at her. It's not Kim-Li, but it's a girl that looks a lot like Kim-Li. Did Brent pick her for that reason? She is very beautiful.

"Why you cry, soldier? You sad? No cry. I make happy." She begins to stroke his forehead, and Scotty likes the feel of it. So gentle.

But he knows she's wasting her time. She can't make the sadness go away. This girl seems nice, but she's not Kim-Li. He discovers he still has the little jar in his hands. But where is the little red straw? No wait, he doesn't need the straw anymore. He reaches into his back pocket and takes out the partly-rolled-up one-hundred-dollar bill. He rolls it up tighter and uses it to snort up a good amount of the powder. He lies back, grateful for the familiar burning at the back of his throat.

He hands her the rolled up bill and closes his eyes to wait for the magic to begin working.

He feels her move away. He opens his eyes.

She stands up and carefully places the hundred-dollar bill somewhere inside her dress. And then she pulls her dress over her head and hangs it on the nail in the wall. She turns to face him.

Scotty stares at her lovely naked body. So very young. So beautiful.

She kneels down beside the bed and starts to unbutton his shirt.

He takes her hand to stop her. "No, wait."

She hesitates, confused.

"I mean . . . You're nice, but you . . . aren't . . . Kim-Li."

She says, "It okay. You want me be like Kim-Li? I do."

She still doesn't understand. She's not Kim-Li, so she won't be able to take the loneliness away. She thinks she can help, but she can't. She's only a very young girl in a strange country where girls are too young to be doing this sort of thing. But how young is this young girl? Brent says they're not really all that young. Is he right? He should find out. He says, "Stand up, please. Could you do that for me?"

She smiles and stands up, her arms down at her sides. This she understands. She knows men like to look at her when she's naked.

Scotty sits up and looks closely at her *mons pubis*. She doesn't have much pubic hair, but she does have a bit of a lump there. How big does the *mons pubis* have to be before you're old enough? He touches it lightly. Does she mind? He looks up at her face. She's still smiling. She doesn't seem to mind. He pushes at it a little to see if it's firm. It is. Did that shrink doctor say how firm it had to be? Scotty wishes he would have thought to ask him that. She still isn't resisting so Scotty carefully feels around the whole area. He wonders what it would feel like from the inside. He sticks his fingers inside of her and feels around.

She giggles.

Scotty wishes she wouldn't giggle. Doesn't she realize this is not sexual. This is a scientific investigation. He's trying to determine her age. He can't feel much of a lump from the inside, but it's hard to be sure; it's too wet and squishy inside her. He wonders what Kim-Li would feel like inside. But that thought makes him sad. Maybe now he'll never get the chance to find out. He pulls his fingers out of the girl.

No need for further investigation, the data is clear: this girl does have a *mons pubis*, even though it isn't very pronounced. She's not a child.

The girl seems disappointed that he has finished his investigation. She takes the hand he was investigating with and licks his fingers.

Why is she doing that? Does she like the taste of herself? Maybe she thinks his scientific investigation was some kind of prelude to sex. She doesn't understand that he was only trying to find out how old she is.

Scotty pulls his hand away and lies back down. The magic powder is starting to work now, and this is all starting to seem like a dream.

She lies down next to Scotty and takes his hand to put it back on her *mons pubis*. She watches him, looking for a reaction.

Scotty tries to think how to tell her he doesn't want her, that he only wants Kim-Li. But the magic powder is confusing things. It's making him feel like maybe she can help make him feel less sad. No, no, no. That wouldn't be right. That wouldn't be faithful to Kim-Li. He tells himself to focus. Otherwise, he might start imagining she *is* Kim-Li, and that would make it even more lonely and depressing. He closes his eyes. He wishes he could just go to sleep. Now that Kim-Li is gone, he's left with nothing. He feels a girl's small hand on his chest, but he's almost sure it's not Kim-Li's hand. Maybe he took too much magic powder. It's making him unsure of where he is and who is lying next to him. Maybe somebody snuck in and put some different kind of powder in his jar, something deep and evil. Maybe it was the puppet master. Maybe it's the puppet master that's trying to make him believe the gentle little hand touching his chest feels exactly like Kim-Li's hand, a soft hand, a gentle hand that comforts, that cares. But he knows the puppet master is lying. This girl is trying to be helpful, but it actually would be better if she wasn't so kind. It would be better if nobody was kind to him. Don't they understand nothing in this world is kind? Everything is cruel, and everyone is only out for themselves. There's a war going on out there in the jungle and nobody cares. All they care about is making money from it. Those headless men lying in the street were headless because of money. Eric wouldn't have had to get shot in the back of his head except that somebody was making money from it. It means we all have to die, all of us Americans, and all of the enemy too. It won't end until we're all dead. It's sad, but it's necessary because the puppet masters want more money. Yes, yes, it's all coming together now: Scotty finally understands. Now he understands what Schopenhauer meant when he said the world is *by its nature* mean and heartless and uncaring. Schopenhauer said the world is what it is, and we have no power over it. He said life is nothing but endless striving with no end in sight except for death. He said the true meaning of everything is that there is no meaning. He said there is no God, and he was right about that too. How could there be? A real God would put a stop to this.

10

Tet

Scotty wakes up with a start. It was a dream about falling down and down through the night. He'd stepped out of an open doorway and fell, passing birds that made strange sounds, passing big airplanes that were on fire, passing an old man with a long white beard who was sitting on a fluffy white cloud laughing and laughing as he worked the strings to make the men down below kill each other. Scotty doesn't want to think about that dream anymore. He looks toward the window. It's morning, another day to be somehow gotten through. He rolls onto his back and looks up at the ceiling. The face is still up there, still watching him. It's trying to remind him of something. There was a girl here last night, but she wasn't Kim-Li. Kim-Li is not here, and it makes Scotty very sad. Without her, it feels like there's no point to anything. He might just as well have died out there in the jungle when the pajama boy—

"Stop! That's a memory."

"Oh, shut up. I don't have to listen to you anymore. Kim-Li said so." But wait, Kim-Li isn't here anymore. Does it mean he *does* have to listen now? He turns onto his side so he can't see the face on the ceiling. He sees his jar of magic powder on the floor, and he thinks maybe if he has some of it, he won't feel so sad. He grabs the jar and uses his finger to scoop some of it out. He puts it inside his nose and the burn of it is so familiar it makes him realize what wonderful medicine it is. He remembers when Brent got it for him. Good old Brent.

He hears something that sounded like an explosion in the distance. It gives him the oddest feeling that he's still dreaming. Explosions don't belong here in Saigon. Explosions belong in the jungle.

"That's a memory. Memories are not allowed."

But what if it isn't a memory? And what if this isn't a dream? What if that was a real explosion? He sits up and listens. No more explosions. Maybe it was a dream after all. But then he realizes it's *too* quiet. He's not hearing any music coming through the wall. And he's not hearing any voices out there, no soldiers laughing, arguing, shouting. Something is wrong. Wong's Bar is never this quiet. Maybe it's another dream. He closes his eyes, but then he hears another explosion. He opens his eyes. This is not a dream That really was an explosion, and the sound of it was very frightening, like hearing a terrible middle-of-the-night crash on a distant highway. Are people dying out there right now? He tries to think what it could mean. That explosion couldn't have been more than a couple of miles away. That would mean it was in this city. Has the war come here? Is it possible that Saigon is being attacked? Then, he hears gunfire, a machine gun. It's far away, but he knows the sound of it. It goes on and on, like some kind of clattering, out-of-balance noisy old factory machine that won't stop.

He stands up, but he can feel the magic powder wandering through his brain. It wants him to lie back down. But he's not going to do it. He has to go see what's going on. What if Kim-Li is out there somewhere? He goes out through the door and starts down the hallway. He is trying to walk in a straight line, but he keeps bumping against the walls, first one side then the other. When he makes it out to the bar, he can't believe what he is seeing: there are no soldiers, and a lot of the chairs have been knocked over, and nobody bothered to pick them up. Wong and the girls are gathered at the front window, looking out. Scotty comes up behind them and taps Wong on the shoulder. "What's going on?"

Wong turns to stare at Scotty. The girls also turns to stare at him. He wonders, why are they are all looking at me like that?

The girl who was in his room is there too. She is very pretty.

She points down at his crotch and says, "Sca-tee, no clothes."

Scotty looks down and sees that she's right. If there is shooting going on out there, maybe he should have his soldier clothes on. But he doesn't know where his soldier clothes are. It seems like a very long time since he was a soldier. The girl takes his hand and leads him back to his room. He doesn't see his soldier clothes anywhere, but the French clothes Brent gave him are on the floor. The girl pushes him down onto the bed and helps him put the French pants on. Then, she quickly runs out of the room. Scotty sits there on the bed trying to make some sense of it all. Why did all the soldiers leave? And where is Brent? It's all very confusing. It feels like his brain is not working right. He slips on the Frenchy sandals, and grabs the Frenchy shirt. He goes back out to the bar and joins the girls at the window. There are lots of people in the street. They're all running in the same direction, away from the city.

"What's going on?" he says.

The girls turn to look at him. They stare at him as if they don't know who he is. What are they seeing? Isn't he the same old Scotty?

They all go back to looking out the window. Scotty pushes his way through them and leans out. He sees smoke is rising into the sky from several different locations near the central part of the city. He hears gunfire from that direction. It really is some kind of attack, but his brain still doesn't want to accept it. How could the enemy be here in Saigon? He wonders if maybe they were here all the time, just waiting to attack.

If so, why did they choose this day? He remembers Mar-lon talking about Tet being a big holiday. Was this big holiday the signal to attack?

Another explosion, louder, and closer, brings oohs from the girls. Scotty leans our farther and sees new columns of smoke. Much closer now. No wonder the people are running away.

He hears a loud noise behind him and involuntarily ducks. But when he turns around, he sees Wong is attacking the wall behind the bar with a hatchet. What the hell is he doing? Has he gone mad? The girls all rush to the bar to watch and Scotty joins them. Wong is furiously chopping away at the flimsy wooden wall. But why? Soon, Wong has chopped away enough of the wall to reveal a steel box that was hidden inside. Wong tears the box out of the wall and runs into the back hallway with it. Scotty hears a door slam back there. He tries to think what could have been in that box. Money? Gold? Secret papers? And what made Wong decide to chop it out of its hiding place now? What does he know that we don't know? Scotty looks at the girls, but they seem as puzzled as he does. He wonders why the girls don't run away too, but then he realizes they don't have anywhere else to go. Their whole world has suddenly changed. A few hours ago, they were happily entertaining American soldiers, but now the soldiers are gone. There is shooting and explosions and people are running in the streets. Maybe Wong was like their foster father, and now he's run away and left them on their own. And maybe, in an odd way, the soldiers were like their big brothers. But they didn't protect the girls like big brother should. They all ran away. Thinking about the soldiers running away makes Scotty again wonder where Brent is. Brent wouldn't run away. Not without coming to get him, would he? Scotty taps the shoulder of the girl he was in the back room with. "Uh, what about my friend? Brent? Where did he go?"

She points out toward the street. "He go. With sergeant." She draws imaginary lines on her sleeve.

Stripes? Brent went off with a sergeant? Why would he do that? The only sergeant he and Brent know is . . . Farkas! Scotty holds out his hands to indicate a fat belly. "This sergeant, was he a big fat guy?"

She nods, making the same gestures. "Big belly. Much fat."

Farkas. It must have been Farkas. But why would Farkas come here to get Brent? And why would Brent go with him? Brent said he doesn't work for Farkas anymore. It doesn't make sense.

The girl has turned back to the window. Scotty touches her shoulder again. "Did Brent seem willing to go with the fat sergeant?"

She looks at him, puzzled. Scotty can see that she doesn't understand the question. She probably doesn't know the English word "willing." He says, "Brent happy? Happy go with sergeant?"

She shakes her head. "Brent no happy. He say no go, but Sergeant man touch gun." She pats her hip.

It means Farkas had a pistol. He forced Brent to go with him. But why?

He asks the girl, "Which way did they go?"

She points in the direction of the warehouse.

Of course. Farkas would take Brent back to the warehouse. That warehouse is Farkas's private kingdom. Brent may be in trouble. Scotty knows he has to go help Brent. He runs out into the street, but he's almost swept away by the hoard of people running toward him. Many of them are carrying large bundles, or pushing loaded-down bicycles, and they keep crashing into him. Normally, they would be very careful not to run into an American, but now it's like they don't even see him. Scotty moves to the side of the street and moves along next to the buildings. He's making some progress, but he's feeling tired and his knee is hurting. He suddenly realizes he forgot his magic powder. He looks back toward Wong's. Should he go back and get it? He turns around again to look in the direction of the warehouse. There's smoke rising into the sky in that direction. Is it the warehouse? He has to go on. He has to go help Brent. He comes to a street that makes him feel nervous. He stops. What is it about this street? Then he remembers: this is the street where the headless bodies were lying across—

"That's a memory. I order you to not remember."

He stops in the middle of the street and shakes his head to make the puppet master go away. "No! You have to go away now." He doubles up his fists and hits himself in both sides of his head, hard. "Go away. I'm not listening to you anymore. Kim-Li said I don't have to."

He looks around. Did anyone hear him shouting like that? Will they think he's gone crazy? But the few people left on the street aren't paying any attention to him. They're so focused on running away, they're not seeing or hearing anything. He hurries on, whispering to himself. "I don't believe in you anymore. I don't believe in you. You are not real. I have to keep going. I have to find Brent."

But did Farkas really take Brent to the warehouse? Why would he do that? Maybe Farkas is the one who's really crazy. He always was mean and petty and vengeful, so maybe he's the craziest one of all. Like when he was tormenting poor Phil. That was a crazy thing to do. And what about how he watched everybody from his office with his big old Army-issue binoculars? Crazy. And now maybe he's gone completely crazy with envy because Brent has the same rank as him and has more powerful connections than him. Maybe that's why he took Brent away. Maybe he's going to turn Brent over to the MPs for selling pot. But no, that won't work; Brent's boss is the major. He wouldn't let them arrest Brent. Farkas must know that. Maybe Farkas was driven crazy because he couldn't get rid of Brent by getting him sent to the jungle like he got rid of me. No way the major would let that happen. Brent has been making too much money for him. Maybe Farkas went crazy because he wasn't making money too.

Suddenly, there's a kid standing right in the middle of the street pointing a rifle at him. He can't be older than eleven or twelve, even younger than the black pajama kid in the jungle.

"Memories are not—"

"Shut up. I need to concentrate." Scotty looks at the boy. Maybe he's just play acting. That rifle looks real, but maybe it doesn't work. He decides to ignore this child and keep going to the warehouse.

But the boy runs to get in front of him. He jabs the rifle into Scotty's stomach and says something in his strange language: *Nuean mong deong*.

"Ow, kid. Quit that. It hurts."

The kid jabs him in the stomach with the rifle again, and Scotty realizes the damn kid jabbed him in exactly the same spot as where that black pajama kid back in the jungle shot him. It hurts, and it pisses Scotty off. He says, "Damn it, kid, stop that. It hurts."

The kid again tries to jab him with the rifle, but Scotty grabs the barrel of the rifle and jerks the gun out of the kid's hands. The gun goes off and the sound is very loud in Scotty's ear. Scotty stamps his foot at the kid. "Go away, kid. You're too young to play with guns. Go home."

But the kid does not go home. He tries to take back his rifle.

Scotty is getting tired of this stupid kid. He points the rifle at the kid and yells, "Go away, damn it."

The kid starts backing away, holding his hands up very high. Scotty looks down the sights of the rifle at the irritating kid. The front sight is covering up the kid's stomach. If he pulls the trigger, the bullet will go right through the kid. T and T. Then, they'll take the kid away to the hospital and patch up the holes inside his guts and the kid will have to have a tube that goes into his nose and down his throat, and he will have to lie very still in bed for a long, long time. Scotty feels his finger slowly increasing the pressure on the rifle's trigger. He knows he's supposed to shoot the enemy, but this boy doesn't look like an enemy. He just looks like a kid, a child who should be in school, or at home with his mother, not walking around on the streets with a gun. Scotty doesn't want to shoot a child. He doesn't want to shoot anybody. He tries to lower the rifle, but it doesn't seem to want to be lowered. His arms and his hands feel locked in place, and his finger is still on the trigger. His brain is telling him he *should* shoot this Vietnamese kid, that he is the enemy, but Scotty knows it's not right to shoot another human being, even if he is the enemy. It's just not logical. He lowers the gun.

The kid turns and runs away.

Scotty is glad to see him go. Good riddance.

But then, he feels outside of himself, watching himself standing in the middle of the street holding a rifle in his hands. It means his brain is not working right. He tries to make his brain think logically. There are buildings on both sides. It means he's in a city. There's smoke in the distance. Is it the warehouse. Is it on fire? Is Brent in the fire? He has to go save Brent. It's like when he had to go out onto that terrible cracking ice to save his friend. He has to do it again.

He notices that his ear hurts. He touches it, and his finger comes away bloody. What the hell? Did that dream kid shoot his ear off? He cautiously feels it again. There does still seem to be an ear, but the bottom part feels like it may be gone, or at least all torn up. Doesn't matter. He will ignore it. Nothing matters anymore except getting to the warehouse.

He hurries as fast as he can, and when he rounds the next corner, he sees the warehouse ahead. It's not on fire, but there's a small group of people out behind it. What are they doing? Is it the enemy? As he gets closer, he sees it's not the enemy; they're just regular Vietnamese people, the kind of people he used to see every day in the streets. So why are they crowded around the back of the warehouse building? Scotty sees a case of food come sliding out from inside the building. A woman picks up the case and runs away with it. Now Scotty understands: they've pried up some of the warehouse's metal siding, and somebody inside is pushing out cases of food. They're stealing food from the warehouse. It means there's nobody inside the warehouse to stop them. The soldier workers must have all ran away. Did they run away to join the fighting? But Brent could still be inside. He has to find out. He stares at the rifle in his hands. It gives him an idea. He hurries to where the people are at the back of the warehouse. He yells at them and points the rifle at them.

They scatter like rats. Scotty remembers the rats that were down in the bathroom hole back at Wong's, and that makes him laugh. The people ran away like those funny rats down there with the *phân bón.*

A case of canned creamed corn comes sliding out of the hole in the building. Scotty gets down on his hands and knees and looks in. An old man is in there. He's pushing another case of food across the floor. He's sweating. It makes Scotty remember how hot it always was inside the warehouse. The old man looks up and sees Scotty. He freezes. Then, he yelps like a kicked dog and scrambles away into the darkness.

Scotty crawls in through the hole. It's dark inside. None of the overhead lights are on. The only light is coming from up at the front. That must be Farkas's office. It's been a long time since he was in this warehouse, but to Scotty, it feels very familiar. It's hot and stuffy, as usual, but now it's dark and silent and spooky. He starts toward the front, but hears a noise behind him. He turns to see the old man scurry out through the hole. Another scurrying rat. He ignores the scurrying rat and heads toward the front of the warehouse again. Oddly, the aisle between the stacks of crates seem narrower than it used to be. It feels like the tall stacks of food cases are closing in on him. He walks faster, heading for the light. He hears a sound ahead: a dull thud, followed by a scary kind of mad laughter. Another thud, followed again by that insane laughing. Scotty slides along next to the wall until he's under Farkas's office window. He cautiously rises up to peek inside, and what he sees makes him feel like he's seeing an old noir crime movie where a cruel policeman is interrogating his prisoner by tying him to a chair and hitting him. The only light in the room is a desk lamp that's shining right in the face of a red-haired man who is tied to the chair. The man's face is all bloody and swollen. Blood is running down both sides of his face, and his eyes are shut. It reminds Scotty of something terrible he once saw: a hurt Marine's chest was all torn up and bloody. Little bloody bubbles of air kept on coming out. Scotty tries to make his mind reach out and grab that memory, but it slips away.

"Memories hurt. Do not remember."

Scotty ducks down and says, "Shh." He listens. Everything is silent. He slowly rises up again to look in Farkas's window. The man in the chair seems to be unconscious, his chin down on his chest. Scotty is having a hard time believing this movie scene can be real, but if a man is being hurt in there, shouldn't he be doing something to help him? The other person in the room is standing behind the desk lamp, only a shadow. He looks like a big man. Could it be Farkas? Whoever he is, he's no longer hitting the man in the chair. He's just standing back out of the light. Is he waiting for something? The man in the chair lifts his head and shakes it. Blood runs out of the side of his mouth. The big man steps out of the darkness. He's swinging something on a cord. It looks heavy. He swings it round and round until it builds up plenty of speed, and then he tries to hit the man in the face with it, but the man in the chair ducks just in time, and the swinging thing glances off of the top of the man's head. The big man laughs very loud. Scotty thinks there was something about the way that man in the chair ducked. He's seen that move before, a well-timed duck that makes the blow glance off. Scotty suddenly realizes the man in the chair does not have red hair; his hair is just covered in red blood. He understands: the man in the chair *is* Brent, the fat man is Farkas, and he's swinging a big pair of binoculars.

Scotty screams, "No!" and rushes into the office.

Farkas turns to look at Scotty. He's smiling a very strange smile. He faces Scotty and starts swinging the binoculars back and forth in front of himself. It's like a pendulum, back and forth. "So it's you," he says. You really ain't dead. When I heard you was dead, I had me a coupla beers ta celebrate. But now here ya are. Figures. Whole damn company gets wiped out and a little yella coward like you gets away. Probly hid somewhere shttin' in your pants while your buddies got shot ta hell, didn't ya? Ga-dam little no good yella coward. He starts moving toward Scotty, swinging those binoculars. Back and forth, back and forth.

Scotty discovers he still has the rifle in his hands. He points it at Farkas. "I'll shoot you, Farkas. I really will."

Farkas stops, but he's still smiling that crazy smile, and he's still swinging the binoculars back and forth. His eyes are wild, but his face looks happy, like he's having the time of his life.

Scotty puts his finger on the rifle's trigger. So smooth. He's amazed at how perfectly it fits his finger. He aims the rifle right at the middle of Farkas's fat belly. All he has to do is pull the trigger, and that will make Farkas stop grinning. He'll shoot him in his fat belly. Make him sorry he made fun of Phil. Make him sorry he hurt Brent. Let him see what T and T feels like. But Scotty is having trouble taking his eyes off of those swinging binoculars. It's almost like Farkas is trying to hypnotize him. The swinging binoculars are coming closer, back and forth, back and forth. The truth of it hits Scotty: Farkas is the puppet master. It all makes sense now. It's been Farkas all the time, hypnotizing him, secretly controlling him, making him do things he didn't want to do. Scotty knows it's good to shoot a bad puppet master like Farkas. One pull of the trigger and this evil puppet master will disappear. It's easy. He did it in boot camp. He shot the human-shaped targets. This is the same. He puts more pressure on the trigger. But something is wrong. The gun doesn't go off. Scotty is finding it's very hard to pull a trigger when it's a real human and not just a human-shaped target. His finger doesn't seem to have enough strength to pull the trigger. He has the odd thought that maybe in this dream, triggers can't be pulled. Maybe in this dream, guns are not real. He lowers the rifle to look at it. It seems real enough. When he looks back up, he's surprised to see that Farkas is no longer there. Where did he go? Did he run away? He looks at Brent. His head is slumped forward. Scotty puts down the rifle and hurries to Brent. He gets ahold of Brent's chin and says, "Brent, look at me. It's me, Scotty."

Brent's head jerks, and he looks up. He manages to get one eye open and seems to recognize Scotty. He works his mouth as if he's chewing on something. Then, he spits out a tooth and grins. Scotty is so happy to see that grin it makes him want to cry. He's seen Brent grin like that before. That grin means, You think that asshole can hit? I've been hit a lot harder than that. And it's true. Scotty has seen Brent get up after he was beaten to the ground by grown men that outweighed him by a hundred pounds. But somehow Brent always struggled to his feet and went right back to fighting. In the end, Brent would either win, or the guy would just get tired of hitting him and walk away.

"Now yer finely gonna get what's comin' to ya, ya yella coward."

Who said that? Scotty turns to see that it's Farkas. He's come back, and he's aiming a large pistol at Scotty's face. Scotty looks into the dark hole that's in the end of the pistol. It looks black in there, but he knows there must be a bullet hiding inside that dark hole. He knows a bullet is soon going to come out of that black hole, and the bullet will be inside of his brain, and he will be dead. He decides he doesn't want to see the bullet coming. He closes his eyes and waits for it to happen. He's not scared. No reason to be scared. It's only the end of this story and the start of the next one. Mostly he just feels tired, too tired to care about bullets coming out of guns, too tired to care about anything. He hears the shot, but for some reason he doesn't feel the bullet go inside his brain. That's odd. When he got shot T and T, he felt the bullet go through. But then he understands: it's because he's already dead. You don't feel anything when you're dead. This is only the dream that follows the other dream. But when he opens his eyes, he sees Farkas lying on the floor. He thinks, that's odd, shouldn't I be the one lying dead on the floor? He hears a sound and turns toward it. Two Vietnamese boys are by the door. One of the boys is the kid from the street, and he's hiding behind an older boy. The older boy is holding a rifle. Scotty recognizes the rifle; it's the same rifle he was going to shoot Farkas with. Scotty looks at the two boys and thinks they look a lot alike. The boy holding the rifle must be the kid's older brother. He must have shot the rifle. Scotty looks down at Farkas. He's groaning and holding his stomach. A puddle of blood is spreading out around him. Did he get shot T and T? Scotty isn't sure how to help him. He decides to help Brent first. Brent will know what to do. He turns back to Brent and begins to untie him, but before he can get it done, he hears another shot, and he feels a sharp pain in the back of his shoulder. He finds himself lying on the floor, right next to Farkas who's still moaning. Scotty feels bad that Farkas had to get shot T and T. He reaches out to pat him on the head. He whispers, "There, there." And then he feels another kind of pain. He opens his eyes and sees it's the darn kid again, kicking him. And to make matters worse, the older boy is pointing the old rifle at his stomach. On no, not again. Not another T and T.

But then there's another shot, and the boy with the rifle falls down. Scotty tries to figure out why the older brother decided to fall down. He tries to be logical. Three of us are lying on the floor. We're lined up like the dead bodies out on that concrete floor at Hanger X. Strange. He notices the dream kid is trying to pull the rifle out from under his big brother. Why is he doing that? Another face appears, leaning down close. The face is Brent. Scotty looks up at Brent's poor beat-up face. It's so sad to see a face all swollen and cut like that. Brent is holding a pistol. It looks like the same big pistol that Farkas was holding, the pistol with the dark hole in the end. Brent shoves the dream kid out of the way and picks up the rifle. Better that Brent has the rifle; that kid is too young to be playing with guns. Brent is pulling on Scotty's arm. Scotty knows Brent wants him to get up, but he's just too tired. He's tired of people getting shot, tired of people dying. In fact, he's tired of this entire dream. But Brent won't stop pulling on Scotty's arm. Scotty finally decides it's easier just to go along with whatever Brent wants. It doesn't matter one way or the other. He lets Brent pull him to his feet. Once he's standing up, he discovers that the back of his shoulder hurts. In fact, it hurts bad. But he knows that doesn't matter. He found Brent and saved him from Farkas, so now they can go back to Wong's. Kim-Li will be there. She will fix his shoulder. She will fix everything.

Brent is pulling him out of the office. He pulls him into the restroom and switches on the lights. He leans the rifle against the wall and goes to one of the washbasins. He pulls off his shirt. Scotty sees that the whole front part of Brent's shirt is covered in blood. That must be Brent's blood. Poor Brent. Brent throws the shirt into the basin and turns on the water. Then, he moves to the next washbasin and turns that water on too. When the basin is full, he plunges his head into the water and scrubs at his hair. The water in the basin is turning red. But then Scotty notices the other basin, the one with Brent's shirt in it, is starting to overflow. The old mopper woman won't like that. Brent puts his mouth under the running washbasin faucet and gets some water in his mouth. He turns and spits a mixture of water and blood onto the floor. Now there's both water *and* blood on the floor. The old mopper lady is *really* going to be mad.

Brent moves to the overflowing basin and turns off the water. He tries to wash the blood out of his shirt. Some of it is coming out, the white shirt is turning pink. Brent shakes out the shirt and puts it back on, pulling the front of it down to hide Farkas's pistol that's stuck inside his belt.

Scotty thinks that wet pink shirt looks nice on Brent. And it must feel nice and cool. Good to be cool in this damn hot warehouse.

Brent turns and pulls at the front of Scotty's shirt. Shrt. Leme see."

"My shirt?"

Brent doesn't bother to answer. He roughly pulls Scotty's shirt over his head and throws it into the overflowing washbasin.

Scotty is shocked to see how much blood is on his own shirt. How did that happen?

Brent leaves the shirt in the running water and turns Scotty around. "Kid got yur shol-dr."

Scotty has no idea what Brent is trying to say. His poor face is so beat up and cut up and bruised, it's amazing his mouth can talk at all. But he still seems to be acting like the same old take-charge Brent. Scotty thinks it's amazing Brent can be so calm and so in control after the beating he took from Farkas. But he's seen Brent do this kind of thing before. Brent can get beat up bad, but he doesn't let it change him. He just keeps going, and Scotty knows why: it's because Brent will never give up. It's important to him to think he's tougher than anybody.

Brent says, "Shit," and turns to spit more blood out onto the floor. He put his mouth under the faucet again, swishes the water around inside his mouth, and then spits it out. Something white comes out mixed in with the blood. He says, "Damn, nother tooth."

Brent goes back to examining Scotty's shoulder. "Nicked shoulder. Toppa bone." He goes to the paper towel dispenser and pulls out a handful of towels. "Here. Keep pressure on. Stop bleedin'." He gives the paper towels to Scotty.

Now Scotty understands. It's what Doc Eric would have told him to do: keep pressure on the wound. Scotty presses the wad of paper towels onto the place where his shoulder hurts. He looks back at Brent and sees he is again at the overflowing washbasin, rinsing out a shirt. That shirt is also turning pink. He pulls the shirt out of the water, holds it up to look at it for a moment, and brings it to Scotty. He helps Scotty put the shirt on, and then makes sure Scotty is keeping the paper towels pressed against his hurt shoulder. The wet shirt feels cool. It feels good.

Brent picks up the old rifle and leads Scotty back out of the restroom. When they get to the front door, Brent tries to open it, but it's locked. Brent immediately shoots the lock twice with Farkas's pistol and kicks the door open. Scotty is impressed. That was a strong kick. At least Brent's legs didn't get hurt when he was getting hit by Farka's binoculars.

Outside, the street is deserted, but there's still shooting in the distance, and there is more smoke in the sky. It makes Scotty feel very tired. It's all too much: the shooting, the smoke in the sky, Farkas and that poor boy getting shot. He just wants to lie down and not think. If only he had some of his magic powder.

"Come on, come on," says Brent. "Gotta keep movin'."

But Scotty is too tired to go on. He pulls the wad of paper towels out of his shirt and looks at it. It's all bloody. He shows it to Brent. "I'm hurt, Brent. And I'm tired. Really tired."

Brent takes the paper towels out of his hand and throws them on the ground. "Your shoulder's hardly bleedin' now. Gotta keep goin'."

"I can't. I'm just too tired."

"No choice. Attacks all over. Gotta keep movin'." He gets ahold of Scotty's arm and pulls him along. But they haven't even made it to the next intersection when an American helicopter suddenly appears and hovers above them. Scotty has a vague memory of a helicopter hovering up above him like that once before. When was that? His brain wants to think about a dead water buffalo, about how bad it smelled, but he notices something odd that distracts him: chips are being torn off of the wall of a nearby concrete building. He watches them fly off the wall, very fast. They're like powdery white moths, darting away. He feels something grab his leg, and then he's down on the ground. He tries to sit up, but something has ahold of the back of his shirt collar and is dragging him back into the alley. The machine gun doesn't stop, and the little white powdery concrete moths are flying all over the place. As he's dragged backwards, Scotty watches them fly. He's fascinated by them. Some of them are bigger than moths, like white birds, fast birds, too fast to even see if it wasn't for the faint trail of white dust they leave behind.

Brent drags him into a building and yells, "What the hell's the matter with you, Scotty? You tryin' to get yourself killed?"

Scotty tries to think how to explain it to Brent. He doesn't understand this is just a dream. It will end soon.

The sound of the helicopter goes away, and Brent gets up to peek out the door. "Damn. Gotta get outta these French duds. Bastards are shootin' at anything."

Scotty is still trying to think how to explain to Brent that it doesn't matter, that this is only a dream, but Brent jerks him to his feet and pulls him out the door. He pulls Scotty down an alley, cursing under his breath. At the next street they stop. The street is completely deserted. Brent throws the rifle under a building's porch and kicks some dirt to hide it. He goes back to pulling Scotty down the street. Scotty feels bad that he's so slow. He doesn't want to cause Brent any more trouble. He can tell Brent is mad at him. He has a hard and determined look on his face. Scotty wonders where Brent gets such strength. But then, he knows Brent has always been like this. He will never give up. If only one person comes out of this war alive, he knows it will be Brent. When it's all over, Brent will go back home, and will be exactly the same person he was when he left. Scotty feels the strength in Brent's arm as he pulls him along, and it makes him remember how strong Brent's grip felt under the ice that day. The river's current was trying to pull him along under the ice, trying to take him downstream. It was like some terrible monster had an icy grip on him and was determined to take him away. Scotty was ready to go with the monster because he thought there was no other choice, but Brent didn't give up. He fought the icy current monster, and somehow he won. He pulled Scotty out of the monster's grip and saved him. Is he trying to do that again? Scotty whispers, "Uh, Brent, where are we going?"

Brent says, "Frenchman's. Gotta get outta this city."

Scotty tries hard to keep up. "But why are we going to the

Frenchman's? Will he know what this fighting is all about?"

"We don't need the Frenchman to tell us, Scotty. It's all over. Or about to be. We gotta get out."

"Out? Out of where, Brent? Out of Saigon?"

"Outta this whole God-damned country. The Frenchman'll know where. Maybe Paris. Or Holland. He says there are hippies in Amsterdam and lots of drugs. Make a damn fortune there."

Scotty thinks about it. Maybe Brent is right. Maybe it would be better to just leave this terrible country, this terrible war. He feels so tired, tired of people dying. And for what? Just for money. Better to just go get Kim-Li and leave. The Frenchman will take us in his car. Maybe to Paris. Paris seems nice, from the pictures anyhow. Kim-Li will like it there. Scotty is still thinking about living in Paris with Kim-Li, when Brent suddenly stops. He's standing in front of a building that has been blown up. Only the back wall is standing. Brent says, "Shit."

Scotty says, "What's the matter?"

Brent points at the destroyed building. "Frenchman's place. Shit, shit, shit." And then he's off down the street again, moving fast.

Scotty hurries to catch up. "Does it mean the Frenchman is dead?"

Brent shrugs. "Don't know. Maybe he blew it up himself."

Scotty looks back at the destroyed building. "Blew it up himself? Why would the Frenchman do that?"

Brent doesn't answer. He's moving fast now, getting way ahead. Scotty wants to keep up, but his knee hurts, and his shoulder is starting to hurt more too. He starts to think maybe Brent doesn't want him slowing them down anymore. Maybe he's going to go on alone.

But at the next corner, Brent stops and Scotty catches up. Brent is peeking around the edge of the building. He has Farkas's pistol in his hand. A building across the street has black smoke smudges above the windows, and one of its walls has collapsed. To Scotty, the rebar spikes sticking out of that wall look like thorns. He remembers thorns in the desert. Cactus thorns that if you get too close will —

"Damn it, Scotty. Are you listening to me?"

"Uh, what?"

"I said it looks like it just happened. We gotta go careful. Stay close, and don't be acting so weird. Just keep up with me, and do what I tell you. Now let's move. We got to get to Wong's."

"Wong's? We're going to Wong's?"

"Yeah. Now let's move."

"Are we going to get Kim-Li?"

"I told you, Scotty. She's gone. Face it."

"She can't be gone. She wouldn't go without me. I want her to come back to Arizona with us."

Brent stares at him. "Arizona? Now I know you've gone nuts. Wise up, Scotty. She doesn't want to go to Arizona. She wants *us* to go back to Arizona. She wants us the hell out of her country."

Scotty is confused. He understands that maybe some of the Vietnamese people might be mad a them for coming here and dropping bombs on their babies in their cribs, but Kim-Li knows he's not like that. "Why wouldn't she want to come to Arizona?"

Brent looks disgusted. "Scotty, sometimes I think you've been asleep ever since you got to this damn country. Why do you think she only sleeps with officers?"

"She doesn't. She sleeps with me."

"Well, I don't know why she sleeps with you, but I do know why she lets those officers do her. It's because she's a spy. Get it? It's her way of getting information out of them. She let's them treat her like a child, lets them beat her up a little, if that's what it takes to get them to talk about their jobs. They complain to her. About their superiors, about how wrong the latest war plan is. Sooner or later, she gets what she wants out of them. The Frenchman tells me, of all the girls the Cong has planted in places like Wong's, she's the best. Those officers confide in her because they think she's only a child. They don't even know she has other lovers. They think she sits there at Wong's all day waiting for them, their own personal hot little piece of ass, a lot like the girls they knew back home in high school, except she knows more tricks."

Scotty's brain is having trouble comprehending what Brent is saying, but he knows for sure Brent is wrong. Kim-Li only lets them look. If they try to do more, she says, Shh, and pushes their hand away. But for some reason, what Brent is saying makes him want to cry.

Brent stares at him. "Now what? You're gonna cry? Jesus, I've about had it with you, Scotty. When are you gonna grow up?" He shakes his head. "Ah, shit. Let's go." He grabs Scotty's arm and pulls him along.

Once again, Scotty feels outside of himself, just floating along. Once again, he's a floating balloon on a string, and Brent is the kid who has ahold of the string, pulling him deep into a dream where precious little girls are spies and people kill each other for money.

"No! You are not allowed to remember people being killed."

"Oh shut up. I don't have to listen to you anymore."

Brent stops. "Fine. You don't have to believe me, but it's true."

"No, not you. I was just . . . talking to . . . myself."

"Oh, great. Now you're talking to yourself." Brent shakes his head and pulls Scotty along. As he floats along behind Brent, Scotty sees an abandoned donkey cart with a broken wheel. It makes him suddenly understand why those students laughed at that scary movie when the man's casket fell out of the horse-drawn hearse. They knew it was just a big joke. When the wheel of the black hearse got caught on the curb, that was funny because it meant you can't go to heaven after you die because the wheel is stuck. When the man saw himself in the casket and got scared of being dead, the students knew is was funny because death isn't real anyhow. And when the cute little wooden puppet shot his friend and put him in a casket, it didn't mean anything because it's all fake, only the puppet master pulling the strings to make things happen. We live and then we die and it's only one more joke in an endless chain of jokes. Death slips on a banana peel and falls down, and everybody in the audience laughs. Reality drops it's pants, just to get a laugh. Scotty finally gets what all those philosophers in his book were trying to tell him: it's all a big joke.

Brent stops. "Scotty! Damn it, why do you keep stopping?"

Scotty points at the side of a building. "Those bullet holes are fake."

Brent scowls at him. "Fake? What's that supposed to mean? If they're fake, then the bullets are fake too, and I can God damn guarantee you they're not."

"Yes they are. None of this is real."

Brent slaps Scotty's face. "God damn it, Scotty, you gotta snap out of it. If we're gonna get out of this alive, you have shape up. Trust me and do what I say."

"Trust you? Trust you for what? Trust you to take me out of that hospital just when they were going to send me back home and send me to the Wonderful Walter to fix me all up? My guts were all messed up inside of me. I would have died if it wasn't for Kim-Li. She's the one who saved me. You'd of just let me die in that room."

Brent gets in his face. "Fine, if you think you can do better without me, you just stay here and see how well you do on your own. I've been dragging you along behind me since that day you fell through the ice. You wouldn't even be alive, if it wasn't for me."

"Yeah, but I wouldn't have even been out on that ice in the first place if it wasn't for you. And you only saved me 'cause you couldn't stand to get blamed for losing another little brother. You think his death was your fault. And it probably was. You were probably off with your hand down inside some little girl's panties when you were supposed to be watching over your little brother. Probably off making some kind of deal, cheating the other kids out of their marbles, or maybe . . ."

This time, Scotty sees it coming, but for some reason he can't seem to make himself duck. He finds himself on the ground watching Brent walk away. He sits up and checks his jaw. It doesn't hurt all that much, but it feels like his teeth aren't fitting together quite right anymore. He watches Brent disappear around the next corner. He yells, "Okay, fine. It's about time I was on my own anyhow." But what now? He looks back toward the sounds of shooting. Maybe he should go back there and wave a white surrender flag or something. Like they do in the movies. He could tell them he's an American soldier. He could say he was kidnapped. Or that he was out of his head and walked out of that hospital by mistake. That doctor probably wrote him up as crazy, so maybe they'll go for that. He turns back to look in the direction Brent went. Brent is going to Wong's. Scotty thinks that before he surrenders, he'd better go to Wong's and get Kim-Li. But which direction is Wong's? He looks up at the hazy sun and realizes he has no idea where he is. He decides it might be better to just rest for a while and think about it. He lies down in the middle of the street and closes his eyes.

"Hey."

Scotty opens his eyes. It's Brent. He came back.

Brent sits down in the dirt next to him. "Okay, let's get this straightened out right now. You're mad at me because I saved you from getting sent back home. Right, I did. But think about it, Scotty. If I'da let 'em send you back, you'd have missed all this. Look around, you're in a foreign country having adventures. If Ida let you go home you'd of missed all this. Right?"

"I guess so."

And what about all that money we made? Wong is holding it for us. He's got a whole shitload of our money hidden somewhere in his bar. You won't believe how rich you are, old buddy. You think you'da got rich if I'da let you go back to Arizona?"

"I guess not."

"And what about Kim-Li? You aren't sorry you got to spend some time with her, are ya?"

Scotty shakes his head.

"I came back to get you just now because I decided you were right. Kim-Li probably is waiting for you at Wong's. I bet she's there now."

That gets Scotty attention. "Do you really think so?"

"It's possible. Let's go find out. What do you say, old buddy?"

"All right."

Brent helps Scotty to his feet and grabs his chin to check him over. "I didn't hurt you, did I? You know I pulled that punch, don't ya? If I'da wanted to really lay you out, you'd still be seein' stars. Right?"

"I guess so."

Brent messes up Scotty's hair like he used to when they were kids. "Okay, buddy. Let's go. Maybe what we're both lookin' for is waitin' for us back there at Wong's."

Scotty lets Brent lead him. He's happy they're going to Wong's. Kim-Li will be waiting there. He can already see her beautiful face.

They go down alleys and they cross deserted streets. Sometimes they have to double back and go a different way because they hear shooting ahead, but finally they round one more corner and there it is, Wong's Bar. Scotty thinks Wong's square box of a building looks lonely without any of the pretty girls standing outside. Did they all run away too?

Brent says, "Let's hold back a minute. Let me get the lay of the land."

But Scotty sees movement inside the bar. Is it Kim-Li? Has she come back? He shakes loose of Brent's grip and runs straight into the bar. Inside, the place looks the same as when he left it, except there are no girls, and no Wong. The place is empty except for three boys sitting at one of the tables. All three are dressed in black and their heads are close together. They're looking at a big piece of paper and whispering.

Scotty approaches them. Maybe they know where Kim-Li is.

Two of the boys jump up and point rifles at him.

The third boy jumps up and shouts, "Dừng!"

But then Scotty sees the boy who shouted is not a boy. The person is dressed like a boy, but the face is Kim-Li's face. For a moment, Scotty can't believe his eyes. He's sure it's Kim-Li's face, but she's dressed in black pajamas just like that boy that shot him T and T back in the jungle, and she has an automatic pistol in her hand.

Brent comes in through the front door with his hands up.

The two boys turn to point their rifles at him.

Brent smiles and says, "*Bonjour. Bonjour.*" He turns to Scotty and says, "*Bonjour*, eh? *bonjour*?" His eyes seem to be saying something.

Scotty gets it. Brent still wants him to play the French person again, so he shrugs and says, "*Oui, oui, bonjour.*"

The two boys act like they want to shoot Brent, but Kim-Li pushes both of their rifles down. She points at Brent and says something to them in her language. They both laugh.

Scotty wants to run to her and take her in his arms, but her eyes are telling him no. Scotty is confused. What is she pretending to be?

She goes up to Brent and pokes him in the chest with her pistol.

Brent stumbles backward.

She pulls Farkas's pistol out of Brent's belt and points it at his face.

Brent keeps his hands in the air, smiling and shrugging and saying, "*Bonjour. Bonjour.*" He's backing toward the door.

Scotty goes closer, wanting to hold Kim-Li. He wants to tell her how much he has been missing her, how glad he is to see her. He starts toward her, but she turns and points Farkas's gun at him.

Scotty stops. He's confused. Why is she acting like this?

She turns back to Brent and again uses the gun to poke him in the chest. Brent backs out the door. She pokes him again, and he stumbles out into the street. She turns to Scotty and gestures with the pistol for him to go outside with Brent. Scotty isn't sure what's going on, but he does what she wants him to. Out in the street, Kim-Li whispers something to Brent, then pushes him away. Brent raises his hands even higher and says, "*Oui, oui. Bonjour, bonjour.*" He looks toward Scotty and waves for him to come. But Scotty doesn't want to go. He doesn't want to leave Kim-Li, no matter what she's gotten herself into. Whatever she is now, he's willing to be it with her. She's dressed in black clothes like the enemy, but it doesn't matter. Even if she really has joined up with the enemy, he still wants to be with her. He wants to take her in his arms and tell her he's willing to be whatever she wants him to be. He starts toward her, but Brent moves quick and grabs his arm. He almost jerks Scotty off his feet as he begins to pull him away.

Scotty tries to pull free, but Brent's grip is too strong. Scotty has never felt Brent squeeze his arm that hard. It hurts.

As they go, Brent whispers between his teeth, "Just keep walking, God damn it. And don't say a damn word."

Scotty looks back and sees that Kim-Li and the boys in black are watching them go. He wants to go back and talk to Kim-Li to find out what's going on, but Brent keeps pulling him on down the street. "I said, don't look back, damn it. Those guys could still shoot us just for the hell of it."

"But I want to talk to Kim-Li. I want to tell her—"

"Just shut up and walk." Brent puts his arm around behind Scotty and forces him to keep going.

"But—"

"No buts! Just shut up and keep walking. And as soon as we get around the corner, we run. Got it? We run as fast as we can."

But Scotty doesn't want to run. He's too tired. In fact, he doesn't want to do anything anymore. He sinks to his knees.

Brent tries to pull him back up, but Scotty is not going to go another step. What's the point? If Kim-Li is no longer *his* Kim-Li, then there's nothing left. He doesn't care if those boys in black do shoot. He falls over onto his side and begins to cry, and this time he doesn't care if Brent or the puppet master or anybody else thinks it's unmanly. The strings have been cut. He's a dead puppet. He will just lie here and die.

Brent is kneeling next to him, talking in his ear. "Scotty, listen to me. I'm pretty sure she told them we were French drug dealers. Not worth bothering with. But French drug dealers don't lay down in the middle of the street and cry. Get up. Kim-Li would want you to get up."

Scotty looks up at Brent? "She would?"

"Of course she would. Don't you get it? She's trying to save your scrawny ass. If it was me, she'd of shot me and said good riddance."

"She would?"

"Damn right she would. She hates Americans, but not you. She loves you. She wants you to live. She told me so."

"She did? She said she loves me?"

"She sure did. She told me to take you back to Arizona. She said that's where you belong, not here."

Scotty remembers that first night he was with Kim-Li. She said he didn't belong in this country. "I saw her whisper to you back there."

"That's right. She told me I should take you away from there."

Scotty sits up and wipes away the tears. He looks back down the street, but Kim-Li and the boys in black are gone. He points back at Wong's. "But what about Kim-Li? Shouldn't we go back and save her?"

"No, she doesn't want that. She has to keep on pretending. For a while anyhow. We'll find her later."

"But how? How will we find her?"

She'll . . . find you. That's what she said. She'll meet us later."

Scotty isn't sure if Brent is telling the truth. "Did she really say that?"

"She sure did. She said to tell you she'd meet up with us later. Now get up. We have to hurry."

"But how? Where will she meet us?"

"In Arizona. She said she'd meet us there."

Now Scotty is suspicious. "Now wait a minute, Brent. How will—"

"We'll send for her. That's the plan. When we get to France, the Frenchman will bring her there. Then we'll go to Arizona."

"We're going to France first?"

"We sure are. We are if you get up on your feet and get moving."

Scotty allows Brent to help him up. Brent leads him down the street, his strong arm around Scotty's waist. "First, we'll go to France and those doctors in Paris will fix you all up. The Frenchman told me they have the best doctors in the world in Paris. They'll even fix up whatever is wrong inside your head. Then we can go back home to Arizona."

But Scotty barely hears what Brent is saying. He's thinking about how happy he will be when Kim-Li comes to join him. He'll show her the desert. Maybe the desert flowers will be in bloom. She won't believe how many tiny little flowers there are on the desert floor in the springtime. Scotty wonders if it's springtime in Arizona right now.

Brent leads them through deserted streets and into a dusty alley that ends at a sort of open-air garage that has a rusty sagging tin roof. In a weedy field behind the garage, old cars are scattered. Most of them have no wheels or windshields. Scotty recognizes the smell of old grease and it makes him homesick for the back lot of the junkyard back home. He wonders what Kim-Li will think of the junkyard? She'll like it, he's sure. He'll tell her stories about how he and Brent used to play there.

Brent leads them through the old cars to a very dirty car that *does* have wheels on it. It reminds Scotty of the car the Frenchman had. Brent looks in the car's window, so Scotty comes to look too. There's nothing inside the car except for a lumpy blanket on the front seat. Brent taps on the window, and like magic, a young man wearing sunglasses comes out from beneath the blanket. It's Mar-lon. What is he doing here?

Mar-lon rolls down the window and looks at Brent. "*Mon Dieu*, Brent. You look like run over by truck."

Brent says, "Never mind that. Let's go." Brent pushes Scotty into back seat and slides in next to him. Mar-lon turns back to them and says, "You take time get here. You think I want die here waiting?"

Brent says, "Kim-Li told me where you were, but we had a hell of a time getting here. Fighting all over the place. Where's the Frenchman?"

Mar-lon says, "He gone. Go to be with family in Cambodia. He make me wait. I tell him no. I say not want wait and die, but he say I have to wait for Brent, so I wait."

Scotty says, "Thank you for waiting, Mar-lon. *Merci.*"

Mar-lon says, "I not wait for you. I wait for him." He points at Brent.

Brent leans forward. "You got papers for us?"

Mar-lon says, "Paper for you, not him."

Brent grabs the back of Mar-lon's shirt collar. "Listen, damn it. Don't be givin' me any shit after what I've been through today. You'd better have papers for both of us, or I'll take yours."

Mar-lon shrugs. "I only have French paper. He not French."

Brent says, "From now on, he is. Besides, he speaks better French than you do. Now let's go."

Mar-lon starts the car, and they go very fast down narrow streets and back alleys. They pull onto a paved street and yet another American helicopter appears in the air ahead of them.

Brent yells, "Go back! Back up!"

Mar-lon stops so fast, it throws Scotty forward into the back of the front seat, and he ends up sitting on the floor. Brent tries to help him back up onto the seat, but it's hard for Scotty to get up because Mar-Lon is driving backwards too fast. Scotty finally gets back up on the seat, but then Mar-lon spins the car around, and Scotty is again thrown to the floor. Scotty decides he might as well stay sitting on the floor because that's where he's going to end up anyway. Mar-Lon is again driving very fast. Scotty can't hear the helicopter anymore, so he carefully gets back up onto the seat and leans forward to try to see where they're going. He sees they're roaring down a narrow street, but the street ends ahead at an empty lot with a rickety wood fence around it. Mar-Lon isn't slowing down. Scotty says, "Look Out," but Mar-lon ignores him and plows right through the fence. When pieces of wood fly past his window, they seem almost like wooden birds taking off. Scotty laughs.

Mar-lon glances back over his shoulder. "What matter with him?"

Brent says, "Just keep driving."

Mar-lon says, "I bet he gone crazy. Whole country gone crazy. Tet make everybody crazy. Frenchman say it all over now. He say Americans go home soon."

Brent says, "Maybe, maybe not. Depends on how they play it. But somethin' big sure as hell is goin' down. They drive on in silence, and soon Scotty is surprised to see they are going out of the city. Are they going to the jungle? Mar-lon is driving very fast on a dusty road, heading toward the setting sun.

Scotty turns to Brent. "She will come later, won't she? She was just pretending not to like me, right?"

Brent pats him on the knee and says, "That's right, Scotty. She was just pretending. Now just sit back and enjoy the ride. We'll be out of this damn country soon, and you'll feel a lot better."

"She couldn't come with us because of those boys in black, right?"

"That's right. If they knew Kim-Li was protecting two Americans, she'd be in danger. She'll meet us later."

Mar-lon looks over his shoulder at Brent. "Kim-Li come later?"

Brent says, "Keep your eyes on the road."

Mar-lon says, "Not worry. I know road. Road go to Frenchman family farm. Other side of border. In Cambodia. I take Frenchman there all time. They stop us at border, but guard know me. No problem."

Scotty doesn't know what they're talking about, and he doesn't care. He's happy to know Kim-Li wants to come to Arizona. He'll show her the desert. She'll love the desert. In fact, that's where they will live, out there in the desert, just the two of them. They'll sleep on the ground in each other's arms, and he will show her all the millions of beautiful stars up in the clear Arizona night sky. He'll tell her the story of Cassiopeia and how the gods punished her vanity by making her sit up there in the sky forever. They'll live on the fish he catches from the Verde river, and they'll be happy just being together for ever and ever.

www.ingramcontent.com/pod-product-compliance
Lightning Source LLC
Chambersburg PA
CBHW062036170626
46813CB00001B/354